BLOOD & SECRETS

HELEN BRIGHT

BOOKS

Vinci Books

vinci-books.com

Published by Vinci Books Ltd in 2026

1

Copyright © Helen Bright 2015

The author has asserted their moral right to be identified as the author of this work in accordance with the Copyright, Designs and Patents Act 1988. This work is a work of fiction. Names, characters, places and incidents are the product of the author's imagination or are used fictitiously. Any resemblance to actual persons, living or dead, places and incidents is entirely coincidental.

All rights reserved. No part of this publication may be copied, reproduced, distributed, stored in any retrieval system, or transmitted in any form or by any means, including photocopying, recording, or other electronic or mechanical methods, nor used as a source for any form of machine learning including AI datasets, without the prior written permission of the publisher.

The publisher and the author have made every effort to obtain permissions for any third party material used in this book and to comply with copyright law. Any queries in this respect should be brought to the attention of the publisher and any omissions will be corrected in future editions.

A CIP catalogue record for this book is available from the British Library.

Paperback ISBN: 9781036707699

The EU GPSR authorised representative is Logos Europe, 9 rue Nicolas Poussion, 17000 La Rochelle, France

contact@logoseurope.eu

By Helen Bright

The Night Movers Vampire Series

Bitten and Bound
Blood & Secrets
Gregor's Reason
Sergei's Angel

Chapter One

Keeley

I love my job! I've been Gregor Antonov's PA for the past five months, and I've enjoyed every minute of it. He's been a fabulous boss, letting me work flexible hours to suit my childcare needs.

My daughter, Daisy, is four and a half now—you have to say the half, or she gets annoyed—and soon she'll be in full-time school. This job allows me to drop Daisy off at her nursery in the mornings and pick her up midday to take her home for lunch. When my boss is over from Russia and work is busier, a friend from my old job at Night Movers collects Daisy for me.

Today Daisy is with Joshua York, one of my old bosses at Night Movers. He's been a rock for me whenever I've needed someone to lean on. He spoils my daughter constantly, and she absolutely adores him. Last week he bought her a swing and slide set for his back garden, so he doesn't have to take her to the swings at the local park. Not that Josh doesn't want to, of course, but he's limited by how much time he can spend in the sun.

You see, Josh is a vampire. So is Gregor, my boss, as well as Nik and Alex—the other two co-owners of Night Movers. And Sergei, Yuri, Finn, and Patrick—all friends of mine, and all vampires. Does this bother me? Surprisingly, no. They are some of the nicest individuals I have ever met. I've been around most of them since I was a young girl, just a few years older than Daisy is now.

My aunt Maggie has worked for Josh, Nik, and Alex in the offices at Night Movers for thirty years, and often took us into the office with her when we used to come and visit. My parents were originally from this village, but they moved to Lincolnshire for my dad's job when Mum was pregnant with me and my twin brother, Daniel.

Sadly, Mum died from breast cancer when we were twelve, and my dad couldn't cope with her loss. He ended up having a breakdown, so Daniel and I had to stay with Aunt Mags and Uncle Dave until he was well enough to look after us again.

Freya Staithes—another vampire, who is also Josh and Alex's sister—used to take me out shopping and to her home for holidays. She became like an aunt to me, and now that I'm a grown woman, she's one of my best friends.

Freya told me about the PA job with Gregor Antonov and passed him my details. I'd met him before, on occasion, but always felt too intimidated to speak to him, which wasn't like me at all, as anyone who knew me would tell you. But Gregor Antonov, the Russian billionaire vampire, has a commanding presence that intimidates even the most powerful men and women.

Now that I know Gregor better, I feel differently about him. He's one of the most charming, respectful men I've ever met. It's like he treasures your company, and he makes you feel as though you're the most important person in the world.

The last time he came over to see the progress on his house, he brought me the diamond earrings I wore today for a job well done.

DIAMOND EARRINGS!

I'd never owned a diamond anything before, and they're not small diamonds either. Gregor said all women should own diamonds, and after seeing how these sparkled in my ears, I completely agreed. If I'm honest, I may have had a bit of a crush on Gregor. Tall, with broad, muscular shoulders, dark-brown hair and piercing blue eyes. What's not to crush on? I melt like butter whenever he says my name in that delicious Russian accent.

Keeleey... He always says it with a slow drawl, and the first time I heard it, I almost swooned.

The house Gregor is having renovated is the old Rothley Manor, which is just outside our little village of Barrowfield in South Yorkshire. He hired a brilliant interior designer who's worked for members of the Royal Family, as well as famous footballers and models in the UK and Europe. His name is Ryan Adamson. He's only twenty-six, just a couple of years older than me, and he's totally gorgeous. Unfortunately for me, he's also gay, and he's recently come out of a long-term relationship.

To help Ryan get over his breakup, me and some of the ladies from my old job took him on a night out around Rothley and Barrowfield.

What a night that was!

Daisy was staying with my ex's parents, so I could let my hair down without worrying about looking after her when I got home. My ex's parents live in Gainsborough, which is only a thirty-minute drive away. My ex, Rick the prick, wants nothing to do with Daisy, so his parents take her once a month when they know he's not going to visit. It's an odd situation, but I wouldn't stop Rick's parents from seeing her just because their son doesn't want to be in her life. Although sometimes, when she's asking me questions, I think it would make life easier for me if she didn't know them.

Our night out was one of the best I've ever had.

We danced most of the night away in Rothley, which I love to do, then came back to the Red Lion and stayed for one of their famous lock-ins. Sergei brought a bottle of absinthe that a friend of his makes. Oh my God! I have never been as drunk as that before. If it hadn't been for Josh, I don't think Ryan and I would have coped. He came with Alex—our designated driver since Julia became pregnant—and ended up taking Ryan and me back to his cottage to sleep it off.

Josh looked after us all night when we were throwing up and brought us breakfast and much-needed painkillers the next morning to kill the hangover. He also gave me a small amount of his blood, which really helped.

Josh wouldn't tell me what happened during the ride home in the minibus, but I ended up losing a shoe and somehow my bra, although I still wore the rest of my clothes. He now calls me his Cinderella, though I doubt I'll get Prince Charming riding up to me with my high heel on a cushion. Not here in Barrowfield. The only Prince Charming I have in my life right now is Josh. But he still sees me as the little girl that Aunt Mags used to bring to the office, even though I've tried to make him see me as the woman I am today.

Of course, there's always Gregor and Sergei. Though Sergei never seems to take anything seriously, whereas Gregor... Gregor is the king of the castle.

Chapter Two

Keeley

I left Ryan at the manor to lock up while I went to get my car from near the old stables. The builders were working late, as were the decorators, so Ryan was staying to make sure they did everything to his specifications. He's only five-foot-seven but has a way of making those big, burly builders and decorators obey his every command. A true professional if ever I saw one. Even Gregor doesn't faze him.

Gregor had brought two of his bodyguards with him last time—Yuri and Maxim. Yuri is lovely, but Maxim is mean. He doesn't speak, he just grunts and looks at me like I'm shit on his shoe. I don't know what I've done to upset him, but he's always so disparaging and nasty towards me. Ryan threatened Maxim that if he heard he'd upset me once more, he was going to tell Gregor. That seemed to do the trick until they all left, and I hoped Maxim stayed away this time. I mean, it's not like Gregor needs a bodyguard in this sleepy Yorkshire village.

I threw my bag in my crappy little car that had long seen better days and sat still for a minute after closing the door, enjoying a moment of peace. Gregor would be arriving in two days' time, so the builders, decorators, and Ryan had really gone for it today. They were aiming for the interior of the manor house to be completed for Gregor's visit. There were still the cottages and stable block residences to finish, but they could be done later.

The noise from the manor today had been horrendous, so I savoured the quiet of my car for a minute before turning the key.

Nothing. That's what I got when I finally turned the key. So I tried again, pumping the accelerator a little to see if that helped—still nothing. After trying for another five minutes, I gave up and phoned Josh.

"Hi, Keeley, are you on your way home? Daisy's been a big girl and ate all her fish fingers and spaghetti."

"That's good. I hope she's behaved for you. Listen, Josh, my car broke down, and I'm going to have to call the AA, so I'm not sure what time I can pick Daisy up. Do you mind dropping her off at the manor with me? I don't want her going back to mine without me. My dad's on one of his benders again."

"I'll come and get you, Keeley. Stay put, me and my little princess will be there in ten minutes. You can call the AA out tomorrow."

"Thanks, Josh, but—"

Too late; he'd already hung up the phone.

I knew he would come for me. I think he would do anything I asked of him, except kiss me, of course. Josh would be the ideal man for me. Yeah, so he's a vampire, which means a beach holiday in Ibiza is out of the question, but in every other way, he's perfect.

Josh is about six-foot-three of pure muscle. His brown eyes often seem to have flecks of fiery amber in them, lighting up bits of me that shouldn't burn for him. Of African descent, his skin is the colour of milk chocolate, and I have more than once dreamed of tasting it. He keeps his tight curls cropped close to his head, and I'd love to run my fingers through them and feel the texture.

He's a beautiful man with facial features a model would be proud of, and where Gregor makes me swoon with a silly schoolgirl-like crush, Josh makes my heart beat faster in my chest whenever I see him. Even sometimes when I can't see him, I can tell you the very moment he walks into the room just from how my body reacts. I know it's because I'm in love with him, but since that love isn't reciprocated, I try to forget about anything more meaningful. But I see Josh most days, and it's getting harder to hide how much he means to me. And how much I want him.

Josh's Honda CRV pulled up beside my car, tugging me away from thoughts of being with my perfect man/vampire. He got out of his vehicle and walked towards me, concern marring his handsome face.

"Hey, Keeley, are you okay?" He opened the door, took my hand, and helped me out of the car.

"Yeah, I'm fine, Josh. It's this bloody thing failing to start again."

"Mummy, you said a naughty word," shouted Daisy from the window of Josh's SUV.

"Sorry, Daisy."

She was like the swear police lately. Not that I choose to swear in front of her, but occasionally something slips out and when it does... Bam! She's in there straight away. Never misses.

Josh popped the bonnet up and we went through the

motions of trying to start my car. But the engine wouldn't turn over even when using the jump leads.

"It's definitely a job for the AA, Josh, but thanks for trying. Would you mind dropping us off at home now? I want to get this little one bathed and in bed," I said, smooching a kiss off the sweetest little girl in the world.

"Of course, but if your dad's being a problem again, maybe you should stay with me?" he said.

"Thanks, Josh, but I want to keep an eye on him so he doesn't end up back in the hospital again."

"Can't Daniel watch him? I can arrange for him to have time off work so he can sort him out."

"No, Josh, it's okay; I'll handle it. Dan's moved out, anyway. He says he's done with him now. They had another big bust-up, and it got all heated. Dad punched Dan, so Dan moved out and lived at his friend's house until he got a flat. He moved in a few weeks ago."

Josh stepped closer and asked in a soft voice, "Keeley, why didn't you tell me it had got this bad at home? Maybe I could have helped."

"There's only my dad that can help himself now, Josh. But I can't leave him on his own. He nearly set the house on fire the last time he was like this. He was so drunk he forgot to switch the grill off."

"Then it's not safe for you and Daisy to be there either," he declared. "Come home with me, Keeley. As soon as one of my properties becomes empty again, you can have it."

Although I was grateful, I shook my head. "No, Josh. Thanks, but no. I need to know that he's going to be okay. He does this and then he gets better. He just needs time to sort himself out again," I insisted.

"Will he go to rehab or an AA meeting?" Josh asked.

"No. Been there and done that. You get him set up to

go, and then he just refuses, so it's pointless. But he seems to come out of it himself, eventually."

Less than ten minutes later, Josh was dropping us off at home. Daisy was in a great mood due to the in-car DVD player Josh had installed for her. She'd been watching a cartoon in the back of the car while Josh and I had been talking. I knew she couldn't understand much of what I'd been saying, but kids tend to pick up more than you think. So in this instance, I was glad that Josh had spoiled my little girl yet again with his thoughtful actions. I got out of the car, grabbed both mine and Daisy's bags, and then went to take Daisy out of Josh's arms.

"Daisy's not tired, Josh. She can walk in," I insisted.

"I'll carry her in, Keeley. You have steps down to the house," he pointed out.

Before I could stop him, he'd gone through the gate and down the path to the door. I stepped past him and opened it, hoping to God my dad was asleep. No such luck!

"Where have you been, Keeley? You're an hour late," Dad yelled, drunk as usual. He came into the kitchen and saw Josh with Daisy.

"What the fuck is he doing holding our Daisy?" he raged.

"Grandad, that's a very naughty word," shouted Daisy. Josh held her tighter against his chest.

"Dad, stop it. Josh looked after Daisy while I worked today, and then my car broke down, so he gave us a lift here."

"Well, he can get his filthy, black hands off my granddaughter," Dad bellowed.

I was mortified. My dad had never been racist. None of us were.

"Dad, just shut up, please. Josh is my friend; you can't speak about him like that."

"So, you're off whoring yourself out to him while you're supposed to be working, are you?" Dad questioned as he stumbled sideways into the wall.

Daisy started crying, and I followed suit.

"That's it. Get your stuff, Keeley. You're coming home with me, and I won't hear any arguments," Josh said as he turned towards me. He put Daisy down to stand on the floor and spoke to her gently.

"Daisy, why don't you help your mummy pack some of your clothes? You can come and stay at my cottage tonight. We can watch Ellie the Fairy Queen again, and you can show your mummy the colouring in you did for her today."

Daisy nodded and took my hand as we walked towards the stairs. I paused for a moment to tell Josh to ignore whatever my dad had to say. He looked at me and smiled, even though I knew he was angry and upset.

Chapter Three

Josh

As soon as I heard Keeley's footsteps upstairs, I grabbed hold of her drunken father and lifted him up in the air by his shirt. He seemed shocked by my strength, even in his drunken state. I let him struggle for a while, and then I spoke.

"If I ever hear you talk to Keeley like that again, drunk or not, I will hurt you so bad the only way you'll be able to take alcohol again will be through an IV drip in hospital. Do you understand me, you drunken bastard?"

"Fuck off, you—"

I knew he was going to be trouble, so I did what I probably shouldn't have done. I bared my fangs and extended my nails into claws on my free hand.

"Wh...what are you?" he asked, shaking.

"I am the stuff of nightmares," I whispered in his ear. Then I flashed my fangs and red eyes once more while hissing at him.

I heard the patter of water hitting the kitchen floor, and when I looked down, I saw that Derek, Keeley's father, had pissed himself. I looked into his eyes once more before I moved away from the puddle of urine that was pooling by my feet.

"Derek, you will forget all about what you've just seen. You understand that I'm a good friend of Keeley's and that she and Daisy will stay with me for a few weeks. You will apologise to Keeley and Daisy when they come downstairs and will promise to visit with your doctor tomorrow to get some help. Do you understand me? Tell me if you do."

Mind control doesn't always work on drunks, but Derek nodded and told me that he understood—repeating everything I'd said.

"Now clean this piss up, then bring any alcohol you have left in the house and pour it down the sink," I commanded.

Derek nodded again, so I put him down, making sure neither of us stood in the puddle of urine.

He brought out a mop and bucket from the cupboard behind him, so I took it from him and filled it up at the sink. I handed it to Derek, but he swayed when he went to grab it. Not wanting him to fall and cause Keeley even more stress, I took it back and opened the cupboard under the sink to search for some disinfectant.

There was some lemon-scented antibacterial cleaning fluid at the side of some dusters, so I poured some into the mop bucket and set about mopping the kitchen floor. When I finished, I went outside and poured the dirty water down the drain. There was an outside tap, so I rinsed the mop and bucket out before I went back inside.

Keeley stood in the kitchen watching her father pour a bottle of whisky down the sink.

"What happened?" she asked hesitantly.

"We just had a little talk. Your dad decided he needs to go to the doctor tomorrow to get some help. It's best if he gets rid of any remaining alcohol to enable him to see that through."

"Did he now?" Keeley turned to look at me, smiling for the first time since I'd picked her up earlier. Then, mumbling something about hidden bottles, she hurried back upstairs.

She came back down with two more bottles of the cheap whisky that Mr Singh sells at the local shop.

"I found one in the airing cupboard under the towels," Keeley said, handing it to her father. "And this one was in the ironing pile."

I watched her father swallow hard as he took the bottles and began pouring them away. The smell of the whisky combined with the lemon disinfectant wasn't a pleasant combination. Out of the mouth of babes, little Daisy announced, "It stinks in here, Mummy. Can we go to Josh's house now?"

Keeley nodded, so I took Daisy's hand in mine.

"I'm sorry for the things I said earlier, Keeley. And I'm sorry for swearing and upsetting you, Daisy. I didn't mean to. I love you both, so don't stay away too long," Derek said quietly.

"I love you too, Dad," Keeley sobbed. "If you can get an appointment in the morning, I'll go with you to see the doctor."

Derek nodded, then turned to me.

"Look after them both. I'm sorry for earlier."

"Apology accepted," I said, completely taken aback because mind control had not made him do that.

After picking up Keeley's small black suitcase and the

girly pink holdall from behind Daisy, I ushered them out of the house.

Daisy chatted away on our journey to my cottage, saying she *really* needed a suitcase with Queen Ellie on it because they were the best ones, while Keeley cried silent tears, doing her best to keep them hidden. Wanting to offer her comfort and support, I clasped Keeley's hand in mine and held it for as long as I could while driving.

I put the heating on as soon as we got home. It was much cooler now, and I didn't want my girls to catch a chill. After checking if they needed anything, I took the suitcase and holdall into one of my spare bedrooms.

Daisy came running in after me and scrambled onto the bed. She'd taken off her shoes in the kitchen and was now pulling off her socks and leggings.

"I'm having a bath," she announced.

"Oh, are you now?" I said, laughing at her enthusiasm. Daisy got her head stuck pulling off her long T-shirt, so I helped her remove it.

I rubbed noses with her. Eskimo kissing, she calls it, and it's currently one of her favourite things.

Keeley stood in the doorway smiling at us, and I kissed her on the cheek as I went by.

"Thank you, Josh, for everything you've done today."

"No problem, Keeley. We all need a little help now and again," I told her.

"Can I run Daisy a bath?" she asked.

"I'll do it while you get her things together. You can use my bath. I'll turn the Jacuzzi setting on so she has bubbles," I said before realising my mistake.

"*Joshua Bubbles*," Daisy shouted while bouncing naked on the bed.

I laughed and shook my head as I walked through to my

en-suite bathroom. Daisy called me Joshua Bubbles because I kept a few bottles of bubbles in my desk drawer for whenever Keeley brought her to visit.

Since Keeley got her new job with Gregor, we've all rallied around and helped with childcare. I was glad she'd let us do this. I'd visited Keeley the day she gave birth to Daisy and had been a small part of her life ever since. She was the light on some very dark days for me, and I loved her so much.

While the bath was running, I called Nik at the office. I explained the situation and asked him to let Maggie know so she could come over and see Keeley later. I also told him I was taking a few nights off. I'd filled in enough for Nik and Alex; they could cover for me for a change.

Keeley's father was Maggie's brother-in-law, so I wanted to let her know and to see if they could accompany Keeley when she went with her father to see the doctor. It was going to take some persuading from them to get her dad to accept some real help.

I thought I could talk to her later about trying to get him into a private rehab centre. I knew the NHS was pretty stretched and that he might have a long wait to get into one of their places, but I could send him somewhere good. Keeley and Daniel wouldn't want me to pay, but I can afford it, and if it made Keeley and Daisy happy, I would do it in a heartbeat.

Daisy came running into the bathroom and stopped at the side of the bath. I couldn't tell whether the bubbling water amazed or scared her. She looked up at me in awe and asked, "Is it a magic bath?"

"Yes," I replied. "It makes you cleaner. Queen Ellie has one."

She gasped, then quickly attempted to climb in.

"Mummy, quick, help me get in. Queen Ellie's got one of these baths. Josh, put my pink bubbles in. They make me really clean."

I watched as Keeley tipped a couple of capfuls in, then I picked Daisy up and placed her in the bubbling bath.

"*Wow!*" she said in such a little voice it was almost a whisper. Then she turned to me and asked, "Josh, how come you've got a queen's bath?"

"I got it for you, Daisy, so that you and your mummy can come and stay with me."

"I love you, Josh," she said, throwing her soapy arms around my neck and soaking my T-shirt.

"And I love you too, Daisy," I replied, smiling. Truth be told, I was a little choked up at that declaration, so I excused myself and went to the kitchen to put a pizza in the oven.

Twenty minutes later, Daisy was squeaky clean and wearing her fairy pyjamas while eating a slice of pizza at the table. Keeley jumped in the shower after getting Daisy dressed, and when I heard her walk into the room, I got up to get her pizza and put it on a plate with the salad I'd prepared. When I turned around, I had quite a pleasant shock. Keeley stood at the side of my kitchen table wearing little pyjama shorts, a tank top, and nothing else.

Keeley is an exceptionally beautiful woman. Standing at five-foot-ten with long, wavy blonde hair that she nearly always wears loose. She has the most beautiful ocean-blue eyes, sexy full lips, and a smattering of freckles across her nose. Keeley has the hottest figure you could ever imagine, with long, toned legs and bigger-than-average pert breasts—

her nipples standing proudly against the material of the top she wore. She looked like a goddess, and it took a while to register that she was speaking to me.

"Josh, hey, I said you didn't need to cook. You've done more than enough for us already."

"It's no problem, Keeley. It's nice to have someone to take care of. I'm usually on my own now that Nik and Alex have their ladies, so it's good to have company."

I pulled a chair out for her to sit on, grabbed the orange juice and glass from the kitchen counter, and poured her a drink. Then I sat next to Daisy and ate without glancing at Keeley at all. As soon as Daisy had finished, she got down from the chair and ran straight towards the TV.

"Please, Josh, hurry. Put Ellie the Fairy Queen on before I have to go to bed."

"Daisy, you need to brush your teeth first before you watch the telly," Keeley insisted.

"Aww, Mummy, do I have to?" whined Daisy as she hid behind my leg.

"If you don't, there's no Queen Ellie. Your choice," her mother warned, trying to sound stern.

"Aww, okay. But only if Josh puts the toothpaste on the brush for me."

I took Daisy's hand and started towards the hallway.

"Sorry, Josh, our toiletry bag is still in your bathroom. I forgot to take it through to the other one after my shower."

"That's okay, Keeley. I'm not bothered which bathroom you use," I reassured her.

I walked into my bedroom, and Daisy ran past me into the en suite to grab the bag containing her toothbrush and toothpaste.

Sitting on the side of the bath, I carefully squeezed the strawberry-flavoured toothpaste onto a pink fairy toothbrush. Only when Daisy began brushing her teeth did she stop talking.

So this was what everyday life was like when you had kids. I loved it!

I hated that Keeley's dad had been giving her all that grief, but selfishly, I was happy that she and Daisy were here with me.

I lifted Daisy up so she could spit her toothpaste out in the sink and rinse off her toothbrush. She told me how important it was to have clean teeth because if you don't, *"the dentist won't give you a sticker."*

Armed with that knowledge, off we went hand in hand back to the kitchen, where Keeley was washing up at the sink. I wanted to walk up to her, wrap my arms around her front and kiss her bare shoulders. But she'd had a tough time today, and the last thing she needed was me making a pass at her. Keeley needed to feel comfortable in my home, so I had to keep my lustful thoughts at bay. To be honest, they weren't all lustful. I would've been just as happy to hold her.

I put the film on and settled down on the sofa with Daisy on my knee. Keeley came to sit beside me and, to my surprise, leaned towards me and put my arm around her shoulder. I placed a kiss on the top of her head, then did the same to Daisy.

"My two pretty princesses," I declared, pulling them in for a hug.

"No, Josh, I'm a queen now, like Ellie," Daisy haughtily declared.

"Oops, I forgot," I replied, trying not to laugh. "My pretty princess and queen."

I felt Daisy smile through my T-shirt, and then we settled down to watch the film. Within fifteen minutes, she was fast asleep.

I was about to get up and put her to bed when there was a quick knock at the door before Maggie walked in. Keeley turned, put a finger to her lips, and pointed to a sleeping Daisy. Maggie nodded and tiptoed towards us. She bent to kiss Daisy, and I joked that I thought she was going to kiss me, so she planted one on my cheek, too. I stood with Daisy in my arms, and Keeley went to take her from me.

"Let me put her to bed, Keeley, then you can explain what's been going on to Mags. I'll make us all a drink when I come back," I whispered, trying not to wake Daisy.

Keeley nodded her head and kissed Daisy before I took her to the guest bedroom.

Daisy had fallen asleep on my sofa several times since I'd begun taking care of her while Keeley was at work. But putting her to bed was just so different. It made me imagine what it would be like to be the little girl's father. To care for her every day—feed her, clothe her, pick her up from nursery, bathe her, brush her teeth, and then put her to bed. I'd love to be such an important part of her daily life.

If only Keeley didn't see me as just a friend or, even worse, family. If only it would be okay to have the thoughts I'd been having about her for so long.

After tucking Queen Daisy in with her pink teddy, I made my way back to the hallway, keeping the bedroom door open slightly so we'd hear Daisy if she woke up. I tiptoed as lightly as I could back to the sitting room, pausing in the doorway when I heard my name mentioned.

"Then we came back here with him and got settled in for the night. I honestly can't thank Josh enough lately, Aunt Mags. He's been a great friend to me," I heard Keeley say.

"Is that all he is, Keeley? A friend?"

"Sadly, yes. I'm sure Josh still sees me as that awkward

teenage girl who got knocked up. I think he'll only ever view me as a friend."

"I wouldn't be too sure about that," Maggie said. "But whatever happens, don't hurt him, Keeley. Josh has a big heart, and I'd hate to see it broken."

"I wouldn't hurt him, Aunt Mags. That's the last thing in the world I would ever want to do," Keeley stated.

So, Keeley wanted me to see her as more than just a friend. If she only knew how I felt about her. I wasn't sure how to play this, but shouldn't the fact that she and Daisy were living with me make it a little easier? I shook off my thoughts for the time being and walked into the room.

"Daisy's out like a light, but I've left the door open a little in case she wakes up."

"Thanks, Josh. I'll make us all a drink. What would you like?" Keeley asked.

"Nothing for me," Mags said, getting up from the sofa. "I'm going back to work. I'm glad you're taking a few days off, Josh; you've earned the rest after all the hours you've put in over the past few months."

"Thanks, Mags. Are you sure you won't stay for a drink?"

"Yes, I'm sure. Let me know in the morning if your dad's got an appointment, Keeley. It doesn't matter what time. I'll make sure I get Dave to go with you. After all, he's your dad's big brother, so he can try again to get him straightened out."

"Thanks, Aunt Mags. I promise I'll call, but don't hold your breath," Keeley cautioned. "You know what he's like."

Mags kissed Keeley on the cheek, and I saw her to the door. Before saying goodbye, she hugged me and said she'd call us tomorrow.

I watched her get into one of the compound's golf-cart-type buggies that we used to get around the place. Then I locked the door and walked back to the sofa.

Keeley came towards me with two cups of tea, so I took one from her and sat down. She sat beside me and picked up the remote control.

"What do you usually watch, Josh?"

"Not much, to be honest. I'm usually at work at this time. What would you like to watch?"

She flicked through the channels and chose *Dark*. I enjoyed that show, too, so we settled down on the sofa as we had before, with Keeley leaning into me and my arm around her.

This was what I wanted every night. To be with Keeley like this, and Daisy asleep in my home after our day together. Simple things, yet perfect, nonetheless.

I finished my drink at the same time as Keeley finished hers, so I took the cups and placed them on the lamp table beside me. Then I pulled Keeley closer.

She smelled like the raspberry body wash she used on her and Daisy. It was lovely, but so was Keeley's own scent. I ran my fingers up and down her bare arm and marvelled at how smooth her skin felt under my fingertips. I moved them around in lazy circles over her upper and lower arm, tracing my name across her wrist.

Another scent hit me, heady and addictive. Keeley was aroused. I didn't know what to do with the knowledge. Should I carry on as I was doing? Did I mention that I knew she was turned on?

In the end, I carried on as I was, trying to stave off an unwelcome erection until Keeley shivered.

"Are you cold, Keeley?" I asked politely, though I knew the real reason behind it.

"A little. I forgot to bring my bathrobe," she replied.

"Well, you aren't wearing much, so here, have my T-shirt." I got up from the sofa, stretched a little, and then pulled it over my head.

Keeley looked up at my naked torso, and I watched breathlessly as she licked her lips. I handed her my T-shirt, but she didn't put it on.

"Suit yourself," I said as I sat down beside her. Again, I put my arm around her, and this time, Keeley ran her fingers over me—all around my chest and down to my abs.

Oh, fuck! My cock was growing harder, and there was nothing I could do to stop it while Keeley still touched me.

"Keeley," I warned through gritted teeth, trying hard to make my saluting cock stand down.

Looking up at me, she whispered, "Josh, will you kiss me, please?"

I cupped my hands around her face and leaned in to kiss her, softly at first, then before I knew it, we were kissing each other with as much passion as either of us could bring, and we couldn't seem to stop.

Keeley moved so that she sat astride me, then took off her tank top, baring her perky breasts. I touched her from her collarbone down to her belly button until she groaned and grabbed my hands, placing them on her full globes. They felt soft and weighty—her nipples begging for my attention. I traced my fingertips over the sensitive buds, teasing and tugging before sucking them into my mouth.

"Yes, oh God, that's so good. Don't stop," Keeley whispered.

I didn't stop. Instead, I slipped my right hand into her shorts. Keeley gasped when I ran my middle finger between her bare folds. I found her clit and rubbed around it as she rocked her pelvis into my hand, steadily building a rhythm.

Her movements suddenly faltered, and Keeley cried out as she came all over my fingers.

When her breaths were back to near normal, I took my hand out of her shorts and put my fingers in my mouth, tasting her creamy essence.

"Take off your shorts. I want to taste you, Keeley," I told her, my voice sounding hoarse.

Keeley shook her head. "Not out here, Josh. Daisy could come out and see us."

"Shit! Yeah, I'm sorry. You got me all carried away there," I admitted. "Will you come to bed with me, Keeley? We don't have to do anything; I just want to hold you."

"Yes, Josh, I'll come to bed with you. But I'll have to get in with Daisy if she wakes up during the night." Keeley sounded slightly nervous.

"Of course," I said, stroking her cheek. "Whatever you need to do."

"Well then, take me to bed, Josh. Love me and make me feel wanted."

I kissed her softly and told her the truth. "I do love you, Keeley, more than you know. And I want you so badly. I have for a long time now."

Keeley gasped, looking a little shocked at my statement. But I could see a smile emerging.

"I love you too, Josh. I've dreamed of us...of a night like this and how it could be between us."

My heart filled with joy at the words I'd wanted to hear for so long.

I kissed Keeley again and couldn't help smiling as I did so. Then I turned off the TV while she went to check on Daisy, joining me a few minutes later in my bedroom.

Chapter Four

Josh

I waited for her by the side of my bed, and she came to me with a look of apprehension.

"What's wrong, Keeley? If you don't want to do this, just say so. I won't put pressure on you because we fooled around out there."

Keeley shook her head. "It's not that, Josh. It's the thought of not being good enough for someone again. I haven't had a lot of experience, and I've not slept with anyone since I found out I was pregnant. Look how that relationship turned out."

"He's the biggest fool that ever walked this earth. You are the most beautiful woman I've ever met, and you're just as beautiful on the inside, too," I said, placing my hand over her heart.

Keeley backed away from me, and I could have torn Daisy's father apart for hurting her. I had to turn my face away so she wouldn't see that my fangs had descended before I had time to retract them.

I heard the rustle of fabric and turned around to find her climbing naked into bed. She was gazing at me, and I held that gaze for a few moments before I unbuckled my belt. Then I removed my jeans and boxers in one and stood naked before her.

Keeley gasped. "Bloody hell, Josh, you are huge. I mean, I know I've had a baby, so I'm obviously no virgin, but that's just not going to fit."

I laughed quietly as I got into bed.

"Do you trust me, Keeley? Do you trust that I would do everything in my power not to hurt you?"

"Yes, I trust you, but—"

"Then let me take care of you tonight. Let me show you how it should be when someone loves you with everything they have."

Keeley bit her lip, then nodded slowly. I kissed her with lazy little presses of my mouth around her lips, cheeks, and eyes, making my way down to her neck, where I licked her collarbone from one side to the other and planted little bites where her neck met her shoulder. When I heard her moan, I transferred my kisses back to her lips and took advantage of her open mouth to thrust my tongue inside. Within seconds, the kiss turned wild. I rolled us over so I could lay my body on top of hers, and she wrapped her legs around my thighs.

She rocked her pelvis up to meet mine, so I placed my cock at her entrance and pushed inside her.

Keeley felt so tight. Even though she was wet, I knew I would hurt her if I went any further. After one more kiss, I rolled us back over so that she was straddling me, then I lifted her up by her hips and brought her up the bed towards my face.

"Josh, I've never... Oh my God!" Keeley groaned as I thrust my tongue inside her repeatedly.

I eased back her folds and found her clit, which was firm from her arousal. I ran my tongue around it, then flicked repeatedly in an up-and-down motion. Keeley seemed to love that and began grinding herself into my face. She tasted so delicious, better than I'd imagined, and I eagerly lapped up the cream she released as her orgasm built. I carried on with the same up-and-down rhythm, and when I slipped two fingers inside her, Keeley came with a near-silent scream before her body dropped forward onto my headboard.

I lifted her and brought her back down to where my cock stood proud and wanting. Then I lined my cock to her entrance and Keeley sank down on it slowly. I could see the outline of her features and her body from the light we'd left on for Daisy in the hallway.

Keeley was stunning, and perfect in every single way.

"You are so sexy, Keeley, so perfect. You are mine now, mine for always."

"I want to be yours, Josh. Don't ever let me go," Keeley said, breathing hard while moving up and down my length.

It was too much. The feeling of her tight, wet heat wrapped around my cock and the way she moaned my name had me about to blow. I stroked her clit rhythmically while she rode me hard, doing my best to make it last—this moment I'd been dreaming about for so long. Keeley cried out as her orgasm hit, and I erupted inside her when I felt the muscles of her sex contracting around me.

She fell forward onto my chest. Her skin was damp, and she was almost breathless as I sought her lips once more.

While we kissed and whispered *I love you* to each other, I heard a quiet little voice in the doorway.

"Mummy," Daisy sobbed.

"I'm here, Daisy, just a minute," Keeley said anxiously as she scrambled away from me.

I reached over to my bedside drawer and pulled out a pair of boxer shorts, putting them on under the quilt. Keeley jumped up out of bed and picked Daisy up. She was holding her close and stroking her hair while whispering everything was okay.

"It's not okay, Mummy; I heard you cry."

"Mummy wasn't crying, Daisy," I told her while walking towards them. "I was tickling her, and she was laughing."

"Were you laughing, Mummy?"

"Yes, love, I was. Now let's go back to bed, or we'll be tired in the morning," Keeley said.

"Can we stay with Josh in his big bed?" Daisy asked.

"Oh no, Daisy. I don't think there's enough room in his bed," Keeley replied.

"You can both stay with me. There's plenty of room," I told them, hoping that they would. I didn't want Keeley to leave my bed tonight, and I didn't want to see Daisy upset, either.

While Keeley tucked Daisy up in bed, I went to the bathroom to wipe my face. I had the taste and scent of Keeley's orgasm all over it, so I wanted to get cleaned up before I kissed Daisy goodnight.

Keeley got up to use the bathroom as soon as I returned. Pulling back the duvet, I climbed into bed and yawned. Daisy scrambled over to me, put her arms around my neck, and lay her head on my chest, yet my little chatterbox never said a word.

By the time Keeley came out of the bathroom and put

her pyjama top and shorts back on, Daisy was asleep. Keeley snuggled up to Daisy and grabbed my hand.

"Sorry, Josh. You probably didn't expect this tonight," she whispered apologetically.

"Keeley, you and Daisy come as a package deal, so don't ever apologise for Daisy being with us. I love you both and would do anything for you." I kissed Daisy on the top of her head, then raised Keeley's hand so I could kiss that too.

For the first time in my long life, I finally felt whole. Like the missing pieces from the jigsaw of my existence had been found and put in place. Keeley and Daisy completed me. They were mine now. Mine to love and protect, always.

Chapter Five

Josh

I woke up at 6 a.m. with something in my mouth.

It was Daisy's foot.

She was lying across the pillows and had her head on Keeley's shoulder. Daisy's mouth was open, and she was snoring softly. I got out of bed as quietly as I could, picked up the jeans I'd worn yesterday, and carried them into the bathroom in the hallway.

After a quick shower, I went to start breakfast. I knew Keeley would want to leave early so she could try to get her father in to see the doctor. After rooting around in my fridge, I put bacon under the grill and whipped up some eggs. Scrambled eggs were Daisy's favourite this week, but I'd learned from experience that her favourite foods could change on a whim.

Just as I was pouring Keeley a cup of tea to take into the bedroom, in she walked holding Daisy's hand. She looked up at me with a shy grin, and I couldn't help but smile right back. Keeley looked lovely this morning. They both did, and when she walked right up to me and planted a wet kiss on my lips, I felt like I'd won the lottery twice over.

"Breakfast is ready, my two sleepy heads," I announced while pulling out a chair for each of my girls.

"This is lovely, Josh. You are spoiling us…and I love it," Keeley declared playfully.

"I like spoiling you two," I told them, serving up the bacon and scrambled eggs.

Keeley cut up Daisy's bacon while I brought us each a drink.

"Josh, are you going to marry my mummy?" Daisy suddenly asked.

Keeley and I stared at her, both of us a little shocked.

"What's made you ask that, Daisy?" Keeley inquired, trying to keep the nerves out of her voice.

"Because you and Josh were in bed and were nudey-rudey, and you gave him a sloppy kiss when you saw him. When people on telly get all nudey-rudey and kiss, they get married and have babies."

Keeley's face went bright red, and she was lost for words, so I seized the opportunity and told the inquisitive little girl the truth.

"I would like to marry your mummy, Daisy. But only if that's okay with you?"

I looked at Keeley when I finished speaking. She sat still with her mouth hung open in utter shock, and I wondered if I'd done the right thing by admitting that.

"I think it's okay, Josh, and I could be a bridesmaid again," Daisy replied with unbridled enthusiasm.

Daisy had been a bridesmaid at Alex and Julia's wedding, and she loved all the attention she'd received.

Keeley still hadn't spoken, and I was starting to get nervous in case I'd just messed everything up between us.

"Ooh, would that mean you'd get to be my daddy too?" Daisy asked, her eyes as wide as her smile.

"Would you like Josh to be your daddy?" Keeley questioned when she finally found her voice.

"Yep!" Daisy nodded. Both she and Keeley turned to look at me.

"Would you like to be Daisy's father, Josh? It's a forever thing, so think very carefully about the answer you give."

"I don't need to think about it, Keeley. I would be honoured to be Daisy's father. To become that would be the best thing that's ever happened to me," I admitted.

Keeley and I couldn't seem to tear our eyes off each other, and I understood at that moment what people meant when they said that time stood still for them.

Daisy broke the silence.

"So, *are* you going to be my daddy, Josh?"

Keeley turned to Daisy and smiled. "Yes, love, you have a daddy now. I think you should give your daddy a big cuddle and say thank you for making you breakfast."

Daisy stood on her chair, and I picked her up to sit on my knee. She put her arms around me as far as they would go and said, "Thank you for making me breakfast, Daddy. Oh, and thank you for being my daddy, too."

"That's okay, princess," I told her, my voice cracking. I tried my best to keep the tears appearing in my eyes at bay.

"Not princess, Daddy. You keep forgetting. I'm a queen now, like Ellie," reminded Daisy as she scrambled off my lap and ran towards the hallway.

"Come on, Mummy. I need to get to school to tell my friend Kelly I've got a dad now, like her, and I'm going to be a bridesmaid."

I looked over at Keeley and smiled. "Thank you, Keeley. I hope you know I'll never let either of you down. I will love you both and take care of you, always."

"I know that, Josh. I just hope you realise that taking care of madam in there isn't always this easy."

"Keeley, I woke up this morning with Daisy's foot in my mouth, and she was lying straight across the pillow. If I can cope with that, I don't think anything else will faze me."

Keeley laughed. "You don't know the half of it yet, Josh."

"No, but you'll be there to hold my hand throughout it all and show me the way," I replied.

"You don't have to marry me, you know. It was just talk," Keeley said.

"No, it wasn't, Keeley. Not for me, anyway."

I knelt beside her.

"Keeley Saunders, will you marry me?" I asked. I took her hands in mine and looked into her eyes.

Keeley smiled hesitantly, then nodded. "Josh, if you're sure this is what you want, then yes. I will marry you."

I kissed her softly, trying to put as much love into it as I possibly could. I wanted to take her back to bed and make love to her slowly, but I could hear Daisy bouncing on the bed and repeatedly singing, "I've got a daddy, I've got a daddy." So I reined those thoughts in until Daisy went to sleep tonight.

I sat back on my heels and sighed while deciding how to broach something that had been in my thoughts since yesterday evening.

"Keeley, I've been thinking about your dad and the best way to help him. Will you allow me to get him into a good rehab centre? Cost isn't an issue for me, and I don't want him getting any worse while we wait for the NHS. If we go private, we might be able to get him regular checks and weekends there, too, so he can keep on the right path."

"Josh, it would be way too expensive and—"

"Keeley, I want to do this for you. And for Daisy and your brother. Think of it as an early wedding present from me so your dad can be well enough to walk you down the aisle and be a good grandfather to Daisy."

"Josh, I don't know what to say," she said. "There's so much to consider and—"

"Let me do this for you, Keeley. I was taken from my family over 270 years ago. For so many years, I wondered what had become of them, and if someone was around to help my father in my absence. It would make me feel good to be able to help your father."

Keeley pulled me in for a hug.

"Thanks, Josh. I hope this works for him. He wasn't always like this. When Mum was alive and well, he was the best dad you could ever wish for. When she was dying, he just couldn't cope, and when she passed away, he lost it altogether. After the funeral, he had a breakdown and ended up in a psychiatric unit. That was when we went to live with Aunt Mags and Uncle Dave for a few months. Once he was well again, we all moved back here permanently. He was coping so well for quite a while, but when I went away to university, he lost it again. I felt so sorry for Daniel for having to cope with him on his own. When I found out I was pregnant and came back home, he got himself well again. He was great with Daisy and used to look after her while I worked. Can you remember how good he looked then, Josh? He looked so different. Now he's just a shell of a man."

"We'll get him healthy again, Keeley. Maybe we can beef him up, like Daniel," I joked.

"That would take some doing—our Dan's proper muscular, like you. My dad's never really been like that. Me and Dan don't take after him at all when I think about it. We're both blond with blue eyes like our mum, and much taller than him too. My grandfather was tall, though, so Dad says we take after him."

"I want to remember how my family looked, but I think my memory of them has become distorted a little over the years," I told her. "I wish I could draw well so I could have an image of my parents and my cousins. I think I resemble my father, but my eyes are like my mother's."

"Mummy, I can't fasten my buttons," Daisy yelled.

"Duty calls," Keeley said while pushing her chair back. Once standing, she tilted her neck from one side to the other, then stretched her arms out in front of her.

I snagged her hand and pulled her back to me.

"I love you, Keeley, and I can't wait to have you in my bed again."

"If it's anything like last night, I will be one satisfied woman," she said, blushing.

I spanked her bottom as she walked away, so she turned around and blew me a kiss.

Chapter Six

Keeley

We managed to get my father in to see the doctor for an emergency appointment, which was an impressive feat. He had to have some blood tests and a full examination. The doctor explained the effects that alcohol can have on the liver, but I knew all that anyway, and so did my dad. It hadn't stopped him drinking before, but this time, it made me think about my drinking on those rare nights out. I decided to limit my own alcohol intake and not be encouraged by handsome Russians to drink their vodka and absinthe.

Dan had picked us up in his car, and Uncle Dave had come to the doctor with us. I explained to them about Josh wanting to pay for private rehab treatment for Dad, and Dan reluctantly agreed.

With Doctor Chandler's help, we were able to place Dad in a privately funded rehab centre in Sheffield. It was only forty minutes from where we lived, but they didn't have a place for him until that evening, so Dan and I went back home with him to get his things together.

Dan was still angry with Dad, but he was making the effort to get along with him, and I was grateful for that. Uncle Dave took Dad out for a walk, so Dan finally asked me what had been on his mind most of the morning.

"What's going on with you and Josh?"

"Well, Josh minded Daisy yesterday, so when my car wouldn't start, I phoned him to let him know I'd be late picking her up. He came to get me, brought me here, then came in the house with Daisy and me." I sighed heavily, remembering Dad's words and behaviour yesterday.

"Dad was awful with him, Dan. He was quite racist towards him. He said I'd been whoring with Josh, and he was shouting and swearing, which made Daisy cry. Josh told us to get our things together so we could stay with him. I left Josh with him while Daisy and I got our clothes and stuff, and when we came downstairs, Dad was pouring whisky down the sink, and he said he was sorry. He also agreed to go to the doctor's today. Josh offered to pay for the rehab so we could get Dad well again, so he could walk me down the aisle as a dad should."

"Why? Are you planning on getting married, Keeley?" Dan asked, one eyebrow raised.

I nodded my head. "Josh asked me to marry him this morning, and I said yes. So I'll be getting married, though I'm not sure when. It's all kind of new, and to be honest, it all happened so fast. Then we had Dad at the doctor's, so I haven't had time to think about it."

Dan gaped and me. "But you're not even going out with Josh. I mean, I know you've fancied him for years, and he's been giving you the eye for a lot longer than he should have. But you haven't been in any sort of relationship with him,

Keeley. People who decide to get married are usually going out together for a while and maybe living together for a bit. You've spent one night at his home, and suddenly you're getting married? What will Daisy think about this?"

"She wants to be a bridesmaid, and she's happy for Josh to be her dad."

I knew exactly what Dan was saying. It's what I'd been thinking all morning.

But I wanted it.

For some insane reason, I knew it was meant to happen. This pull that I had for Josh, these feelings, they weren't going to go away or die down just because society deems that you shouldn't rush into marriage.

At the end of the day, I was marrying someone who'd become my best friend, my protector, and the man I wanted in my bed. I love Josh, and I believed him when he said he loved me too. In my mind, that was the requirement for marriage. We didn't have to rush into it; we could live together until we tied the knot. I wasn't that bothered about when I'd become Mrs York.

"Well, he's great with Daisy," Dan conceded. "He always has been. But Josh is black, and Daisy might get some taunts at school from kids who don't understand when she tells them he's her dad. You know how small-minded people can be. You should talk to her about it so she can let you know if anyone says anything. Then we can nip it in the bud. I have no doubt he'll be a brilliant dad to her. I mean, he's practically been that over the last few months anyway since you got your new job."

"I know. He's a great guy," I said with a contented smile.

"He's also a vampire, Keeley. And not the same type as your new boss, or Alex or Nik, because he can't stay out in the sun for more than a few hours. He will never age, and

Gina explained to me that if she drinks Nik's blood regularly, then she won't age, either. How will Daisy feel when she starts to look older than her mum and dad? How will you feel about drinking blood? Have you really thought this through?"

No, I hadn't thought much about that. My heart had ruled my head when we were thrown into that conversation by Daisy this morning. But I wasn't letting go of the decisions I'd made. They'd just need a few tweaks, maybe.

"There is one thing, Keeley. You'll be well off if you marry Josh, that's for sure," Dan stated.

"That's true, I suppose. If not for Josh's money, Dad wouldn't be getting the help he needs today."

Dan nodded in agreement. "I'm grateful for his help, Keeley, and I hope this works like it's supposed to. Did Josh take Daisy to school today?"

"Yes. He said he'd take her after I left. He's got a car seat for when he looks after her, which is a good thing because mine's still in my car at the manor. I'm going to get the AA out to it later. Josh says he'll put me on the insurance for one of his cars, so at least I'll have transport."

Dan gave me a kiss on my forehead before going to put the kettle on. "He's a good guy, Keeley, and I know he'll be a good father for Daisy. I'm happy for you both, but I think you need to get used to being a couple before you get married."

"I know, and I promise I'll make sure we talk about stuff tonight," I assured him. "How are you doing? Will you move back here while Dad's away?"

Dan sighed heavily. "I'm okay. I hate being on nights, but the money's better, so I'll have to suck it up for a few more years. It's just hard to have a relationship with someone when you're going to work just as they get home."

"I thought you were enjoying sowing your wild oats. You seem to have had more women than Hugh Hefner if the gossip in Barrowfield and Rothley is anything to go by."

Dan had a reputation as a stud, and it embarrassed me to hear women talking about him and how good he was in bed. That's what happened on my last night out. I was in the toilets at a bar in Rothley when a couple of women came in and were talking about him. One was telling the other how he had kept her up all night having sex, and the other woman said she'd never had as many orgasms as Dan had given her with just his tongue. I was so embarrassed and stayed in the toilet until I heard the women leave. That's something you don't want to hear about your twin brother.

But it seemed like Dan wanted more than casual sex—like maybe he was finally going to settle down. I hoped he could meet someone, though I think he'd already gone through most of the single women in a ten-mile radius of Barrowfield, so they probably wouldn't come from around here.

"I wouldn't listen to all the gossip, Keeley. If you did, you'd be asking Josh questions about Mel from the Red Lion," Dan said.

I suddenly felt sick. Had he been seeing Mel? Why hadn't I heard about it?

"What do you mean, Dan? I wasn't aware that Josh had been seeing anyone."

"You know what gossip is like, Keeley. It went around the canteen at work that Mel came back with Josh, Nik, and that Russian guy, Sergei. They say she stayed the night at Josh's cottage, and he's sometimes seen nipping in the Red Lion after closing."

"Thanks for telling me, Dan," I said, although I wish he

hadn't. What I had with Josh helped me to cope with my dad this morning, but I could kick myself for not asking him about his previous relationship history.

"Hey, don't be upset, Keeley. If there's one thing I'm sure of, it's that Josh would've never committed to you if he was involved with someone else."

"Yeah, you're right, Dan," I agreed, and prayed that it was true.

Chapter Seven

Keeley

It was after 7 p.m. when I walked into Josh's cottage. It had taken a lot longer to get my dad sorted at rehab than I thought, but the staff were lovely, and I had much higher hopes for his recovery than I had this morning.

I'd called in at the manor to see how work was progressing and to get some paperwork sorted for tomorrow when Gregor flew in. While there, I got the AA out to my car, and they told me it would cost way more to fix than it was worth.

Ryan had been down in the cellars doing his thing. The width of the cellar spanned the entire house, and though part of it had been divided up for wine and storage, there was a huge section that was currently having extensive remodelling that I hadn't been able to see the plans for. Very secretive and a bit strange, too, as this was the only part of the house where Ryan had brought in a different team of specialist contractors. And it didn't have the planner's approval.

I was exhausted and had a headache, so I was happy to see that Daisy had been bathed and was in her pyjamas waiting for me.

I also felt guilty for being out this late, so I picked her up and apologised for not being home earlier.

"It's okay, Mummy. Me and Daddy have been too busy to miss you anyway," she said, very matter-of-fact.

Daisy seemed to love saying the word daddy, and it surprised me that she hadn't slipped up and called him Josh again. In a way, until I had a good long talk with Josh, I kind of wished she hadn't called him Daddy yet. I needed to know the truth about Mel at the Red Lion first. I mean, I trust that Josh would never hurt me, and especially Daisy, but I'd trusted my ex, too, and he still broke my heart and ignored Daisy's existence.

Instead of giving in to her watching Ellie the Fairy Queen again, I opted to read Daisy a story. I sent her into the bathroom so we could brush her teeth, and Josh handed me a cup of tea and gave me a kiss. I pulled away before he could deepen the kiss any further and walked into the bathroom after Daisy.

After brushing her teeth, Daisy picked out a book from her backpack. It was a board book she'd had since she was a baby. She liked me to read it to her at least once a week.

Even though Daisy had lots of new books, she still loved this one. So I started telling her the story about a little nut-brown hare and a big nut-brown hare. When I got to the end for the second time and told her I loved her to the moon and back, she was looking sleepy.

After kissing her on the cheek and wishing her sweet dreams, I put the book on the bedside table. Daisy insisted she wasn't tired, but her eyes told a different story. After telling me she'd be able to sleep much better if she had some Queen Ellie pictures and bedding in her new room, Daisy turned on her side and was asleep within minutes.

I lay next to her for a while, thinking about how I could bring up the conversation about Mel from the Red Lion. A few minutes later, Josh opened the bedroom door and said he'd put my supper on the table, so I kissed Daisy goodnight and went to eat.

Josh had made baked potatoes with chilli and a side salad. He asked about my dad, and I told him about the rehab clinic and how nice it was. He held my hand across the table and said he was sure it was going to work out okay, and that the next time we saw my dad, he would be much better than he'd been in a long time.

I told him about my car; he said I should scrap it as I could have his Toyota. Josh said he didn't use it much since he bought the SUV, and he'd feel much better if Daisy and I were in a bigger, better vehicle than what we had. I nodded my head and kept on eating my supper. Josh was watching me intently, and it made me a little nervous. His mobile phone rang, so he got up to answer it.

"*Hi, Mel,*" he said in a cheery voice.

Mel! So was the gossip right? Was there something going on between her and Josh? I tried to listen to the conversation, but Josh walked towards the bureau and rifled through a drawer for some paperwork. He read out the details of a company, then looked at me as he said, "*No, sorry, Mel. Tonight's not good for me. Perhaps tomorrow night. Yeah, that would be great. I think I have it sorted, anyway, so don't worry. I'll make sure you're in good hands. Yeah, okay. See you soon."*

He hung up the phone and placed it back in his pocket. I felt his eyes follow me when I got up to scrape the remaining food in the bin and place my plate and cutlery in the sink. When I turned around, he was behind me, blocking my way back to the table.

"Keeley, what's wrong? You've been off with me since you came home. Have I done something to upset you? Did you want to get Daisy bathed and ready for bed yourself? I know you missed her, but you had a long day today, and I wanted you to rest when you came home.

"Daisy kept asking to get in the magic Queen Ellie bath with the bubbles ever since she got home from school. Oh, and I've found a whole new phenomenon. A child's doll will end up holding more water than the actual bath it was in. How does that happen? I thought I'd got all the water out, then I went to lift it out of the bath and even more came out. It happened again when I turned it over. It went on for about five minutes before I just gave up and left it to drain away."

I had to laugh at his bewildered expression. It was safe to say that would be the last time Josh allowed Daisy to put her doll in the bath.

"No, Josh, it's not that. I just…I heard some gossip today. I know we shouldn't listen to gossip, but I noticed something too, the last time we were at the Red Lion. I heard today that you might have had something going on with Mel. That she stayed here overnight, and you've been visiting her late at night at the pub. Then I hear you arranging to see her tomorrow. What am I supposed to think?"

"That when I said I would never do anything to hurt you, I meant it," he said.

"Well, I've heard that line before, so forgive me if I don't put much stock in those words," I argued.

"Not from me, Keeley. I meant what I said. I'm nothing like Daisy's father, so don't treat what I say like it was him saying it."

"Were you in a relationship with Mel?" I questioned.

Josh shook his head. "No, I wasn't in a relationship with her. But we slept together a few times."

I was both shocked and upset to hear that. I think it was the casual way he said it that got me the most.

"You said that like it was nothing. And now you're going to see her tomorrow night. Do you have a friends-with-benefits relationship?"

"What? No, Keeley, you have it all wrong," Josh stated, running his hands over his hair in frustration. He let out a heavy sigh and said, "Keeley, come and sit with me and let me explain it better."

I let him lead me over to the sofa, then he switched on a lamp. I shut my eyes against the light and placed my hand level with my eyebrows to stop the glare.

"Can you turn it off? I have a banging headache," I said, utterly fed up. My mood was completely opposite to how I started my day. He switched it off and turned back to me.

"Why didn't you say anything, Keeley? I could help you with that," Josh chided, frowning as he bit into his thumb before pressing it against my lips.

I didn't want to take his blood until I heard what he had to say, but he was pretty insistent, so I took the few drops that he offered and immediately felt a little better. Josh stood up, got me some water, and asked if I had any painkillers in my bag. I fished out two paracetamol and swallowed them down with the cold water, before placing my empty glass on the lamp table. When he sat beside me, he took my hands in his and ran his thumbs over the back of them.

"I own the Red Lion, Keeley. That's what that phone call was about. I was thinking of selling the pub, which I've told Mel about because she's the manager. She might not have wanted to stay on under new owners, and I have someone who's already expressed an interest in purchasing the business."

"When did you stop sleeping with her?" I asked.

"We only hooked up a few times, and it only started when something terrible happened. It was just a way to find some comfort, that's all."

"You could have come to me for comfort, Josh," I whined. I would have offered it to him gladly.

He shook his head. "Not then I couldn't. I'm going to tell you something now, and I don't want you to freak out on me, okay? Believe me when I say that we don't normally go around killing people or other vampires."

I sat up a little straighter and waited for him to carry on speaking.

"Last year, when Alex got involved with Julia, we found out that both she and Alex were being watched by another vampire, although we didn't know who at the time. The vampire kidnapped Julia when she called into the Red Lion to see Mel about something. It was after a delivery, and he found them in the cellar. He knocked Mel unconscious and was going to take Julia away with him so he could force her to be his Bonded woman. We learned he'd done the same to another woman in the village years before, but she'd managed to escape him when he went back home. The vampire used mind control to force the woman to sleep with and Bond with him. He even got the poor woman pregnant, but as I've said, she left the village and escaped him."

"Who was he, and why did he want Julia?"

"He was Brandr, the man Alex once thought was his father, but it turned out that he wasn't. His father was called Sebbi, and Sebbi had been having a relationship with Alex's mum—fathering Alex and Freya and using mind control on Brandr so he wouldn't know. It's a long story, but because Alex's real father had turned Brandr into a vampire and left him out to burn in the sun, Brandr came back to get his revenge.

"As Sebbi was dead, he waited until Alex was Bonded to a woman so he could steal her instead. That was a bloody quick way to explain it, and even I found it confusing," Josh stated.

"He was a monster," I said, horrified. Josh nodded.

Poor Julia. The woman had been through enough before she met Alex. She must have been so frightened. And the other woman was lucky to escape him.

"Mel called me to tell me what had happened, and I called Alex. We got to the Red Lion and…well, Mel had a gun and some knives, and we stayed behind the bar while Alex tried to talk Brandr out of it. He was also communicating telepathically with Julia through their Bond."

"Gina told me about that. I suppose it was a handy thing to have right then."

"Yes, it certainly was," he agreed, pausing for a moment before continuing with something that left me speechless. "Mel shot Brandr in the head, and Julia was able to stake him in the heart, which rendered him in a death-like state.

"To kill a vampire, you must stake them in the heart, chop off their head, and burn them. The head and the body must be separated because if not, they can heal if they become re-joined and the stake is removed."

I nodded as if I understood, but this was all new to me and quite creepy, if I'm honest.

"Alex took Julia away so that she didn't see the rest. I volunteered to remove the vampire's head, and Nik, Sergei, and I burned the head and body where we'd had the bonfire at the back of the pub. After that, we tried to clean the place up. Mel ended up coming back here with me rather than be on her own where everything had happened. We ended up having sex that night and then just held each other. It was a cathartic release. We'd both seen and done some terrible things that day, and we needed a way to forget. We hooked up again a couple more times, but it was just sex for both of us, and we knew there'd never be anything more."

Josh looked so sincere, and I knew he was telling the truth.

"I've been so lonely, Keeley, and I needed some company. So I was thrilled when you let me watch Daisy for you while you worked. I was falling for you but trying not to because I've known you forever. I thought you'd think I was a bit of a pervert to be fantasising about you all the time."

"You fantasised about me? What did these fantasies involve?" I wondered if they were anything like mine were about him.

"I could show you, but maybe not tonight," he said with a sexy smile.

"Why not tonight?" I asked, disappointed.

"Keeley, you came home from work upset because you thought I was seeing someone else, and you have a headache. The type of fantasies I have of you don't involve any of those things."

"My headache's nearly gone, and I'm sure I read in a magazine that sex is good for them," I insisted.

"Oh, really?" Josh smiled and raised his left eyebrow. It seemed he didn't believe me.

"How about I run you a bath," he said, "You can relax your day away and we'll see how you feel after that?"

"Sounds good to me, Josh. I'll wash the dishes while you run the bath. Perhaps you could relax in there with me?" I suggested.

Josh walked towards the hallway and gestured for me to follow.

"Leave the dishes, Keeley. I'll wash them. Just get yourself in here and get naked," he demanded in a voice that made me melt.

I watched him leave the room and missed him as soon as he was out of my sight.

Was it right to want to be with him so much?

Maybe I felt this way because I'd desired him for so long, and now he was finally mine, I needed him close.

I thought I knew what love and need between two people should feel like. Evidently, I was wrong.

The feelings I'd developed for Josh over the years were so different from anything I could have imagined. Stronger, deeper, and so real they could almost take on a life of their own.

I could hear the bath running, but instead of doing as he asked, I went to the sink and did the washing up. Then I walked to the guest room to check on Daisy before going into the bedroom. When I began removing my clothes, I heard Josh muttering to himself over the sound of the water bubbling, so I went to the bathroom to see what that was about.

The bathroom was bathed in candlelight, and a shirtless

Josh stood against the sink, holding Daisy's doll upside down and shaking it.

"What's up, Josh?" I asked with a smirk, knowing full well the doll would still have water in it.

"I thought it was all out, but when I lifted the damn thing it started trickling again. I'm going to have to buy her another one because, at this rate, it will take a week for it to be dry enough for her to play with."

The puzzlement on his face set me off laughing, and I couldn't stop. He looked at me and smiled before morphing his features into an expressionless gaze. He didn't blink or move at all, and when I could finally stop laughing, I became a little nervous.

"Strip for me, Keeley," he commanded.

I didn't hesitate. I was only wearing my blouse and underwear now; I'd left the rest in the bedroom. I tried to make it a sexy striptease, but my nerves and clumsiness got the better of me, and I ended up fumbling with the buttons.

Josh came towards me and stilled my hands. He undid the rest of my buttons slowly, while at the same time planting baby kisses on the side of my neck in a spot that turned me on as much as any foreplay could.

"I can't wait to sink my fangs into this bit here when I'm making love to you," he whispered while biting gently on that same sensitive spot.

With his words and actions combined, my sex flooded with arousal, and my knees grew weak.

"Leave the bath, Josh; take me to bed, *please*," I begged.

Josh shook his head. "No, babe, we have all the time in the world for that. Let's have a bath together and just chill for a while."

He kissed me slowly on the mouth, then backed away

and unbuckled his jeans. I removed what was left of my clothing and sank into the soothing bath.

I glanced over at Josh as he climbed in at the opposite end of the bath, and *WOW!* Josh seemed to have the world's biggest hard-on. I was as impressed as I was stunned.

"Josh, you're hung like a horse. I've only seen a couple of actual…you know," I said, pointing at his cock. "But I doubt many men could rival that."

Josh laughed and said, "Well, you seemed to like it last night."

"Oh my God, what does that say about the size of my vajayjay to have fit that in? I mean, I know I've given birth and everything, but I thought I'd go back to nearly normal, at least," I said while realising I must have a massive vagina.

Josh threw his head back and laughed even harder.

"It's not funny, Josh. I've just learned I have more room in my vagina than in my gym bag."

Why was he still laughing? This was a serious issue. I may need some designer vagina surgery.

"Keeley, believe me when I tell you that your vagina is perfect. In fact, I thought it was a bit on the tight side, to be honest. I had to work to get you extra wet before I could get more than the head in," he assured me. But he was still grinning broadly, his perfect white teeth standing out against his dark skin.

"You're not just saying that to make me feel better, are you?" I questioned while trying to remember how to exercise my pelvic floor muscles.

"No, love, I'm not. Why do you think I did all this?" He gestured at the candles and the bath. "I want you nice and relaxed and properly turned on before I even attempt to get inside you tonight." He looked sincere, so I decided to believe him.

"I was so turned on when you were kissing and biting my neck. And when you talked about sinking your fangs in, that really got my juices flowing," I admitted.

"I noticed," he said. Then he seemed to hesitate before asking, "Would you let me take your blood tonight? I'd only do it if you wanted me to. No pressure."

Josh's eyes told me everything. For some reason, he was nervous. Like he thought I'd only do it to please him. Well, he'd got that wrong.

"Gina and Julia were talking about it with me a few weeks back," I told him. "They said when Nik and Alex bite them during sex, it makes them orgasm harder and longer than normal. Gina says Nik likes to bite the inside of her thigh after he's gone down on her."

"Bloody hell, Keeley. That's way too much information about my brother, best friend, and their women. I can't believe all the personal details you ladies tell each other."

"Well, they said it was amazing, so I wouldn't mind it at all…however you'd like to do it."

Josh stared at me for a moment before saying, "I think I'd like your neck the first time, then I'd probably go for the inside of your thigh or your breasts."

My mouth went dry, and I licked my lips as I watched him rise onto his knees and lean towards me, water dripping off his dark, muscular body. I reached out to touch his biceps and shoulders, marvelling at how hard they were as he braced his hands on either side of my head.

Josh leaned down to kiss me, and I met him halfway. His lips were soft and warm when they first touched mine, and then passion took over. I grabbed the back of his head, pressed my lips harder against his, and kissed him with all I had. All too soon, he pulled away from me and sat back down at the other end of the bath. I could see in his eyes that he wanted me as badly as I wanted him, but tonight he felt that this was his dance, so I let him lead.

"Have you ever drunk from a woman you've had sex with before?" I asked, dreading the answer before he gave it.

"Years ago, I paid prostitutes for sex and their blood. As soon as they felt the pleasure it gave, they always tried to make us regular clients."

"You paid to have sex? Why does someone as good-looking as you need to pay for sex?" I asked in surprise.

"Keeley, I know I told you about my background, of how Alex saved me when I was brought to Liverpool as a slave. Now think about how a black man would have been treated in England 271 years ago. What respectable English woman in their right mind would want to be seen associating with a black man, never mind having a committed relationship with one? Most wealthy families with slaves wouldn't allow them to get married, so there was no one other than prostitutes for me at that time."

"Did you sleep with many?"

"No. Even prostitutes were picky about sleeping with black men. But at least with me, they knew they couldn't catch diseases, and I could help them heal from theirs with my blood.

"Then there were the women in Gregor's club. They weren't prostitutes, but it was their sexual fantasy to get a vampire to take their blood after sex—or some of the other kinky shit that Gregor's into."

"What do you mean by that?" I asked, curious to find out something about my normally secretive boss.

"I suppose I shouldn't be telling you this," he said as he looked at me warily. "Gregor owns a kink club in Moscow. It's a discrete, high-end place, and loads of important Russian dignitaries are members. Anyway, some of the female members who are submissive like us to drink from them during sex, or during one of their specific kink sessions."

"Oh my God, so my new boss is some sort of Dom or whip-wielding fetish guy?" I asked, shocked yet also a little intrigued as the image of Gregor wearing nothing but leather trousers sprang to mind.

"I'm not saying any more about Gregor," Josh said with a sigh. "I had sex with women there, but that was as far as I went. I'm not into all that flogging, paddling, and tying women up to wooden contraptions while you test how much pain they're willing to endure in the name of pleasure. I just never got any of that, and it doesn't turn me on like it did some of the other guys."

"I've read a few books about that kind of thing, but I've never done anything like it," I admitted. I wasn't opposed to some of what I'd read, though.

"Did you want to try any of what you read?" he asked a little nervously.

"Maybe some stuff, although I wouldn't like any real pain. Maybe a little spanking or tying me up and teasing me." I was embarrassed to admit that, but I was being honest about my thoughts on the subject.

"We could try it, I suppose," he said, though he sounded downhearted.

"What put you off about it, Josh?" I asked, sensing there was a lot more to the story than he was telling me.

Josh lay his head back and stared at the ceiling. "When I was brought over on the slave ship, there was also a young woman from the village who'd been captured. One day, two of the guards held her down and raped her in front of us. Me and another guy I was shackled to tried to stop them, but they tied us to a post and had us whipped and beaten.

The woman tried to fight them, but she was in chains, and there were two of them. They brought her back down with the rest of us below deck later that day when they'd had their fill of her. She was bleeding from every orifice and was beaten beyond recognition. They'd broken most of the bones in her face and jaw and quite a few in her body. They left her there to die that night and didn't come for her body until the following day."

Tears appeared in Josh's eyes before he blinked them away.

"So I don't like the idea of women being tied up and beaten in the name of pleasure and sex."

"Oh, Josh, I'm so sorry. And I'm sorry for the poor woman who had to endure that before she died. I hope her ghost came back to get her revenge on them."

"It didn't need to. Freya, Alex, and I saw to that," he said in a hardened tone.

"I don't need any of that kinky stuff, Josh," I reassured him. "It's just that earlier, you mentioned fantasising about me. One of mine is where you tie me to the headboard and blindfold me. Then you tease me by kissing, touching and licking all over my body, making me beg for you to fuck me."

His pupils dilated; I could tell my fantasy appealed to him.

"I think that could be arranged," Josh said. Then he added, "Keeley, I'd do anything for you, but I could never hurt you. Not even if you wanted me to."

"Does it hurt at all when you bite someone?" I asked.

"I'm told it's a fleeting pain that turns so quickly to pleasure, and you feel it for less than a second," he replied.

Somewhat warily, I asked, "Josh, have you ever drunk from a woman you were in a relationship with?"

"No. It's never felt right before. And to be honest, I've never had a full-on relationship. Not where we've given each other a commitment to be exclusive."

This pleased me. I wanted to be a first for him in something, and it appeared that I was.

"Come on, let's get washed and get out of here," he said, passing me my raspberry body wash.

After removing my make-up with my facial cleanser and cloth, I washed my breasts, arms, tummy and between my legs while Josh watched hungrily. Then I lay back and swished the fragrant bubbles away. Because the Jacuzzi jets were bubbling, the soapy wash took a little longer to rinse off than it usually did.

Josh's body wash was Versace Eros and matched his aftershave. It was a fragrance that tempted me whenever I'd been near him at work and when I saw him on a night out. Now here he was, washing his body with it in front of me, running his big strong hands all over his chest, his muscly abs, right down through the black pubic hair and all over his hard length.

I'd seen enough. Feeling flustered, I grabbed a towel and stepped out of the bath.

"What's up, Keeley?" Josh asked, washing the suds from his body before following me.

I said nothing, just dropped to my knees in front of him and took as much of his cock in my mouth as I could. Josh groaned as he placed a hand on the back of my head. I had to wrap one of my hands around the base of his cock to help me build a rhythm; he was too big for me to use my mouth alone. I flicked my tongue around the head, then all along his shaft from the base to the tip, tasting the salty fluid leaking from it.

"Enough, Keeley. You're killing me here, love. I don't

want to come in your mouth. Not tonight. I want to come buried balls deep inside you with my fangs in your neck and your blood flowing through me."

Josh pulled me up and dried us both while I touched him everywhere I could. When we were both dry, he led me over to the bed and kissed me, urging me to lie down. I was glad of the low light from the bedside lamps as I watched him lie beside me. I hoped he couldn't see the stretch marks I had from my pregnancy and that I wasn't as smooth-shaven down below as I like to be. Josh stroked my body lazily from my neck to my thighs.

"Keeley, you are perfect. How no one has snapped you up before now is beyond me," he said as he looked into my eyes.

"I was waiting for you," I answered honestly.

For years, I waited for Josh to look at me like I was everything to him. Now I'd finally got my wish.

I stilled his hand and placed it at my core. I was wet for him, but as Josh was a vampire, he'd have known that already. When I took my hand away from his, he slid his fingers into my dampness and found my clit. My eyes closed, and I moaned softly when he began teasing me there.

I pulled him down for a kiss that made my toes curl, and I knew Josh liked it too; I could feel a sticky trail over my leg from where his hard cock rested. He planted kisses and nibbles over my neck, collarbone and down to my chest. Then he licked and lightly bit the soft flesh on each of my breasts, teasing me—as if he had all the time in the world to do just that. When he sucked a nipple into his mouth, the orgasm slammed into me, and I came all over his fingers.

In my orgasmic stupor, I was vaguely aware of Josh bracing himself over me. I tried not to tense when he attempted to enter me, but he felt too big and thick, so I held my breath and froze.

"Don't be scared, Keeley. I'm not going to hurt you. I would never hurt you." He kissed me softly and whispered, "I love you."

When I told Josh I loved him in return, he kissed me again, over and over, without moving his mouth from mine. I moaned his name, and a sudden force of need had me tilting my hips, taking him inside me. Josh threw his head back and groaned as he thrust deep, and I felt stretched to the very limit. It was perfect. Even better than last night.

"Please, Josh," I begged. And that was all it took for him to let go and move between my legs with harder, deeper thrusts. I felt another orgasm building with each passing second, and when I came, Josh bit deep into the side of my neck. The sharp, slicing pain disappeared when he took the first pull of blood into his mouth, and as soon as that happened, I orgasmed again.

I felt as though I was floating away on a cloud of pleasure, and I never wanted to come back down. When he removed his fangs, I whimpered with the loss, putting my hand on the back of his head to try and keep him there. Josh quickly flipped me over onto my hands and knees, pushing into me from behind.

It was rough, unrestrained, and deliciously deep. I loved it. Craved it, even. Josh slowed the pace as he ran his fingers up and down my spine. "You're so beautiful, Keeley, and you're all mine," he declared. Then he pulled out of me and rolled me over onto my back, adding, "I need to kiss you and see you when I come."

He sank inside me slowly, beginning a deep, consistent rhythm I felt at my clit every time the base of his shaft dipped inside me, triggering yet another orgasm, albeit less powerful this time. Gazing up at him, I saw a look that seemed like pain at first, then I felt his release hit deep inside me, and the look changed to one of pleasure, then peace. It was mesmerising, and I wanted to make love again so I could see it once more. I touched his face, and he turned his head to kiss my fingers.

"That was beautiful, Josh. I knew it would feel good when we finally got together, but these last two nights have been more than I've ever dreamed of. And when you bit me...."

"Yeah, I could tell you enjoyed it," he said, smiling. "You taste so good, Keeley. Not only your blood, but everywhere. Your kiss, your skin, and your sex...they're all my favourite things rolled into one."

"Well, I'm glad you like it all because I *l*ove you tasting me. I want you to do it again, and soon," I told him.

"I want to Bond with you, Keeley. Do you know what that means?"

"Gina told me it's where you take my blood at the same time as I take yours, and that makes us sort of married forever."

I remembered her telling me a few other things, but I wanted Josh to explain them.

"The exchanging of our blood part is right, and it usually happens during sex. But it's so much more than being married forever. We'll have an unbreakable link and will sense when we need each other. Or if we feel happy or sad. Eventually, we'll be able to communicate telepathically with one another. As long as you take my blood regularly, you'll never get ill or age—so you'll live as long as I will."

"When would you want to do it, Josh? Would you want to get married first?" I asked.

"No, love. I want to do it as soon as possible. But it will

have to be when Daisy's away at her grandparents because the urge to touch each other and have sex is much too strong when you first Bond. So it would be best if Daisy wasn't around to catch us in the act because, in the first few days, there will be many, many acts."

I giggled at his words and the dreamy expression on his face. He smiled and kissed me before whispering, "Let's make love again."

This time, our lovemaking was more frantic, and I wrapped my legs high around his waist as he drove into me. We came together when he once again bit into my neck.

Afterwards, he carried me into the bathroom to get cleaned up in the shower. I felt a bit sore when he rinsed away all the sticky evidence of our lovemaking, so he gave me a little of his blood to help me feel better.

After we dried ourselves, I slipped on a nightshirt before going to check on Daisy. She was sound asleep, and I was grateful for that. It meant that tonight I could fall asleep in Josh's arms. And after telling him I loved him, that's exactly what I did.

Chapter Eight

Josh

I woke at 3 a.m. to Daisy tapping on my shoulder. I turned over carefully, removing my arm from around Keeley's waist.

"Daddy, I need a wee, and my cover's come off my bed," she said with a light sob.

Keeley was sound asleep, so I got out of bed as quietly as I could, glad that I'd remembered to put on some boxer shorts before I went to sleep. I took hold of Daisy's hand and led her back towards the guest bathroom so we wouldn't wake her mother.

She pulled down her pyjama bottoms, and I lifted her up onto the toilet.

"I want Mummy to sleep with me," mumbled Daisy as she finished her wee and scrambled off the toilet. I pulled her bottoms back up and turned on the tap to wash her hands.

"Mummy's tired, Daisy. It wouldn't be fair to wake her

when she needs her sleep," I said, yawning.

"But you aren't asleep, so maybe you could sleep with me instead?" Daisy suggested, putting far too much soap on her hands.

I washed off the soap and dried her hands before carrying her back to her bedroom. When we got there, the quilt was on the floor to the left side of the bed.

"How did this happen, Daisy?" I asked while making up the bed again.

"I think a tree monster wanted to steal it," she replied, taking my hand in hers.

"There are no tree monsters, Daisy. I think you've been watching far too much Ellie the Fairy Queen, and your imagination's running away with you."

"Like the tree monster running away with my cover?" she asked.

"No tree monsters, remember?"

I picked her up and put her back in bed, and after covering her up, I lay on the bed beside her. Daisy turned over and put her hand on my arm.

"Daddy, why do you get to sleep next to Mummy now and I don't?"

Now, how did I answer this? I wasn't sure what to say or if I should let Keeley tell her, but I decided to explain things in a way I thought she would understand.

"Well, Daisy, when a mummy and daddy love each other, they get to sleep in the same bed so they can cuddle each other if they need to."

"But I love you and Mummy, so that means I can sleep with you too."

Drat. That didn't go as well as I thought it would, so I had another go.

"When a mummy and daddy have a big girl like you

and Queen Ellie, that means the big girl gets her own bedroom because only babies need to sleep with their mummies and daddies. And you, Queen Daisy, are certainly not a baby," I stated, kissing her on her nose.

Daisy rubbed her nose against mine and said, "Eskimo kisses, Daddy."

She was the sweetest child ever, and I was so blessed that both she and Keeley had allowed me to be her father.

Daisy cuddled up against me and yawned. I held her until she fell asleep, and then I went back to my bed where the only woman I'd ever been in love with lay sleeping soundly.

Chapter Nine

Keeley

I couldn't believe I hadn't heard Daisy get up last night. I was so tired after everything that happened yesterday; I slept until my alarm clock went off. Josh woke up as soon as he heard it and wanted to make love again. It was tempting, but I didn't have enough time this morning.

Daisy didn't have school today, so we let her sleep in. Gregor was due to land at Doncaster Airport, and I wanted to get to the manor and make sure everything was ready for his arrival.

I knew they'd almost finished the renovations in the main residence, and the business I'd been dealing with on Gregor's behalf was progressing well. I just wanted to keep up the good impression I'd made when I met him the first couple of times.

I genuinely enjoy everything about my job, and I wanted to keep it because my work impressed Gregor, not because he was friends with Freya and she'd asked him to employ me.

After showering and dressing, I looked in on Daisy. She was still fast asleep, although I willed her to wake up so I could see her before I left. Today would most likely be another long day, so I wouldn't see her until just before her bedtime again.

Josh's cottage felt like home already. Decorated in calming, neutral colours but with tasteful, luxurious furnishings, it was somewhere I'd always felt able to relax and de-stress. Josh favoured grey and stone colours on the walls and fabrics; solid, exquisitely carved rustic oak for the kitchen and bedroom furniture, and his bathrooms were epic! I wasn't used to living in such comfort. My dad hadn't maintained our home since before Mum died, and I never had the time or spare cash to make it anything other than liveable.

Walking into the kitchen, I saw that Josh had made us both mushroom omelettes, and though I was nervous about Gregor arriving, I was extremely hungry too.

"I could get used to this, Josh," I said as I finished my omelette and drank the best cup of tea I'd ever had.

"So could I, Keeley, although things will be different when I go back to work."

Josh sighed heavily and sat back in his chair. He seemed to be carrying the weight of the world on his shoulders.

"What's wrong, Josh?" I asked while going over and hugging him. He pulled me onto his lap, so I lay my head against his shoulder.

"Think about it, Keeley. I work twelve-hour nights, and you work full-time days. I'll be asleep when Daisy gets up and at work when she goes to bed. I can see her when I get up at around three, but we'll never have much time together as a family because when you arrive home, I'll be off to work."

"We'll sort something out, Josh. Families have to deal with this kind of thing all the time. It'll be okay, I promise," I reassured him.

"But that's the thing, Keeley; our family doesn't have to deal with it. I could sell my share of Night Movers. I know Sergei has expressed interest, as has Gregor. I'd have to talk to Nik and Alex, but to be honest, I can't see any other way to work this out." Josh looked miserable, and it was clear to see he was struggling with what to do for the best.

"Promise me you'll think about it before you rush into anything," I pleaded. "I'd hate to see you lose something you love because of me and Daisy."

"But I want to build our Bond together, Keeley. Daisy needs me to be a father, not just someone she sees in passing and on weekends. That's how families end up when they have no choice. Well, I have a choice. *We* have a choice. I have enough money for us to live off for a long time, even if I didn't sell my share of the business. And then there are the houses and the pub…"

I kissed his cheek. "Stop worrying, Josh. We can talk about this later. Now give me a proper kiss; I promise to give you a nice relaxing massage when I get home tonight."

"Can't we have a quickie now? I'm sure that'll relax me more than any massage would," Josh asked hopefully.

"No, Josh, you randy sod. It's okay for you men because you don't have the messy part of sex to deal with, and I'm not getting back in the shower now that I've done my hair and make-up."

"You could let me have a little play to get me through the day… Come on, Keeley. You know you want to," he mumbled against my throat.

Josh gifted me with the sexiest yet still playful look I'd ever seen. He traced his fingertips under my skirt until he reached the lace edge of my knickers. Flecks of amber appeared in his chocolate-brown eyes as he became even more aroused. He nuzzled the hair at the side of my head, and I could feel the hard length of him growing against my bottom. I had to kiss him; I couldn't seem to do anything else. When his tongue snaked into my mouth, Josh slipped his fingers into my underwear, finding the very spot that throbbed for his touch.

"Open your legs, Keeley," he commanded, and despite my earlier reservations, I obeyed. He pressed his thumb against my clit and moved it in slow but firm circular motions. I waited for him to push the fingers he held at my entrance deep inside, but he didn't. He stroked my wet opening gently, the complete opposite of what his thumb was doing to my clit. I couldn't help the moan that escaped into his mouth while he kissed me softly.

I rocked against his hand, trying to force his fingers to penetrate me, but he held fast and wouldn't let me set the pace. I had no control over this encounter, and it was too much for me to handle. The tell-tale signs of my impending climax had me breathless and shivering with anticipation, calling out his name when I came. Josh thrust two fingers inside me mid-orgasm, and I came again. One orgasm blended into the other in a seamless parade of spasms and flutters, my juices flowing over his fingers as he pressed them against that special spot inside me that only he seemed able to find.

I whimpered when he withdrew his fingers. I couldn't help it. It was involuntary, the same way my sex tried to grip his fingers to keep him in place. Josh held the two digits that had just been inside me against my lips, wanting me to lick them. I flicked out my tongue and lapped the tips, then he put them in his mouth and sucked.

"You taste so good, Keeley. Especially when you come. I want to lap it all up, but if I do that, I'll have to fuck you. And you're right: we can't right now. So go and change your wet undies, and we can avoid touching each other before you leave. If we do, I'm going to lose my resolve, and you won't be leaving for work anytime soon."

I got up from his lap and immediately felt how wet my knickers were. After slipping them off, I went to the bedroom and put them in the laundry hamper, then I gave myself a wipe with a damp washcloth before putting on fresh underwear.

I should have made love with him when he'd asked me earlier. I was still so turned on, even though I'd just had two orgasms. I'll know next time not to deny my man.

My man... I loved the sound of that. I wish we'd both acted on our feelings for each other much sooner instead of denying our attraction and love. But maybe it was better this way because our love had time to grow and become everything we needed it to be.

The sound of the front door opening pulled me out of my daydreams, along with Freya's voice as she yelled, "Hello!"

I left the bedroom and walked towards her welcoming hug.

"How are you, future sister-in-law?" she asked with a wink.

"I'm good, Freya; how are you?"

"I'm quite excited, actually. Julia, Gina, and I are going shopping for things for the baby today. I was hoping we could take Daisy with us. I thought we could stop off at the toy store so Auntie Freya can spoil her little niece."

"She's always called you Auntie Freya, but you'll officially be Auntie Freya when Keeley and I get married," Josh said as he handed Freya a cup of tea.

"That will make me an aunt twice over in one year." Freya beamed.

"I wish I could come with you. I need to get Daisy's feet measured for some new shoes," I told her.

"I can get them measured and buy her a pair. What colour do you want her to have?" Freya asked.

"I have the money here," I said, reaching into my bag for my purse. "And either pink or pale blue would be good. She'll probably pick blue because of Queen Ellie's wings, though."

Before I could take out the money, Josh handed Freya a wad of notes.

"I'll buy Daisy whatever she needs from now on. I'm her dad, so I get to provide for her. Freya, whatever she wants, take it out of that. And buy her a new doll, especially if it says, *will not absorb twelve litres of bath water.*"

"Okay. I'm guessing you bathed the doll," Freya said with a laugh.

"Yes, I was conned into it last night, and I'm still draining the water out," Josh stated, frowning.

"I remember when we took it into the sea last year at Hornsea," said Freya. "We carried it around in a sandcastle bucket for the rest of the week at my house until it was completely dry. That reminds me, will it be all three of you coming for a holiday at mine this year?"

"Our first family holiday on the east coast of Yorkshire," said Josh with a smile. "Of course, I can't spend a full day in the sunshine, but enough time for a good paddle in the sea and fish and chips on the promenade or around Bridlington Harbour."

"Perfect. Just let me know when and I can get your rooms ready," Freya replied.

I stared at them both as they were making plans for my and Daisy's life, and it felt odd. It was usually me that decided everything that Daisy and I did. But now we had Josh.

Our family of two was now a family of three. Even more, if you count Freya, Alex, and Julia. Daisy and I had always had Freya in our lives, so that wasn't something we had to get used to. But Alex and Julia will become my brother and sister-in-law. Daisy's uncle and aunt. I wondered if Alex would want Daisy to call him uncle. It would have to be a discussion for later because time was ticking, and I needed to get to the manor before Gregor arrived.

As if reading my thoughts, Freya said, "If you need to get off to work, I can get Daisy up and ready."

"Thanks, Freya, that would be great. I was hoping she'd be awake before I left, but I think she had a bad dream last night about tree monsters, so no cartoons for her today."

I grabbed the keys for Josh's Avensis, planted a big wet kiss on his lips, and then turned to hug Freya before I left.

"Is everything okay, Keeley? You aren't stressing about Gregor coming over, are you? I know he can seem quite intimidating, but he's incredibly sweet when you get to know him."

"No, Freya, it's not Gregor. It's Maxim. Yuri is lovely, but Maxim is just awful. I don't dislike many people, but I hate him. He's a bully who decided he didn't like me for some reason, and every time I see him, he makes that known. Never in front of Gregor, of course, but others have noticed."

"I'll have a word with the moody fucker if you want,"

said Josh, his hand clenching into a fist by his side. This was the last thing I needed in my new job—my boyfriend beating up my boss's bodyguard. I'm sure I could keep my job if that happened. Not!

"I don't want you interfering in this, Josh; I can sort it out myself. So promise me you won't do anything. Please."

Josh held up his hands in a placating gesture. "Okay, but if he hurts you, Keeley, I'll take him down hard, and he'll never get back up."

I could see his eyes start to change; a red rim surrounded the amber-flecked brown of the iris. I went over and hugged him tightly, and when I kissed him, the tips of his fangs grazed my lips. It didn't bother me, though. Strangely enough, I found it slightly arousing. Freya pulled out a chair, which scraped the floor noisily, reminding us of her presence.

"Thank you for looking out for me, Josh," I whispered in his ear.

"Anytime, Keeley. I'll be there whenever you need me."

I walked to the door and gave them both a quick wave before I stepped out into the bright sunshine.

As I closed the door behind me, I could have sworn I heard Freya say, "Well, *I* never promised not to hurt him."

Chapter Ten

Keeley

When I got to the manor, it appeared as though all hell had broken loose. Ryan was running around getting his team to fetch and carry everything from the old ballroom into the main lounge and study.

I managed to catch him for two minutes, and he confirmed that all would be in order on the inside of the house by the time Gregor landed, which was half an hour from then.

Nik was picking up Gregor, Sergei, Yuri, and Maxim; they'd be arriving at the manor in just over an hour. I checked my email to find that Gregor had requested I accompany him to buy a car, which he could use while here in England.

He'd specified that the car must be a Volvo or an Audi. But it had to be a four-wheel drive so that he wasn't restricted in winter. I phoned around and made an appointment with Luxury SUVs in Doncaster, which specialised in Volvos. But the nearest Audi centre that could fit us in was in Sheffield, and that wouldn't be until tomorrow.

Another email came from a member of the Rothley Boys' Football Team. They cheekily suggested that Gregor should support their team and fund the cost of the new football kits because, and I quote, *'That's what rich Russians like to do.'* I thought that nine-year-old Tommy Hedley had shown some initiative by finding my email address and sending me his suggestions, so I was going to mention it to Gregor. He was keen to be accepted by the town of Rothley and the village of Barrowfield, where most of the acreage that came with Rothley Manor lay.

There was a twenty-thousand-pound fund that Gregor had set aside for such requests. He didn't have to do that, but Gregor was a generous man and knew that in a small village and town such as Barrowfield and Rothley, a little money can go a long way.

I heard a clatter and a yell from the hallway, so I went to investigate.

Ryan was chastising a young man who was down on the floor, picking up a copper tray. I put my hand on Ryan's arm and led him away for a moment.

"Maybe I should let my staff know they're working for a vampire. They might not drop anything then," Ryan huffed.

"Don't you bloody dare. I'm surprised you know," I told him truthfully.

Ryan smirked. "Well, love, when you're paid as much as I am for a job, it ensures the utmost discretion at all times."

"Weren't you scared or even slightly disturbed when you first found out?" I asked.

"Keeley, I've worked for some of the highest-paid footballers, models, and royalty from all over the world. Trust me when I say that being a vampire has nothing on them."

Another clatter sounded in the dining room, and Ryan dashed off to confront the clumsy one.

I went back into the office Gregor had assigned me and went through the schedule of business he'd need to attend to during his visit.

Most of it revolved around the new supermarket being built by Gregor, Sergei, and the Night Movers team. I knew how much it would benefit the community, but the main supermarket giants were far from happy about it.

There'd been quite a few hold-ups with the planning permission in the beginning. We found out that one reason for the delay was a supermarket chain lodging a complaint. But thankfully, the council was able to discount all further objections, and we hoped to begin building soon, subject to their conditions.

After nearly an hour had passed, the house became quiet, so I went to see if anything was the matter. I found Ryan just about to go down to the cellar.

"Oh, hey, Keeley. We finished everything on the ground floor and in the first six bedrooms. Do you want me for anything else?"

He was looking a little sheepish and seemed to be inching his way below the stairs.

"Ryan, why aren't I allowed to go downstairs?"

"Now, Keeley, you know that Gregor stipulated there's only him, me, and a select team of workmen allowed down there," he replied, shaking his finger.

"Are you replicating something from his kink club? Is that why he flew you out to Russia?" I asked hesitantly.

Ryan frowned. "I'll pretend I didn't hear that, Keeley, and if not knowing bothers you so much, take it up with Gregor."

He marched down the steps without looking back, and I knew I had my answer.

I heard a vehicle pulling up the gravel driveway and went to meet them at the door. The first person I saw was Maxim. He was scowling at me, as usual, and I had to work hard to keep a smile on my face to greet my boss.

"Keeley, my darling. You look even more beautiful now than on my last visit," Gregor said.

Oh, this man was smooth, but I accepted his compliment and went over to shake his hand. Gregor pulled me into a hug instead and said, "Thank you for everything you've done here while I've been away." Then he kissed me on the cheek.

"It's good to see you again, Gregor. Everything is prep—"

Before I could get the rest of the sentence out, Sergei picked me up and spun me around.

"Keeley, I have missed you. Please tell me we are all going out to the Red Lion again on this visit. I have brought much alcohol this time."

"I think I'll give your alcohol a miss after the last time, Sergei, although a night out sounds good."

I'd be going as Josh's girlfriend or fiancée this time, which would be the first time I've been out as part of a couple in five years. I couldn't help the silly grin that spread across my face until I happened to glance in Maxim's direction. Yuri came around the back of the car with Nik. They both carried two suitcases and stopped just in front of me.

"Hello, Keeley. I am happy to see you again. How is your lovely daughter?" asked Yuri. He was a great guy. Although tall and muscular, Yuri didn't have that bodyguard look to him that Maxim had. He had a kind of dishevelled rock star appearance that came with a friendly manner. I'd warmed to him instantly.

"She's good, Yuri. Thank you for asking. And how are you?"

"All the better for being here in England because you have the sun. Russia is having so much rain."

"Well, don't expect it to last, Yuri. Our summers aren't usually this good," I stated.

It was the truth. We typically have around three weeks of scattered sunshine in South Yorkshire, which is considered a pleasant summer, although we seem to be doing well of late.

I followed everyone inside, keeping my distance from Maxim.

Ryan walked up to Gregor and shook his hand. "Everything is as you requested, Mr Antonov. There are still the old coach house cottages, stables, and estate cottages to complete. Although, the estate cottages have had their first fix and are just waiting for the electricians to finish."

"Excellent news, Mr Adamson. When do you expect completion of the cottages?"

"About three weeks, if the kitchen units can be delivered on time."

Gregor turned to me and asked, "Keeley, will you chase

up all the suppliers on Mr Adamson's list so that there are no delays? I am happy to pay for prompt service if that helps. Until that time, both Maxim and Yuri will stay at the manor with me."

"Yes, of course," I replied, hurrying along behind him. Gregor had long legs, which equated to even longer strides than my five-foot-ten frame was used to taking.

"I'm sure you'd all like something to eat and drink after your flight. Would you like me to bring something in from the kitchen?" I asked, glancing around at everyone.

"That would be wonderful, Keeley," said Gregor with a smile. "If you give us a moment, we will join you."

I smiled back and walked towards the kitchen. Nik and Sergei followed me, and it was only a few seconds later that Nik said, "So, Keeley, you and Josh have finally got it together then. It's about bloody time."

"You are with Josh? Why did you not wait for me, Keeley?" Sergei joked as he took my arm in his.

"There's been something building between you for a long time. I guessed as much after you had your daughter, but Josh kept denying it. I had to put up with him mooning after you when you weren't looking," Nik said.

"Josh was mooning you?" questioned Sergei, alarmed. "I thought baring your ass was an insult."

"Not that type of mooning," Nik replied, shaking his head. I turned and hugged Sergei.

"Sergei, you make me laugh. Thank you, I needed that."

"Anytime, Keeley. Although, I do not know why you would laugh. And you can tell Josh that I do not wish to see him bare his ass at you when I am near. I feel it is wrong to do so."

Nik shook his head as he filled the kettle. I'd bought two

platters of sandwiches and some pastries from the Night Movers canteen on my way to work. I'd also picked up some cupcakes that Moira, one of the Night Movers kitchen staff, had made. Sergei made a beeline for them, so I slapped his hand away and indicated to another box at the side of them.

"Those are yours, Sergei. When I asked Moira if she'd bake for today, she told me she'd promised to make you cupcakes for your next visit."

Sergei placed his hand over his heart.

"Moira is a wonderful lady; always bakes for Sergei." He opened the box and took two out. Then he passed the box to Nik, who also took two.

"Gina's dieting again," Nik announced before biting into a cupcake and groaning.

"We had better eat them all before you take me to your cottage," replied Sergei as he took out another cupcake and licked the frosting from the top.

"I've hidden chocolate chip cookies and red jellies in your room," Nik said before putting a whole cupcake in his mouth.

"Are they the sour, fizzy jellies?" asked Sergei.

"Of course," replied Nik, licking the frosting from his chin.

Gregor, Yuri, and Maxim walked into the room while I was pouring the tea.

"There's also fresh coffee in the pot if anyone would like some," I informed them.

"Thank you, Keeley, but I fear only Yorkshire Tea will do for most of us now. My dear Freya has me addicted." Gregor smiled when he mentioned Freya.

I used to think that Gregor and Freya were involved, but Freya insisted they were just good friends. It's obvious they're extremely fond of each other. The same can be said of Gina and Sergei. If I didn't know that Nik and Gina were together and very much in love, never mind Bonded, then I'd say that Sergei and Gina could be a couple.

Everyone gathered around the table in the huge country-style kitchen, and it wasn't long before there was very little food left.

"There's fresh blood supplies in the small refrigerator inside the old walk-in pantry. They were delivered yesterday," I added.

I'd ordered blood from the same provider that Night Movers used. That part of the job was quite new to me. I mean, I knew they were vampires and obviously drank blood, but other than the donations we made at the monthly blood drive on the Night Movers compound, I wasn't aware there were any other ways to obtain fresh blood. Apparently, there are donors throughout Europe who regularly donate to vampires and are paid well for their services.

"Gentlemen?" Gregor asked. All but Maxim shook their heads. Maxim knew where the pantry was, so I left him to fend for himself.

"Keeley, shall we go to the SUV dealership? Do you have your own car here to take us, or should I ring Alex?" asked Gregor.

"I have a car we can go in," I said. I was eternally grateful that Josh had given me his Avensis to use. My old car had been a tiny rust bucket.

Nik looked at me knowingly and smiled. I think the look of relief must have been visible for all to see.

"I wish to have a four-wheel-drive vehicle so that we are not restricted in bad weather. I will purchase one for myself, one for Yuri and Maxim to use when they are here, and one for you, Keeley," Gregor said nonchalantly.

I think my jaw hit the floor when I heard him say that, and I quickly turned to let him know I had my own transport. Gregor held up his hand to silence me.

"Keeley, I am going to buy you a vehicle. I would like to know that you are safe when driving yourself and your daughter around, and Volvo has some of the safest cars on the road. I did not bring you a gift on this visit. Instead, my gift to you will be a vehicle of your choosing at the dealership today."

When I shook my head, Gregor came over to where I stood and said, "Indulge me a little, my darling. I like to reward those who work for me, and you have been more than capable in your role as my PA."

What could I say to that? Gregor was a man who wasn't so easy to refuse. It seemed that only Freya could put him in his place. Maxim was not impressed, however, and he barged out of the kitchen in an almost child-like strop. Laughable, really, for someone his size.

"What's with him?" asked Nik.

"He's a fucking dick," replied Sergei. Yuri nodded his agreement.

"Sergei, do not use those words in front of a lady. How many times do I say this to you? It is not good manners," Gregor admonished.

"I am sorry if you are offended, Keeley," said Sergei as he leaned in for a hug.

"No worries, Sergei," I told him before kissing his cheek. "And you're right; he is a fucking dick."

During the journey to Doncaster Luxury SUVs, Gregor asked me why I was driving Josh's car. I told him that Josh and I were a couple now, and I'd moved in with him. I explained about my car breaking down, and Josh giving me the use of his old one.

Gregor was thrilled that Josh and I were together, as was Yuri, although Gregor said I should have told him about my car situation sooner. He said he hadn't realised that my other car was so old and felt bad that he hadn't bought me a new one before now. I told him it was down to me to sort out my transport issues, not him. But I could tell by the expression on Gregor's face when we walked into the showroom that he wouldn't be swayed from buying me a car. I just hoped that Josh was okay with it.

I walked up to the reception desk and advised the salesperson that I was the PA to Mr Antonov, and we were here with the intention of purchasing three brand new four-wheel-drive vehicles. I also informed Mr Andrews—the salesperson—that it was a choice between Volvo and Audi, and we hadn't yet made up our minds.

I used my special professional, *don't bullshit me* voice, which seemed to do the trick, as Mr Andrews immediately jumped up and took us to an office area. He arranged for hot drinks to be brought over as we perused brochures, colour charts, and specification leaflets.

When Gregor advised Mr Andrews that cost was not an issue, and he would like to pay for them in full today, I had to suppress my laughter and keep a professional demeanour. The salesman wore a look that said all his Christmases had come at once.

After test driving the XC90 and the XC60, Gregor decided on two XC 90 Inscriptions: one in Onyx Black for himself and Savile Grey for Yuri. He also bought a top-of-the-range XC60 SE LUX in Ice White for me. Gregor wanted me to have the same as him, but I liked the smaller SUV and told him I would feel more comfortable driving this one.

As the vehicles were each to Gregor's specifications, they had to be ordered. We were told it would take at least a week, so I informed Mr Andrews we'd require two XC90 courtesy cars to be supplied free of charge until the new ones arrived. I also told him we needed three years of free servicing with parts and labour to be thrown in with each vehicle at no additional cost because that's what Audi was offering. It was a lie, of course, as we hadn't even been to Audi, but he didn't know that. Mr Andrews went away to ask his boss about servicing and how soon they could have the courtesy cars ready.

Gregor turned to me and said, "You are an excellent negotiator, Keeley. I may have to take you back to Russia with me so you can sit in on some of my business deals there."

I blushed and told him I would if I could speak Russian. But I also had Daisy to think about, and now Josh, so maybe Russia just wasn't on the cards for me.

Mr Andrews came down with his boss, Mr Halliday—although we were to call him Roger. He thanked us for choosing his company, Luxury SUVs.

I reminded him that we hadn't settled on the deal as we'd yet to hear whether we could have our service plans and courtesy cars. Gregor went with me on this and started to put his platinum credit card back in his wallet.

Roger immediately agreed to our terms, so Gregor handed over his card.

Mr Andrews informed us they were readying a courtesy vehicle straight away, and that they would deliver another to an address of our choosing tomorrow morning. Yuri handed over his details for insurance purposes, as he would be driving the vehicle back. Gregor gave them his details so they could organise the second. After all the boxes had been ticked on our purchases, we returned to Rothley Manor.

Gregor came back in my car instead of going with Yuri, which surprised me. I thanked Gregor for buying me the car so many times on the way back he had to tell me to stop, but I couldn't help it. I was thrilled. It was a lovely thing for him to do, and I was awed yet again by his generosity.

We pulled up to the front of the manor with Yuri right behind us. Maxim approached the car and opened the door for Gregor.

"Ladies first, Maxim," Gregor admonished. But I was already out of the car and walking towards Gregor, who held out his hand for mine and kissed it.

"I think your new car will suit you, Keeley."

"I think so too, Gregor, and thanks again for buying it for me. I hope you know just how much I appreciate it."

"Now, now, my beautiful one. You deserve the very best of everything, and something tells me that's just what you will get from now on," he said with a smile.

Maxim huffed as he walked away, but when he turned back, the look he gave me made me stop in my tracks. My good mood plummeted, and the sickening sneer he left me with didn't make me feel any better.

I found Ryan in the kitchen and told him about the car. He was over the moon for me and said it was a shame I'd fallen for Josh because Gregor would make a great catch. I laughed and told him that money and expensive gifts weren't everything. Ryan said, "Come on, Keeley. You can't tell me that you don't get even a little turned on when you hear him say your name in that sexy as fuck Russian accent."

I had to agree with him on that score, and I was giggling so much that I didn't see Maxim standing behind us.

"Do you think he wants you, English woman? Do you think you could satisfy a man like Gregor?" Maxim snarled.

Ryan spun around to face him. "Why? Do you think *you* could satisfy him, Maxim? Because from where I stand, Gregor is all man—as straight as they come. Whereas you... Well, you are as gay as me, just not as camp. Isn't that right, Maxim?"

"You do not know what you speak of, decorator," Maxim spat.

"Honey, I've spent years honing my gaydar, and you, Maxim, are not a straight man. I think you're jealous of Gregor's affection for Keeley."

What the hell? Ryan must have it wrong. Maxim wasn't gay; I was sure of it. I turned to Maxim to let him know I was already in a relationship, but he left the room with vampire speed before I could even speak.

"Well, now you know why Maxim hates you so much," Ryan remarked. "Maxim has feelings for Gregor, but I can't see him getting anywhere with that one. So he'll have to stay his angry, frustrated self forever. I know what that feels like, believe me."

"I just can't believe he's gay!" I said, shaking my head.

"What's he like when Freya comes, Keeley? Think back to how he acts when Gregor and Freya are together. He's even moodier when she's around than he is with you."

He had a point there.

"So what do I do about him?"

"Nothing you can do, babes. Just let him get on with it," he shrugged. "Anyway, Keeley, I've got to go. I'm meeting up with a guy from Sheffield who's *definitely* gay, and he *most certainly* has the hots for me."

"Well, I hope you have a great night, and you'd better fill me in on all the sordid details in the morning."

"Back at you, girly," Ryan said with a wink and a smile as he left me behind in the kitchen. I wasn't sure what to do about Maxim, but I decided that the best course of action would be to confront him and let him know I had zero interest in Gregor other than as my boss.

I found him in the entrance lobby, about to go upstairs, so I called out to stop him from leaving.

"What do you want, bitch?"

"Maxim, it's not what you think. I have no romantic interest in Gregor at all. In fact, I'm in a—"

"I don't fucking care what you have to say. Do you think you know Gregor? Gregor does not do romance. He likes to play with his women. He makes them believe they are special to him, that they matter. But just when they think they have a good man, he whips them, fucks them and feeds from them. Then they fade away like daylight when he loses interest. You will be this way, *Keeeleey*," he said, mimicking how Gregor says my name.

"Gregor is a good man, despite what you say, Maxim. Freya wouldn't be his friend if he wasn't," I declared.

Just as I finished speaking, Maxim pushed me up against the wall.

"Do not speak that woman's name in my presence. She is a distraction for him, nothing more. She is not what he needs. The world would be a better place if she were gone."

I was scared, but also angry. Was he making threats towards Freya?

"I won't let you harm Freya. I'll tell Gregor, and he'll—"

Suddenly, Maxim let out a choking gasp.

"Maxim, were you threatening Keeley and calling me names?" Freya asked while lifting Maxim up by the throat. "Come on then, you bully; let's see how you fare against a woman now. Just go for it, Maxim, vampire to vampire. After all, this has been a long time coming, and I'm sure you've often dreamed of the moment you'd get to hurt me."

I moved away from the wall just as Freya slammed Maxim against it.

"I bought Daisy a pair of pink sandals and a matching pair in blue. And I couldn't resist buying her some trainers with a fairy on them. They were just too cute," Freya said while squeezing Maxim's neck even harder.

"Oh, okay. Thanks, Freya," I replied, both shocked and impressed by Freya's strength and the ability to hold a normal conversation when she was choking the life out of someone.

She leaned into Maxim. "If I ever find out you've hurt Keeley in any way, I will hunt you down and take your head. Do you understand me, Maxim?"

He tried to speak, but he was unable, so he nodded his head.

"Good. I'll let you go then," Freya said before throwing him twenty feet across the hallway effortlessly.

Gregor came out of his study and shouted, "What on earth is going on around here? Maxim, why are you on the floor? Get up, man." He turned, spotted Freya, and smiled.

"Freya, my darling, I have missed you so much. I'm glad you are here to see how the manor is progressing. And now you get to stay with me at my home instead of yours. Come, let me show you around."

Before he reached us, Gregor said, "You have been such

a great help to me today, Keeley. Go home to your little one and have a lovely evening."

I nodded and opened my mouth to say goodbye, but no words came out. Freya winked and waved back at me before taking Gregor's arm in hers.

After grabbing my bag out of my office, I got in the car and drove home, still unable to comprehend what had just taken place at the manor.

Chapter Eleven

Josh

When Keeley walked in through the cottage door, she was a little overwhelmed, to say the least. Sitting on the sofa in front of the TV were Alex, Nik, and Keeley's brother, Daniel. They were watching something musical, and dancing away at the side of them were Sergei and Daisy. My cottage is open plan, so from the sofa, you can see straight through to the kitchen table, where Gina and Julia sat drinking cloudy lemonade. I was in the kitchen stirring the chicken curry I'd made, ensuring the accompanying rice didn't overcook.

As soon as Daisy saw her mother, she squealed and ran straight up to her. Keeley lifted her in the air and then hugged her tightly. I walked over to where they stood, my blonde-haired, blue-eyed angels, before kissing them both on the cheek. Keeley turned her head at the last minute and kissed me on the lips, so I kissed her back, the taste of her igniting the want and need I'd had to keep buried earlier today.

"I've missed you today, love," I told her when I pulled them close.

"I've missed you too, Josh, and though I'm home earlier than usual, I'm absolutely exhausted."

"I'm cooking for everyone, so after they've eaten, we can give Daisy a bath and settle in for the night."

"Sounds good to me. Have you eaten yet, Daisy?" she asked the little whirlwind, who was struggling to get down so she could join Sergei again.

"Yes, I've had lots to eat today, and I got a toy and some fairy trainers."

"She's just had a jacket potato and cheese," I told Keeley.

Then Gina piped up with, "She's also had an ice cream, a chocolate chip muffin, a packet of crisps and a banana."

"Yeah, it's been a real junk food day for all of us, and this heartburn is giving me hell," Julia remarked, patting her chest.

"*I* was good today," Gina stated. "I'm determined not to break my diet this time."

I saw Nik and Sergei give each other a look, but it seemed Gina hadn't noticed. I'd probably get visits from the two of them so they could raid my biscuit barrel again.

My table only seats four people, so Gina, Keeley, Daniel, and I sat there. Alex, Julia, Sergei, and Nik sat on the sofa and in armchairs. Julia wasn't eating due to her indigestion and heartburn, so she began reading Daisy a story while the rest of us ate the curry and rice with naan bread.

Once we'd finished eating, Alex addressed everyone in the room.

"I've been thinking about something that will affect Josh and Nik in particular. There's no easy way to say this, so here goes... I'm considering going part-time at Night Movers."

Before anyone could say anything, I jumped straight in.

"So am I. I have a family now, and working twelve-hour nights doesn't fit with Keeley and Daisy's hours. I don't want to give up on the company altogether, but I need to work fewer nights."

I looked around and saw Alex nodding at me.

"It's the same with me, too. When the baby comes, I'll need to regulate my hours around what's healthy and natural for them. It'd be okay for a couple of years or so to work the hours I do, but what about when they start nursery and then school?"

"You can make me a partner...then I can work the hours you don't want to do," said Sergei. Everyone looked at him.

"I appreciate the offer, Sergei, but I want to speak with Freya first to see if she wants to take on half my share. I'll also have to ask Finn; he expressed an interest a few years ago," Alex informed him.

"I know that Finn is your cousin, Alex, but I do not like him. He annoys me. He is too serious," Sergei told him.

It was true there was no love lost between them, but I, for one, didn't care about that. I walked over to the sofa, extended my hand to Sergei and said, "I accept your proposal; you can take half my share in Night Movers. We can meet with our solicitor to get the finer details worked out."

"Thank you, Joshua. You will not regret this," Sergei declared as he stood and gave me a manly hug.

"What about your businesses in Russia, Sergei?" asked Gina.

"I will have to go back as planned in three months, but there are people who I can delegate to if needed, and we can run the Russian end of Night Movers from anywhere. I, too, would like to be near my family," he said, gesturing to Nik and Gina.

"Oh, Sergei..." Gina walked over to him and held him tightly. "I'll be glad to have you here with us every day. I miss you when you're gone."

"I miss you, too, my Gina." He kissed her forehead and put his arms around her.

I understood Nik's relationship with Sergei. They were cousins who were brought up together in a Romanian orphanage run by a relative who was also a priest.

The priest kept their identities safe for nearly fifteen years until their paternal grandfathers came for them after the war with the hunters—the same war in which each of their Born Immortal fathers and their witch-born mothers were killed. So obviously, they were close—more brothers than cousins. But the way Sergei was with Gina sometimes, I would have said there was more going on than I would be comfortable with.

Keeley looked at me and asked, "Are you sure about all this, Josh?"

"Positive, love. Now let's get our little miss in the bath and ready for bed." Picking Daisy up from Julia's knee, I carried her to the bathroom. Then I set the bath running for her while Keeley gathered up Daisy's night clothes. Leaving Keeley to bath Daisy, I went into the kitchen to wash up, but Gina had beaten me to it.

"Thanks for doing the washing up, Gina," I said gratefully.

"*Thank you* for cooking for us," she replied. Everyone else chimed in and said thank you too.

Daniel asked, "Would it be okay if I went in to say goodbye to Keeley and Daisy?"

"Yeah, Dan, of course. This is Keeley's home, too, so you are welcome here anytime." He nodded his head and made his way to the en suite.

I heard Daisy yell, "Look, Uncle Daniel, it's a magic queen bath!"

"What on earth does she mean by that?" asked Julia.

"It's the Jacuzzi setting. When Daisy first had a bath here, she didn't look too sure about it, so I told her Queen Ellie had one, and then she liked it," I replied.

"Good thinking," said Julia. Then she stood and mumbled, "I've got to see this," as she waddled her way into the bathroom.

"So, what's it like to have a ready-made family?" asked Alex.

"It's the best thing that's ever happened to me," I told him truthfully. "Hearing Daisy call me dad makes my heart jump with joy. I can't wait to have more kids with Keeley. She's an amazing mother, always has been."

Alex nodded in agreement. "I can't wait for our baby to be born. It's changed all the priorities I once had in my life. That's why I need to scale down the work a little. I want to be there for my child whenever they need me throughout their life, and especially their childhood."

"Joshua, this is not one of those times when you feel the need to show your ass, is it?" Sergei asked while backing away from me.

"What on earth are you talking about, Sergei?" I replied, confused.

Nik huffed. "Sergei, I told you, it's not the same type of

mooning you are thinking about." He turned to Alex and me and said, "I was talking to Sergei and Keeley earlier, and I happened to say you'd been mooning over her for a long time. And this muppet thought I meant you'd been pulling a moony at her."

Alex and I laughed out loud while Sergei continued towards the door. "Come, Nik, let us go to the office; you can put me to work. Gina, you are to come also," he said as he backed out of the door.

"I can't believe I have to work with him, Josh. What have you done?" Alex groaned.

"He'll be fine, Alex. Don't worry about him." Sergei sometimes acted the joker, but he was always there when needed. There was a lot more to him than most people knew, Alex included. So I just let it be and waved goodbye to Nik and Gina.

Daniel walked out of the hallway and made his way to the door. "I think you've lost your lass in there, Alex. Our Daisy has her smitten."

Alex nodded and got up from the sofa. "I'd better get Julia settled at home before I leave for work," he said. "I know she says I fuss too much, but I like to know she's okay before I leave the cottage."

I followed him into the bathroom to see both Julia and Keeley sitting on the floor covered in bubbles.

"Look, Daddy, it's like Queen Ellie does when she magics the fairy dust," shouted Daisy. Then she stood, scooped up some bubbles and flung them into the air while singing the fairy song at the top of her voice.

Julia and Keeley sat giggling away as little Daisy flung the bubbles at Alex and me. I looked at Alex and saw the strangest expression on his face when he glanced between Julia and Daisy.

He whispered, "She looks more like a baby without her clothes, and her hair all wet away from her face."

And thinking about it, I suppose she did. With her still babyish frame, big blue eyes, chubby cheeks, and cute little nose. Alex bent down and rubbed Julia's swollen belly.

"She's lovely, isn't she, Julia? I wonder if our baby will be like her."

"Uncle Alex, I'm not a baby," Daisy said crossly. "Tell him, Mummy. I'm going to the big school soon, and I'm four and a half."

"I know you're a big girl, Daisy. I just meant that if we have a baby girl, it would be nice if she was as pretty as you," Alex replied.

Daisy pursed her lips and frowned, as though considering what he'd said.

"Did you put the baby in Auntie Julia's tummy when you got married and I was a bridesmaid?" Daisy asked thoughtfully.

I'd never seen Alex blush before. It happens so rarely with vampires.

"Something like that," he mumbled, looking anywhere other than at Daisy.

"Well, if you put the baby in Auntie Julia's tummy, you should know whether it's going to be a girl or a boy," reasoned Daisy with a huff.

We all tried our best not to laugh, but it was impossible. In fact, Julia laughed so hard she was in tears. Suddenly, she stopped laughing and said, "Quick, Alex, get me up. I need to pee."

I picked up Daisy's nightclothes from the cabinet while Keeley scooped her up in a towel, then Alex helped Julia up off the floor.

Later that evening, with Daisy all tucked up in bed fast asleep, Keeley and I sat on the sofa with a glass of wine. She was wearing the little pyjama shorts and tank top she wore the first night that she and Daisy came to stay with me. It was hard for me to keep my hands to myself, but there was something that I needed to do.

You see, Freya and Daisy weren't the only ones in the family to go shopping today.

I'd rung through to a jeweller in York that I knew. They supplied beautiful pieces of jewellery that were anything but ordinary. I'd spoken to them earlier and requested an engagement ring with a blue topaz stone, as that reminded me of the colour of Keeley's eyes. They agreed to set aside some rings for me to view around midday. I rang Keeley's brother to tell him what I was doing, and to ask for his blessing. I don't think her father would have readily agreed to give me his blessing, even if I could have got in touch with him. But the conditions of his rehab state no contact for at least a month, so it wouldn't have mattered either way.

Daniel agreed to drive me to York so that we could pull up alongside the shop and I could run inside. My vehicle has specially tinted windows, so I could do it all without spending much time in the sun. Daniel joined me in a back room after he'd managed to park up, which wasn't an easy task in York. The selection of rings in blue topaz was quite limited, but I narrowed it down to three choices.

I initially thought I'd choose a platinum ring setting, but I saw the perfect ring for Keeley in yellow gold. It wasn't an overly large stone, just short of a centimetre in total. It was princess cut with two small princess-cut diamonds on either side of it. Daniel agreed that it would be perfect for Keeley.

Luckily, he'd brought Keeley's *'leave me alone I'm married'* ring from her jewellery box that she'd left at her father's house. It was a fake gold wedding ring she put on when on a night out so that men wouldn't try to pick her up.

The jeweller used it to size the engagement ring, and luckily for me, they had one to fit. I remembered Alex bought Julia matching jewellery with her ring, so I asked the jeweller for earrings, a pendant, and a bracelet. I selected a perfectly matching pendant and chain, but the earrings and bracelet had to be ordered, as they would be bespoke pieces.

While I was there, I bought Daisy a little pendant and chain in the same colour. I knew she'd love to have the same as her mother. Daniel went to start the car while I paid for all the jewellery, and after less than an hour in York, we were on our way home. I was confident that Keeley would love the ring when I bought it, yet I felt so nervous now.

"What's up, Josh?" Keeley asked, looking concerned. I didn't answer. Instead, I got down on one knee and took her hand in mine.

"Keeley Saunders, will you do me the honour of becoming my wife?"

I'd had a big speech planned, but at the last minute, the words I wanted to say seemed to leave my mind.

"Yes, Josh, you know I will." Keeley leaned forward and kissed me softly. I pulled away from her and handed her the open ring box.

Keeley gasped.

I took the ring from the box and placed it on the third finger of her left hand. It was a perfect fit, and the colour looked so pretty against her skin.

"It's beautiful, Josh, thank you," she almost whispered, tilting her hand in different directions, admiring the way the blue topaz and diamonds sparkled.

"That's not all," I informed her, taking out the box with the chain and pendant.

"Oh, Josh!" Keeley clasped her hand over her mouth as I removed the jewellery. She lowered her head so I could place it around her neck, brushing my fingers against her skin as I fastened it. I watched her shiver as she turned her face to mine and kissed me.

"Take me to bed, Josh. Make love to your fiancée."

I took her lips with an open-mouthed, soft kiss, then scooped her up in my arms and carried her through to the bedroom.

I placed Keeley by the end of the bed and took off her tank top, kissing her neck while I did so. I could smell the raspberry body wash from the shower she'd taken earlier, but it was her own unique scent that attracted me more. A scent made even more perfect by the fact that she'd become highly aroused. I carried on kissing all over her neck from front to back, occasionally licking from her throat to her earlobe, which I took gently between my teeth.

My kisses, licks, and nibbles moved to her shoulders and collarbone. She seemed to like harder nips with my teeth for those areas, so I stored that information away to use later. I stood behind her, kissing up and down the length of her spine until I got to the elastic waistband of her pyjama shorts. Dropping to my knees, I traced above the waistband with my tongue, making her turn around to treat her hip bones to the same gentle licks and nibbles.

The scent of her arousal surrounded me, and I couldn't help but press my face against her mound and inhale. My cock was now so hard it was uncomfortable to keep my jeans on, so I stripped naked before her. She reached out to touch me, but I grabbed her hands and held them around her back, kissing her hard, pulling her body up tight against mine. I knelt once again and turned her around.

I kissed the back of her thighs down to her knees, where I traced my tongue in circular motions. She moaned as I went from one leg to the other until they began to shake. Then I tugged off her shorts and lifted her up onto the bed.

Keeley pulled me down for a kiss, our tongues duelling and dancing as the heat in my body rose once more. My cock throbbed, desperate to be inside her.

Pulling away from our kiss was hard to do, but if I hadn't, this would have been over far too quickly. I grabbed her hands and pinned them above her head with her arms outstretched, awaiting my mouth.

"Grab the edge of the mattress, Keeley, and don't let go," I told her, then I kissed the inside of her upper arms down to her inner elbow, where I licked in the same small circles as I had at the back of her knees.

"Aahhh, Josh, please," Keeley cried, but I wouldn't be rushed tonight.

I wanted to taste every inch of her skin, to memorise every moan and sigh as her need for me reached its peak. I wanted to satisfy my woman like she had never been satisfied before, and until this night was through, I would do it many times over.

I made my way down to her breasts, kissing and gently biting the fleshy mounds before licking all around her areolas. Then I took her nipples into my mouth one after the other, gripping them between my teeth and flicking the tips with my tongue.

Keeley's orgasm took me by surprise. I hadn't touched her sex once, so she'd come from nipple play alone. This turned me on more than ever before, and I quickly kissed my way down her belly towards her hot, wet folds. I parted them with my fingers, revealing the swollen bud of her clit sticking out from its hood, just waiting for my tongue.

With the first lap from her wet entrance to her clit, I was in heaven. The taste of Keeley's come was making my mouth water for more, so I carried on licking her, every now and again pausing to nibble gently on her folds and the top of her mound. Her breaths came in heavy pants, escalating onwards as I fastened my mouth over her clit and flicked my tongue rapidly.

She almost screamed my name as she came over and over. By now, I was so hard it was painful, and I couldn't wait to be inside her. But my need for her blood was rising, scrambling my senses. I turned my head to the inside of her thigh and sank my fangs in deep, thrusting two fingers inside her and curling them slightly, tapping at that most sensitive spot. Keeley came again, a small squirt of female ejaculate hitting my cheek, making me feel like a fucking king. I withdrew my fangs from her thigh and licked at the puncture marks.

After removing my fingers, I placed her legs around my neck and entered her swiftly. I fucked her hard and deep in an unrelenting rhythm that had us both cresting the wave of a powerful orgasm, crashing down on it together as I filled her with my release.

I rested on my elbows with me on top of her, and her legs now wrapped around my back. We were both still panting hard, our skin damp with sweat and my cock still semi-hard inside her. She opened her eyes and looked deep into my own. No words were said, but I knew she wanted more of me. The expression she wore told me that much. I placed my hands in the middle of her back and lifted her towards me as I knelt, then sat back on my calves.

With her legs still wrapped around my back and my cock still buried deep inside her, I picked her up and made my way to the bathroom.

I stood in front of the shower with her in my arms and my cock flexing inside her as she kissed me. Within seconds, I was rock hard again and ready for round two.

Instead of getting us in the shower as I had originally planned, I walked over to the sink and sat her on the cabinet that surrounded it. I closed my eyes as I sank inside her, the pleasure so strong I moaned out loud. When I opened my eyes, I saw myself in the mirror. My eyelids appeared heavy, and my expression was tense as I tried not to give in to the pleasure and come too soon. I could see the muscles in Keeley's back flex, and the flesh of her arse as it moved against the countertop.

"I can see myself in the mirror while I'm fucking you, Keeley. It's turning me on so much that I think we need to slow down and change places." She whimpered as I pulled out of her, so I soothed her with kisses before turning her around to face the mirror. Then I lifted her hips until she was at the right height to push my throbbing cock inside her.

"Open your eyes, Keeley, and see what I see," I whispered in her ear. Keeley moaned breathlessly while she watched our lovemaking. I pulled her body upright and ran my fingers over her breasts, loving the contrast of her pale, full globes against my dark hands. I watched with fascination as the dusky pink areolas puckered and made her rosy nipples stand proud.

I placed two fingers of my left hand over her lips, so she opened her mouth and sucked. I felt the pull directly on my cock, and my balls lifted. Oh fuck, I had to stop moving. If I carried on, I'd come in seconds. Keeping my lower body still, I removed my wet fingers from her mouth and used them to tug firmly on her nipples, one after the other.

"Ah, Josh," she gasped. Her eyes became glassy, and her sex quivered. Dropping my other hand down to her sex, I ran my index and middle finger around the opening, gathering some of the wetness that surrounded the base of my cock. I slid them up to circle the hood of her clit and thrust inside her once again.

Keeley threw her head back onto my shoulder and chanted my name with each firm stroke of her clit and thrust of my cock. When I felt the first spasm of her sex as she came, I could hold back no longer. Bending her over onto the sink, I fucked her as though my life depended on it, watching the bounce and swing of her breasts with each hard thrust.

Glancing in the mirror as I came, I saw her watching me with a look that spoke of love, desire, and a promise of forever. A look I wanted to see on my woman's face every day of my life from now on.

After showering each other off, I went down on her once again. It seemed I couldn't get enough of Keeley's essence—a fact she wasn't likely to complain about.

When we got back in bed, she linked her hands through mine and sighed.

"I've got something to tell you, and I don't want you to be mad," she said, turning towards me.

"What is it, love?" I asked warily.

"Gregor bought me a car," Keeley replied. She hunched her shoulders and closed her eyes, almost as if she expected me to shout at her.

"I know. Sergei said he was going to. What has he bought you?" I asked.

"A brand-new Volvo XC60 in Ice White," she said, excitement in her voice. I whistled and shook my head.

"He's always been an extravagant bastard, our Gregor."

"Josh," she scolded, tut-tutting at me and shaking her head. "I thought it was a lovely thing for him to do, but I was worried that you'd be mad."

"Why would I be mad, Keeley? You've done nothing wrong. And I'm your fiancé, not your keeper. Don't ever be frightened to tell me anything."

"Okay," she said, biting her lip. The look on her face said I wouldn't like whatever else she had to tell me.

"Maxim had another go at me and pushed me against the wall."

"What the fuck, Keeley? Why didn't you say something earlier?"

"Freya came in and caught him pushing me. She threatened him, then threw him down the hallway."

"Good," I grunted angrily. "I want to find him and rip his fucking head off."

"Josh, it's sorted now. I don't think he'll come after me again now that Freya's had a go at him."

I wasn't so sure. Freya was going back home tomorrow, so I thought I'd pay him a visit, just to warn him and hurt him a little. I pulled Keeley against me and held her tightly.

"He's a vampire, Keeley. He could hurt you—or kill you if he wanted. Let me talk to him at least. He needs to know you're mine, and I always protect what's mine."

Keeley sighed in resignation. "All right, you win. Come and pick me up tomorrow afternoon. You can say hello to Gregor before you threaten his bodyguard."

"Okay," I replied, happy that she'd let me help.

"Oh, and, Keeley?"

"Yes?" she answered sleepily.

"I would have bought you any car you wanted."

"I know," she mumbled. Then she turned on her side and fell asleep.

Sleep didn't come for me as quickly, though. I kept thinking of all the ways I could punish Maxim, and with my lively imagination, there were quite a few.

Chapter Twelve

Keeley

When I got to work the next morning, Gregor had gone out for an early breakfast with Freya. We were in the process of finding a cook/housekeeper for the manor, and Gina suggested that we interview her aunt for the position.

Linda was a lovely lady in her early fifties. She'd never worked before as her husband wouldn't allow it, but he passed away two years ago, and she found herself needing work. So Gina got Linda a cleaning job at Night Movers, but she fancied a change.

Gina thought working at Rothley Manor would be perfect for her, and she was coming to be interviewed at the end of the week. Until then, I had to provide a fully stocked kitchen and light meals if needed.

As soon as Ryan saw my engagement ring, he started asking about wedding plans and dates. Josh and I hadn't discussed *when* we were going to get married. I wanted my father well first, and Josh knew that. It was so upsetting not knowing how he was getting along in rehab, but we had to trust that the clinic knew what they were doing when they said no contact.

A text message pulled me out of my sad thoughts. It was Gina offering to bring me a few sandwiches so we could have a picnic in the manor's secret garden. I texted back that I would love a picnic with her today. There were more things I wanted to ask Gina about Bonding with Josh, and this would give me time alone with her to do that.

I'd had some of his blood before when I was hungover, or a bit sore after you-know-what. He gave me some in the shower last night—a little more than I'd had previously. But we'd been very active in the bedroom yesterday, and he assured me that it wasn't enough to start the Bonding process.

Apparently, once we Bond, we'll need to make love often, and we won't want to be away from each other for days. To be honest, I was starting to feel that way about him anyway.

I've enjoyed everything that Josh and I have done sexually, and I couldn't wait until I saw him later so I could have a repeat of last night. He's *extremely* good at what he does to me, and each time seems better than the last.

I went out to bring my laptop in from the car and noticed the large truck in front of the old coach house. The builders were taking a step back from those buildings today, and the windows were currently being installed. I didn't have time for more than a quick glance inside the first one, so I decided to check on them once the window company had left.

The coach house was being turned into cottages, and I thought the builders had done an excellent job restoring what were essentially ruins for many years.

I made my way back to the manor and saw Gregor's car in the driveway. So with my laptop in hand, I went to his study and knocked on the door.

"Come in, Keeley," shouted Gregor.

"How did you know it was me?" I asked, walking towards his desk.

He looked at me with some amusement and said, "I doubt very much that Yuri and Maxim have taken to wearing high heels, or that they smell as beautiful as you do."

"Oh," I murmured, looking down at my black stiletto heels. "Are they too noisy going across these floors?"

"Not at all," replied Gregor. "I like a woman in heels, Keeley. I find it extremely sexy. The way they make her legs look and how they sound as she moves across the floor…it does things to a man. I am glad that you wear them. Often tall women avoid them because they don't want to tower above their men, but you embrace your height, and I find that confidence alluring."

"Gregor, you flatter me today." I fanned my face to cool my heated, blushing cheeks. Some women might find Gregor's words disconcerting, but he hadn't made me feel uncomfortable. Quite the opposite. I felt empowered.

"Keeley?" Gregor said in a questioning voice. "Is that what I think it is?"

Taking my left hand in his, he ran his thumb over my engagement ring.

"Yes. Josh proposed to me properly last night."

"It is beautiful, and it suits the wearer so very well. Now *I* shall make a proposal. Would you allow me to host an engagement party here for you? We can open the ballroom and have music and dancing to celebrate the occasion."

"That's very kind of you, Gregor, but I'll have to speak to Josh first."

"A formality, Keeley. You own the man now, so he is yours to command," he stated while waving his hand dismissively.

I laughed but said, "Then I accept. Thank you for your offer, Gregor. I'll speak to Josh and tell him we can have our engagement party here."

"When will you Bond with him? You must take some time off work because I do not wish to walk into a room to find my PA in a compromising position with my friend."

"Gregor," I gasped with embarrassment. "I wouldn't dream of messing around with Josh in your home."

Gregor laughed out loud at my denial. "Keeley, my darling, Bonding is a very important time for a couple. Your will, your hormones, and your bodies are taken over by such powerful feelings that you cannot deny their effect. The Bond consumes you while it is new and keeps you wanting that person for the rest of your days. It is a wondrous thing."

"Gregor, why haven't you Bonded with anyone? I mean, look at you. You're good-looking, sexy, generous to a fault, and could charm the knickers off a nun with mere words. I'd have thought you'd have women lining up to be with you."

"Ah, Keeley, now it is *you* that flatters *me*. However, as much as I like to see love and Bonding in my friends, I appreciate that some people were never meant to be part of a Bonded couple."

"How do you know that, Gregor? You and Freya would make a lovely couple. It's obvious you adore each other."

"My beautiful Freya. I fear we are one and the same. Freya has her demons to fight when it comes to love and commitment, and I have mine. Now, let us discuss what is on today's agenda. I see that the windows are going in at the coach house this morning."

With that last statement, Gregor had effectively dismissed the conversation about him finding love.

We went through the day's agenda quickly, and I mentioned that Gina would be coming to have lunch with me in the secret garden at the back of the coach house. Gregor said he'd join us with champagne and strawberries to celebrate my engagement. Then we ended our meeting and walked into the hallway.

Gregor hugged me and said, "Thank you for accepting my proposal, Keeley. The engagement party will be a wonderful occasion. I cannot wait to celebrate with all our friends."

He took my hand and kissed the ring. "It matches the blue of your eyes perfectly, and this, too." He lifted the matching pendant and then kissed me on the cheek.

"I fucking knew it," yelled a voice from the staircase behind me.

"You said you had no romantic interest in him, but I knew it all along," Maxim almost screamed.

I turned to face him and tried to calm him down. "Maxim, it's not what it looks like. Gregor has offered to—"

"Marry you, yes, I know. I heard everything," he panted.

I tried to speak again, but I was silenced by a confused Gregor.

"What is the meaning of this, Maxim? What are you talking about?"

"Why would you want someone like her, Gregor? She could never be enough for you. I have seen how you are with women, and I know you can never be fully satisfied with them."

"Maxim, I don't understand what any of this has to do with you, or why my love life should concern you at all," Gregor declared, shaking his head.

I hurried towards the kitchen out of their way; I didn't want to be around to hear what went down next. I realised too late that I'd left my laptop in Gregor's office, but there was no way I was going back for it.

Feeling frightened and out of sorts, I made myself a cup of tea with shaky hands. When Ryan entered the kitchen and held open his arms, I could no longer keep my emotions in check and ended up sobbing quietly in his embrace.

Chapter Thirteen

Gregor

I took hold of Maxim's shirt and dragged him into my study. I didn't know what the fuck he was talking about, but I was damned sure I'd find out within the next few minutes.

"Maxim, explain to me the meaning of this outburst. Why did you yell and upset my Keeley?"

"Your Keeley? Does *'your Keeley'* know what you usually do to the women you get close to? I wonder if she would still want to be *'your Keeley'* if she did?" he said, using his fingers to represent quotation marks each time he said your Keeley.

"Maxim, you are really pissing me off. I have no fucking clue why you are angry with Keeley, or with me. But I advise you to calm down before you cause a reaction in me you are not likely to forget."

"What will you do? Beat me? Use a whip or a flogger until you make me submit?" he ranted.

"You are crazy. Why would you speak to me this way? What gives you the right?" I shouted.

"Because I'm sick of being overlooked for some blonde with breasts and a cunt."

"Maxim," I warned, pointing my finger at him.

"Let's face it, Gregor. Freya is more of a match for you than this human woman will ever be. Although Freya cannot give you an heir."

A look of recognition came over Maxim's face when he spoke those last few words.

"That's what all this is about, isn't it? You want the human woman to bear your children?" he said.

"Maxim, I do not wish for any woman to bear my children, so I do not know where this is coming from. But I warn you not to disrespect either Freya or Keeley. They are more precious to me than any jewel, and I will not hear you speak ill of either of them."

"I know why you have chosen the human woman over Freya," Maxim said. "She will submit to you in all ways, whereas Freya would not submit to anyone."

"I do not wish either of these women to submit to me. You have the ramblings of a madman, Maxim," I yelled, still no wiser as to what had caused this outburst from him.

"Oh, I know I am mad, Gregor. Believe me, I have tried not to let this madness take over. But alas, I cannot seem to stop. And do you know what the worst thing is? There are people like me who would welcome my madness with madness of their own. But I do not want to be around these people. No, not Maxim. Maxim chooses instead to fall in love with someone who would not embrace the madness in him."

"Madness? Love? Maxim, are you telling me you've fallen in love with Keeley? Or Freya?"

"Ha! If only it were that simple. No, this is where my madness lies," he said, and with a speed that only a vampire possesses, he crossed the room and kissed me hard on the mouth.

Within a second of his lips touching mine, I used all my strength and threw him across the room.

He laughed bitterly and mumbled, "At least you didn't throw me as far as Freya did yesterday."

"You attacked Freya yesterday?" I questioned, my rage building as I stalked towards him.

"No, I was going for your precious Keeley, but Freya intervened," he spat.

I saw red, literally, as my irises became red-rimmed and my fangs descended. The first punch I threw landed square on his jaw and sent him flying into the bookcase against the wall. With the second punch, I felt three of his ribs break, but I didn't stop there. I carried on punching him until I heard shouts from Ryan at the doorway.

"Perhaps you want to fuck now that you have used violence," wheezed Maxim. "After all, that is usually what you do to the women you whip in your club."

"Get out, Maxim, and keep away from me and the women I hold dear. If you dare to come anywhere near me again, I will kill you."

Maxim laughed between coughing up blood, then he got up and left. Ryan glared at me from the doorway before walking away.

I closed the door to my study and sat at my desk, hardly believing what had just occurred. I tried to replay everything Maxim had ever said or done that would indicate any of what just happened, but I couldn't.

Maxim had been my loyal bodyguard in Russia for over twenty years. He and Yuri had often accompanied me to my club and had seen me perform in a few scenes with women. I thought they knew that any punishment given was not a form of violence against those women—but to enhance the experience for both of us until I had their complete submission, their orgasm, and their blood. I did not consider anything I'd done to the women who submitted to me to be in any way violent. Yes, I used whips, floggers, paddles, and canes. But the women wanted these things, craved them even.

Did Maxim honestly believe that the reason I used those implements was because I secretly hated women? Did he think that the women I fucked did not satisfy me? Surely, I gave no indication that I could ever be satisfied by a man?

I remembered the feel of his lips against mine and the scratchiness of his stubble, even though it was only for a second. It almost made me vomit.

I glanced down at my white shirt splattered with his blood. After ripping open the buttons, I threw the shirt in the bin. The skin over my knuckles—which had split from the punches to Maxim's face and jaw—was almost healed. He hadn't retaliated. My anger was such that it would have been futile, especially when I found out he'd tried to hurt Keeley. If I had known that last night, I would have sent him away then.

I got up from my chair and made my way towards the stairs. I needed a shower. I wanted to wash away the confusion, the blood, and the sickening feel of Maxim's kiss.

Chapter Fourteen

Keeley

Gina texted me to say she was on her way to the manor, so I texted her back and said I'd meet her in front of the coach house. If I was totally honest, I just wanted to call Josh and tell him to come and pick me up. I wasn't a coward by any means, but two pissed-off vampires are two too many in my book, and due to Maxim's stupid assumptions, I seemed to be the cause.

In the end, I didn't call Josh. Instead, I tried to take my mind off what had happened by checking on the progress of the window company before Gina arrived.

By the time I got to the coach house, the last couple of men were leaving, and the windows were fully installed.

The difference that the windows made to the converted building was remarkable, and you could now clearly see that there were separate cottages. The windows had been specially crafted in hardwood and had a chestnut-coloured finish that complemented the old stone building.

I stepped inside the cottage on the left and worked my way around the builder's leftover tools. They should have been removed or cleared away, as leaving them could have caused a tripping hazard to the window installers. I made a mental note to tell Ryan about it.

I heard a noise behind me and turned quickly to find that Maxim had entered the cottage.

My heart began beating way too fast, and my hands were shaking, yet I stood my ground with my head held high, trying to explain away the earlier misunderstanding.

"Maxim, listen to me when I—"

"No, you fucking whore, you listen to me! I accept that Gregor will never want what I can give, but that does not mean I will stand back and let you have him. He would tire of you, anyway, I am sure of it. But because of you, I must leave the man I have served loyally for decades. Because of you, my life as I know it is over. Therefore, I must take your life away. It is the only way I will find any peace."

I tried pulling out my phone while backing away from him, but it fell to the floor in my haste.

"No, Maxim, please. You have it all wrong. I'm engaged to J—"

Before I could say anything more, Maxim leapt across the room and grabbed my shoulders. His fangs tore into the side of my neck, and he sucked hard at the wound he'd made.

I struggled to get away, but it was no use. He was just too strong. And the more movements I made, the more his fangs savaged me. I screamed as loud as I could, but I hardly heard the sound due to the growling noises coming from Maxim.

Josh's bite was something I found arousing, and I welcomed the significance. This was anything but. It was frightening and painful, and I knew I would die today.

I thought about Daisy and how I wouldn't see her first day of school or watch her grow and learn all the important things in life. I thought of my brother and my father and wondered how they'd cope with the loss of yet another woman in the family. And as my vision darkened and my breaths became shallow, I thought of Josh, and how I wished I could have him hold me one last time…

Chapter Fifteen

Gina

After visiting my mother in Rothley, I made my way over to the manor. The sun was high in the sky by the time I reached the coach house. I decided to look inside and see how the builders had sectioned it off to make two separate cottages. As I approached, it looked so different. It didn't even have windows and doors the last time I saw it, but now the building was unrecognisable. It looked like someone had taken two cottages from a fairy tale and placed them on the grounds of Rothley Manor.

A woman's scream came from inside the building. It was loud and shrill, and a tingle of fear raced up my spine. I dropped the bag of food and drinks I was carrying and ran towards the building. I could hear sounds coming from the cottage to the left and froze when I got to the doorway. Maxim grasped Keeley from behind and was feeding on her neck. In the seconds I stood there taking in the scene, I saw her lose consciousness.

Yelling for Maxim to stop what he was doing, I ran towards them and jumped on his back. He threw me off him with little effort, and as panic set in, I tried to remember the self-defence training Nik had me doing every week. Picking up a wooden-handled chisel, I started back towards Maxim. When I got close enough, I swept his legs out from under him, causing him to fall to the side with Keeley still in his grasp. I noted she was still unmoving and was deathly pale.

Refusing to believe it was too late to save her, I focused all my efforts on separating the two. I stamped as hard as I could on Maxim's head, but he grabbed my calf before I could repeat the action, pulling me to the floor. Kicking my foot out, I caught him hard in the temple; Maxim cried out in pain, releasing Keeley in the process.

I quickly flipped myself upright and launched myself at his chest with the chisel in both hands. It sank into his flesh, and he let out an unholy roar as he tried to pull it out. I leapt away from him, but I realised that with the amount of movement he was making, I hadn't sunk the chisel deep enough to pierce his heart.

Glancing around, I saw a thick plank of wood to the side of me, so I picked it up and brought it down on the chisel with as much force as I could manage.

Maxim coughed out blood before going completely still, and then his eyes glazed over. I watched him for a few more seconds while I got my breath back, just to make sure the chisel had really hit its mark. Then I threw down the wood and went over to where Keeley lay.

I tried to feel for a pulse, but my hands shook so badly that I couldn't keep still enough to feel anything. There were two deep holes and a tear in the side of her neck, and I could see she still had blood trickling out of them. I noticed a sharp blade from a retractable knife on top of a workbench, so I reached up and grabbed it.

Pulling my phone out of my pocket, I called Nik before sliding the blade across my wrist.

"Gina, where are you? What's wrong? I could feel your fear, but I couldn't communicate through our Bond." Nik's panicked voice came through the phone as I placed my wrist in Keeley's mouth.

"Nik, please come to the coach house," I sobbed, hitting speakerphone with my free hand before using it to massage Keeley's throat, forcing her to swallow my blood.

"Gina, what's happened? Tell me you aren't hurt?" I heard Nik pick his car keys up and the squeak of our front door opening.

"Maxim attacked Keeley. I think I've killed him, Nik, but he was draining her, and she won't wake up. There's so much blood, and I'm trying to make her swallow mine, but—"

"Alex, get Josh and drive him to the coach house. Now, Alex! Keeley's hurt. Julia, you sit with Daisy," I heard Nik yell.

"Gina, what do you mean you can't get her to swallow?" he asked.

"I'm trying to get her to swallow my blood because she's lost so much of hers, but she's not moving. Nik, please hurry."

I heard Josh let out an anguished cry as car doors were opened and closed in the background.

"Gina, did he hurt you too? Why are you bleeding, love?" Nik asked, and I could clearly hear the alarm in his voice.

"No. I've cut my wrist, and I'm trying to give her my blood so that she'll be okay. I drank your blood today, so I thought mine would help her."

"Fuck, Gina, you shouldn't have done that—you can't help her that way. Tell me it's not deep, Gina? Please, baby, tell me you're okay?"

I was feeling a little dizzy, to be honest, but I didn't want to worry him, so I said, "It's okay, Nik. I'm moving her throat, so she's swallowing some down now."

"No, Gina, listen to me. You need to stop what you are doing and tie something tight around your wrist to stop the bleeding."

Nik must have had me on speakerphone because I heard Alex giving orders to Gregor down his phone.

A wave of nausea swept over me, and black floaty spots appeared before my eyes. I suddenly found it hard to swallow, and I had to focus on hearing Nik speak.

"Talk to me, Gina. Stay on the line, love."

"Nik." My voice sounded so far away, and my head felt like it was filled with cotton wool.

"I love you, Nik," I said breathlessly. And just before I thought I would pass out, Gregor's tall, imposing frame came into view.

Chapter Sixteen

Gregor

I had taken the call from Alex less than a minute ago, but my race to the coach house seemed to last an eternity. I couldn't believe I'd been stupid enough to think that Maxim would just pack his bags and return to Russia.

Keeley lay bloody, motionless, and pale, with Gina swaying over her. Gina's wrist was placed over Keeley's mouth, and I could see her trying to work her throat to make her swallow down the blood. Not that it was going to do any good.

I quickly moved Gina away and bit deep into my wrist. Mimicking Gina's actions, I forced Keeley to swallow my blood. I didn't know if I could save her, but I had to try. Even though she'd be forever changed, at least she'd be alive. The alternative was unthinkable.

I gave orders to Gina so she could stop the bleeding from her wrist, but when I turned around, she just sat there, staring.

She was covered in blood, and I could hear that her heartbeat was perilously low.

"Gina," I yelled, trying to snap her out of her stupor.

Keeley hadn't taken nearly enough of my blood, but I couldn't let Gina die either. With the way her wrist was rapidly pumping out blood, I knew that's what would happen if I didn't intervene.

Taking away the hand from Keeley's throat, I bit into that wrist and placed it over Gina's mouth.

"Come on, Gina, you know how to do this. Take blood from me so that you can heal. Please, Gina. Do it for Nik and your children. Do it for Sergei—because none of us could deal with him if anything happened to you."

Gina drank—almost imperceptibly—from my wrist, and within a minute, her own wrist had started to heal.

Although she still needed more blood to help her regain the amount she'd lost, Gina pushed my hand away and said, "Please, Gregor. Keeley needs it more. Daisy is too young to grow up without a mother."

I nodded my head and began once again the task of getting my blood into Keeley's system. In no time at all, a vehicle pulled up outside the building, and Josh, Nik, and Alex appeared before us seconds later.

For as long as I am on this earth, I will never forget the sheer devastation on Josh's face as he knelt beside Keeley's still form.

"Give her your blood, Josh," I told him, removing my wrist from her mouth.

As he got to work on Keeley, I turned to see Nik biting into his wrist as he held Gina in his arms, rocking her gently, whispering soothing words to her while she drank.

Alex stared at Maxim's body, then turned to me and

asked, "What happened here, Gregor? Why did he attack Keeley?"

"There was a misunderstanding earlier. We argued and fought. I told him to leave, but he must have come out here and found Keeley instead."

"I should have killed him yesterday when Keeley first told me about him," Josh yelled, his voice a mixture of anger, helplessness, and fear.

"I only found out about it this morning," I told him. "I did not know he had this much violence in him. I never imagined he was capable of hurting a woman." How could I not have known this?

"Why, Gregor? Why did Maxim have problems with Keeley?" Alex questioned.

"Because he thought I was in love with her. He thought I wanted to marry her."

Josh growled, and his eyes went red as his fangs descended.

"Was Maxim in love with Keeley?" Alex asked, confused.

"No," I answered. "Maxim was in love with me."

They all gasped and turned to look at me.

"It was not reciprocated in any way. I only found out today." I went to stand but stumbled to my left until Alex grabbed hold of me.

"Gregor, you'll need blood before we get you out of here."

"The kitchen has a refrigerator in the old pantry. Please bring blood for all of us. And if you can find Ryan, the decorator, tell him to have his men take a few days off, starting now," I told him weakly.

Alex nodded, then left. I turned to look at Josh, who was

cradling Keeley in his arms, his tears falling into her blood-soaked hair.

"Do you think she can be saved?" Nik asked, nodding towards Keeley.

"She won't be human," Josh replied, his voice croaky from tears and blood loss.

Nik closed his eyes tightly, but not before I saw a lone tear escape and run down his cheek. My heart broke for these vampires and the women they loved. What they had gone through today should never have happened.

I should have followed Maxim and made sure that he left. I could have put him on a plane back to Moscow myself.

"You need to take his head, Gregor. When all your builders have gone, you need to make sure his head and body are burned," Nik growled.

"I will call Sergei and Yuri to do it when you leave with Gina. I don't want her to see any of it," I told him. Nik nodded and placed a kiss on Gina's cheek. She was pale and sleepy but looked better than she had a few minutes ago.

"Keeley can have one of the guest suites for now. You cannot take her home until she's fully transitioned and can be trusted enough to be near her child," I told them.

It was agonising for all concerned to realise we'd have to keep Keeley away from her daughter, but everyone here knew that recently transitioned Made vampires find the blood of children far too tempting to let them near.

Chapter Seventeen

Alex

I dismissed all the building contractors and went to the blood store in the old pantry. Ryan followed me in, asking why I'd just told everyone to take a few days off.

Reluctantly, I told him what had happened. Mostly so he didn't go to the coach house, but also to keep him away while we disposed of Maxim's body. Ryan was distraught, yet I offered no assurance that everything would be okay.

I couldn't see things being okay ever again.

Just yesterday, I was looking at Josh and seeing all the love he had for his new little family, and a bright future was on the horizon for all of us. Now there would be tears and heartache for Keeley, Josh, and that innocent little girl, whose mother would have to be kept away from her for a long time.

I'd switched off the Bond with Julia when I heard Gina tell Nik what had happened over the phone. Because of the panic, Gina hadn't been able to communicate through her

Bond with Nik, but it was probably for the best, so she could concentrate all her energy on fighting Maxim.

Who would have thought that a human as small as Gina would be enough to disable a Born Immortal bodyguard like Maxim?

Nik had done the right thing in training Gina. As soon as Julia was fit enough after the birth of our baby, I would train her, too.

As I headed back to the coach house with the bags of blood, I called Freya and explained what had happened. She was devastated and set off back to Rothley straight away.

We discussed what would happen to Daisy in the immediate future. Freya said she would take her back to Aldbrough with her. She also asked about Keeley's brother, Daniel. I knew we had to tell him what had happened to her as soon as possible, and I dreaded that conversation. Maggie would be heartbroken too.

I had Daniel's number on my mobile, so I sent him a text and asked him to meet me at my cottage in an hour.

When I got back inside the coach house cottage, the scent of Keeley's and Gina's blood hit me hard. Adrenaline and the sickening sight of what we'd stumbled upon had prevented it from affecting me earlier, but now it knocked me sideways. I was glad I'd brought so many blood bags and handed them to Josh, Gregor, and Nik before taking one myself.

I told everyone about my phone call to Freya and her plan to take Daisy. Josh didn't comment, but Gregor and Nik agreed it was for the best. I could see that Josh was barely holding it together, so I tried to put a plan into action to get us all out of the building.

Gregor said Keeley and Josh could have a room at the manor for however long they needed it, and I was glad. I didn't want a newly turned vampire anywhere near Julia.

"Josh, do you need any help with carrying Keeley?" I asked, even though I knew what the answer would be.

"No. I'm good now that I've had the blood." I watched him stand with Keeley in his arms and wobble slightly. Gregor held him steady while he took a few deep breaths. I wondered just how much blood Josh had given Keeley to make him so weak.

Glancing at Keeley, I could see that the holes and the tear in her neck had virtually healed, so she wasn't losing any more blood.

"I'll book you in for an extra blood delivery as soon as possible, Gregor. In the meantime, I'll bring you some from our stock," I informed him as I made my way over to Nik and Gina.

Gregor nodded and waited until Josh started walking to the door with Keeley held tightly in his arms.

"I'll bring you some clothes later, Josh," I shouted as he walked towards the manor. He didn't turn and acknowledge me, but I hadn't expected him to. His body was weak, and he was emotionally drained. The sad thing was, there would be no quick fix for the latter.

I held the door open to the back of Nik's SUV, took Gina from his arms while he got in, handed her to him carefully and covered her up with my jacket. Nik nodded his thanks but said nothing.

After closing the door, I walked around to the driver's side. I had Gina's blood on my hands and shirt, so I quickly wiped my palms on my trousers before I started the car and drove home.

After parking the vehicle outside Nik's cottage, I walked with them to his front door and left them once they were inside. Then I made my way over to my cottage, taking a deep breath before I went inside and faced Julia and little Daisy.

Julia gasped when she saw my bloodstained shirt.

"Alex, you switched off the Bond. What's happened?"

Lowering my voice so that Daisy couldn't hear, I explained what had happened to Keeley.

Sergei sat at the table with Daisy, drawing pictures with coloured crayons. When he heard Gina's name mentioned, he came towards me with a questioning look, but he suddenly stepped away.

"That's Gina's blood," he said, making his way to the door. "Where is she, Alex? Where is my Gina?"

"Home with Nik," I yelled after him. But he'd already left before I could finish the sentence.

Chapter Eighteen

Nik

I held Gina under the warm shower stream, rinsing the blood from her hair and arms. The bathroom door suddenly flew open, and Sergei dashed in, staring at Gina's torn, bloody clothes on the floor. He slid open the door to the shower and stepped inside, fully clothed.

"Sergei, what the fuck are you doing? Get out," I yelled while trying to keep Gina from falling.

But Sergei didn't move. Instead, he looked Gina over from top to bottom before he asked, "Where was she injured, Nik? Did you give her enough blood?"

"Yes, Sergei, she's had enough for now. She can have more later. Gina cut her wrist to get blood into Keeley, but she cut into it too deep."

Just then, Gina became aware that Sergei had joined us.

"Sergei," she said, sounding way too out of it for my liking. Then Gina burst into tears as Sergei turned her around and held her tightly.

"My Gina," he murmured, kissing her cheek before breathing in her scent. "You are okay now. You are safe, and we will take care of you."

What scared me the most about this situation was that Gina wasn't the slightest bit bothered by Sergei seeing her naked, or that he was holding her. Gina was normally so self-conscious about her body, so her not being fazed by Sergei's presence made me realise how far she'd gone into shock.

"Wash her quickly while I hold her, Nik, then we can get her into bed with a hot drink," Sergei commanded, checking her wrist once again.

I was angry at him for taking over with his commands, but also grateful to have him hold Gina up so I could wash her and Keeley's blood away.

A few minutes later, Gina was thoroughly clean. Sergei told me to wait a few moments while he cleaned the blood-stained clothes away from in front of the shower.

As soon as he stepped out of the shower, he removed all his wet clothes and picked up the bloody ones before wiping the floor with his shirt.

I watched him exit the bathroom with the bloody, wet clothing, then I switched off the shower and carried Gina out.

I stood Gina up so she could lean on the wall for support before I quickly towelled her dry, then I helped her into bed and pulled the quilt up before finally drying myself.

Sergei wore a dry pair of boxer shorts when he entered the bedroom with the quilt from his bed. He covered Gina and left, returning two minutes later with a cup of her favourite hot chocolate before getting in bed beside her.

"Nik, hurry and get into bed. You need to hold her and keep her warm."

"Sergei, thanks for helping, but I would appreciate it if you got out of bed. Gina's naked under there, and when she finally gets her bearings back, she'll go up the bloody wall when she knows you've seen her without her clothes."

"Nikolas, I do not care what Gina gets angry about when she is well again. I just want her to feel better, and right now, she is still in shock."

"I can hear you both," said Gina in a weak voice.

"Gina, sit up a little and drink this hot chocolate," Sergei encouraged, reaching over to the bedside drawers to retrieve the cup.

I helped Gina sit up so she could drink, but she shook so much that Sergei had to take the cup away before spilling any. She lay back down and turned towards me.

"Hold me, Nik. Make me forget what happened today."

I held her close and rubbed my hands up and down her back to generate some heat. Within a few minutes, Gina had warmed up. After sighing heavily, she fell asleep in my arms with Sergei at her back.

When I told Sergei what had happened in the coach house, I saw a noticeable change in his demeanour. An ice-cold need for vengeance replaced the worry in his eyes.

"Did you finish Maxim?" he asked.

"No, I didn't want to leave Gina. She was too weak—even though she'd had blood from Gregor and me. She must have been so frightened, Sergei. I could feel some of her fear through our Bond, but she held most of it back from me."

"Our Gina is brave and good, Nik. She is always thinking of others before herself. You must make her take better care, Nikolas, because I cannot lose her. I would not wish to be in a world without Gina."

I didn't want to be in a world without her either, but she

was my woman, my Bonded mate, and soon she would be my wife. Was there more than simply friendship for Gina in Sergei's heart?

"Sergei, what are your feelings toward Gina?"

"I love her. She is my best friend," he replied.

"I thought I was your best friend," I joked.

"You are my brother, Nikolas. We may not have had the same parents, but our mothers were cousins, so we are blood. You have been in my life since I was born, and we have shared many times, good and bad. You are my best friend, too, but Gina is more than that to me. She is everything. I can tell her anything, and she does not judge. She is a beautiful woman inside and out, and she makes my life worth living." He kissed the back of her neck before resting his head on her shoulder.

"Are you in love with her, Sergei? I know you won't lie to me, and I need to know exactly how you feel."

Did I, though? I honestly didn't know how it would affect my relationship with Sergei if he told me he was in love with Gina.

"In a way," he replied. "I love her more than I should, I know that, but it is impossible not to."

"How long have you loved her?" I asked through gritted teeth.

"Around fourteen years. You told me you had met her and knew she was yours. She'd only just come to work here after I had gone back to Russia. You told me all about her and the fact she had a husband and children. But you said you could tell she wasn't happy, and you would wait until she left her husband, no matter how long that might take. When I came over three months later, you introduced us, and it felt like a lightning bolt had hit me. I was so affected by Gina; I wanted to kidnap her and take her back to Russia with me. And if she'd not had children, I probably would have done so.

"One day, during my visit, I was driving Josh's car through the village when I spotted her. She was walking to school to pick up her children, and I offered to give her a lift. I could tell she didn't really want to get in, but it was raining, so I persuaded her to let me take her. We chatted for a while outside the school gates, and when she went in to get her children, I waited to give them a lift home. Her kids were happy that they wouldn't have to walk in the rain, and they talked about what they had done at school that day. I imagined how it would be if they were my family and Gina was my woman. It was a happy thought, but I knew it could not be. You were already so in love with her, and I would never risk our friendship. I knew I couldn't have her—not as I wanted. But that day never left me. So I settled for whatever I could have from Gina, even if it were only the type of love that good friends bring."

I couldn't believe what I was hearing. I felt like I didn't know Sergei at all. Though I knew he thought a lot of Gina, I didn't realise his feelings went that far.

"Does Gina know about this, Sergei? Did you ever tell her how you feel?"

"No. I tell her I love her often, but she does not know that I feel more than friendship towards her."

"I won't share her, Sergei," I stated vehemently.

We'd shared women in the past, but that was nothing more than a bit of kink with women in Gregor's club. Or casual sex on a night out. I could never do that with Gina.

"I know you won't. I'm not asking you to," replied Sergei.

"This is so fucked up," I said with a heavy sigh.

"It does not have to be, Nikolas. I love Gina, and I will

do nothing to upset her. We can go on just as we are; it does not change anything."

"How can you say that, Sergei? How can I go on knowing that when you look at the woman I love and tell her you love her, it means so much more than it should? How can I watch you cuddle Gina and kiss her cheek, knowing you want to take it further? Do you want to fuck her, Sergei? Do you want to taste her and take her blood?"

I was angry now, thinking about Sergei wanting Gina sexually, and my raised voice caused Gina to stir in her sleep.

"I do not think of these things anymore," Sergei said, getting out of bed. "I accepted that would never happen years ago.

"Then you never wanted her as much as I did because I wouldn't ever get past wanting Gina in that way. To never know the feel of her lips on mine, the way her body moves against me as I make love to her, and the taste of her... I could *never* not want that."

"Yet another reason why Sergei and Gina were meant to be friends and nothing more," he said. "I must go now and take Maxim's head. I will ensure he burns well and has no chance of returning."

Sergei paused in the doorway and glanced my way. "Do you want me to stay with Gregor for the rest of my visit?"

I looked at Sergei—my best friend and brother—and felt as though I should hate him for what he'd just told me. But I couldn't. I had loved him far too long for that to happen. He saved my life when we were boys, putting himself in harm's way by doing so. And he hadn't acted on his love for Gina because he knew I loved her first. I couldn't hate Sergei; it just wasn't possible.

"No, Sergei, you can come back here. You are always

welcome in our home; you know that. But if you'll be staying in England more than Russia now, you'll have to think about building your own home. We have the land out back that has planning permission. Speak to Alex about it when things calm down. Then we can come to yours and eat *you* out of house and home."

"And you would be more than welcome," he said with a smile. Then he went to his room to get dressed before disposing of Maxim's body.

Chapter Nineteen

Sergei

I left Nik and Gina's cottage and headed to Gregor's home. Once again, I had to do a job that no one ever wanted. Only, this time, I was glad to take the vampire's head and burn him.

My Gina's life had been put at risk because of him, and the lovely Keeley was no longer human. Maxim needed to die a painful death, but he was already staked. The quicker we got rid of him, the lesser the chance of being discovered. Russian politsiya turn a blind eye to our activities, but I am not so sure you could explain them to English police.

Yuri met me outside the cottage where Maxim lay. He appeared confused, scanning the area around the cottages as he approached me.

"Sergei, do you know where Maxim's body is?" he asked.

"Yes, it is in the cottage on the left. Why?"

"It's not in there, Sergei. I have checked both cottages in the coach house, and they are both empty. I can see the blood from the two women, but Maxim's body is gone. Did Gregor take care of it already?"

I made my way past Yuri into the cottage. The stench and stains from the dried blood were clearly apparent, but there was, indeed, no body. Something glistened in between all the dried blood, so I went over to see what it was. A pretty blue pendant caught the fading sunlight, so I bent down to pick it up. It was on a gold chain that had been snapped apart, and I suddenly had an unwelcome vision of Maxim tearing into Keeley's neck—ripping the chain apart as he pulled away. What the poor woman must have suffered at the hands of that vampire…

I took out my phone and called Gregor, but he did not pick up. So I called Josh, but it went straight to voicemail.

I had a terrible feeling about this, and Yuri concurred. We ran using vampire speed towards the manor and used our senses to locate Keeley. She was in an upstairs bedroom, along with Josh and Gregor. Keeley had yet to regain consciousness, and as a Made vampire, it could take days before she came around.

It appeared that Josh and Gregor had been trying to clean her up for some time. There was blood all over the bath and in the shower, as well as on the floor and walls. Keeley had long hair; I imagine it would've taken many washes to get it all out.

The pain in Joshua's face was clearly visible. He was going through hell right now, and Yuri and I would probably make it worse.

"Gregor, where is Maxim's body? Did you dispose of it already?" I asked, hoping he had, yet my instincts told me that was not the case.

"No, I texted you and Yuri to do it. It's in the coach house cottage on the left."

"But it's not there, Gregor," replied Yuri. "Sergei and I have just come from the cottage, and there is definitely no body."

"Fuck!" shouted Joshua. "He was staked. You could clearly see he was incapacitated. There was no way he was getting up from that."

"I checked around the perimeter before Sergei arrived. He must have been moved at least fifteen minutes ago," said Yuri.

"Joshua and I have been here with Keeley since we came into the house. Alex and Nik stayed for a few moments after us. Maybe they moved him?" Gregor suggested.

"No, it was certainly not them," I stated. "I have just come from Nik and Gina's. He told me what had happened and that they left Maxim's body where it was."

I walked over to Joshua and handed him the pendant and broken chain. Keeley lay motionless in his arms, covered in a soft white bath sheet.

"I found this in the cottage, Joshua. I thought it might be Keeley's."

He nodded his head, then lifted Keeley's left hand.

"We got engaged last night. I bought her the pendant to match the ring."

It was a beautiful blue topaz, and I knew he had picked it because it would match her eyes. Keeley had the prettiest blue eyes, like the colour of the Mediterranean Sea. My heart broke for both of them and that beautiful little girl.

Gregor crossed to Yuri and asked, "Did you remove Maxim's stake? I know you were friends, but—"

"No, Gregor," Yuri shouted angrily. "I only tolerated Maxim; he was not my friend. But even if he was, what he did to Keeley is a crime punishable by death. I will take his head without question or remorse when I find him—staked or not."

"I had to ask, Yuri," Gregor said as he sat on an ottoman at the bottom of the bed. A white towel stained with blood was wrapped around his waist.

Both men were wearing towels to cover their nudity. They needed to put on clean clothes and get something to eat before we tried to find Maxim.

"Why don't both of you go and get dressed and bring something for Keeley to wear? We will stay here with her until you get back," I suggested.

"I'm not leaving her," said Joshua. "If Maxim is still around without the stake in his heart, he will heal. He could come back for Keeley to finish the job."

"Or Gina," added Gregor. "After all, it was Gina who fought and staked him. He will not like being bested by a human woman."

I pulled out my phone and called Nik. When I explained about Maxim's disappearance, he let out an angry roar. He knew that Gina would now be a target, but I assured him I was on my way back and we would both guard Gina.

"You cannot leave, Sergei. You will either find Maxim or guard Keeley," Gregor commanded.

"Gregor, you do not command me. I answer to no one other than my Gina and Nik. You are here with Yuri and Joshua. Keeley has enough men guarding her tonight. I can search the surrounding area before I leave, and I will come back later with some clothes for Joshua and Keeley. When I do, I will search again. I do not think that Maxim will stay near here tonight. He will need blood, food, and rest before he has his full strength back. Make sure your blood store is locked and your home is fully secure for the next few days."

"Thank you, Sergei," said Joshua quietly. "Keeley's clothing is still in Daisy's room. She'll need everything, including shoes. I'll bin all our clothes from today. We'll never be able to get all the blood out, so it's no use trying to save them. Freya will know what to pack for Daisy. Just give her a kiss from her mummy and daddy if you see her."

I nodded my head and tried not to show too much emotion. The man was holding on by a very thin thread, and I did not want to see it snap.

"Also, Sergei, tell Gina thank you. She put her own life at risk to save Keeley today. She's a brave woman."

I nodded at Joshua. "She is the very best."

I knew it would be pointless to search around the grounds for Maxim, but I did it anyway. When I concentrated hard enough, I could pick up many scents, Maxim's included. But they were all faint traces scattered around by the wind and damp evening air.

The threat to Gina's life could be genuine, while Maxim was unaccounted for, so I wanted to get back to her quickly.

After I revealed my feelings for Gina, I thought Nik would ask me to stay away from her. I was happy he hadn't done so. Even if he wanted to, the fact that Maxim could still be alive would change all that for him.

Nik would keep Gina safe no matter the cost.

I was glad that I had told him. I could not lie to him about anything, so there was no other way. I will always love Gina, but the type of love I feel is different now—more acceptable.

Maybe one day, I will find happiness with someone and share a love that can be returned freely.

I called Alex to let him know about the current situation at the manor and heard little Daisy scold him for cursing at my words. My heart hurt for that innocent child. I would give her anything she asked for to ease her sadness when she found out about her mother's fate.

Chapter Twenty

Alex

Julia was heartbroken, but she was trying her best to keep a cheerful expression on her face in front of Daisy. The poor little girl was oblivious to what had transpired at Rothley Manor today and was currently sitting at our table eating jacket potatoes with cheese—her favourite food.

Sergei rang, so I answered immediately. He told me that Maxim's body wasn't there anymore, and they believed him to be alive.

"Oh, fuck no," I cursed. I'd seen his body, and Gina had undoubtedly staked him through the heart.

"Uncle Alex, you said a naughty word," yelled Daisy from the table.

"I'm sorry, Daisy," I replied, turning away from her and Julia.

Sergei asked who was still at the manor when we left. I said I'd dismissed everyone and informed them they could all have a few days off. I'd made Ryan aware of what had happened and why it was safer for everyone not to be there, and he was upset about Keeley. He'd wanted to see her, but I'd asked him to leave so we could get things sorted.

Sergei told me that he and Yuri had searched the entire property and grounds, but he couldn't find anything. He also said we should be vigilant in case Maxim came back to kill Keeley or Gina, and I agreed that was entirely possible. I told him we should think about Daisy, too, as she could be a way to hurt Keeley. At that statement, Sergei cursed. He told me he was on his way back and would call in when he returned. He was going to collect some clothes to take to Keeley and Josh—theirs were too bloodstained to salvage.

I ended the call when I heard a car outside the cottage. It belonged to Daniel, Keeley's twin brother. I hated to be the one to tell him what happened today.

Just as Daniel approached my door, Freya and Sergei pulled up in front of Josh's empty cottage. I breathed a huge sigh of relief, knowing I wouldn't have to break the news to Daniel on my own.

I opened the door and let them all in. Sergei knew what I was about to do and asked if he could take Daisy to see Nik and Gina.

After kissing everyone goodbye, Daisy took hold of Sergei's hand and waved to us. She was so trusting. I had to watch them walk to Nik's cottage to give myself peace of mind that she'd be okay.

Daniel knew something was going on because of our sombre expressions, so I didn't waste any time and told him what Maxim had done to Keeley.

"Is she dead?" he asked in a whisper.

"No, Daniel, she's not dead. But she won't be human, either. Keeley will be a Made vampire, like Josh, but it will take some time for her to get to that stage."

"What do you mean?" he asked, confused. "I know there's a difference between you and Josh, but isn't it just that Josh can't stay out in the sun as long as you?" He pointed at Freya and me.

"We were born to a vampire father and human mother," said Freya. "When we made the change, we drank human blood and went to sleep overnight. The next day we woke up as you see us now, changed in ways that, apart from our strength and longevity, are mostly invisible…until provoked. Although we were hungry for blood, we didn't experience blood lust, so we could be around humans without hurting them.

"We can walk in the sun without harm, but it takes years for that to happen with a Made vampire. When a human is turned, that's what they are called: a Made vampire. The change is so significant that they'll need to feed on blood often—for several days, at least. Their ability to keep away from human blood is very fragile, especially children's blood."

"So what are you saying, Freya? That my sister will hurt Daisy? Her own child?" he demanded.

"That might not happen, Daniel, but it would be a strong possibility. She wouldn't mean to do it, but if Daisy was to fall and cut her knee, Keeley could react to the scent and accidentally drain her blood."

"She would murder her?"

"No, Daniel, it wouldn't be murder, it—"

"Yes, it would be murder. You can dress it up as much as you like, but it would still be murder," he yelled.

His anger and hurt were palpable, and he had every right to be upset. This was a terrible situation, and there would be no easy way out of it. I explained that Maxim's body was missing, and Freya went ballistic.

"Alex, you should have taken his head immediately. You should have burned him," she stated.

"Freya, he wasn't going anywhere. We had to get the women out of the way first. Gina was in a bad way, and Nik couldn't leave her."

"You should have finished him, Alex; you know how this works. Now he could be lurking around waiting for a chance to hurt Keeley, Gina, or even Daisy."

"What?" yelled Daniel. "I'm taking Daisy away somewhere safe until you've all got your shit together."

He tried to leave, but Freya stopped him at the door.

"Listen to me, Daniel. Daisy will stay with me. I can keep her much safer than any human, family or not, and I have staff who will guard her with their lives. You are more than welcome to come with us, but I won't let you take her anywhere on your own."

"Or what, Freya? Will you attack me the same as this Maxim did with Keeley?"

Freya reeled back in shock.

"No, Daniel. I could never hurt you or anyone in your family. How could you say such a thing?"

"Well, forgive me if I'm not '*pro-vampire*' tonight, everyone. But what do you expect when my sister had her human life taken away today and will crave her daughter's blood?"

Dan put his head in his hands and let out a sob. Julia approached him, putting her arms around his back. He turned and held her as close as he could without her baby bump getting in the way.

I remembered the day my sister was forced to take the blood and make the change, and an icy shiver went down my spine. Freya must have guessed what I was thinking because she held my gaze for a few moments before stepping towards me. I pulled her into my arms and held her tightly.

There we were, two grown men finding comfort and strength from women—actions as old as time.

Freya broke away from me and went over to Dan.

"Come with us, Daniel. Daisy will feel better if you are there. We can tell her we're taking her on a little holiday until her mum gets better. She'll understand that Josh has to stay behind and look after Keeley."

"Will you wait until I pack a few things up from home?" he asked, a little calmer now.

"Yes, of course I will. I need to pack some clothes and toys for Daisy, anyway. Does she have anything at your dad's house that would be good for a holiday?"

"Yeah, she does. I'll get some stuff together and meet you back here. I've never been to your place before, so I'm not sure how to get there."

"You can go in my car with me. I can get Daisy's car seat from Josh's SUV," said Freya.

"Can we call and see Keeley before we leave?" he asked.

"No, Dan," I told him firmly. "Not with Maxim still unaccounted for. None of you would be safe."

Daniel nodded his head. He knew the right thing to do was to get Daisy out of the way as quickly as we could, so he didn't push it. He glanced back at me as he reached the door.

"Alex, what about staffing? We're going to be short if I go away."

"Don't worry about that, Dan. Take as much time as you need. I'll make sure you're on full pay, and it won't affect any other holidays you've booked."

"Thanks," he said, walking out of the door.

Freya collected some of Daisy's clothes from Josh's

cottage while Julia and I went to find Sergei. He was going to take some things over to Gregor's for Josh and Keeley, and I wanted to see him before he left.

I may not always get along with Sergei; sometimes, I could bloody throttle him. But whenever there's a crisis, you can rely on him to get the job done.

I knew his priority would be Gina and Nik, but I needed him to consider Julia, too. Julia and I would have to go to work tonight, and I also wanted Sergei there. Maggie wouldn't stay at work when she found out about Keeley, so I'd need him to keep an eye on Julia if I had to go out to the compound.

Speaking of Maggie, I heard one of our compound's golf buggies come hurtling down the lane towards our cottages. Maggie was driving and was clearly upset.

"Alex," she yelled as the buggy came to a squealing stop.

"She must have spoken to Daniel," I remarked as Maggie stormed towards me. I noticed Sergei coming to the door of Nik's cottage, obviously wondering what all the commotion was about.

"When were you going to tell me about my niece, Alex? I've just spoken to my nephew, and he's heartbroken. What the hell happened up there today?"

"Maggie, please, calm down. We didn't know what was happening until it was too late."

"Bullshit, Alex. Keeley told me herself that she was dreading Maxim coming over. She just didn't want to let Gregor know that Maxim was bullying her. Keeley was afraid she'd lose her job because Gregor would think she wasn't up to it. I told her to tell him. I thought he would sort it out if he knew."

"I had a run-in with Maxim over it, Maggie," said Freya. "I threw him down the hallway at the manor yesterday after I caught him having a go at Keeley. I thought it would sort him out. Obviously, I was wrong."

"Obviously," yelled Maggie. "Didn't you think to tell Gregor?"

"It wouldn't have made a difference, Maggie," I informed her. "Gregor fought with him today over it and told him to leave, but he found Keeley instead."

Maggie started crying. "I'm going over to the manor to see her right now, so you better get cover for me at work tonight."

I grabbed her arm to stop her from leaving. "No, Mags, you can't go and see her—"

Before I could finish the rest of my sentence, Maggie raised her hand and slapped my face. I stepped back in surprise. I'd never once argued with Maggie and wouldn't have expected anything physical from her.

I didn't let go of her other arm. I just pulled her close and held her against my chest.

"She's my niece, Alex. Who are you to tell me I can't see her?" she argued.

"Mags, the only reason I won't let you go is that Maxim is still missing. The stake must have been removed before anyone could dispose of his body, and now we don't know where he is. It's not safe for you to go to the manor on your own, especially not tonight. Sergei's going to take Josh and Keeley some clothes over soon. Why don't you help him get their things together, and maybe you could go with him?"

"Keeley's so young, Alex," Maggie said between sobs. "She'll be devastated when she finds out she could hurt Daisy."

"Shh, Maggie, come on now. Keeley needs us to be strong for her. We need to show her we love her no matter what. It will all work out in the end. Everything always does," I assured her, though it was almost certainly a lie.

"You are her aunt—the nearest thing she has to a mother. She'll need to know you are on her side, Mags. There will be many changes to get used to in her world over the next few days."

Maggie nodded, and I tilted her head back to wipe the tears from her cheeks.

"I'm sorry I slapped you, Alex," she murmured.

"Don't worry about it, Mags. Although maybe you should think of a career change. Perhaps boxing or cage fighting," I joked.

"Very funny," Maggie grumbled as she walked towards Josh's home. When she spotted Sergei, she said, "Come on, Sergei. Let's get cracking."

"Maggie, what is cracking?" Sergei asked. "It is not something kinky, is it? You are a beautiful woman, Maggie, but I am sure your husband would not like me to…OW!" Sergei yelped when she clipped him up the side of his ear.

"Behave yourself, Sergei."

"Yes, Maggie," he murmured while following her into Josh's cottage, winking at us before closing the door.

Julia and I went into Nik's cottage and found Daisy sitting on the bed eating biscuits with Gina and Nik.

"How are you feeling?" asked Julia.

"A lot better now," Gina replied. "I keep randomly bursting into tears, though."

"It's only to be expected. You've had quite a shock, and then with the blood loss…." Julia remarked.

"But I shouldn't feel so sorry for myself when there's poor Keeley…." Gina closed her eyes and shook her head.

"Have you seen my mummy, Auntie Gina? Uncle Alex says she's poorly, and she doesn't want me to catch it, so Auntie Freya's going to take me to her house to stay with her."

We all exchanged sorrowful looks, and I could feel a lump in my throat when I glanced at little Daisy.

"Uncle Dan's going to Auntie Freya's with you too, sweetheart," Julia told her.

Daisy gave Julia the most beautiful beaming smile and said, "I'm glad Uncle Dan's coming. I miss him lots because he has a flat and I live in my new house. But I'm glad I've got a daddy, and I hope he can make Mummy feel better soon. Uncle Alex, you could take her my cough medicine to see if that will make her feel better," Daisy suggested. Julia and Gina blinked back tears.

"Come on, princess, let's get you to Freya and make sure she's packed all your toys," I said, picking her up and carrying her next door.

"Uncle Alex, I'm not a princess. I'm a queen, like Ellie," she declared with a huff.

Duly chastised, I apologised to the little queen and handed her over to Freya so that Julia and I could go into the office and start the night shift.

Chapter Twenty-One

Freya

About half an hour into our journey to my home in Aldbrough, Daisy fell asleep. I tried conversing with Daniel, but he didn't want to talk. That was understandable, considering what had happened today, but it meant there was an awkward atmosphere throughout our drive.

When we pulled into my driveway, I could tell that Daniel was surprised. My home is much larger than Gregor's manor house, but it doesn't have as much acreage as his. I suppose Daniel expected something small and quaint—like the cottage Alex lives in. But even though I have other smaller properties, this one has always been my favourite—and one I will always consider my home.

Leonard, my butler, came to the car and immediately opened the back door to take Daisy out of her car seat.

"I knew she'd be asleep," he said as he lifted her into his arms. "Millie's been baking all her favourites, and Sally's been to the supermarket in Hull to get all the food she likes.

She also bought her a large paddling pool, so I hope the weather's good tomorrow."

"Leonard, this is Daniel, Daisy's uncle," I said, introducing them.

"It's a pleasure to meet you, Daniel," Leonard replied, closing the car door behind him. "Now, let's get this little one inside out of the damp night air. Frank will come out and collect her things later."

"I'll get them," said Daniel as he made his way round to the boot of my car.

I drive an old Subaru Forester, and I love this car. It's an all-wheel drive, which is perfect for the harsh winters we sometimes get on the east coast of Yorkshire, and it's never let me down in the eight years I've owned it. Gregor is always on at me to get a new one, but you get used to things, and I'd hate to let this one go.

Frank, my gardener, came out of the house, closely followed by his wife, Sally. Frank offered to take Daniel and Daisy's luggage, but I think carrying it inside my house made Daniel feel useful. I believe he was a little overwhelmed by his surroundings, so I told him I'd take him on a tour of the house once we had Daisy settled.

Daniel stopped to look at some photographs hanging on the wall in the hallway. They were of Keeley, Daisy, and me on the lawns outside when Daisy was just a baby. It was a lovely sunny day when they were taken, and we were relaxing after a walk on the beach near Mappleton. Further on, there was a photograph of the three of us building sandcastles on Hornsea beach. I remember asking a lady to take the photo and trying our best to get Daisy to look at the camera and smile.

I hoped the photographs set Daniel's mind at rest regarding Daisy being here. She's used to having holidays with me. The only difference this time was that Keeley wouldn't be with us.

Leonard carried the sleeping Daisy upstairs to the bedroom we'd had decorated for her last Christmas. We knew she was potty about Ellie the Fairy Queen, so we had the room decorated with fairy wallpaper and matching paint colours. Frank built her a four-poster bed and painted it white, while Millie made the drapes from a shimmering blue voile material I'd sourced from India.

Being in the business of buying and selling fabrics meant it was easy for me to source the perfect Queen Ellie colour. The room was enchanting, and I could tell it impressed Daniel when he saw it.

"The room next door is the one Keeley normally stays in, so you can take that one if you like," I offered. "It has an adjoining door to this room, and Daisy normally sneaks into bed with Keeley if she wakes through the night. But if you want, I'll sleep in that room, and you can take my bedroom or one of the others," I told him.

"How many bedrooms are there?" he asked.

"Ten on this floor, and most have en-suite bathrooms, then four downstairs, but my staff have those rooms. Leonard is married to Millie, my cook, and Frank is married to Sally, my housekeeper. The staff quarters are just off the kitchen and are separated into two wings. There are also two more bedrooms, a sitting room, two bathrooms, a study, a dining room, and a small kitchen. At one time, we all lived here, Alex, Josh and I, but they moved further inland to manage their business."

"How far from the sea are you?"

"About half a mile, give or take, although with how fast the coastline is eroding, it won't be long until we're much too close for comfort."

The coastline is deteriorating at an alarming speed, and many homes have already gone as the land has fallen into the sea. The North Sea can be a beast when the weather is rough, and it seems there's little to be done to prevent it from attacking the surrounding cliffs. Although, along the coastline at Mappleton, enormous boulders have been placed on the beach in front of the cliff, which has slowed down the erosion for the time being.

"I can show you around the area tomorrow, and weather permitting, we can take a walk along the cliffs," I suggested.

"Thanks. That would be great," he replied.

"Daniel, I want you to feel at home here during your stay. You've always been welcome in my home, even if you didn't come along with Keeley. I know the sheer size of this house can be a little daunting, but you'll get used to it eventually."

"Oh, I'm sure I won't be here that long, so you don't have to worry about me," he replied with a sharpness that made Leonard turn to him with a hostile glare. I caught Leonard's gaze and shook my head.

Daniel had such devastating news today, so obviously, he was upset. I busied myself by getting Daisy's night things out of the suitcase I'd packed for her, and Daniel went through the interlocking door into his room.

When Daisy was tucked up in bed, fast asleep, I knocked on Daniel's door and asked him to join me for supper. On our way down to the kitchen, I gave him a quick tour. He seemed particularly impressed with the large ballroom.

Looking at it from a stranger's point of view, I suppose it

was impressive. Highly polished dark wooden floors, intricate cornicing, and mouldings adorning the ceiling. A row of floor-to-ceiling windows and glass doors covered by heavy, colourful drapes made it look like a room that would belong in a fairy tale.

Chandeliers lit the room, but to me, it was at its loveliest in natural light—with the midday sun shining through the windows. Apart from a few chaises and sofas against the walls, it was basically unfurnished.

Whenever Gregor came to stay with me, he insisted we light a fire in the enormous fireplace and dance around the room like we used to centuries ago. It always makes me smile when we do that.

Millie had prepared a chilli with rice and homemade garlic bread. It had taken me a while to get Millie to add foreign foods to her culinary skills, but my goodness, it was worth it!

Daniel complemented Millie, and I think it made her day. She began fussing over him as she did with Alex, Josh, and Gregor. I offered him a beer, which he accepted with a smile, and I saw him relax for the first time since he'd found out what had happened to Keeley. I knew it would be pointless to push further conversation this evening, and I was happy to sit for a while in silence.

Sally was upstairs watching over Daisy, so I asked if Daniel would mind if I caught up with some work emails. He asked what I did for a living, and I explained how I sourced the best fabrics from around the world and sold them to fashion houses.

We got involved in the fabric trade three hundred years ago. Alex and I would travel to Liverpool and meet with traders on ships from overseas selling beautiful silks, vibrant coloured fabrics, and spices. We quickly built up a good trade, and although Alex left the business to pursue other ventures, I kept buying and selling textiles.

I own two clothing warehouses and other related businesses, but there's something about discovering new materials and fabric colours that inspires me to carry on. Over the years, I've met many designers from world-famous fashion houses, and I love seeing their modern, if not sometimes bizarre, designs.

Daniel asked how often I travelled for business and how many countries I'd been to. I told him about my visits to the Far East and how exciting it was to learn about different cultures. He said he'd like to travel more because he'd only ever been as far as France and Spain with his family and, more recently, on a few lads' holidays to party resorts, such as Magaluf in Majorca.

I told him he had plenty of time to travel since he wasn't quite twenty-five yet. Daniel said he didn't think there was much chance of travelling too far when he had a flat and a car to pay for on his wage. He seemed down about his job, but I didn't want to get into it too much tonight. Daniel had mellowed a little, and I didn't want to spoil his mood, so I carried on with my emails while he sat by the fire drinking his beer.

I occasionally sneaked a peek at him to make sure he was okay. Daniel is just so handsome. He has wavy dirty-blond hair, which is usually quite short, but he'd recently let it grow, so it covered his ears and neck. He has the most amazing blue eyes framed by long brown lashes, and his full lips and strong jaw are edged with thick stubble, giving him a sexy, rugged appearance. Daniel is at least six-foot-three and is muscled to perfection.

I knew he regularly went to the gym at Night Movers because I'd seen him working out there a few times. But he's not overly muscular, if you know what I mean. I can't stand those over-muscled guys whose veins stick out and have no necks. I know some women find that attractive, but I certainly don't. Let's just say that Daniel has all the right muscles in all the right places, and if the women I saw ogling his six-pack were anything to go by, then he's not short of female attention.

He looked up and caught me staring at him, and I saw something in his gaze that I hadn't seen for some time. It was lust.

I knew that Daniel had a bit of a crush on me when he was younger, but I hadn't seen him look at me like that since he was a horny fifteen-year-old.

I was twenty-seven when I was forced into immortality, so my looks hadn't changed since then—even though that was hundreds of years ago. But to see Daniel looking at me like that again threw me for a loop, and I suddenly felt weird about admiring his body earlier. Like he was still a teenager—although clearly, he wasn't. So I feigned tiredness and told him I was off to bed.

Daniel followed me upstairs, saying it would be better if he could get some sleep, as no doubt Daisy would be up early in the morning. We said goodnight without our eyes meeting, and I told him to let me know if he or Daisy needed anything.

Chapter Twenty-Two

Daniel

My room at Freya's house was huge. In fact, you could just about fit our entire upstairs at my dad's house in it and still have room to spare. Although it was a sizeable space, it didn't feel cold. The whole place had good central heating, with large radiators and an open fire if needed.

I don't normally wear pyjamas, but I'd packed the only pair I owned to bring here. I hadn't known if Daisy would have been sleeping in my bed, so I wanted something to wear just in case.

The bedroom had an en-suite bathroom, which still held some of Keeley's toiletries, like toothpaste, shampoo, conditioner, and that raspberry-scented body wash she uses. I thought about calling Josh to see how she was, but they'd said earlier that she might be out of it for days yet.

After brushing my teeth, I got into the enormous bed—amazed at how small I felt in it. It was great not to have to keep my tall, broad frame in the single bed I'd had for most of my life.

I thought back to when I was sitting by the fire in the kitchen with Freya. I was sure I'd caught her checking me out, but I must have been mistaken. I know I'm good-looking, but Freya's in another realm in the looks department.

I'd fancied her since I was about twelve years old and used to fantasise about all the filthy things I wanted to do with her when I had my nightly wank. In fact, I think most of the muscles in my right arm came about because of Freya.

Being a vampire, she hadn't changed over the years, and she still did it for me in a big way. But I've seen her hanging around with that filthy-rich boss of Keeley's. The powerful, mega-wealthy, good-looking bastard is plainly her type. My teenage fantasies would never come true. I knew that.

Still, it didn't hurt to dream, I thought, as I stroked my hard-on through my pyjamas—thinking about all the ways I could take Freya. Her laid bare on the rug in front of the fireplace in her kitchen came to mind. I wondered whether her hair down below would be as pale as the blonde on her head, or maybe she wouldn't have any covering her folds. I thought about how she would taste when I lapped at her slit and ran my tongue up to her clit. How her back would bow off the floor when she neared her peak, making me hold her hips down with both hands to keep her in position.

I pictured her full breasts topped off by proud pink nipples that hardened at my touch, and the feel of her tight, wet heat when I sank my hard cock inside her. Taking out my painfully hard erection, I stroked myself to the brink, which didn't take long. Hot, rhythmic spurts shot into my hand and over my belly.

I used the tissues at the side of my bed to clean up the

best I could, then I went into the bathroom to get rid of them and wash my hands.

That's all it would ever be for Freya and me: a fantasy spilled over from my teenage years. And frankly, after what happened to my sister, maybe that was a good thing. Because no matter how great Freya and the others were, every one of them had the strength and speed to kill us in seconds. Now my sister could do the same, and I wasn't sure how to deal with that.

Chapter Twenty-Three

Keeley

It was dark when I woke, and I wondered what the time was. Josh had his arms wrapped around me, and I was glad because I felt quite cold. For a few moments, I let myself relax in Josh's embrace. I was thirsty, and my head and throat ached, but this feeling of being loved and protected made everything seem better.

"Keeley?" said Josh, in a voice thick with emotion. I tried to turn my head to see him, but my neck and throat hurt too much.

"Josh, I think I'm coming down with something. I don't feel so good," I croaked.

I felt strange. Detached, maybe. Not quite in the here and now. Floating between the past and the present.

I thought about asking him for a few drops of blood to make me feel better. And that's when it hit me!

Blood. I needed blood. A raging thirst like no other I

had ever experienced tore through me, and I began to shake.

"Keeley, it's okay. I've got you," Josh said, turning me over to face him and biting his wrist.

I don't know what came over me in that instant, but his blood smelled so good. I snatched his wrist and brought it to my mouth, lapping and then sucking at the blood that flowed. My gums throbbed, and something slid down them. A red haze tinged the darkness of the room, and I felt compelled to bite down on Josh's already bleeding wrist.

I couldn't help the groan that escaped my mouth as I drank from Josh; no more than I could stop myself from climbing on top of him so I could grind my sex against his. And still, I drank.

"Keeley, that's enough," he insisted, his tone firm. He gathered my hair in his free hand and pulled.

I let go of his wrist as I cried out—the orgasm taking over me completely. But as I was coming down from the waves of pleasure, something happened. Memories of yesterday flashed through my mind. Like swiping through the images on my phone, they kept coming and didn't stop. I heard a scream, which I realised was my own when I relived the moment that Maxim tore into my neck.

I placed my hand over where he'd bit me but felt nothing, just unbroken, soft skin. I looked around, confused and frightened. This wasn't our bedroom in Josh's cottage. I was at Rothley Manor, naked and in bed with Josh. I was still sitting astride him, and he was holding me tight to his chest.

"Josh, why are we at the manor? Why—?"

Oh, God, no. I finally figured out what was wrong with my aching gums.

I had fangs!

"No, no, no," I screamed as I pushed away from Josh and leapt out of bed.

"Keeley, you need to calm down. Please, come and sit with me so we can talk about what happened."

"Oh, I know what happened, all right. Maxim attacked me and turned me into a vampire," I spat. My voice sounded strange to my ears as I spoke around the elongated fangs.

"No, Keeley, not quite, but if you calm down for a second and come over here, I'll tell you exactly what happened yesterday. I don't want to upset you, but I won't lie to you, either."

He held out his hand, and after a moment's hesitation, I took it and walked over to the bed with him. We sat down and faced each other. Josh took my hand in his and kissed it before he spoke.

"I don't know how much you remember about yesterday, but Gregor fought with Maxim and told him to leave. Instead, Maxim sought you out and tried to kill you by draining you of your blood. Luckily, Gina came to see you and discovered what was happening. She fought with Maxim and staked him in the heart. Gina let us know what had happened and tried to give you her blood for some reason. She cut her wrist and forced you to swallow, but she'd cut too deep and couldn't stop the bleeding. Gregor got to you just before we did, and he gave both of you his blood.

"When Nik and I got there, we took over from Gregor. I'm going to be honest with you, Keeley. I wasn't sure if we could save you in any capacity at the time. But I kept going like Gina and Gregor had, working your mouth and throat so you could swallow. After a while, I noticed the deep holes Maxim had left in your neck begin to heal. I knew then that you'd live, but you'd be a Made vampire, not a human anymore. I'm sorry, Keeley. I'm truly sorry that you have to deal with this. If there were anything I could have done to keep you human, I would have done so. But letting you die wasn't an option for any of us. I know it's going to be hard getting through these next few months, but we can do it together."

"You, me, and Daisy," I said, looking into his eyes. I watched the slight flicker in them that told me I wouldn't like what he had to say next.

"Keeley, until you can be sure you have full control over the blood lust, it's best we keep Daisy away from you."

"What do you mean? Where is Daisy?"

"She's gone to stay with Freya for a little while. Daniel's gone with her too, so you know she's being looked after and probably spoiled rotten as well."

"And who made that decision, may I ask? Was it you, Josh, a Made vampire? Or was it Freya, who is also a vampire? Tell me, Josh, what makes me any different from you?" I retorted.

"Because a Made vampire has less control over their need for blood when they've just transitioned. And…they find the blood of children even harder to resist."

"So what are you saying? That I'm a risk to my daughter's life? That if she accidentally falls and cuts herself, I'll want to bite her? Kill her, even?"

For the second time in two days, I felt like my life was over. Yesterday it nearly was, and today, the way my heart was breaking, it might as well have ended, anyway.

"Why didn't you just let me die, Josh? If Daisy would be better off without me, you should have let me go."

"No, Keeley. Daisy still needs you. It will take time to get you to a stage where you can control your need for blood, but we'll get you there. You just need—"

"How long, Josh? Are we talking days, weeks, months, or years?"

"Well, everyone's different, Keeley. It may take a few months, that's all."

"MONTHS?" I yelled. "Months to a child seems so much longer than it really is. And then what? Will I still have the occasional slip? If she accidentally hurts herself, will she have to run away from me instead of running to me to make it better?"

"Keeley, however long it takes, we will deal with it, I promise," he stated while tucking my messy bed hair around my ear.

Josh looked so sincere right then—like he genuinely thought this would all turn out okay. But I knew differently. I knew it would never be okay again, and I wished that Gina had never stumbled across Maxim and me in that coach house cottage. It would have been better if they'd let me fade away because I couldn't contemplate being a danger to my daughter.

I heard a knock at the door and realised I was still naked. I saw a bathrobe placed over a chair, so I picked it up and put it on. Then Josh called out for whoever it was to come in.

Gregor opened the door carefully. He had a tray full of cups and a plate of toast in the other hand. Josh jumped up to take the tray from him as he entered the room.

"Good afternoon, Keeley. How are you feeling?" he asked as he came towards me and inspected my neck.

I wanted to say, *'not fucking good at all because I've just been told I could kill my child,'* but good manners and respect for

Gregor had me saying, "I'm okay, I suppose, all things considered."

"I'm surprised to see you up so early. It can be days before a Made vampire comes around after they've been turned. Your injury and blood loss were so great, I didn't expect to see you up and out of bed for some time. I've warmed you some blood. It's under here," he said, lifting the lid on a serving platter.

"You may find it easier to take if it's warm...until you get used to it, that is." He smiled nervously—as if he didn't know how I would react.

"Thank you, Gregor. That's so thoughtful of you. But I've just had some of Josh's blood, so I'm good for now."

I found the idea of drinking from a blood bag utterly gross, but I supposed it would be something I'd have to get used to.

Gregor and Josh looked at me oddly as I picked up a slice of toast and started eating it. Thank God my new fangs had gone back into my gums, or I wouldn't have been able to chew. My mouth felt so weird when they'd come down, like when I was a child and had a tooth out at the dentist's, and they'd put cotton wool between my gum and upper lip. My mouth felt full, and my gums tingled.

Josh picked up a bag of the blood that Gregor had brought and downed it quickly. I felt guilty that I'd taken so much blood from him earlier. He must have been exhausted after giving me his blood yesterday. Gregor, too.

"Thank you, both of you, for saving me yesterday. You gave me your blood to keep me alive, so you probably need it more than me right now." I tried to be sincere, but they both knew I had mixed feelings about being alive.

"Keeley, you are so precious to me; I would have done anything to save you yesterday. You are a wonderful young woman with people in your life who love you dearly. You deserve to live a long and happy life. Yes, you will have to make significant changes, but you can live forever with the man you love," Gregor said.

"But I can't be a mother to my daughter, Gregor. She's not five yet and still needs me to love and care for her. Apparently, I can't be near her yet because I might snack on her if she gets hurt. There's no way I can live that long, happy life without Daisy. She's my world, Gregor."

I began to cry; huge gulping sobs wracked my whole body. Josh picked me up and sat on the bed with me on his lap, holding my head against his shoulder.

"You'll get there, Keeley. We just have to get you to a stage where you can control your blood lust. Your love for Daisy will help you. I know you can do it because you're a strong woman. Look at how much you've achieved in your life so far. You've been a single parent for nearly five years, and you've coped so well. During that time, you've worked hard and dealt with all your dad's problems. You are an inspiration, Keeley, and I'm so proud of you."

That little speech didn't help with the sobbing. In fact, it just got worse. I seemed to cry forever, but in reality, it couldn't have been more than ten minutes. When I finally stopped, I realised Gregor had left the room, leaving Josh and me alone again. He held me tightly and occasionally placed kisses on my cheeks and lips.

"Your lips are so soft, Keeley; they're even softer when you cry. It breaks my heart to know that you suffered yesterday, and I couldn't protect you."

"I was going to call you and tell you about the argument with Maxim and Gregor, but I worried it would cause problems in your friendship with Gregor if you interfered, and I didn't want to risk losing my job," I admitted.

"I would give up anything for you, Keeley. You and Daisy are more important to me than anyone," he said softly.

I wiped my eyes and sighed. "I can't help thinking things will never be the same for us again. I should have known that good things weren't meant to happen to someone like me. Maybe I should have been content with having Daisy and working at Night Movers instead of falling in love and going after a better job."

"You can't stop love happening, Keeley. Whether it builds up slowly or hits you like a bolt of lightning, there's very little you can do to stop it when it's right. And ours is so right, Keeley. I tried to hide my feelings—as did you. But I'd never even consider letting you go now that I know what life could be like with you and Daisy. Whatever silly ideas you have in your pretty head about us being better off without you can stop because it's never going to happen. Daisy and I are in it with you for the long haul, and we *will* get our happily ever after; I promise you that." He flashed his beautiful smile and hugged me a few moments longer.

I got up off his lap and walked over to the window. Gregor had said it was afternoon, and I wanted to see the sunlight.

"NO, KEELEY!" yelled Josh when I pulled the first curtain back.

"What the hell are you doing?" I shouted as he tackled me to the floor, my body under his.

"The sunlight, Keeley…it will burn you from the inside out. You won't be able to be in sunlight for years, love. I'm so sorry; I thought you realised that."

Apparently not. But he needn't have worried in this instance.

"Gregor's had all the window glass covered with a

special film that filters out the harmful UV effects of sunlight. It's similar to what you have, but it lets more light through than the ones at your cottage and the Night Movers building. It had to be virtually unseen because this is a listed building, and English Heritage wouldn't have passed it otherwise."

"Oh, right. Sorry, love," he replied, looking down at me. "You are so beautiful. I won't ever tire of looking at you."

"Even with puffy eyes after all that crying?"

Josh said nothing, kissing me full on the mouth, pouring all his love for me into that one sensual act. I closed my eyes and let it take me to where all the hurt and sadness didn't exist. To a place where the only things I could feel were love and desire.

Josh undid the sash on my robe and kissed me from my throat to my sex. Then he removed his boxer shorts and slowly pushed his hard length inside me. He told me he loved me with every thrust, how he was so scared that he'd lose me, and finally, how I was his for always. Not only could I see the love, desperation, and fear in his eyes, I could smell it, too. The love was pure and heady, but the fear was sharp and bitter at the back of my throat. All my senses were amplified—like Josh's quickening heartbeat.

It was a steady and gentle build to our climax, but when it happened, it seemed to heal something inside me, and I thought that maybe things could work out as Josh had promised.

Some minutes later, we moved our tangled limbs, and Josh pulled me up for a shower. The bathroom held a deep, claw-footed, cast-iron bath with a shower over the top. It had a white shower curtain that draped all around it. So pretty, and very romantic.

"Sergei brought your shampoo and conditioner, as well

as some of our clothes. We'd already washed you and shampooed your hair before putting you to bed," Josh informed me as we stepped into the shower. I turned around quickly when his words finally registered through the shower spray.

"We?"

"Gregor and I brought you in and showered you because you were covered in blood, both yours and Gina's. We had to wash your hair several times because the blood had dried and matted it."

I groaned and put my hands over my face.

"So my boss has seen me naked, then?"

"It wasn't like that, Keeley. We were all fully clothed to begin with, and both Gregor and I kept our boxers on when we finally got your clothes off. I didn't think any were salvageable, so I told Gregor to bin them. I was too weak to do it all by myself yesterday, love. Gregor and I had two bags of blood each before we brought you back to the house. But we'd given you so much of ours before you showed signs of healing, and I wouldn't leave and get more blood until I had you clean and resting in bed. Even then, I didn't leave you. Gregor brought more up when you were settled, and Sergei delivered my own supply along with our clothes.

"I don't think it was just blood loss that caused my weakness, but also the realisation that I nearly lost you. And the fact that, after waiting so long to find a woman who meant the world to me, the perfect life I thought we'd have could've been taken away from us, just like that. I never wanted this life for you, Keeley, but I'll take you any way I can have you. Human, vampire, or some fucking sci-fi alien, I don't care. As long as I have your love, I'll be happy."

I placed my hand over his heart, my pale milky skin against his beautiful deep brown. His jet-black chest hair flattened under the shower spray until I ran my fingers through it, his bulky pectoral muscles flexing underneath.

He was glorious, this man/vampire of mine, from the top of his head to the tips of his toes and everywhere in between. I didn't want to break his heart, but the healing I felt when we'd made love had disappeared when he told me about washing the blood away after my attack.

I didn't want to feel like this, so lost and alone, when I knew deep down that I was loved. But then I wondered what he really loved.

Josh fell in love with a human woman. A devoted mother and daughter. A friend to all—apart from the vampire that took my human life. Would I still be the same Keeley Saunders now I was no longer human? Somehow, I didn't think so.

I didn't want to give Josh false hope, but I couldn't stop myself from holding him again. If my world was going to be so utterly fucked up that I didn't recognise it anymore, I would enjoy the love and comfort he offered for as long as I could before I finally gave up everything I ever wanted.

Chapter Twenty-Four

Freya

Daisy and I had been up for half an hour when we finally decided it was time to wake Daniel. It was 8 a.m., and after coming into my room to wake me with a storybook earlier, Daisy told me she wanted to have breakfast in bed with her uncle and me.

Millie made us all a lovely English breakfast of lean bacon, sausage, fried eggs, mushrooms, and beans with lots of toast. Leonard and Sally brought it up on two trays, and we knocked on the door to Daniel's room before Daisy opened it, then ran and jumped on his bed.

Daniel lay asleep on his front with the covers kicked off towards his feet. Black pyjama shorts clung to his waist and arse, his muscular arms on either side of his head. He was so sexy like this, and even Sally looked her fill before placing the tray on a side table and opening the curtains.

Daniel groaned a little at Daisy's bed-bouncing and the sunny glow from the window, and he asked Daisy to bring the covers up from the bottom of the bed because he was cold. It was perfectly warm in his room—stuffy, even. But the real reason that Daniel hadn't turned over onto his back until he was covered didn't hit me at first. Why would it? It had been years since I woke up in a man's bed, and I'd forgotten the fact that men often wake up with an erection.

I was embarrassed, yet also a little turned on. I could scent his arousal, and was that…? The scent was faint, but I was sure that Daniel had been masturbating at some point during the night. I felt my nipples pebble against my nightshirt, and I knew he'd noticed.

My mouth became parched, and I felt a little lightheaded. I would need blood later because I was sure I wouldn't be able to get through the day otherwise. A near-naked Daniel had my hormones twisted into knots by doing nothing more than looking as sexy as sin in the bedroom next to my own. I should have moved him further down the hallway because the man was temptation itself.

An age seemed to pass while we stared at each other, but Daisy shouting, "I want my toast cut into soldiers," broke into my thoughts.

"Daisy wanted us to eat breakfast in bed, so I arranged for a cooked breakfast to be brought up. If you would rather it be you and Daisy, I can eat on my own," I offered, my gaze holding his.

"Wow, thanks. I'm impressed," he said as his stomach growled.

Sally took the tray off the table and walked around the bed to place it in front of him. She smiled and asked, "Would you like me to pour tea for you, Daniel?"

He shot her a dazzling heart-racing smile before taking her hand and kissing the back of it.

"No, I'll do it. Thank you, Sally. It's not often I get

someone wanting to look after me like this. I do appreciate it."

Sally, who was all blush and fuss, patted Daniel on the shoulder. "Well, you'll be looked after while you're here, young man, that you can be sure of."

Leonard shook his head before he turned to me and asked, "Will there be anything else, Freya?"

"No, Leonard. Just say thank you to Millie for the lovely breakfast, would you, please? We'll see you later before we leave for Hornsea."

Leonard nodded, and both he and Sally left us to have our breakfast. I sat on the bed and took the teapot and cups from Daniel's tray, placing them on his bedside table. Then I took a plate of breakfast and toast from the tray before lifting the legs underneath it, so it was high enough for Daisy to eat her breakfast more comfortably. I looked up to find Daniel watching me closely.

"Do you do this often when Keeley comes to stay?" Daniel gestured at the breakfast trays.

"At least once per holiday," I told him while cutting Daisy's sausage and bacon into smaller pieces.

"You're really good with her," he observed, taking a sip of his tea.

"She's a joy to look after, aren't you, Daisy?" I laughed as she dipped her toast in the runny egg yolk and tried in vain to catch it in her mouth before it ran down her chin.

"Didn't you ever want your own kids?" he asked innocently. "You'd make a great mum."

And just like that, my appetite vanished. I placed my knife and fork down on the plate and rose from the bed.

"I'm not as hungry as I thought I was," I said, trying to hide my hurt. "I'll go and get ready first, then I can get Daisy dressed when she's finished her breakfast."

"Freya, wait," he replied, confused yet concerned. But I didn't stop moving until I was inside my room with the door closed.

Daniel had done nothing wrong. Obviously, Keeley had respected my privacy and hadn't told Daniel how my children had lost their lives. But I couldn't help the pinch in my heart when I thought of having my own children around me. Cutting up their food, getting them dressed, and all the silly mundane things that don't seem important to you at the time, yet add to the memories you keep locked in your heart and mind about good times long passed.

I would give anything to spend one more day with my daughter. To hold my baby son in my arms and feel his breath against my cheek. Something I never got to feel.

The tears came like they always did, falling silently down my face as I washed them away with the spray from the shower. But unlike most other days, I had to pull myself together. I had little Daisy to think about for a while. Daniel, too. Their lives had been disrupted by someone taking Keeley's choice away from her, forcing her into immortality just like I had been. I needed to help them make the best of a bad situation, and I couldn't do that if I were alone in my room, grieving.

I quickly dressed and tied my shoulder-length blonde hair in a ponytail. It hadn't taken long for the puffy redness from crying to fade from my grey eyes—courtesy of being a vampire. I didn't want to leave my room and risk running into Daniel, so I dialled Leonard to bring me up a bag of blood.

Going out during the day always made me tired—I'm a vampire, after all—but being a Born Immortal means I can tolerate the sun. Poor Keeley wouldn't have that option for another century, at least.

Leonard knocked on my door before walking in. He guessed I'd been crying. I swear that man knew me better than I knew myself at times. He'd brought me the bag of blood but offered his wrist first.

"No, Leonard, it's okay. Bagged stuff will do today," I told him with a smile. My staff let me drink from them if I ever needed to.

Unlike at Night Movers, where the staff donated blood in a clinical environment, my staff donated straight from the vein. They, in turn, were offered enough of my blood to replenish theirs, keeping them fit and well and preventing them from ageing.

Unlike when a bonded couple donates during sex, there is no emotional or hormonal response from myself or my staff during the giving and taking of blood. And it's not needed that often. Once a week is enough to keep these humans with me.

Leonard and Millie have been with me for over a hundred years, although Frank and Sally came later. I depended on them as you depend on family, and I love them all dearly. Especially Leonard. If I could have chosen a father from anyone ever to grace this earth, it would have been him.

"What's wrong, Freya?" he asked, cupping my cheek, then pulling me in for a hug.

I told him what had happened when Daniel asked about me having children—how I'd become upset and left the room without explaining.

"Well, Freya, maybe it wasn't the right time to tell them, what with little Daisy being all ears. But you can talk about your children, even if you don't speak about how they died. You could tell Daniel they passed away in an accident many years ago, but it shouldn't stop you from talking about them.

"From what you've told me, your Brisa was a beautiful, lively little girl who'd so much love for everyone in her heart. I've said it before, and I'll say it again. It's not good to keep your memories of her to yourself and Alex. Share them with others, Freya. Let them know how special she was. How you and your husband adored her, and how excited you were to be expecting again. I hate to see you unhappy, my dear, and I'd love to see the day when you find that special someone who can share your life and your memories, *and* help you make new ones. I always thought that Gregor would be the one to capture your heart in that way, but maybe a human will sweep you off your feet. Maybe someone not too far away," he suggested, raising his eyebrows as he nodded towards the room where Daniel and Daisy ate their breakfast.

"Behave yourself, Leonard," I groaned.

"Oh, I wasn't implying anything, Freya," he said with a smirk. "I just found it highly amusing how you and Sally seemed quite taken with a certain blond male this morning."

"Out, shoo." I gestured towards the door. "I bet you all had a good gossip in the kitchen."

"I never gossip," Leonard declared with mock outrage. He pecked me on the tip of my nose before leaving, and I watched as he walked down the stairs.

I wondered just how much meddling my staff would do over the next few days. God knows they did it often enough with Gregor. We've both found their attempts at matchmaking pretty funny over the years, with Gregor playing up to their secret endeavours to see me fall in love. I suppose it was a shame that couldn't happen. Gregor is a wonderful man, but I could never fulfil some of his baser needs.

Gregor and women are a complicated equation. He's

kind, respectful and endearing… outside of the bedroom, at least. I know how hard he tried to be the kind of man I needed, but it wasn't to be. I am too strong a woman to submit to him, and Gregor accepts this. Yet still, to the outside world, he and I would have made a good couple. Instead, he's my best friend—someone I share my past and present with—a man who's seen me cry but has never made me feel vulnerable.

Daniel made me feel vulnerable.

A human male with all the weakness they possess made me feel vulnerable with an innocent question. Because answering truthfully would have brought me back to a time when I was human—weak and vulnerable enough that my family was taken from me. That's something I do not miss about my humanity. I like the fact that I'm physically stronger and have the age and wisdom to see past things that blind emotional humans to the danger that surrounds them.

Still, I'd been caring for a human family in my home for less than twenty-four hours, and I'd already shed tears. I also had a strong feeling that things in my relatively uncomplicated life were about to change significantly, and for all the power I possessed, it wouldn't be enough to stop it.

Chapter Twenty-Five

Daniel

Daisy was exhausted. She'd fallen asleep on the short journey back from the beach at Mappleton and was still sleeping as I carried her indoors. I'd enjoyed our day out, although I felt guilty that Keeley wasn't with us. Freya was quieter than usual, though, and I think it was because of something I'd said this morning. Everything was going okay until I asked her about having children. She'd clammed up and said she wasn't hungry anymore. I felt terrible, but with Daisy around us, I hadn't had a chance to ask her about it…or to apologise for upsetting her.

This morning, we went to a shopping centre called Hornsea Freeport. Freya wanted to buy more clothes for Daisy, but I made her put her money away. If Daisy needed something, I would buy it for her. Freya seemed put out, but she didn't argue about it.

I bought some swim shorts and put them on in the fitting rooms after I paid for them. I hadn't brought any from home because I didn't think it would be beach weather, but today was warm and sunny.

After visiting Hornsea Freeport, we went along to the beach. Near the car park, a few small shops sold toys, towels, and flip-flops. We bought Daisy a bucket and spade, and two small tennis racquets with a soft ball.

Freya's housekeeper had brought a cool box to the car with plenty of food so that we could have a picnic on the beach. I carried the cool box, picnic blanket and towels while Freya carried the rest.

I suppose to most people, we looked like an average family—husband, wife, and child, and it gave me a thrill to think of us that way.

I wanted that now. I'd been living the single life for too long and felt it was time to settle down. Of course, I'd have to find someone to settle down with because I knew the woman walking alongside us wouldn't want someone like me.

She had a massive home with staff to help her run it, and she owned a successful business. Freya should never have to lower her standards for someone like me—working a permanent night shift at her brother's company and only just able to pay for my flat and car.

We stopped at a spot on the beach that gave us enough room to lay the blanket down and play a few games. Then Freya stood and took off her sundress.

How on earth was I supposed to last the day looking at Freya in the little flowery bikini she wore underneath it? She only had to smile at me, and BAM! Instant hard-on. Seeing more of her fucking sexy curves was pure torture. Suddenly swim shorts didn't seem like such a good idea, because even with careful adjustments I couldn't hide the stiffy I sported.

Daisy asked me to go to the sea with her so she could fill

up a bucket with seawater, but I couldn't move until I got myself under control. Freya took her hand and led her down to the sea, which gave me another magnificent view, because Freya from behind was just as sexy as Freya from the front.

Just breathe, Dan, and think about what today is about: letting Daisy enjoy herself and not miss her mum too much, I told myself. After a few deep breaths and thinking about work, I could finally stand and get the towels ready for Freya and Daisy to come back to.

After taking Daisy to bring water another couple of times, I built a few sandcastles with her. I hadn't built sandcastles since before my mother died. Keeley and I used to build big ones with moats around the outside, and we'd also bury Dad's feet in the sand. Mum used to walk us along the beach looking for interesting shells we could put on the outside of our sandcastles, and Dad would take us to rock pools and tell us about all the creatures we found in them. But now my mother was gone, and my dad was an alcoholic going through rehab.

I realised that Daisy wouldn't get those kinds of memories anymore because Keeley couldn't go out in the sun, and Josh had to limit the time he was out in it too. So I vowed to make this week extra special for Daisy, and to take her on holiday every year to give her the things that made me happy as a child.

"Penny for your thoughts," said Freya as she leaned her shoulder into mine.

"I was thinking about making some happy memories with Daisy today. She won't be able to do this with Keeley anymore."

"I know, and I'm so sorry about all of it, Daniel. For Keeley more than Daisy. She's young yet, and children can be very resilient about some things. But Keeley will really suffer not being able to do the things most of us take for granted, and she'll worry about how Daisy is feeling. Let's make some videos and take pictures of this week, then we can send them to her so she can see Daisy's okay and having a good time," Freya suggested.

So that's what we did. The video we sent was of Daisy making a sandcastle, but we had to have three goes at it before we got one where the turret stayed on when she pulled the bucket away. Then Freya took one of Daisy and me attempting to play tennis, although again, Daisy made us redo that video until she could finally hit the ball.

We got someone to take a photograph of us having our picnic together. I had to put my arm around Freya so we all could fit in the picture, and it felt good to hold her against me. I noticed she shivered a little when I did that, so I told her we could head back to the car if she felt cold. Freya said she was okay but would put on her sundress.

The dress didn't have any sleeves, so I handed her my T-shirt to wear. When she put it on, the hard-on I'd tried to keep in check since we arrived at the beach would not stay down. Something about her wearing my clothes made me feel as though Freya was mine. That she belonged to me as much as the T-shirt she wore, and would fit my body better than any clothing ever could.

After a few hours on the beach, we decided it was time to go.

On the way back, Freya took us to the beach at Mappleton—the village next to where she lived. She pointed out the enormous rocks and boulders that had been brought in to slow down the rapid coastal erosion happening all over the east coast of England. Freya promised to take me on a walk by the cliffs near her home later, so I could see how they'd been affected.

I looked forward to it, not only because I found it interesting, but because I'd be with Freya. I enjoyed her as a person and the passion she had for things she was interested in—not just because she was gorgeous.

On the way back to Freya's car, we each held one of Daisy's hands and swung her a little. Both Daisy and Freya were giggling away, and I was grinning from ear to ear. I'd thought today might be awkward and I wouldn't enjoy it, but that couldn't be further from the truth. It was only last year I went on two lads' holidays—one to Ibiza and the other in Magaluf—and I thought sun, sea, booze, and sex made for the best holiday ever. But today, being on the beach with my niece and Freya had given me more pleasure than any lads' holiday ever could.

Chapter Twenty-Six

Freya

We had to wake Daisy up for her bath, and she yawned the entire time. After a sandwich and a warm milky drink, she went off to bed so that Sally could read her a story. Sally and Frank were going to watch over her while I took Daniel for a walk around the cliffs and the village before it became too dark. I was a little nervous, if I'm honest. I wanted Daniel to fall in love with Aldbrough.

I knew he'd spent his teenage and adult life in and around Barrowfield and the small town of Rothley, which wasn't exactly a social hub—then or now. But Aldbrough village is tiny, with only a post office that has a small general store attached, a fish and chip shop, two pubs, a guest house, and a church. Other than the small caravan park, that was it. Some people might find it boring, but I loved it. I wanted Daniel to see its quaint beauty and how friendly everyone was. I wanted him to love it as much as I did.

We first walked alongside the cliff around the caravan

park, as we only had about an hour of daylight left. The sea was calm, and the sunset shone pink hues throughout the sky.

"It's so peaceful here, Freya," Daniel remarked as we made our way back to the village from the cliffs. "It's no wonder you don't want to live in Barrowfield, though I know Keeley would love it if you did."

"Alex would like me to live there too. Especially with the baby coming. And to be honest, that's the only drawback of living an hour's drive away. I can't just pop round to see my family, but it's not like I live at the other end of the country, either. So I'll have to make up lots of excuses to be in Barrowfield more, then I can get my hands on the new baby and Daisy for lots of cuddles."

"You could always come and see me," he suggested as he took my hand. "Then maybe I could show you a good night out around Rothley."

"I'd like that, Daniel," I told him, smiling at the eagerness in his voice. I don't know whether it was the invitation he gave me for the night out or the fact he was still holding my hand that kept the smile on my face, but I suddenly felt so happy.

"You can call me Dan. Keeley and my friends do," he said.

"Okay. Dan it is."

"I think this morning I said something that upset you, Freya, and I'm sorry for that. I didn't mean to."

And just like that, my happiness vanished. I tried to pull my hand away, but he held on to it tightly and tugged me towards him.

"I want to know what upset you, Freya, so I don't do it again. You don't have to tell me, but I swear I'm a good listener. And I'm not one to spill secrets, either."

I looked around at the rugged coastline and the darkness edging its way through the sky. Could I do this? Could I tell one more soul about the day my human life ended?

Dan turned my face towards him and swore. He must have seen the glaze of tears forming in my eyes because he said, "I'm sorry, Freya. You don't have to tell me anything if you don't want to. I should never have brought it up."

I leaned into him, and he put his arms around me, holding me tight to his chest as he kissed the top of my head. My tears were silent, but there were many of them.

I decided Leonard was right. Maybe I should let more people into my life and not hide my past. So I took a deep breath and said, "Let's sit down on that bench. This may take a while."

Dan nodded and walked me over to the bench. It had a brass plate with an inscription dedicated to a treasured wife from her loving husband. A declaration of love for all to see. They weren't a local couple, but they'd holidayed at the caravan park for years. I'd known them but only by sight and the occasional *hello*. The husband passed away the year after his wife. He couldn't function without the love of his life, and I knew how that felt. It had been so long ago for me, and I *had* learned to function again, but lately…

Dan was still holding my hand, which he turned over and kissed. He didn't say anything or hurry me; he just sat patiently and waited for me to speak.

I began by telling him about finding out that Brandr wasn't my biological father, but Sebbi, who had been like an uncle to us, was. We'd discovered that Sebbi was a Born Immortal who had taken the blood and become a vampire. This meant that Alex and I were also Born Immortals, although human at the time. I told Dan about our journey to England, and that my mother had drowned during the storm that hit us just before we arrived here.

He said he was sorry to hear that I'd lost her while I was so young. Almost the same age as he and Keeley were when their mother died.

I described our way of life in the settlement near the village of Staithes and how I met and married my husband. Then I told him about my daughter, Brisa, and how Alex, my father, and my uncle Gamall doted on her. I also told him that my father would pressure me to take human blood so I could be fully immortal, and I didn't want that because I wanted to grow old with my husband and children.

I bit back the tears and told him about the fire that raged through my home and killed my husband and daughter. And how the devastation caused me to lose my baby boy, who was stillborn when I was five months pregnant. I said that I'd haemorrhaged due to problems with the birth, and I was dying—a fact I welcomed at the time because I couldn't live without my family. But my father wanted me to live—against my wishes—and he forced me to take both his blood to heal, and human blood to make me a Born Immortal vampire.

Then I took a few deep breaths and told him how I'd found out that my father got someone to start the fire that claimed their lives. He'd done it because he thought my husband was the only one stopping me from becoming fully immortal. My father wasn't aware my little Brisa would be at home that night; she should have gone to his home with me like she always did.

I confessed that I couldn't let my father live knowing what he'd done to my family, so I plotted to end his life. I looked Dan in the eyes and told him exactly how I'd killed my father, and how I'd asked my brother to end my life so I could be with my husband and children.

"Obviously, Alex refused because I sit here today telling you my story. But it's why I got upset this morning when you mentioned me having children. As far as I'm aware, a female immortal cannot reproduce. Although, I'm not sure why, as male immortals can father children to human females."

Dan didn't say anything at first. He couldn't seem to look at me, either.

"Dan, do you hate me because I killed my father?" I asked. Although I wasn't sure what I would do if he said yes.

He shook his head. "No, Freya, I could never hate you. I'm not a parent, but I know if anyone—no matter who they were—hurt Daisy, I would tear them apart with my bare hands. Does that make you hate me?"

"No, of course not."

"Well then, don't hate yourself for what you did to your father because he deserved it as far as I'm concerned. And how he forced you into becoming immortal was awful. You've had to live with your grief all this time. I'm surprised you're as strong a person as you are."

I shook my head. "I'm not strong, Dan. Not emotionally, anyway."

"You are strong, Freya, and thoughtful, caring, generous, and utterly gorgeous. And so bloody sexy, especially in that bikini you wore today. Even when you were covered up in my T-shirt, you looked sexy as fuck."

I giggled at his dreamy expression, and he raised one eyebrow as he looked at me.

"Are you laughing at me, Freya?"

"It's the look on your face that did it. I can't believe you thought I looked sexy in a man's T-shirt," I said, my heart rate kicking up a notch as he leaned towards me.

"Not just any man's T-shirt, Freya; it was my T-shirt. Knowing you wore what had been on my skin made me hard as a fucking rock. In fact, I'd been fighting a stiffy since we got to the beach. I was going to check if men could die from having a constant erection because if that's true, then I'd better go home for my own safety. Being around you makes me hard. You don't have to do or say anything other than just be you. It's been the same since I was about twelve years old. As a teenager, you were my ultimate fantasy, and that hasn't changed."

His eyes were a stunning sparkling blue, his lips so kissable and full. I couldn't help but lean over the few inches between us and kiss him. My kiss was soft and chaste, but that only lasted a few seconds.

Dan grabbed me by the back of my neck and pulled me flush against him as he kissed me passionately, his tongue thrusting into my mouth, flicking against my own. I couldn't help the moan that escaped my mouth as I wound my arms around his neck and let him take complete control. It felt so good to give in to his demanding kiss, and how he held me made me feel wanted and protected.

Why had Daniel made me feel that way? I've kissed a few men over the years—all Born Immortal men, not human. But I never felt this much passion and need, not since my husband all those years ago. It shocked yet thrilled me and gave me hope I might find the other half of my soul again.

A springer spaniel jumped onto the bench and interrupted us, his owner not far behind, apologising for disturbing us.

When we were alone again, I chanced a look at Daniel.

I found him gazing at me with a look that told me exactly what he wanted. Could I do this? Would I be able to have sex with him without developing feelings? I didn't think that was possible because I already felt something for him, although I wasn't sure what that was. I knew I wanted this blue-eyed man who epitomised sexy, but I also enjoyed just spending time with him.

"Freya, tell me we're going to do more of what we just did when we get back to your place," he said in a raspy voice.

"Where do you want it to lead to if we do?" I asked, desperate to hear his answer.

"Well, to start with, I want to undress you slowly, tasting every inch of your skin as it's revealed. When I have you fully naked, I want to tease your perky nipples with my fingers and tongue until they feel hard enough to cut glass. Then I'll work my way down your body, kissing every inch of you I encounter. And then I'll part your folds and taste you, lapping at you until your clit stands proud. Then I'll—"

My body reacted instantly, so unbelievably turned on by his words.

I got up from the bench and tugged on his hand. "Come on then, Dan. Take me home and show me some action."

"Your every wish is my command, sexy Freya." With little effort, he picked me up and carried me over his shoulder.

I laughed out loud, yelling at him to put me down, but he kept me there until we arrived on the road away from the village. Dan pulled me into a covered bus shelter and began kissing me again. This time, he ran his hands all over my fully clothed body as he pressed me against the wall. He grabbed my hand, placing it over his denim-covered erection, and groaned as I rubbed up and down. Even through his jeans I could feel how big he was, and it gave me such a thrill to know I'd caused this reaction in him.

He undid the buttons on the jeans I'd put on before we left the house, and I secretly wished I still wore my sundress so he could have better access to my sex. But Dan didn't let my tight jeans stop him. He pulled them down along with my knickers to mid-thigh, then traced my sex with his fingers, teasing me before kicking my legs apart as far as they would go.

"I can't wait till I get my tongue and then my cock in here," he said as he slowly slipped a finger inside me. Then he pulled the finger out and moved it up towards my clit, which he circled rapidly; the wetness from inside me made it easy for him to do so.

Dan changed the movement to a firm up-and-down motion as he thrust his tongue inside my mouth, kissing me hard—like he was desperate for more. An orgasm began to build, rising rapidly with the firm rhythmic strokes of his fingers until I cried out my release into his mouth. Dan swallowed the sounds as he kissed me, his fingers slowing gradually until my orgasm was done.

He was still kissing me as he pulled my undies and jeans back up and fastened them. Then he moved his mouth to my ear and said, "The next time you come, we'll be on your bed with you on your back and my face between your legs."

Then he took my hand and led me the rest of the way home.

It took forever to get to my front door, but when we did, Daniel pushed me up against it and kissed the breath right out of me. I pulled away from him and turned the handle, the warmth from the hallway a welcome change from the damp night air. Leonard stepped out from the shadows and offered to take our jackets. I looked for signs that he'd spotted our kiss, but he gave nothing away.

"I've just taken a hot cup of cocoa up to Sally. Little Daisy was sleeping soundly when I left the room. Can I get either of you anything?" Leonard asked.

"I'm fine, Leonard," I replied, then I turned to Daniel and asked if he needed anything.

"No, thanks, Leonard. I just need to go to bed." He gave me a sexy grin, and I knew the last thing he wanted to do was sleep.

"Yes, I'm sure you do," Leonard mumbled as he turned to me and winked.

Busted! I was so embarrassed I didn't know where to look, but I couldn't meet Leonard's eyes at all.

"Well, goodnight then," said Daniel as he took my hand again and led me up to Daisy's room.

We opened the door as quietly as possible so as not to wake her. Sally put her book down and removed her reading glasses, raising a finger to her lips as we entered the room.

"She woke up earlier and asked for a drink, but she went straight back to sleep. She's been out like a light for about half an hour now," Sally whispered while gathering her things together.

Daisy lay with her blonde hair fanned behind her on the pillow, her hands in front of her face, looking like a little angel. Daniel and I kissed the top of her head before tiptoeing out of the room and closing the door.

"Well, goodnight, Sally. Thanks for watching her for us," Daniel whispered.

"It was a pleasure. She's such a joy to be around."

Daniel bent down and kissed Sally's cheek, thanking her again for being such a star. She blushed and fluttered her eyelashes at him before saying goodnight and walking down the stairs.

Daniel, or Dan—as he'd asked me to call him—was such a charmer. No wonder he had women everywhere falling at his feet, me included, and I told him so. His answer to that was to whisper in my ear, "I wouldn't mind you kneeling at my feet, Freya. I'm sure I could think of an activity you could do so you didn't get bored while you were down there."

I feigned shock, but he picked me up and threw me over his shoulder again, urging me to keep my voice down so I wouldn't wake Daisy up. He stood me upright on the floor at the side of my bed and gave me a look that just about melted my knickers off. I looked at the bed and suddenly became nervous, although I'm not sure why.

Daniel was a big guy, but I was a Born Immortal. I shouldn't get scared or nervous around him. But for some reason, I was.

"Do you want a drink?" I asked, moving over to a cabinet that held Frank's homemade honey whisky. That, along with a fine brandy that Sergei buys me, is what I use for a nightcap if I need one.

"Is that for Dutch courage, Freya? Do I make you nervous, or is what we're about to do making you nervous?"

"A little of both, if I'm honest, Daniel," I admitted when I handed him a whisky.

"You find it hard to call me Dan. Why is that?"

"Why is it important to you that I shorten your name?"

"Because I want you to see me as the man I am now

and not the lanky teenager I once was," he replied, standing in front of me.

"Oh, I don't think you have to worry about that. Whether Daniel or Dan, I can see you're all man," I assured him.

"I hope you tell me we don't need condoms because I desperately want to feel you bare."

"No condoms needed," I told him.

He took the drink from my hand and ordered, "Strip for me, Freya, don't be shy. Show me what was hidden from me on that beach today."

"Only if you do the same for me," I challenged.

Dan smiled and took off his long-sleeved black T-shirt, throwing it on the floor. I'd seen him shirtless today at the beach but seeing him in my bedroom when we were alone was an entirely different experience.

I wanted to touch his chest and abs, first with my fingers, then with my tongue.

The sound of his belt unbuckling pulled me out of my thoughts. Watching every button on his jeans come undone made my mouth water, and when I looked up, I noticed him eyeing me intently.

"Freya, I seem to be the only one getting naked here. If I have to strip you bare, I can't say how well your clothes will fare when I remove them."

I picked up my glass and took a huge gulp of whisky before removing my T-shirt. I wore a pale lavender bra that unclipped at the back, but I didn't remove it. By the time I looked up, Daniel was only wearing dark-grey boxer trunks, which did nothing to hide the erection he was sporting and the damp spot where the tip of his cock was positioned.

He stalked over to me and pulled my body flush against his, the heat from his chest burning into my own. His hand went to the back of my head, and with one hand under my bottom, he lifted me enough to kiss me without dipping his head. His lips were soft yet demanding, his tongue dancing with mine as our mouths moved together. Daniel's kisses left me wet and aching to be filled.

The back of my legs touched the bed and he lowered me onto the mattress. Nerves hit me again, but when I opened my eyes and looked at him, he took my breath away. In his eyes, I saw want, need, and something I couldn't identify. It chased away any apprehension I had about what was to come next. He removed my jeans and lace knickers in one go, my bra next, which left me naked before him. He looked his fill of me from my toes up to my eyes, and from the way his cock was twitching madly in his underwear, I could tell he liked what he'd seen.

His fingers traced up my feet and legs, around my hips and thighs and over my sex until he reached my breasts. Then he did the same with his talented tongue. When his mouth reached my nipples, I could feel the evidence of my arousal coating the inside of my thighs.

I really wished I'd shaved down there. Being blonde, I'd never had that overly bushy look, but I wished it was shaped neater. Or like a landing strip or whatever they call it.

He climbed over me and kissed me on the mouth. It was slow and gentle, and I felt cherished. I had a feeling that this was the calm before the storm, and I wasn't wrong.

A minute or so later, Daniel began kissing my neck and throat, then across my collarbone, which he licked and nibbled to the point of near pain.

I put my arms around the back of his head and shoulders as he worked his way down to my breasts. He sucked the fleshy part all the way around, avoiding my nipples until I was panting and trying to buck my hips towards his. Then he zeroed in on the hard buds, using his tongue and teeth to lap and bite. I swear I nearly orgasmed through that alone. But then he ventured lower, kissing a line down to my belly button and below. When he traced a line with his tongue from hipbone to hipbone, I just about shot off the bed.

Carrying on lower with his licks and kisses, he nuzzled my mound, breathed in the scent of my arousal, and groaned. That turned me on just as much as any foreplay ever could. He parted my folds and zeroed in on my clit with rapid flicks of his tongue, and I orgasmed in less than thirty seconds.

I expected him to crawl up the bed and have sex with me straight after my orgasm, but it seemed that Daniel was only getting started down there. After licking and nibbling on each of my folds, he thrust his tongue inside me repeatedly, and I cried out with unabashed pleasure. He flattened his tongue and gave me long, firm licks from the opening of my sex straight up to my clit, and the sensations made my legs tremble.

Dan's broad shoulders held my legs open, even though I tried to close them around him. His right hand made its way up my belly and settled over my left breast, pulling and twisting on my nipple. His tongue teased my clit with the same firm strokes and sucks, and this time, when I screamed his name as the orgasm hit, he finally came up the bed to place his body over mine. He wiped the glistening wetness coating his stubble on my lower belly, then kissed his way up to my mouth.

He still wore his boxer trunks, so I helped him push them down his thighs using my feet. When the head of his cock touched my entrance, I braced myself. I knew from the outline on his underwear earlier that he was a good size, but when he pushed inside me slowly, the fullness stole my breath, and I was grateful that he'd taken the time to get me so wet. It had been a long time since I'd had sex, and with Daniel being so big, it may have been a little painful for me if he'd been a selfish lover and not prepared me enough to take him.

But I think it was much more than that for Dan. It appeared he'd enjoyed giving me pleasure—like it was important to him that I was satisfied before he was.

I could taste myself as he kissed me, and it made me feel wicked and wanton. For the first time ever, I wanted to taste myself on a man's cock. But there was no way I'd stop him making love to me. Because that's what it felt like. Real lovemaking. His thrusts were slow and even. The base of his cock was hitting right where I needed it, and with every thrust, he seemed to touch something inside me that made me moan into his kiss.

"Hold on tight to my neck," he whispered, and I obeyed—not once questioning his hushed command.

Dan placed his hands under the cheeks of my bottom and lifted me as he sat back on his heels, then he pulled me onto him as he pushed himself inside me. The feeling was exquisite. He widened his legs but carried on with the same movement, pulling me onto him as he thrust, hitting my G-spot and clit each time.

The orgasm blindsided me. I swear I saw stars and angels and, possibly, heard heavenly music. I'd never climaxed like that in my whole life, and I'd lived a very long time.

He lay me back down on the bed, and it took a few minutes of him kissing me to realise that he hadn't actually come himself. He broke the kiss and whispered, "I'm coming with you this time, Freya."

Dan's movements became hard and forceful as he took

what he needed from my body. I loved it. Seeing him lose control after he'd controlled my pleasure so thoroughly was thrilling and made me tingle in all the right places.

I thought this part was all for him despite his words, but when his breathing became ragged, and he groaned in pleasure, the last thing I expected him to do was place his thumb over my clit and rub.

This time, when I came, he did too. His release seemed to go on forever and with a look that spoke of pure pleasure.

When he finally opened his eyes and looked down at me, I couldn't tear my gaze away. He was beautiful, this man who gave me the most pleasurable sexual experience I'd ever had.

A wave of guilt hit me hard because that accolade should have gone to my husband. But although many of my memories of him were a little cloudy now, I can safely say that sex was never as good as this, although it was always good.

The difference that made it special with my husband was love. Something that Daniel and I didn't share, although I could certainly see myself falling for him if we spent any more time together.

"What's that look for, Freya?" he asked, his body still above mine.

"I realised that was the best sex I've ever had," I admitted. "Then I felt guilty, as that should be something I shared with my husband, not someone I'm not even in a relationship with."

Why did I tell him that? Had sex scrambled my brain?

He grinned before kissing me in a long, wet, tongue-filled burst of pleasure. Then he pulled back, knowing the effect it had on me, and said, "I'm glad I gave you the best sex you've ever had, but you don't have anything to feel guilty about. Your husband has been gone a long time, and if he loved you as much as you told me he did, he wouldn't want you to be unhappy and alone. And if I had more to offer you, Freya, I would love to be in a relationship with you. But I'm just a nobody. You deserve someone who can treat you right and give you everything a woman like you should have."

"What's that supposed to mean? And why would you think you're a nobody?"

"Freya, I work nights in your brother's company. I'm waiting for George to retire so I can be a full-time supervisor. How sad is that? My only aim in life right now is to become a supervisor so that I can earn another couple of hundred a month in my take-home pay after tax.

"I live in a one-bedroom rented flat that costs me over a full week's wage, and by the time I pay my bills and car insurance, I don't have a great deal left. My dad's an alcoholic, and despite falling out with him, I still try to sort out his bloody life so that it doesn't all fall on Keeley. I want someone to share my life, Freya, but at the moment, I'm not a good prospect," he said sadly. "And you deserve someone who can treat you right... Buy you expensive jewellery and fancy clothes, that kind of thing. I can't do that, Freya, even though I'd like to."

"I don't want someone who can buy me expensive jewellery and fancy clothes, Daniel. I can buy those if I want. Material things aren't important to me; they never have been. What I *do* want is someone I can trust not to hurt me or abuse the love I give them. Someone who makes me feel safe and protected, giving me emotional strength when needed. If they were willing, I'd want to bond with them…to share our lives and love forever. They'd have to accept that I can't have children, though."

"Julia is pregnant."

"A male vampire can get a human woman pregnant, but as I've said before, I have never known an immortal female managing to conceive."

"Then you could adopt a child. You see adverts on the telly and in newspapers for people to foster and adopt. Those poor kids look so lost. There are orphanages abroad on the news—three or four kids in a single cot with dirty sheets. It chokes me up to see them like that. You look at Daisy and see how much she's loved by all her family and everyone else in her life. Makes you want the same for all little kids."

I could tell by the way Dan said it that he felt passionate about it. Like Sergei and Nik did, but they'd been brought up in an orphanage. They donate a lot of money to Romanian orphanages and help close the disreputable ones.

"You have a big heart, Daniel," I said as I touched his cheek. "I'd love it if you'd find room in there for me."

Daniel's eyes opened wide, and he seemed quite shocked by my words, but then he shook his head and said, "There's no need to make room for you in there, Freya. You've owned my heart for years; you just didn't know it. But that doesn't mean I'm the right man for you, even though I want to be."

"Maybe I can convince you otherwise, *Dan*," I said, and he smiled.

"Finally, you use my grown-up name again. You called me Dan a few times last night when you brought Daisy and me here. And you screamed it when I was balls deep inside you."

"Well, we need to get cleaned up, *Dan*, or I swear you're sleeping in the wet patch tonight."

"What was that you said, Freya? You want me to bend you over the bath and fuck you senseless? Well, it's your lucky night tonight, my sexy blonde vampire, because I'm raring to go again." He laughed as his cock flexed inside me.

He carried me into the bathroom and did exactly that before getting me into the shower and using the spray from the shower head to do some uber-satisfying things to my clit. After drying off and getting his pyjamas, Dan climbed back into my bed with me. He spooned in behind me and held me until I fell asleep in his arms, happier than I'd felt in centuries.

I'd do anything I could to stay this way.

Chapter Twenty-Seven

Josh

Keeley had grown increasingly despondent throughout the day, which was something I'd expected. Being unable to make things right for her was hard to handle. When you love someone as much as I love her, you'll do anything to make them happy. But I couldn't see Keeley being truly happy ever again.

I thought back to how I'd behaved when Alex turned me into a vampire. I remember being scared and constantly hungry for blood, but Keeley didn't have that. She'd fed from me this morning, and I had to make her feed from a bag of blood this afternoon. But she hadn't wanted it. Keeley didn't possess the ferocious need for blood that all Made vampires were afflicted with, which concerned Gregor and me.

Gregor spoke to someone in Russia about it earlier. They said that Keeley should have fed every two or three hours since she awoke, and it was highly unusual that she'd woken so early after transitioning, anyway. He also said that Keeley should have been out for at least thirty-six hours after such a traumatic turning, and her case sounded more like the transition of a Born Immortal, not a Made one.

Keeley's mother was human and had passed away from breast cancer years ago. Her father, who I was currently funding rehab for, was certainly not a vampire. So this whole situation seemed strange to all of us.

Keeley was a vampire now, of that there was no doubt. I'd seen her irises take on a red rim and felt her fangs in my neck, so there was no argument there. And yet, something was definitely off about her transition, though we were at a loss as to what that was.

Freya and Dan had sent some videos and a few photos through earlier. They were taken this afternoon on the beach at Hornsea. I was happy to see Daisy enjoying herself, although I couldn't make out Keeley's reaction to them. Not how she truly felt, anyway. Of course, she'd said the right things—like how she looked like she was having a good time and that Daisy loved building sandcastles. But she'd had a sort of detachment to the video. Like it could have been anyone's child running around with a bat and ball on the beach.

I sent Freya a text asking if we could video call them tomorrow. It would be good for Keeley to talk to Daisy, and vice versa. I hoped she'd realise she had something to aim for when she saw how much our daughter had missed her.

It was getting late, but Keeley was restless again. She hadn't fed since this afternoon, and I think I was getting on her last nerve asking if she needed blood again.

Sergei was due to call shortly. He'd worked in the Night Movers offices alongside Alex and Julia last night. Nik had stayed home with Gina.

I was keen to find out if everything was okay at work. Partly because I wanted something to take my mind off my worry about Keeley, even if it was just for a short while. I also wanted to know if Sergei had any questions regarding the partnership. He'd agreed to take half my share of the business, but neither of us thought he'd have to step into the role this quickly.

Keeley got up from the bed and opened the windows. The night felt humid now that the wind had dropped. Keeley took a deep breath before turning to face me.

"I want to go out for a walk," she declared.

"I don't think that's a good idea, Keeley."

I looked out over the grounds of Rothley Manor, closing one of the windows slightly.

"Why not? You've kept me cooped up in here all day, Josh, so why can't I go outside now it's dark?" she whined.

"It's not safe, Keeley."

"Why isn't it safe? There's no one here at the manor other than you, me, and Gregor, so I can't suddenly go into blood lust and attack anyone."

"It's not you attacking someone that we're worried about, love," I told her, hoping Keeley would leave it at that.

"Look, Josh, I don't see what the problem is. I'm not desperate for blood and I feel okay. I just want to stretch my legs and breathe fresh air. Please, Josh, let's go for a walk," she begged.

I let out a heavy sigh and told her, "We need to wait until Sergei gets here."

"I'm sure Sergei will wait or call us." Keeley looked out of the window towards where the coach house cottages were.

"Josh, is there something else you aren't telling me?" she

asked with anxiety in her voice. "What are you hiding from me?"

I didn't want to tell her. I wanted her to feel safe for a few days, at least until we found Maxim. But I didn't have a choice.

"Gina staked Maxim in the heart. It was enough to stop him and render him in a death-like state. But to truly end a vampire, you must remove their head before burning the head and body separately. We left him in the coach house cottage so we could get you and Gina out of the way before we finished him. Alex sent the builders and decorators home before we left the cottage, and Gregor put a call through to Sergei and Yuri so they could deal with Maxim. Sergei and Yuri arrived almost an hour after we left, and when they did, Maxim's body had gone."

"So what are you saying, Josh? He was dead. Gina staked him. How did his body just up and leave?"

"Vampires aren't truly dead until you remove their heads and burn them. If someone had removed the stake and given him blood, Maxim would've been able to recover. As I said, even when you remove their head, you must ensure it stays separated while it burns."

"Who would have removed the stake? I can't see Sergei doing it, and I'm not sure Yuri liked him that much, either."

"Well, someone did because Gina had definitely staked his heart. We've gone over everything, Keeley. Alex got rid of the staff. Gregor was with me the whole time, apart from when he went to get us more blood. I know he didn't leave the manor, Keeley. Gregor was devastated by what happened to you."

"Why didn't you tell me about him sooner?" she asked.

"I didn't want you any more upset than you have been," I replied. "This has been hard enough for you as it is,

Keeley. You didn't need to know that the vampire who tried to kill you was still at large. Besides, Sergei and Yuri are trying to find him."

"So you decided I didn't need to know. Tell me, Josh, is there anything else you decided I didn't need to know?" she shouted angrily.

"No, Keeley. Fuck no. It wasn't like we wanted to deceive you. Gregor and I discussed it, and we thought it best not to stress you with it. All your reactions have been a bit off since you awakened from your transition."

Keeley glared at me. "So what does that mean, Josh? That I'm some kind of vampire freak?"

"No, of course not, Keeley. For fuck's sake. Will you stop with the fucking arguing and calm down?" I said as I grabbed her arms.

Quick as a flash, she pulled her arms out of my grasp, and with her new-found vampire strength, she threw me across the room. I hit the wall with a loud thud that took my breath away and brought down the expensive-looking paintings that decorated it.

"Oh, no, Josh, I'm sorry," she cried as she dashed to my side. "Please tell me you're okay. I only meant to push you away, and I swear I didn't know that would happen."

Keeley was genuinely upset. Although it hurt to see her that way, it felt good to have her concern and hugs.

"I'm okay, Keeley. It just took me by surprise, that's all. I think it surprised you, too. You'll have to get used to having extra strength now. You'll learn to adjust to this like everything else, but at least you know you have the strength to fight Maxim if he comes after you again. We don't know if he'll come back for you—or go after Gina for staking him. We thought Daisy might be a target, too, but—"

Keeley stumbled back, a look of horror on her face.

"Oh, fuck no, Josh. You need to go to Daisy and keep her safe."

"Freya will keep her safe, Keeley. You don't have to worry about that," I assured her.

"I know she will, but surely having you around would be better than just Freya. We need to find him, Josh; I won't be able to rest until we do."

There was a knock on the door before Sergei and Gregor walked in, looking first at me slumped on the floor, then at the damaged wall and paintings.

"I do not think Mr Adamson has finished with the decorating in this room yet, Keeley. We shall have to get him back to sort it out," Gregor said, so very matter-of-fact.

"I'm sorry, Gregor. I didn't mean to cause any damage. I just got angry and pushed Josh and—"

"Joshua! How dare you piss off my Keeley and make her push you into the wall? You should be ashamed of yourself," Sergei admonished. He came over to us and put his arm around Keeley. "Do not worry, Keeley. Sergei is here now, and I will not piss you off like Joshua. Would you like to go for a walk outside with Gregor and me?"

"I would love to go for a walk, but what about Maxim?" she inquired.

"Josh can stay here and watch over the manor, my darling. Sergei and I will be your guards tonight," said Gregor with a smile.

"What? No way are you taking her outside without me," I voiced angrily, jumping up and marching towards Sergei. But Keeley had already run over to the other side of the room to put on her shoes.

"You need a break, my friend. Both of you," Sergei stated. "This has been a traumatic couple of days for all involved, and if you do not take a break when tempers are high, it can only get worse. You know I am right, Joshua."

I nodded my head as I looked at Keeley, who was chatting happily with Gregor. I wanted to rewind time a few days so that it was me putting a smile on her face like that. Like when I proposed to her or when she caught me singing and doing the actions to Daisy's favourite song.

I wanted to find Maxim and kill him slowly, making him suffer for what he'd put Keeley through. And for what he was putting me through now because I was suffering too.

My heart was breaking all over again. I had a feeling in my gut that I wouldn't have my happily ever after with Keeley and Daisy. Don't get me wrong; I would fight tooth and nail for us…for the happy family life we wanted. But I knew the fight would only be one-sided, which hurt more than any physical pain I have ever endured.

Chapter Twenty-Eight

Sergei

After being at the manor with Gregor, Joshua and Keeley, I returned to the Night Movers compound. I did not know what to make of the atmosphere surrounding the couple. Keeley was trying to distance herself from Joshua, physically and emotionally, and maybe that was to be expected. It had been two days since Maxim tried to take her life, and who knew what the short-term effect of an attack like that could be?

Everyone is different, be they human or vampire; therefore, we all cope differently.

Keeley was worried about being around her daughter, and rightly so. We all know that young Made vampires find the blood of children too tempting to overcome.

But Keeley was not behaving like most newly Made vampires I had encountered.

She wasn't constantly craving blood, and she did not

lack energy or coherent thought. Keeley had not suffered the delirium that Made vampires experience. In some ways, a newly Made vampire can appear in looks and behaviour like a drug addict fighting addiction. But apart from her strength, eyes and fangs, there was no difference in her appearance or behaviour.

I spoke to Joshua about everything before I left. He worried he might lose what he had with Keeley and was distraught. I assured him I would do everything I could to help them both, but there would be no quick fix to their situation. In the meantime, I could find Maxim and eliminate any threat he posed to Keeley or my Gina.

Gregor and I had set things in motion with Viktor to find a monetary trail that would lead us to Maxim. He must have taken his travel documents and wallet with him when he left the manor to find Keeley. They weren't in his room with the rest of his things.

Viktor had just informed me that Maxim used a credit card to withdraw money in Southampton, so it is possible he boarded a cruise ship to leave the country.

Viktor had already flagged Maxim's passport, so they should have refused him travel, but with mind control, you could easily make someone let you through customs if there were no other witnesses. It is harder to do at airports as security is tighter, but for night-time sailings, it can be much easier to get away with.

New passports are a problem, too, as it is no longer as easy to fake those documents, although it can be done. Maxim had an old Ukrainian passport—a much easier one to fake. It hardly matters to us anymore as we always used the private jets to travel in, all owned and shared by myself, Gregor, Viktor, Nik, Josh, Alex, and Freya. Although Gregor and Viktor also have several of their own. We had all formed a silent part of the Night Movers business that was hidden away from the UK company's legitimate import/export and transportation side. We regularly transport both Made and Born Immortal vampires all over Europe and beyond. I do not know of any other vampires operating a flight transportation service like ours, so Maxim's only way to get back to his Ukrainian home or his apartment in Moscow would be by sea.

Even if he did manage to get back, we had guards in Moscow and Lviv with orders to kill him, and Maxim would know this.

Until we could confirm he had left the country, I would not rest. Even then, I would still want to be sure my Gina and Keeley were safe from any threat.

I arrived back at Nik and Gina's cottage for a bite to eat before I finished my shift in the Night Movers' office. Gina said she was okay to go back to work tonight, but Nik refused to let her, and I had agreed with him.

Gina still seemed tired and weak, even though she had taken blood from Nik and me a few times in the last twenty-four hours. I'd been to the pharmacy and purchased iron and vitamin supplements for her. I knew our blood would heal Gina, but I thought she might benefit from taking iron in the long term. Humans that bonded with vampires who drank more regularly from them did this, and they said it helped.

I found Gina in the kitchen in her nightshirt when I returned. It was after midnight, but she was used to working the night shift with Nik, so I suppose Gina found the change to her sleeping pattern difficult when she had been so inactive throughout the day.

"Hey, Sergei, how was Keeley?" she asked as she took

out a third mug from the cupboard and put a tea bag in it for me.

"Physically, she is okay; after all, she has vampire healing now, but I am not sure about her emotional state. I'm worried she will want to distance herself from Josh and little Daisy," I answered truthfully.

"But Nik said that she had to be away from Daisy for a while until she's able to control any blood lust."

Gina had that little vertical line that appeared next to her right eyebrow when she was worried or trying to figure something out. It wasn't there all the time, and for a forty-three-year-old, it was the only sign of age she had. Of course, now that Gina had Nik's blood regularly, she would not age anymore. She would always possess the pretty features I loved so much.

"I think it is more than that, Gina. I'm not sure how to help them, but I do not want to see something so right become broken. Joshua has been the happiest I have ever seen, and I have known him for nearly two centuries."

Gina came towards me and hugged me close. I kissed her cheek and wrapped my arms around her. She is only around five-foot-four, and as I am a little over six foot, she had to tilt her head back to look me in the eyes.

"Sergei, she probably just needs time to adjust. I mean, her whole way of life will have to alter now. She won't be able to walk in the sunlight, so even a simple thing like taking Daisy to school is out of the question—as is taking her to the doctor or the dentist. Simple, normal things that most mothers take for granted. It's heartbreaking for her. People need to give Keeley time and support her. We may not like the decisions she makes, but at the end of the day, we have to let her live her life as she sees fit. If we push her, she will just dig her heels in. Keeley has always been a strong young woman, and I have a lot of respect for her. I think Josh should give her the freedom to choose, even if it isn't what he wants. Keeley can always change her mind; we women often do."

I didn't need to see Nik to know he'd joined us a few minutes ago, and I asked his thoughts on the matter.

"I think Gina is right, Sergei. We need to listen to what Keeley wants. Josh will want everything to be the same as it was, but in the short term, at least, that's not going to happen. And we all know that Gregor—*Mr Large and in charge*—might try to influence her. It won't go down well if that happens."

Nik never took his eyes off me while I was holding Gina. Since our talk the other day, he hadn't said anything about my feelings for her. But he watched our physical interactions closely—like he was waiting for me to make a move on her. That was something I would never do. For one thing, it would upset Gina and make her feel differently about our friendship if she thought I wanted her sexually, and also, I couldn't do that to Nik.

Another thing was, although I loved her more than ever, I felt that the type of love I had for her had gone beyond sex. That probably sounds strange to most people, but to see Gina happy and contented made me happy too. It was enough for me, and I hoped that, in time, Nik would understand this.

"I'm going to grab something to eat and get back to the office," I told them. Then I gave Gina one last kiss on the cheek and let her go so I could make a sandwich.

"Come back to bed, Gina. We'll be back at work tomorrow night, so let's make the most of this one." Nik grabbed Gina's hand and pulled her towards their bedroom.

I knew what would happen, even before I heard the little moans and sighs that Gina tried so hard to keep quiet. Nik was letting me know that Gina was his woman in every way. It didn't bother me as long as he made her happy. I wanted what Nik and Gina had, but I couldn't imagine myself loving another woman like I loved Gina. I hoped my feelings would change because I cut a lonely figure as I sat eating my sandwich, while a few rooms away, my best friend made love to the woman who held my heart.

I left the cottage and made my way to the offices, checking over my shoulder as I walked in case Maxim was around. Although Southampton was a long way from Yorkshire, I had a feeling that Maxim was going to come back to this village. But for what purpose, I did not know.

Alex approached me and asked how things had gone at the manor. I wanted to tell him truthfully, but Julia was listening, and I didn't want to upset her. She'd cried on and off most of last night, and I didn't think it was doing her any good to be that upset when she was so heavily pregnant. So I told them Keeley was doing well and that we'd been for a walk together around the grounds of the manor.

I followed Alex to the conference room and told him my thoughts about the situation. I said he needed to visit Joshua tomorrow. He was a brother to him, and Joshua needed his support. I offered to stay with Julia when he went so that she wasn't left unattended while Maxim was missing. Alex said he'd take me up on that and thanked me for my help. He patted me on the shoulder as we walked back to the office, and the moment felt surreal. Alex and I had never got along that well. It was partly my fault, as I loved to torment him.

Also, he once caught Freya kissing me. It was nearly sixty years ago, and as far as I am aware, he never told anyone. But he'd found it hard to tolerate my company ever since.

It wasn't until last year, when I helped dispose of the body of Brandr—the vampire who'd been his stepfather—that he seemed to tolerate me more than he had previously.

Maggie was on the phone when we went back into the office. Julia said they would wait until she'd finished her call before going for something to eat.

"Why don't you both stay home?" I suggested when I noticed Julia's tired eyes. "I'm sure Maggie will show me what needs to be done tonight."

"No, Sergei, we can't expect you to come and do our work like this. It's not fair," argued Julia. She offered me chocolates from the large box on her desk.

"Julia, you do look tired, love, and I know Sergei will be able to cope. After all, Maggie taught you, and it didn't take you long to learn the ropes," Alex prompted.

"That's because I'm a woman, and we are amazing."

"Yes, you are, my love, and I'm a fortunate man to have you as my wife." Alex gazed lovingly at Julia, then gave her a peck on the lips and helped her put on a jacket that didn't quite fasten around her baby bump.

I waved goodbye to them both and went to sit with Maggie at her desk.

"They're in a loving mood tonight," I commented, nodding towards the door Alex and Julia had just left through.

"I'm sure that big box of chocolates had nothing to do with it at all," she said with a smirk.

"Ah, I see. To appeal to Alex and Julia's good nature, I should ply them with sugary treats?"

"You see, Sergei, you're learning already. I'm such a good teacher—I should probably get a pay rise," she declared with a wink.

Chapter Twenty-Nine

Daniel

"Ow," I moaned as something poked me in the face.

"Uncle Dan, why are you in Auntie Freya's bed? Are you going to get married now?"

Oh, shit! Daisy was here. I hadn't meant to stay the whole night in Freya's bed for this exact reason, but at least I had the foresight to put on my pyjamas last night.

I opened one eye and looked at Daisy. Her long blonde hair was sticking up at the fringe and side. Her big blue eyes darted from me to Freya, then back again expectantly.

"Why would you think we'd get married, Daisy?" I asked, yawning.

"Because you're sleeping in Auntie Freya's bed. When Mummy slept in Josh's bed and we had our breakfast the next day, they asked if it was okay if they got married and I could be a bridesmaid and then Josh could be my daddy and now he is my daddy," she said all in the same breath.

God, this child could speak fast. I'm sure she did it to confuse adults first thing in the morning.

"Good morning, Daisy," said Freya as she sat up and stretched her arms above her head. Her grey eyes were mesmerising in the sliver of sunlight peeking through the gap in the curtains, and she still looked sexy as sin first thing in the morning. I was pleased she hadn't kicked me out of her bed last night, even if Daisy seeing us together was awkward.

"Auntie Freya, are you going to get married to my uncle Dan?"

"Why do you ask that, Daisy?"

"Because he sleeped here in your bed," she said in a babyish voice while pointing at me.

Sleeped... Daisy was so forward for her age that the odd slip-up made my heart melt.

"Goodness me, you're right," gasped Freya in a mock shocked voice. "Whatever are you doing sleeping in my bed, Dan?" she asked, trying hard not to laugh.

"Erm, I..." What the hell did I say to that? I shot Freya a look that told her she was in for it later. She winked at me and laughed.

"I want to go sailing today. Can we go sailing in Frank's boat, Auntie Freya? *Please?*" Daisy asked, giving Freya the cutest little pout ever.

"We'll have to ask him if it's okay, but I don't see why not. Would you like to sail with us at Hornsea Mere, Dan?"

"I don't mind going sailing," I said, picking Daisy up and tickling her. "Let's get you dressed, and then we can all have our breakfast."

It turned out that Freya's gardener, Frank, had a sailboat that he'd built himself. It was around fifteen-foot-long and had two sails—a large mainsail and another much smaller. He named his boat The Sally Ann, after his wife. For a man of few words, that seemed to say a lot.

Hornsea Mere is the largest freshwater lake in Yorkshire and lies to the west of Hornsea. It's around two miles long and was dotted with other smaller sailboats by the time we got there.

I helped Frank get the boat into the water from the trailer while Freya fastened Daisy into a lifejacket. As I've said before, Frank was a man of very few words, so when he gave instructions on how to operate the sails, I was all ears. To be fair to Frank, he saw my confusion after he used words like batten and jib, so he broke down the basic operation and different parts of the boat in a way I understood.

I want to say that, with my help, we got the sailboat over to the other end of the mere without issue, but I had some problems with the first sail. It was a breezy day, but I wouldn't have said it was a strong wind, yet I was not prepared for how hard the sail would toss me to the other side of the boat when it billowed out and the ropes I held pulled me over.

Freya was part concerned, part amused at my mishap and asked if I was hurt. I thought I'd have some bruising later, but male pride forced me to say I was fine. Daisy said I was just being silly, and that you weren't allowed to be silly while you're on Frank's boat.

Apparently, Keeley and Daisy had sailed on this boat a few times before, and Frank said that my sister had mastered the use of the sails on her first go, which dented my pride even further.

It didn't surprise me, though. Keeley was much smarter

than me, always had been. My dad used to say that you didn't have to tell Keeley anything twice; she always got it the first time.

Although we were twins and were both tall, blond, and blue-eyed, that's where a lot of our similarities ended. Keeley excelled in school and was going to university when she fell pregnant.

I, on the other hand, hated school and wasn't academically gifted. I didn't do well in my exams, and the only thing I liked about the place was the sports I got to play and that all the girls fancied me.

I wish I hadn't found the academic side so hard because there aren't many well-paid jobs for someone who got a D in every subject apart from art.

I'd always been able to draw and paint well, and a few of the older lads said it meant that I was gay, like our art teacher. Being tall and having as much muscle as I had when I was a teenager soon put a stop to that, but the fighting didn't go down too well with my dad and Aunt Mags. And being constantly grounded because of it wasn't fun either.

I hoped that Daisy took after her mother and not me. Not only was my sister smart and beautiful, she also had a big heart and was kind and friendly to everyone. I hoped that being a vampire wouldn't change that side of her.

Looking at Freya, with her pale blonde hair flying behind her as we sailed across the mere, I had high hopes that my sister could retain the same personality and strength of character. After all, Freya was kind, thoughtful, and generous to a fault with her time and wealth to those she loved. Freya was a beautiful woman, inside and out, and although she was a vampire—which meant she was ridiculously strong—it didn't stop her humanity from shining through.

The loss of her family at her father's hand had almost destroyed Freya, and she'd carried that hurt and betrayal for all those years, still crying over it even yesterday.

Although Freya could snap me in half if she wanted, I still felt the need to protect her. But I couldn't tell if that was going to be a good or bad thing in Freya's eyes.

After two hours of sailing, we headed back to Freya's house. Millie had cooked a huge dinner with roast beef, Yorkshire puddings, and all the trimmings. I was glad because I'd been ravenous when we got back.

After our dinner had settled, we played a game of cricket on the lawn at the side of the house, and I felt myself warming to Freya's male staff. It was obvious they adored her, and although they were her staff, they were all like one happy family. I was glad that Freya had these people in her life.

Seeing them with Daisy was great, too. Keeley and I no longer had our grandparents, and my dad had been too drunk during the last year to do anything like play cricket with Daisy. So having all these people wanting to play and enjoy the outdoors with her was a gift. More memories for my niece to take with her throughout her life.

After at least an hour of attempting to play cricket—with a little girl who made up her own rules about any sport she was playing—it started to rain, so we packed up our things and headed indoors.

I was glad the rain stopped play on this occasion

because my side and hip were hurting from the fall I'd had on the boat.

When Millie suggested that she and Daisy make play dough in the kitchen, I said I'd go upstairs and have a bath.

When I took off my clothes, I couldn't believe how bad the bruising was around my ribs and hip, but I hoped the warmth of the bath would ease the ache taking over my side.

I yawned loudly. We'd been on the go non-stop since Daisy woke us this morning, and despite having youth and fitness on my side, running around after my niece was exhausting.

I still couldn't believe I'd made love to Freya last night. It was an incredible experience and one I wanted to happen again soon. Although, with how much I ached, I didn't think it would be anything like the athletic sex we'd had over her bath and in her shower. My cock sprung to life just thinking about it. I ignored it as best I could, washing my hair and body before climbing out and getting dry.

Wrapping the towel around my waist, I walked into the bedroom and was surprised to find Freya lying on the bed. She was fully clothed but wore a smile that said she appreciated my near-nakedness.

"I thought I'd come up and check on you while Daisy was busy playi—"

Freya stopped mid-sentence and jumped off the bed when she noticed the bruising on my side. She came towards me and pulled the towel away from my waist.

"Is this from your accident on the boat?" she asked

while tracing her fingers over the bruising on my ribs and hip.

"Yes," I replied, trying to sound calm. As though the fact that she was touching me wasn't making my cock twitch.

"Why didn't you say anything earlier, Dan? I could have helped you."

"It's just bruising, Freya. You couldn't have helped with this."

"I could give you some blood to take it away."

I took a step back, unsure how I felt about accepting blood from her.

"You wouldn't have to take much. Just a few sips would probably do it," Freya said.

I looked at her warily. She seemed a little hurt by it, which made me feel terrible.

"Please, Dan, don't be scared of me or my blood. I would never do anything to hurt you. I feel so guilty knowing you've been aching all day. You must have hit something hard when it swung you over."

"Yeah, I hit the box with the lifejackets and rope," I told her, wincing as I recalled the pain I felt on impact.

Freya walked over to the door and locked it before returning to me. Then, taking my hand in hers, she led me to sit on the bed.

Freya removed her top and jeans, leaving her in a white satin bra and pink lacy knickers. She kissed me softly, sighing against my lips. Cupping her face in my hands, I kissed her right back.

Freya's kisses were a great pain reliever in themselves, but she pulled away from me and asked again if I'd take some of her blood. Her grey eyes were glassy and looked directly into the blue of my own.

"Please don't cry, Freya," I said, pulling her in for a hug. "Honestly, it's not that bad. But I'll have some of your blood if it makes you feel better."

"Thank you, Dan," she replied with a sniffle. "I can't bear the thought of you hurting."

A few seconds later, she'd removed her bra and knickers and straddled my cock.

"Don't be alarmed at what you see next. Remember, I will never hurt you," Freya repeated. The nail on Freya's left index finger grew to a sharp point before she made a cut in her left breast near her nipple. Then she sank onto my cock, enveloping it in her tight, wet heat before rising back up to place her bleeding breast in my mouth.

I thought her blood would have the same metallic taste as mine, but after I swallowed the initial few drops, it took on a sweeter taste entirely, and I was hooked. Freya sank back down on my cock and rode me while I sucked on her blood. The ache in my side disappeared, and I thrust my hips up to meet her downward moves, slamming into her hard and deep.

The sex was out of this world, and judging by the noises Freya was making, she felt the same way.

She grabbed my hair, pulled my mouth away from her breast, and then kissed me hard. It was too much for me, and I knew I'd come soon, so I used the back of my knuckle to rub her clit. Freya grabbed my hand and showed me how much pressure and speed she needed to get her off, and with her help, it didn't take either of us long to get there.

I didn't stop kissing her as we came, partly to hide the sounds of pleasure we were making, but also because kissing Freya was pure pleasure in itself. She stopped kissing me and licked her way up to my ear.

"Next time, I'll be swallowing *your* blood right after I swallow your come," Freya whispered breathlessly.

My already semi-hard cock rose back to full attention inside her with those words. I rolled her over and made love to her with a deep but gentle rhythm, which Freya matched, meeting me thrust for thrust. I peppered kisses all over her face until I recognised that little hitch in her breathing that told me she was coming.

I watched her come apart beneath me; her mouth open as she gasped and said my name, a pink flush spreading over her chest and throat, and her eyelids becoming heavy—almost sleepy.

I'd never seen Freya look more beautiful, and I'd looked at this woman many times over the years. But I knew this look would stay with me forever…because I realised right then I'd fallen madly in love with her.

Chapter Thirty

Keeley

Josh set up my laptop on the bed while we awaited a video call from Daisy. My heart skipped a beat when I heard her shout *"Mummy"* in her excited little voice. Josh adjusted the laptop screen so Daisy could see us both, and I tried not to cry when I told her I loved her.

Freya and Dan were on either side of Daisy, so I said hello while Josh sat down and got comfortable beside me.

"Hello, Daddy," Daisy yelled in Freya's ear as she leaned forward and waved at us. It pushed her out of view of the camera on the laptop, so Dan made her sit down next to them again so we could see her.

"Hey, pretty girl. What have you been doing on your holiday?" asked Josh.

"Well, I went to the beach and built sandcastles, then I beat Uncle Dan at tennis. And today we went sailing in Frank's boat. Uncle Dan was silly and had a fall," Daisy replied, rolling her eyes. "I won everyone at cricket, and I made play dough with Millie, too." She held up a pink lump.

"It's a dog," Daisy announced proudly, although I couldn't see a likeness to any animal.

"Wow, that's great, Daisy," Josh and I replied in unison. Daisy laughed.

"Are you better now, Mummy? Did you have a cough?" she asked, trying to get closer to the screen again.

"I'm getting better every day, love, but not well enough to look after you yet. So you'll have to sleep at Auntie Freya's for a bit longer if that's okay."

"Uncle Dan slept in Auntie Freya's bed last night, but I don't think they're going to get married and let me be a bridesmaid yet," she sighed.

Dan tried to put his hand over Daisy's mouth to stop her from saying anything else, but the damage was already done. Josh appeared part shocked, part furious, and I could see him struggling to find the words he wanted to say.

"Leave it be, Josh. This is our time with Daisy. Don't spoil it for me," I whispered in his ear.

"What have you got planned for tomorrow?" I asked, changing the subject.

"I thought we could take Daisy to the aquarium in Hull. What's it called, Freya?" Dan asked.

"The Deep," Freya replied. "Keeley and I went a couple of years ago, but I think it will be better for Daisy to go at this age."

"I'm going to see the fish, and there might even be a shark," Daisy declared, making a funny, biting face at the camera.

"I'll get Uncle Dan to take some pictures for you, and you can look at them when you get better. I love you,

Mummy and Daddy," Daisy said. She leaned forward again and kissed the screen.

"I've got to go now because I want a wee. BYE…" she yelled, her voice getting lower as she ran out of the room.

"So, you slept in Freya's bed, Dan!" Josh stated angrily. "What the hell are you two playing at, doing something like that with Daisy under your roof?"

"Don't even go there, Josh. This has nothing to do with you," Freya replied just as angrily.

"I can't believe you slept with my sister. She deserves someone who'll treat her with more respect than you will, Dan."

"Yeah, well, I couldn't believe you slept with *my sister* either, Josh. And what's with all this respect shit? I do respect Freya."

Josh huffed. "The difference is that I love your sister, so I obviously respect her."

"Well, I love your sister too, Josh, and I've always respected her," Dan stated.

Freya gasped, and I watched with bated breath as she turned Dan's face towards her and asked, "Do you love me?"

"Yeah, I do. I can't help it," he said as he touched her cheek.

"I've fallen for you, too. It's only the second time in over nine hundred years that I've said that to a man, and I didn't think it would ever happen to me again," Freya admitted before kissing him.

I think they'd forgotten we were still there because their kiss progressed into something special that only people in love can truly experience.

"We have to go now, guys. Talk to you again soon," I said, closing our connection.

"Well, that was unexpected. I'm happy for them, though. Aren't you?" I asked Josh. He got up from the bed and stormed over to the windows.

"Dan's no good for her, Keeley. He'll hurt her when he finds another conquest," he replied.

I shook my head. "What are you talking about? You just saw exactly the same as I did there. Those words of love were genuine and said from the heart. Anyone could see that."

"They've only been together two days. How can they fall in love as fast as that?"

"Oh, I see what this is. Double fucking standards. Have you forgotten that I slept with you the first night that Daisy and I stayed at your home? And that you told me you loved me that night? Then let's not forget the next morning when we agreed that we'd get married and that you would be Daisy's father," I reminded him.

"That was different, Keeley, and you know it. We've known each other for years, and I fell in love with you a long time before that night. Your brother has screwed around with most of the single women in Barrowfield and Rothley. He never has a shortage of women to keep his dick wet, and he loves the single life."

"Not anymore, Josh. Dan told me he was fed up with being single. He wanted to change his life. To find the right woman and settle down. And it looks like he's done just that."

"She's too good for him," he retorted.

"Excuse me?" I yelled. "You're talking about my brother here, Josh, unless you've forgotten. The same lad that helped me take care of a baby when I was a young, single parent. The very same guy that helps me out financially when my dad's wasting all his money on whisky so we can keep a roof over Daisy's head. My brother has never once let me down, and I will not stand for you bad-mouthing him. Ever!"

I was so angry I was shaking. How dare he speak about my brother like that? As a family, we went through hell when Mum died and Dad had his breakdown. Dan and I were always close. We were friends as well as twins, and when all the bad stuff happened, it felt like the only people we could truly count on were each other, even though we had Aunt Mags and Freya. Although Dan never used to go with Freya and me because he had such a big crush on her.

"Dan has fancied Freya for years, by the way. I once caught him doodling their names on a piece of paper. We would have been fifteen at the time. I teased him about it, and he got mad. He would never go on those holidays and shopping trips she used to take me on. I thought he just had a big crush on her, but who knows, maybe it was much more than that?"

Josh said nothing, just carried on staring out of the window.

I left the bedroom and went to find Gregor. He sat in his study drinking whisky and appeared deep in thought.

"Gregor, can I talk to you for a moment?"

"Of course, Keeley. What do you want to talk about?" He motioned to the chair across from him, then offered me a drink. I wasn't a big whisky drinker, but I took one anyway to be sociable.

"Gregor, could I have my own room for tonight, away from Josh? I don't want to impose, but I feel like I could strangle him at the moment if I don't have some space."

"I heard your argument. You have to realise that Josh is very protective of Freya. She's been through so much in her life, and he only wants what's best for her," he said, swirling the whisky around in his glass before drinking it.

"And he has to realise that I feel the same way about my brother. We've also had a lot of sadness in our lives, Gregor. As a family, we are no strangers to heartbreak. I think they will be good for each other," I told him, then quickly realised how Gregor must be feeling. He denied there was anything going on between him and Freya, but as friends went, they were extremely close.

"Are *you* okay with what's happened between Freya and my brother, Gregor? Or are you going to jump on the *'I hate Dan'* bandwagon?" I questioned.

If he was going to say the same as Josh, I'd head back to my dad's house. I'd rather take my chance with Maxim than listen to people putting my family down.

"All I have ever wanted was for Freya to be happy. If your brother is the person to make that happen, I will be pleased for them both. We live a long, lonely life when we don't have someone to love. You are immortal now, so you would do well to remember that, Keeley. If you want to take another room here, that is okay with me. But remember, despite what Joshua just said about your brother, he loves you dearly."

"I know that, Gregor, and I love him, too. But I'm loyal to my brother, and I'll not have him spoken about like that by anyone. My brother is a good man who deserves to be loved, just as much as Freya does."

Gregor nodded, then poured another whisky. I declined the offer of another and got up to leave. I looked down at Gregor, and he seemed so forlorn that I walked over to him and hugged him tightly. After kissing him on the cheek, I said, "Thank you for being such a good friend to me, Gregor. I'm glad I have you in my life."

He looked up at me and smiled. "Keeley, you are an exceptional woman, and I am also very happy to have you in my life. I feel that our friendship will only get stronger as the years go on, and that is something I will treasure. You will always have me to come to if you need anything. Never forget that," he said as he stood and held me. We stayed that way for a while until I heard someone at the front door.

"Excuse me while I see who that is," Gregor muttered as he left the office.

I saw Josh on the stairs as I followed Gregor. He stared at me like he wanted to say something but couldn't find the words. Well, I wasn't going to help him with that. Love or not, he could take a running fucking jump if he didn't apologise to me, Freya, and Dan for what he'd said.

Gregor greeted Alex at the door, and I groaned inwardly. Alex was going to be more protective than Josh over Freya. The last thing I needed was him ranting on about my brother.

"Joshua, I know you will want to tell Alex about the news you found out tonight. But know this… If I hear either of you disrespect Keeley's brother, you can both leave this house and not return. Do you understand me?"

"What's wrong, Gregor? Why would we disrespect Daniel?"

"Your sister has fallen in love with Keeley's brother, and it appears he feels the same in return. By disrespecting Keeley's brother, you disrespect your sister and her choices, and that is unacceptable to me. I will also not allow Keeley to become upset. She has been through enough these last few days and does not need any more stress from small-minded individuals. Now, I know you have a lot to talk about, so I suggest you do that while taking a walk around the grounds. It is a lovely evening now that the rain has stopped, and the fresh air will do you both some good."

Gregor held out his arm and smiled at me. "Come with me, Keeley, and tell me the best programmes to watch on digital TV. There are hundreds of channels, and I don't know which I should view," he said as we walked to the TV room.

I decided there and then that Gregor was my hero. Josh talked about respect, but as far as I was concerned, this man had it in droves. Whoever captured Gregor's heart would be a very lucky woman indeed.

We watched a Michael McIntyre show on a comedy channel, which Gregor found funny. After that was over, we watched Micky Flanagan doing the *out-out* joke. I found it hilarious, but Gregor just didn't get it. I put the show on pause and tried my best to explain it to him.

"It's because there are different levels to going out," I told him. "Obviously, he said he was only going out to the shops and didn't mean to go out to the pub, but he was asked, so he went. Then someone asked if he wanted to go to a nightclub, so Micky explains he wasn't meant to be out, although he ended up out anyway. But going to a nightclub would be taking it one step further, hence out-out."

"But surely, whether you are at a pub or a club, you are still out?"

He was more confused by my explanation than he was when Micky did it.

"I do not find that one as funny as the other jokes," he stated, shaking his head.

"They're all good, Gregor," I told him, laughing at his confusion. "But comedy is subjective."

I noticed Josh in the doorway watching us. Gregor stood and gave me a kiss on the top of my head.

"Perhaps I'll watch this comedian again on the internet, and I will see if I can make sense of his repetitive words. I do not like to think I cannot get the joke. Goodnight, my Keeley. I will see you in the morning. And goodnight to you, Joshua. I have told Keeley that she can have the room next to mine tonight if she wants."

Josh stared at me, open-mouthed. I ignored him, took the TV off pause, and resumed watching. He came and sat down next to me on the sofa, sighing heavily.

"I'm sorry, Keeley. So fucking sorry for my words and actions today. You didn't deserve any of it, and neither did Dan. I called him and apologised. Both he and Freya have forgiven me, and I hope you will too."

I put the TV back on pause and turned to look at him.

"Josh, I don't know what to say to you tonight. I'm still a little hurt that you carried on like that, but I appreciate your apology, and I'm glad you apologised to Dan and Freya."

He held my left hand in his, rubbing his thumb over the centre stone of my engagement ring.

"Don't move bedrooms tonight, Keeley. Stay with me, please. I never want to spend a night without you if we can help it. Obviously, work will mean we sometimes have to be away from one another, but a couple should never spend a night apart in anger."

Josh was sincere; I could tell that from the look in his eyes. But I also needed a little breathing space, and I wasn't sure how to tell him without it coming out sounding bad.

"Josh, for tonight, I want to sleep on my own. I have a lot of thinking to do, and I'd like to come to terms with all the changes I have to go through myself before I can share this new life with anyone else. Do you think you can give me the time and space to do that?"

He looked like I'd just slapped him, so hurt and surprised by my words. But I couldn't back down now.

"I love you, Josh, and I don't want to hurt you. But if you love me as much as you say you do, then you'll do as I ask and give me some space. Please."

"I do love you, Keeley, more than you could ever know. But I feel like I'm going to lose you, and it's making me crazy. I knew I should have stopped all that ranting earlier; I just couldn't control my anger and my words."

"We've known each other for years, Josh, but I think we rushed into being a couple far too soon, and we made excuses that it was okay because we'd wanted each other for so long. Gina told me that a vampire will know when they meet the one, and that will be it for them. But we went from sleeping together to getting engaged within a day."

"Are you saying you want to break up with me?" he asked, the tone of his voice showing how anxious he'd become.

"No, that's not what I am saying. I enjoy being your fiancée. I love that you're mine. But maybe we could take a little time to date each other. Because of Daisy and work, our time was limited, but I—"

"You want me to take you out somewhere? Like a night out or something? Keeley, we can do that as a married couple. We don't have to be dating."

"I know that. But I haven't had much dating experience, Josh. I'm almost twenty-five, and I was barely an adult when I got pregnant. When you are a mum, your every waking moment is about pleasing your child. And while that's a great thing to do, it's also exhausting, and it leaves you little or no time for yourself.

"Over the past year, I've had a night out with the ladies from Night Movers every couple of months, and that's the only time I've felt the thrill and excitement of doing something for myself. Like doing my hair and makeup and wearing going-out clothes instead of work ones. I've never once in all that time gone on a proper date. I'd love to have the excitement of knowing that the man I've fancied forever wanted to take me out. I could take my time getting my hair and makeup just right, and put on clothes I look super sexy in, so I'll feel more confident. You could come to the door to collect me and tell me I look nice, and maybe sneak a quick kiss. Then you could take me to a restaurant or a club so we could dance. You could flirt with me all night and make me feel wanted, then when you brought me home, you could kiss me for ages on my doorstep. And maybe, after we've been seeing each other for a while, you could invite me back to your place and seduce me."

"We can definitely work some of that into our relationship, Keeley," he said.

Josh raised my hand to his lips and kissed it.

"You are right: it was a quick move for us. But know this, Keeley. The excitement and anticipation you speak of, well, that's what I experienced every time I knew you were coming by the office, or when I saw you after I looked after Daisy.

"Over the last few months, every time I put on my best shirt and came down to the Red Lion, knowing you ended up there after your nights out, that was all for you, too. And I know you need to do all this girly preening stuff you've just been talking about, but for me, you always look beautiful and sexy. Whether you're hot and sweaty after your exercise class with Gina, when your hair is all windswept after you've walked Daisy to school, or when you're fully made up on a night out—you take my breath away and make me want you every single time. I'm not going to argue with you, Keeley. I accept you need your space tonight but do me a favour."

"What?"

"Let me hold your hand and walk you to your room."

"Okay," I replied, glad that he wasn't trying to change my mind.

Josh had made sure all the doors were locked when he came in earlier, but he checked the digital security system just in case. We walked up the stairs, and I stopped outside the room next to Gregor's.

"Well, thanks for letting me walk you home, Keeley. I'd like to see you again tomorrow if you're not doing anything," he said with a sly smile.

"Umm, okay. I think I'm free tomorrow," I told him, playing along.

"Maybe I could pick you up and take you for breakfast?" he suggested.

I nodded my head and smiled. "I'd like that."

"Great. Well, goodnight, Keeley."

"Goodnight, Josh."

"Just one more thing," Josh said as he took me in his arms and kissed the smile right off my lips. His lips were firm against mine, forcing my mouth open so his tongue could lap around my own. My back hit the door as he pinned my arms above my head, still kissing me like our lives depended on it. I moaned and felt myself becoming wet. Josh broke his mouth away from mine and kissed and nibbled my jaw and neck before coming back to kiss my lips again. My nipples hardened, protruding through my top, and I tried to grind my pelvis against his to relieve the ache in my sex. But the moment he felt me do that, he pulled away.

"See you tomorrow, my love," he said before kissing my engagement ring and walking away.

I opened the bedroom door and locked myself inside. Then I leant back against the door, still panting with lust. I'd enjoyed every kiss I'd ever had with Josh, but that was something else.

He'd done exactly what I'd asked by giving me some space tonight, but with how he had me feeling, I could beg him to make love to me. Josh had known what he was doing, of course, and I had to smile at that.

I wondered if he was in the room we'd been sharing and was feeling the same way I was. Probably.

I'd felt how hard his cock was when I ground against him. How the hell did he expect me to sleep tonight after that performance? Well, I'd started this separate room thing, and it would do me no good to back down now. So I took off my clothes and climbed into bed, wondering just how long it would take to fall asleep.

Chapter Thirty-One

Gregor

I took my breakfast in the office this morning. Keeley was in a much better mood today, although with the potent scent of arousal and pheromones she and Josh left behind last night, none of us was able to get much sleep. The fact that I hadn't had sex since the week before I left Russia wasn't helping. The same could be said about seeing the new toys and furniture in my cellar.

I was even considering flying out one of the human submissives who go to my club in Moscow. But if I did, they might read too much into it, and it would only ever be a sexual encounter for me. I didn't do committed relationships. I just wasn't built that way. If I had been, I would have wanted the lovely Freya by my side. She'd just begun a relationship with Keeley's brother, and I was about to call the woman who had become my dearest friend so many years ago. She answered on the third ring, and I could hear a child's laughter in the background.

"Gregor, how are you?" she asked in a light, happy voice.

"I am all the better for hearing your voice, my darling Freya," I answered truthfully.

"Gregor, I have so much to tell you, but after speaking to Josh and Keeley yesterday evening, I suppose you've heard some of it already."

"That you have found love with Keeley's brother?"

"Yes. Are you happy for me, Gregor?" she asked hesitantly.

"If you are happy, my darling, then I am happy too. If this is the right thing for you, Freya, then it should not matter what anyone else thinks. Did Alex speak to you last night?"

"Yes. Well, sort of. He rang to ask me if it was true that I was involved with Dan, and I told him it was. He was quiet for a while, and then he told me he loved me. Julia grabbed the phone and nearly burst my eardrums. She kind of squealed, and then she told me that Daniel was one of the sexiest guys she had ever seen. I heard Alex growl, and Julia said, 'apart from Alex, of course.' Then Alex mumbled something, and Julia said prove it—then the phone went dead. So at this moment in time, I'm not sure what Alex thinks, although I can guess. Josh rang us back last night and apologised to Dan and me, and I appreciated that."

"Will you bring him to meet me, Freya? I'm sure I saw him at Alex and Julia's wedding, but I would like to be introduced to him formally."

"Yes, of course, Gregor. It's important that you both meet. After all, you are my best friend, and I need you to like him."

"I adore his sister, so if they have similar personalities, I'm sure I will like him," I told her.

"How is Keeley? Josh seemed really worried about her, Gregor. He said she appeared to be drifting away from him last night."

"I can safely say it doesn't appear that way anymore. Keeley needs to make her own choices, Freya. Like you have done. And we all need to respect that—Josh included."

"I know. I just worry that—"

I heard Keeley's daughter in the background say, "Come on, Auntie Freya. I want to see the sharks."

"Gregor, I'm sorry. I have to go. I'll call you tomorrow. Bye."

"Bye, my darling. Have a good day."

Before I could think any more about the phone call, I noticed a vehicle pulling up the driveway. It was a little white van with the words, *'Chloe's Flowers and Gifts'* written on the side.

I went to the front door and opened it before a dark-haired woman had the chance to ring the bell.

"Oh, hi there. I have a flower delivery for Keeley Saunders," she said while walking back towards the side of her van. She opened the sliding door and took out a large floral display in various shades of blue with white accents. After handing me the display, she then turned back to the van to retrieve a dozen red roses in a crystal vase, which was encircled with a bow in the same colour red as the roses.

"After you," I told her.

We walked into my dimly lit hallway. I wasn't worried about the little human woman being around Keeley. I knew she had taken blood before breakfast this morning, and she'd exhibited zero signs of blood lust.

"Keeley is in the dining room with her fiancé. I will just let her know of your arrival," I informed her warily. We'd left the front door open, and I didn't want Keeley to be affected by the sunlight if she came out into the hall.

I knocked on the dining room door before opening it. Although they were both fully clothed, Josh and Keeley were in quite a compromising position. Josh sat on a dining chair, his hands under Keeley's pretty cami top. Keeley sat straddling him, kissing him passionately. She jumped away from Josh's lap and turned to face the window while adjusting her top. Josh stood behind the high-backed chair, trying to hide the bulge in his jeans.

Again, the scent of arousal hit me hard, so I quickly closed the door on the couple and told them I would leave the flowers on the hall table.

"Is everything okay?" asked the woman with the roses.

"Keeley is just finishing something and will be along shortly," I replied. Then I made my way over to the front door and closed it.

I put the display I carried on the hall table, then I took the roses from the woman and placed them alongside.

"I'm Chloe," she said, holding out her hand for me to shake.

I took her hand in mine and felt a burst of heat rising inside me as I did so.

"Pleased to meet you, Chloe. I'm Gregor Antonov," I told her when I finally found my voice.

"Is this your home, Gregor?"

"Yes. I'm having it renovated so I have a place to stay when I am over here for business."

"Oh, I read about you in the local paper. You're the Russian billionaire everyone's talking about."

I was trying to concentrate on her words, but the perfume she wore distracted me.

"Your scent is intoxicating, Chloe. What perfume are you wearing?" I asked.

"I'm not wearing any perfume," she replied with a blush. "It must be the aroma from all the flowers and candles in my shop."

I studied her for a moment. Chloe was short in height, I'd say about five-foot-four in the flat summer sandals she wore. She was quite curvy, although wider at the hip than the bust, yet they were still much more than a handful. She wore stonewashed jeans with a navy blue, V-necked T-shirt, showcasing her ample cleavage.

Chloe blushed at my open appraisal of her body, and the blush carried on from her cheeks to her chest. The pink hues from the blush suited her pale skin tone. She had a Celtic look about her and wore her chestnut brown hair in a pixie style. Chloe's eyes were an amazing blue-green colour, like the sea around Fig Tree Bay in Cyprus. Her lips were full and coated with a natural-coloured gloss, though I feel red would have looked better. Her nose was covered in a smattering of freckles, making her appear younger than she probably was.

Chloe wasn't someone who'd stand out in a crowd, but there was something about her that I found intriguing. Her beauty was natural, understated, and most certainly feminine.

Chloe was a little too voluptuous than she should be for her height, not something I was used to. The women who attended my club were generally lithe and firm, which helped them keep a bound position for longer. But for some reason, I wanted to see the swell of Chloe's large, shapely breasts when they were bound in leather.

"My business card," she said, handing me a white card with a fancy floral pattern. "I hope Keeley likes the flowers."

Chloe smiled at me, then took hold of the door handle.

I didn't want her to leave, not yet, anyway. I wanted to look upon this curvy woman for a little while longer.

"Chloe, if you are not in any hurry, could I take you on a tour around my home so that you can design some displays for a few of the rooms? I assume you did the beautiful arrangements for Keeley?"

"Yes, I did the arrangements, and I happen to have a spare five minutes. What kind of arrangements do you have in mind?" she asked, taking a small writing pad and pencil out of her back pocket.

"Nothing too feminine, just something to…how does my interior designer put it? Oh yes, *'accent the rooms.'* If you get to know the rooms and do a few displays for them every two weeks while I'm in England, I think that would be enough. Obviously, if I am to host a gathering here, I'll want displays that would suit the event."

"Of course," she replied, scribbling down a few notes, her blush from earlier gone. I liked the pink hue, so I decided to encourage a little more of it, placing my palm at the bottom of her back to guide her to my study.

I leaned in to whisper in her ear. "My dear, this is a very masculine space. Can you think of any special touches you could offer me in this room?" I let my breath coast over her ear and the side of her neck before standing up straight again.

"Well," she began before swallowing nervously. "The tones in here are all neutral, Mr Antonov. You have the almost hessian colour of the walls, the oak of your desk and bookcases, and the tan leather of your chair. I think keeping the theme neutral would work best. We could use terracotta colours in the flowers, possibly carnations and gerberas, along with decorative twigs. Maybe some ferns to bring out the green of your desk lamp. I can supply a coloured vase in a shade of brown or dark green, and I could also supply you with fragrant, decorative candles with a masculine scent, such as sandalwood," she said, writing something down on her notepad.

"I like those suggestions very much, Chloe. And call me Gregor, please. When women call me Mr Antonov, it makes me feel old."

"You're definitely not old, Gregor," Chloe remarked, and there was that blush again.

If she only knew.

I was nearly forty-seven when I took the blood and became immortal, but that was over five hundred years ago.

"Should we go to the next room?" I asked, once again placing my hand on her lower back and guiding her towards one of the sitting rooms.

After taking her to four of the downstairs rooms, I led her back towards the front door. I had agreed to every colour and design she'd suggested for each room, trusting her choice, as her suggestions seemed to fit the criteria I'd specified for each of the chosen spaces.

Chloe gave me a rough estimate, which I agreed upon. It was a reasonable price for the amount of work involved. She was surprised when I also gave her another two hundred pounds contingency, in case she thought of anything else that would be in keeping with the decorative aspect of this old house.

As she turned to leave, I took her left hand and noticed

she wasn't wearing a ring. I kissed the back of her hand and smiled at her.

"Would you consider going out to dinner with me next week, Chloe?" I asked.

She stared at me for a moment, as if she was trying to figure out what my motives were.

Perceptive woman.

After all, I did have a motive where this little goddess was concerned. I decided to put her at ease.

"All my friends in the area have little time to spend with me at the moment, and I find myself lacking good company. I know you are busy running a successful business, but I would be thrilled if a beautiful woman such as yourself could find time to have dinner with me," I said, knowing how women loved a little flattery.

"I'm not sure if I have the time, Gregor. Can I let you know when I bring the displays?" Chloe gave me a friendly smile and then got into her van.

What? Was she turning me down? This was a new experience for me. Chloe wound down her window and called me over.

"Here are some suggestions for you to take a look at when I'm gone," Chloe instructed. She handed me a folded piece of paper from her notepad before driving away.

I unfolded the piece of lined paper and looked at her suggestions, which read, *'I'm free most nights after 8 p.m. My mobile number is on the back of my business card. Oh, and Gregor, you are a terrible flirt.'*

I laughed so hard while walking through the house that Keeley came to check on me. Chloe seemed shy and submissive yet had an edge of boldness about her. A potent combination in my world.

Chapter Thirty-Two

Freya

After tucking Daisy into bed and reassuring her that we'd go to the beach tomorrow if it was sunny, I finally managed to get her off to sleep.

I made my way to my bedroom, pausing outside the room where Dan had slept on his first night here. I didn't hear anything at the door, so I assumed he was downstairs.

I wanted a nice long bath and some chill-out time after being so busy with Daisy today. She'd loved the aquarium and had asked all sorts of questions about the marine life we saw. She's so forward for her age. You have to remember sometimes that Daisy's not even five yet.

I walked into my bedroom and knew he was there before I could see him. The pure male scent of him hit me hard, and when I turned to look at him, the view I saw didn't disappoint. Dan sat in my reading chair with a glass of whisky in his hand. His chest was bare, and his dark jeans were open at the waistband, revealing the top of his boxer shorts. Dan wore nothing on his feet, and his hair was still wet, which told me he hadn't been out of the shower long.

"We need to talk about where we go from here, Freya," he said with a sigh.

That didn't sound too good at all. It was only yesterday that he told me he loved me. Was he having regrets already? I went to sit on the bed across from him, and he offered to get me a drink.

"Why? Do I need one?" I asked, preparing myself for an *"it's not you, it's me"* scenario. He got up and poured me a whisky, then sat back in the chair.

"Just spit it out, Dan," I told him, preparing myself for the brush off. Obviously, Josh had been right all along.

"Freya, I've been talking things through with Keeley today. She was telling me how she feels that she and Josh jumped the gun a bit and that they should have dated in the traditional way before deciding to get married." He sighed again and ran his fingers through his wet hair.

"I have my job and home in Barrowfield, and you live here. I work twelve-hour nights, which doesn't help when you're in a new relationship. So I was thinking…maybe you could stay at my flat with me for a few days during the week, then I could come here on my days off. I will warn you, though, my flat is tiny, and I haven't been in it long enough to decorate. So don't expect anything fancy."

I sat there stunned, and no words came to me at first. Daniel's gaze drifted towards the floor.

"Am *I* jumping the gun a bit, Freya? Only, after yesterday, I thought you wanted something more with me," he said nervously.

"I thought you were giving me the brush off," I finally

admitted. "When you said you wanted to talk, I thought you might regret saying that you loved me."

"Do you regret saying it back to me?" he asked.

"No, of course not."

"Then why would you think I'd regret saying it to you?"

"I don't know. I suppose I'm just wondering why someone as young and gorgeous as you, who can have any woman he fancied, would want someone like me."

"You mean someone I've wanted since I first saw her? A sexy, blonde-haired, grey-eyed goddess, with the most tempting body I've ever laid eyes on. I mean, why would I ever want someone like that?"

"Dan, I may still look twenty-seven, but I'm so many centuries older. I also can't give you children. Not your own children, anyway," I reminded him.

"First of all, you must have great genes because you don't look a day older than I do," Daniel joked. "Secondly, although I admit I'd like to have kids one day, whether they come along naturally makes no difference to me. Daisy's biological father wants fuck all to do with her, yet Josh has always doted on that girl. Who should get to be called Dad? Certainly not Rick the prick. Josh will be her dad in all the ways that count. They might have to do some explaining when Daisy gets asked why her dad has a different skin colour than she does, but the thing they have on their side is genuine love, and that will overpower anything, even biology. And Freya, just so you know, I'm not against *practising* making babies," he said, winking at me.

"So, you want me to be your girlfriend?" I clarified.

"For now."

"Are you sure you want to be done with the single life, Dan?" I asked. He took another sip of his whisky before answering.

"Let me tell you a little story, Freya. Can you remember what I was like at fifteen years old? I was going on for six feet in height, and I'd started to build muscle even then. I'd always been a good-looking kid and had no shortage of girlfriends. And I'd played around with a lot of them. You know what it's like with young lads…always trying to cop a feel of a girl's tits and slipping them a finger or two. As long as I got a wank out of it, I didn't care. And let me tell you, Freya, you've always been the star of every wet dream I've ever had."

I laughed while recalling Daniel as a young teen.

"Anyway, during the summer holidays that I turned fifteen, my best mate's mum gave him and me a job painting all the woodwork throughout their home. He'd started in his mum and dad's room; they had some cupboards in a built-in wardrobe that Aaron was painting. He moved a few boxes so he wouldn't get paint on them, and some books fell out. They were all books about sex, eight of them in total. He shouted me in, and we laughed at first while looking through all the pictures.

"When we looked at a few of the others, we realised we'd stumbled on a goldmine of information, detailing all the ways to get women to have an orgasm. Like I said, being young lads, we looked at all the pictures and diagrams first. Then we put the books back where we found them and got on with the painting. The next day, we got them out again and began reading. I wasn't a big reader. Never have been. But I read each and every one of those books front to back over the six-week school holidays. And I don't even think Rain Man could have memorised their content better than me.

"We also found a lot of porn in the same cupboard, but although watching it was a serious turn-on, it didn't match what we'd read in the books as far as giving women what they wanted.

"When we went back to school, Aaron and I decided we'd put our reading to good use. The first time I got a girl off with my fingers on her clit was awkward and took forever, but when she came, I could have beaten my chest with pride. Straight after, she took my cock out and gave me a wank without me even asking.

"Aaron and I soon found out that the more we got girls off—the further we were able to go with them. By the time we left school and were going out drinking, we'd both become a bit of a legend with the ladies. I was over six-foot-tall by this time and getting more muscular by the day. Being well-endowed helped as well. Women loved me, and I found the better I got at giving oral sex, the more I got away with in the bedroom. I could pretty much fuck any woman in any hole I wanted. Sometimes I had more than one woman. In fact, on one bank holiday weekend, I ended up with three women in bed with me.

"Over the last couple of years, I got bored with all that. To go out and pull was just too easy, and women only wanted me because they knew about my reputation for being good in bed. Even when we went out a few towns away, they didn't seem to want to spend a few hours chatting and getting to know me or anything. When I was eighteen that suited me, and even up to being twenty-three, it was okay. Then I hit twenty-four, and although Aaron and I were still single, a lot of our mates were settling down. Some were even getting married. They seemed happier somehow, and the thought of having someone special in my life really appealed to me. My shift pattern didn't help with trying to establish a relationship, and because I'd been a bit of a man slut, most women said they'd find it hard to trust someone like me."

He got up and walked towards the windows. Without looking at me, he said, "I was lonely, Freya. When I had that last bust-up with my dad, I went to stay with Aaron in his flat for a bit. I was sleeping on his sofa, wondering what the hell I was doing with my life. Two days later, I rented the flat next door to him and decided it would be a new start for me. But although Night Movers pays well, I have to keep doing the better-paid night shift so I can afford to keep my flat and run my car. That's why I'd need you to come and stay with me a few days a week. My job dictates my lack of normal couple time."

I walked up behind him, put my arms around his waist, and rested my head against his shoulder.

"I don't mind coming to stay with you, Dan, if that's what it takes. Although I have another proposition for you."

I turned him around to face me. "You could always come and work for me."

"What do you mean? I don't know anything about fashion or fabrics, Freya, and I'm not smart enough to learn, either."

"It wouldn't be in that capacity, not in the way you're probably imagining. My job involves a lot of travelling, as you know. Lots of the places I travel to are filled with lovely people, some of whom I've known for many years. But there's always the odd one or two men that think it's okay to take advantage of women. Even women like me who have a strong managerial role and own the company.

"There's this one guy in France who I loathe. His company is the place to go for delicate lacework in Europe. The people who work for him are highly skilled and work the lace by hand, embroidering it onto any fabric, even the finest silk, and with workmanship that's second to none.

"I have a designer to whom I supply the finished product, and he pays me an outrageous amount to get this done for him. The French company is the only place I can go to for such skilled, detailed work. The owner is called Thierry, and he's a male chauvinist pig.

"I worked on and off with his father, Jean-Claude, for years, and he was so sweet. If you're wondering how I got away without him noticing I hadn't aged…we use mind control to place images in the minds of people we need to have long-term relationships with—other than family and friends who know and understand what we are. In Jean-Claude's mind, he'd worked with my mother before me. I used mind control to make him think my mother passed away suddenly, and I'd taken over the business. Of course, he knew what he thought my mother looked like, so as we normally do, I planted seeds of doubt in his mind. This convinced him that, although I looked like my mother—the person he'd been dealing with for years—I had things about me that were very different."

"Such as?"

"Well, he would say, 'My dear Freya, you look so much like your mother.' And I'd say, 'Yes, I do, but my mother had the prettiest blue eyes you'd ever seen, and mine are so grey.'"

"And that would work?"

"If your mind control is strong enough, and you put many seeds of doubt in their minds, it can create a different picture than their own memory has stored away. For instance, Alex, Josh, and Nik have known Mr Singh at the post office in Barrowfield for years. Whenever Mr Singh comments to Alex that he looks just like his father, Alex says,

'I do, apart from the terrible squint you remember my father having.' Then the next time Mr Singh sees him, he says to Alex, 'If it wasn't for that squint your father had, you'd look just like him.'

"Josh tells him that his father was a lot shorter and stuttered. Nik always says like I do—different coloured eyes. And I've heard him say something about a limp, too. Before we did this, we had to move around a lot so our immortality wouldn't be revealed. But when you like an area and want to stay, you have to come up with different tactics.

"That's where I think the old legend comes from. You know the one I mean—where vampires don't have their photographs taken because they've no reflection. Obviously, that's untrue. As you've seen, I'm in lots of photographs with all the family and friends I hold dear. But if you can avoid public photos, then there's no public record of your likeness available for people to exploit. You must have noticed that it's always your aunt Maggie who gets photographed by the newspapers at Night Movers' charity events."

Dan's brows drew together as he tapped his finger against his chin, as though pondering what I'd just told him.

"I've never thought about it before, but yes, you're right. The bosses at Night Movers are never in the local paper, even though they sponsor a lot of stuff."

I nodded in agreement. "Anyway, getting back to Thierry. When his father passed away suddenly after a heart attack, he took over the business. He's a handsome man, I suppose, but he's well aware of it and had previously used his family's wealth and status to help gain his playboy reputation. But he's also condescending and cruel. He thinks nothing of trying to undermine women who have important roles in this industry. Thierry tried it on a couple of times with me, and I had to fend him off. I hit him so hard in the chest that he collapsed on the floor, struggling to breathe.

"I used mind control to convince him he'd collapsed with chest pain. But unbeknown to me, the large amount of cocaine he'd snorted, combined with the mind control I'd used, had scrambled his perception of what happened even further. Thierry doesn't know exactly what happened, but he's extremely wary of me. That hasn't stopped him from making sexual advances towards me, but he does it when his bodyguards and others are present. They are paid to turn a blind eye to whatever misdemeanours he commits. But, unless I use mind control on all of them, there's nothing I can do but accept his lewd remarks and inappropriate touching—when he steers me to my seat, for instance.

"My contract with the designer has another eight months to run, and then I'm done with Thierry's company. It's a shame because all the hard-working people he employs will suffer. I'm an extremely wealthy woman and can afford to take the loss, but I have several up-and-coming British designers working with the fashion houses I supply. They need me to keep going until they're established. So I need to see the eight months out. It's all very complicated and cut-throat, as the fashion business often is, and I've never enjoyed that side of it. The fabric-buying side I love but getting to the end product is something else entirely."

"What would you want me to do?" he asked.

"Work as my bodyguard, so I have protection against men like Thierry."

Dan looked deep in thought for a moment, as if contemplating what to say.

"Freya, for a normal human bloke, I'm big and strong, I get that, but you could wait for these men somewhere dark and isolated and snap them in half if you wanted. And if this slimeball is as bad as you say, then maybe you should think about that."

"You think I should kill him?" I asked incredulously.

"No, I didn't say that. But maybe you could break his legs or something. Make sure he's on his own and just jump him. I'd want to. I bet Alex and Josh would do it without hesitation. And your Russian friend, Gregor."

"You mustn't tell them, Dan. They'd be furious to know my staff and I have to put up with the likes of him. Things are different now. There are cameras everywhere, and if they ever caught any acts of retribution on film, it could spell the end of our kind."

He held me tightly, his chin resting on the top of my head.

"Freya, will you be honest with me when I ask you this next question?"

I think I knew where this was going, but I would answer him truthfully. If he didn't want to be with me afterwards, then I'd just have to accept it.

"Other than your father, have you ever seriously hurt or killed anyone?"

"Yes," I admitted. I felt his body tense for a few seconds, then he relaxed again.

"I know you wouldn't hurt me, Freya, so I won't ever fear you. But I want you to tell me about your answer."

Pulling away from him, I perched on the edge of the bed, gesturing for him to sit on the chair opposite. I needed to look into his eyes when I told him. I had to know that he truly held no fear.

"When Alex first saw Josh, he'd been captured and brought over to England to be sold as a slave. While on the journey over, he witnessed a young girl he was familiar with being raped by some of the sailors. He and another man tried to stop them; they were whipped and repeatedly beaten for their efforts. They brought the young woman back below deck with the rest of the captured and left her for dead. She'd been raped in every way possible and was badly beaten, leaving her with multiple broken bones. She died in front of them that night. The captives were all chained, so they couldn't even give her comfort in her last hours.

"Infection set in with Josh and the other man who tried to help the woman. Unfortunately, the other man dropped dead while being lined up to be sold on Liverpool Docks. Alex spotted that Josh was in a bad way and wanted to help him, so he bought him, then took him to his lodgings to try to save his human life. When he knew there was no way possible to do that, Alex turned him.

"When Alex brought Josh home, he became our brother. We taught him how to cope with being a Made vampire, and how to speak English and get by in our world. He had a good life with us and knew that we loved him, but he was plagued with nightmares that wouldn't go away. When he told us that the men who'd abused the woman and had beaten him still haunted his dreams, we took him to Liverpool to get his revenge. We hoped it would stop his nightmares."

I got up and poured another whisky before sitting back down and continuing.

"We took the men involved somewhere quiet. I handed them knives and ordered them through mind control to cut off their cocks and balls." I carried on looking at Dan to see if he felt any disgust with my actions, but apart from a visible wince, he showed no sign that my story affected him.

"After they'd been screaming for a while, Alex slit their throats, killing them instantly. Josh knelt on the floor and cried. He thought it would give him peace when he witnessed their suffering, but that didn't come to him. I, on the other hand, was glad they were gone. They'd hurt my family, and I wanted them to pay."

I looked down at my fingers, recalling the next story.

"Many years later, we were in Lancashire doing business with a mill owner. Some of the new machines could create patterns in fabrics that had never been seen before. We only used to deal with the progressive mill owners who gave their workers a fair wage and good working conditions, but we somehow found ourselves in the company of one real scumbag. We knew he still had young children working for him, and we wanted to broker a deal in which he provided better working conditions and some schooling for his employees.

"We thought that was a reasonable request for the amount of business we were offering. He wouldn't do business with a woman and wasn't happy to work with Josh, either, but he relented to Josh at the last minute. We thought about backing out, but we'd heard something about the owner that sickened us. So, Josh and Alex went to a meeting with him at his home to investigate and, after finding nothing wrong, managed to secure the deal. The mill owner was pleased with the outcome and offered drinks all round and some entertainment.

"Two children, a boy and a girl around eight years old were summoned into the room. The mill owner motioned towards Alex and Josh, and the children went towards them. The girl in front of Josh was frightened by his skin colour and hesitated, but the boy in front of Alex dropped to his knees and went towards the opening of Alex's trousers. Alex jumped up out of the boy's way, and the child cowered, apologising to the mill owner for displeasing him."

"Fucking hell, Freya, that's awful. Please tell me they killed the paedophile?"

"Josh leapt at him and pinned him down, but the children were screaming, frightened because Josh was so enraged he'd revealed his vampire side. Alex told him to keep the mill owner secure without hurting him, then he took the children out into the hallway and gave them each a bag of coins—enough to buy them food and lodgings for a year. He used mind control to make them forget that they'd ever even seen Alex and Josh and that, instead, a gentleman in the street had given them the money. He also tried to make them forget the mill owner and the horrors he had put them through.

"Then Alex went back to Josh and told him to use mind control on the mill owner. He convinced the owner that he wanted to sell us the mill and all its contents for a ridiculously low price. Alex told the owner to arrange it with his solicitor that the sale should go through within two days. He carried on with mind control, asking him to reveal if he knew of any other men who used children for sexual gratification. The mill owner gave up two further names, and my brother took note of them."

I rubbed the tears out of my eyes and carried on speaking. Dan sat beside me now, his palm resting on my thigh.

"After the sale had gone through, my brother used mind control on the owner again and arranged for him to set up a meeting with the other paedophiles in a field a few miles from the town. Alex had researched the other two *gentlemen* and found out they were indeed using their young employees for sexual gratification. They both had female heirs to their businesses, so Josh and Alex weren't worried about the despicable acts carrying on. Of course, we now know differently, but at the time, we thought that men were the only sexual predators. But very few females ran a business in those times as it was considered unseemly, so it was likely their daughters would sell up anyway. Maybe their daughters were victims themselves?

"Once all three men were in the remote meeting place, Alex quizzed the sick predators about their wrongdoings, and told them we'd brought them out of the way to finish them. Unbeknown to us, one man had brought a pistol, which he took out and aimed at Alex. I snapped his neck before he could take the shot, and Alex and Josh killed the other two. We set it up to look like a highway robbery gone wrong. I was sick to my stomach, but not for killing them. It was for all the suffering those children had to go through."

"What did you do with the mill?" Dan asked.

"We sold it on to one of the new progressive mill owners, even cheaper than the ridiculous price we'd paid for it. Children had to be much older to work there with the new owner, and those that did were given free schooling to help them learn to read and write. I would have liked to find all those children who were abused and wipe away their bad memories, but that would have been impossible."

Dan took my left hand and placed it between both of his. I found it as comforting as a hug, and it pleased me greatly that he wasn't judging me.

"Have you killed anyone since?" he asked.

"I can let you in on a very well-kept secret now, Dan. No one else knows this, except Keeley."

"Is that because it was recent?" he asked apprehensively.

"No, but would it bother you if it was?"

"I'm not sure, Freya. If it was because of something similar to what you've just told me, then it wouldn't bother me at all."

"It's still taking a life, Dan. No matter the reason, that fact doesn't change," I stated.

"Does it affect your life? The memory of taking a life, I mean?"

I looked him in the eyes as I answered honestly, "Killing my father has never left me, but the rest have no impact on my life whatsoever."

After a long pause, Dan took a deep breath and said, "So tell me about the last one, then."

"It was 1888. Alex and I had travelled to London to meet with Gregor, who was there for business. Josh stayed here. The logistics of getting him to London without the risk of sunlight endangering his life were immense. It involved several stops via coach and rail, and only travelling at night, which was okay when we journeyed to Liverpool, but getting to London seemed to take forever.

"We had a great time with Gregor. His uncle owned a house in Mayfair, and he would throw extravagant parties and elaborate balls. Everyone was talking about the murders in Whitechapel, and there were theories even then about who Jack the Ripper was. But it was so far removed from the area we were staying in, it seemed like it was happening in another city altogether.

"One evening, Gregor was taking Alex to a club he frequented when he was in London. In other words, they were going to an upmarket whorehouse where Gregor could indulge in his preferred brand of kink. Gregor would never let me tag along. He always maintained that kind of thing shouldn't be something a lady would know about, which was as hilarious then as it is now. If he'd only known what those ladies in high society talked about, he would have been shocked. Alex knew because he'd slept with most of them, married or not, but Gregor liked to compartmentalise them. Whores or ladies, he could deal with that.

"Anyway, after they'd left, I waited a few minutes, then went the opposite way. It was easier when we travelled to use mind control on a prostitute and feed a little from them than it was to take staff along with you. I could have used some of Gregor's Mayfair staff to feed from, but I went in search of a prostitute instead. I paid well for a small amount of their blood, and it meant they didn't have to stay out the rest of the night so they could be safe at home with their families.

"After a short carriage journey, I found myself walking towards a seedier part of London. There was much more noise there, and the stench was horrendous. I walked into a pub and took a drink of ale before continuing my journey. I found a relatively clean prostitute named Catherine and told her my intentions. She was alarmed, but I offered her more than she'd have made on the streets in a month. In the end, Catherine agreed, although she was worried and questioned whether I could be the infamous Jack the Ripper. I assured her I wasn't and used mind control to keep her calm while I fed.

"After I'd taken a little of her blood, she began telling me all she'd heard about the killer. Her friend had known Mary Kelly—the woman who'd been killed the week before. The manner of her death was gruesome, to say the least. There was a theory that the killer could be a surgeon because some of the victim's internal organs had been removed. I was fascinated, and I also felt protective of the women on the poorer side of London. They were all someone's daughter, sister, or mother, and were doing what they could in order to survive.

"After my dealings with the lovely Catherine, I set about

trying to find the elusive killer. I didn't come across him that night, or the rest of the week, and Alex was starting to get suspicious of my whereabouts. I'd been giving him the excuse of visiting a sick human friend every evening, but I knew he didn't believe me.

"On the evening before we were due to leave, Gregor's uncle threw a magnificent ball, where everyone who was anyone was invited. I was able to sneak out of the house undetected and made my way over to visit Catherine again in Whitechapel. She couldn't believe how pretty my ball gown was and spoke to me like she would an old friend.

"Truth be told, I felt more comfortable talking to her and her colleagues than most of the people at the ball. I took blood from Catherine and her friend Sarah, paying them well and giving them some of my jewellery. After chatting with them for another ten minutes, I made my way into the pub. My dress that night turned many heads, and I got a bit fed up with all the attention I was getting, so I came out of the pub and began my journey back to Mayfair.

"I hadn't gone far when I heard a scream that came from where I'd been visiting with Catherine. So I used my vampire speed—despite the fact that there were people around—and ended up in the midst of a horrific scene.

"A man was slicing a knife down Sarah's stomach slowly, but with precision. Sarah was unconscious on the floor, and I feared I was too late. I broke the man's neck before he even knew I was there, and then I sank to the floor and bit into my wrist. Placing it over Sarah's mouth, I forced her to swallow my blood. Luckily, the cuts on her stomach were only skin deep and hadn't punctured any organs. Sarah's wound began to heal, and she slowly regained consciousness.

"Catherine came running seconds after I started to give

Sarah my blood, and I had to use mind control to keep her calm. I explained the body of the man and what I'd caught him doing. I told her what was happening, that my blood was helping heal Sarah, and that I would never harm her.

"When Sarah was fully healed, Catherine and I wrapped the man's body in the excess fabric of my ball gown, which I'd torn away. Catherine didn't recognise the man and I had never seen him before either. We deduced that he was indeed some sort of doctor or surgeon by the knife he'd used to cut Sarah. It was kind of scalpel-like, and he also had various other implements on him, which could have been medical. Although I had no need for doctors, so I couldn't be certain. But Catherine seemed pretty sure.

"We could have gone to the police, but what would they have said? There was a wealthy-looking man with a broken neck and a perfectly healthy prostitute. Who would believe their story? They'd have been more inclined to believe that Catherine and Sarah had murdered an innocent man.

"We stole the nearby grocer's cart, which had been locked away for the night, and I bent the man completely in half, severing his spinal cord so his body would fit inside. Then I wheeled the covered cart through the streets of London as quickly as I could, ending up at the River Thames, but it still took me around twenty minutes to get there. I weighed the body down with rocks and threw it as far into the water as I could. Then I returned the cart and went to check on Catherine and Sarah. I promised them I would be back before I left London the next day.

"Because my dress was torn and filthy, Catherine gave me her cape to keep me covered, and Sarah gave back some of the money I'd given her that evening so I could get a carriage back to Mayfair. When I finally returned, Alex and Gregor were livid. They could smell blood and the scent of death on me, and Catherine's scent from her cape. But I wouldn't be bullied into revealing my actions. That's the only time in the hundreds of years I've known Gregor that I ever came close to falling out with him.

"My anger and frustration with their demands brought tears to the surface, and while more a show of my temper than of weakness, Gregor was horrified that he'd made me cry. In the end, I used it to my advantage and gained his sympathy, although my brother knew me well enough not to be taken in. I told them I'd been helping some of the destitute young women of London and said I would reveal nothing more. It was the truth, after all; I just left out a few important facts.

"I told Alex I'd be stopping in Whitechapel on our way home to give clothing, money and jewellery to two of my friends so they could make a better life for themselves. And that's exactly what I did. I have no idea what became of those two women, but at least I know they weren't fatal victims of Jack the Ripper—if that's who he was."

Chapter Thirty-Three

Daniel

I wasn't sure what to say to Freya after all those revelations or if words were even needed. But I knew she required comfort. Her hand felt cold in mine, and now and then, a shiver ran through her.

I turned her to face me and put my arms around her. Freya sighed heavily, but not from contentment. It seemed more like she was expecting a negative comment from me or, at least, some distance.

She wasn't getting either of those. As far as I was concerned, Freya had removed murderers and rapists from this world, which could never be wrong.

However, I felt relieved that Freya hadn't killed anyone for some time. Yet, I knew without a doubt that if a similar situation presented itself, she'd have no hesitation in taking the life of someone evil to save one of an innocent. But then again, we were all capable of that, no matter how much the do-gooders protest differently.

In the end, I tried to say what I felt without words, showing Freya I accepted all sides of her and her past—however dark that may have been.

I kissed her gently, trying to convey that I loved her and wanted to be with her no matter what. I didn't deepen the kiss; I just kept it soft and sweet until she broke away from me and looked into my eyes.

"You still want to be with me?" she asked. I nodded, then smiled.

Freya smiled back at me, and it lit up her whole face, making it even more beautiful. I could see all the tension and worry of the last half-hour lift away, and my heart felt lighter, too.

I cupped her face and told her how much I loved her. This time, the kiss I gave her was full of desire and need. I flicked my tongue against hers, tasting her sweetness and love for me, and I couldn't get enough.

"Oh, God, Dan, I need you inside me right now," Freya moaned breathlessly.

I had us naked in record time, but she took me by surprise when she dropped to her knees in front of me. My hard cock was bobbing about in front of her face, and when she licked her lips and took hold of me, my balls drew up tight against my body. I wanted her mouth on me, but with the way I felt, it would have been my undoing. Freya must have sensed this because she said, "Do you trust me, Dan?"

I looked down at the beautiful woman on her knees in front of me and replied, "With everything I am."

She smiled wickedly, then licked my cock from root to tip before moving down and sucking gently on each of my balls. I felt my legs give way a little, but she slipped her hands around my thighs and pressed firmly against them, steadying me. Freya took my cock almost to the back of her throat, sucking as she pulled away. She kept her lips firm and wet as she slipped back down my cock, taking me deeper into her throat each time. It was so fucking amazing, and I didn't want her to stop. But after only a minute, I was ready to come.

"Freya," I warned as I tried to pull back to prevent my impending release.

Freya didn't stop. Seconds later, I was coming down her throat, my head thrown back and eyes shut tight while wave after wave of pleasure swept over me. My knees were trembling; my legs felt almost boneless.

Freya stood and kissed me deeply, letting me taste my come on her tongue. I wanted to reciprocate and make Freya come with my mouth, but she had other ideas. She pushed me onto my back on the bed and made me scoot up towards the headboard, following me as I went. Freya straddled me and slid my already semi-hard cock inside her wet heat. Running my fingertips over her breasts, I tugged on her pointed nipples. Freya gasped, so I did it again, harder this time, before taking one of the firm nubs into my mouth. With every suck I gave, I felt my cock grow harder, and soon I was fully erect again.

Freya rode me hard, taking me deep, her sex seeming to suck on my cock as her eager mouth had. I slowed down the tempo, wanting to savour the feeling of being inside my woman. Placing my thumb in her mouth, I ordered her to lick it. She did so without question, and when it was wet enough, I pressed it against her clit and moved it up and down firmly. Freya moaned as she rocked against me, so I pressed down even more on her pink pearl until she cried out her release, the spasms from deep within her tight sex milking me once more.

Before I could get my breath, she grabbed me by the

hair and pulled me upright, my chest flush against hers. With her hand still in my hair, she tilted my head over to the side and licked up my neck towards my ear. Freya was still horny, yet I needed some recovery time. I started to tell her I'd take care of her needs, but Freya silenced me by whispering the same question she'd asked earlier.

"Do you trust me?"

"I do," I replied, enjoying the feel of her tongue lapping at my earlobe, then lower. Seconds later, I felt the sharp points of her fangs as they slid into my neck. My body tensed, and I sucked in a quick breath.

I almost pushed Freya away from me, but when I felt the strange pulling sensation of her sucking my blood into her mouth, I held her even closer.

Raw pleasure shot through my body, making me instantly hard again. I don't know who moved their body first, but within seconds I began thrusting up into her as she rocked against me. My cock throbbed, desperate for release, and although I tried to delay it, when Freya sucked my blood into her mouth again, I was done for. I came with a roar and several grunts and groans, my climax lasting longer than any I'd had before, only ending when Freya removed her fangs from my neck and licked the wounds closed.

I collapsed back against the headboard, pulling Freya with me. She placed little kisses on my jaw and up to my lips before murmuring, "Thank you, Dan."

I smiled up at her, exhausted and more sated than I'd been in my entire life.

"It's me who should be thanking you for that, Freya. I haven't had such a speedy recovery time since I was a teenager. But when I felt the first pull of blood leaving me, I was instantly rock hard. I came, and you carried on sucking. Fuck! I felt that thrill everywhere."

"I bet you never read about that in those books," she said with a giggle.

Laughing with her, I confirmed, "You're right; they never mentioned that."

Freya moved a little, and I felt the wetness sliding out of her and over my balls as I softened inside her.

"I hope you've got spare sheets in here, Freya, because I came loads, and it's already feeling a bit messy."

"I know. I need to get up, but it feels so right to be in your arms." Freya sighed, trailing her fingers through my chest hair.

"It does," I agreed, feeling the rightness of what we had together wash over me. It was a good feeling to know that you belonged to someone like they belonged to you. And that's how I felt about us—that we belonged together.

"But we do need to get cleaned up," Freya said.

"After three, okay," I told her, readying myself. She giggled again but said, "Okay."

"One, two, three," I counted, then lifted her off my body.

I laughed as she tried to walk to the bathroom without opening her legs too much, and I slapped her arse on the way past her.

After a leisurely shower, we made the bed and went downstairs for a bite to eat. I still wasn't sure whether she was serious about the job offer, and what it would mean for us if I took it.

"What's on your mind, Dan?" Freya asked as she

cleared our plates away. "You've gone all quiet on me since we came downstairs."

"I'm just wondering if you were serious about the job offer and how it would affect our relationship. You don't travel that often, so if it's just as and when required, it wouldn't be enough for me. I need full-time employment," I told her truthfully.

"Well, I go over to the sewing factory once a week to check in on things there. When a shipment is ready to be dispatched, I'm normally running around between the designers, the factory, and the warehouse for a few weeks beforehand. And it's anything up to sixteen hours a day. I spend most of those hours with my designers while they panic over the finished items. I'd need you to be on call and ready to leave at a moment's notice. Obviously, I wouldn't want you to appear as my bodyguard unless I meet with someone who warrants it, but I'd appreciate you being my driver and general go-to guy."

"I don't know, Freya. I get the impression you're creating a job for me, and I don't want to feel like I'm a kept man." I told her this in all seriousness. I'd always had a job, and it was important to me that I pay my way.

"Dan, you have to accept that I'm an extremely wealthy woman. I never have to work again if I don't want to. But I need to do *something* to fill my days, so I deal with fabrics and fashion. Alex has offered me a part share of the warehouse and distribution side of Night Movers, but I don't think it's right for me. You could take over it for me if you want. After all, you know the business."

She seemed sincere, but I could never be a pen pusher. Warehousing, I can do; office work is something I'm not smart enough to deal with.

"I don't think I could do it, Freya. I'm not like Keeley. I

hated school and didn't leave with qualifications suitable for a job in an office."

"It can all be learned, Dan. After all, my brothers and Nik didn't go through the British education system."

"Yeah, but you've either got it, or you haven't, and I don't think I've ever had it."

"Oh, I think you've definitely got it, Dan." Freya winked at me.

I smiled, but I was also a little sad at that statement. I wanted to be more than just good sex to Freya, but I knew I wasn't being very helpful with her suggestions.

I think Freya realised where my thoughts had gone because she took my hand in hers and said, "You have a lot of great qualities going for you. You are hardworking, have a brilliant personality and are loyal to your friends and family. You are kind, generous and loving, and for the first time in centuries, I feel like I could have a future with someone. If you want to be with me, you'll have to get over thinking that a man always needs to provide financially for his woman. There are many other roles in a relationship than a provider. A real man will fill as many of those roles as he's able."

She was right; I knew that. But it was hard to change the ideals I'd been brought up with.

"Here's a bit of information for you," she said very matter-of-factly. "In the late 1970s, Gregor told me about an up-and-coming venture which involved transporting gas from Russia to Europe. The project began construction in 1982 and meant that Western Europe could have a steady gas supply from Russia. I invested what I could, although not as much as Gregor or Sergei's family, and within a few years, my investment paid off. I also invested in fuels exported from Ukraine, but I'm glad I pulled out of that while the going was good.

"Gregor was a star managing all those investments for me. I'm glad I put my trust in him—I became a billionaire from those investments alone."

To say I was shocked was an understatement. I knew Freya was wealthy. I mean, her home could house a small army. She even has a cook and a butler, for Christ's sake. But even knowing all that, I didn't think she could be a billionaire. Freya didn't act like you'd imagine one would. She's so lovely and down to earth, and she always has time for others.

I ran my hand over my face and contemplated what it would mean to us as a couple. Freya didn't think that money was an issue, but how couldn't it be? I didn't want her brothers and the staff at Night Movers to think that was why I was with her.

As if reading my mind, Freya said, "Don't let what other people might think worry you or prevent you from being with me. Earlier this evening, you suggested splitting our time between Barrowfield and here, so you could keep your job if you wanted. But the offer of being my driver, bodyguard, and the guy who helps take some of the strain from my day—just by being there when I need support—still stands. If you aren't opposed to me taking your blood, it will be easier for me when travelling because I won't need to take it from anyone else."

I'm not normally a jealous person, but picturing Freya taking blood from someone else after the experience I'd had with her upstairs infuriated me.

"You won't be taking blood from anyone else, Freya. Not anymore."

She laughed at me and shook her head.

"Dan, it's only like that if you're intimate with someone. Otherwise, it's just giving and receiving blood," she assured.

"I don't care. You're not having blood from just any fucking stranger," I insisted. "I mean it, Freya. Don't cross me on this."

"I take blood from my staff, Dan. I feed from the wrist of one of them every few days, and they, in turn, take a small amount of mine to remain healthy and ageless. There is nothing sexual in that at all."

"So if you took my blood every few days, you wouldn't need theirs?"

Freya nodded. "But if you aren't here, I might need to feed. If we're overstressed or hurt, we need more blood than usual. We can have bags of blood delivered, but I rarely order for myself."

"It looks like I'll be taking the job then, Freya," I told her. "Because there's no fucking way I'm letting you drink from another man. Staff or not."

"I didn't know you had a jealous streak, Dan," she teased.

"Neither did I," I admitted. "It's never happened before. But then again, I've never been in love before."

"I think being with vampires is starting to rub off on you," Freya teased. "We are known to be extremely possessive, after all."

"I might do all the biting later," I said with a wink.

"That's what Bonded couples do," Freya replied, looking down at her fingers. I lifted her chin so that she looked directly at me.

"Explain what you just said," I demanded, curious to know what she meant.

"Well, when an immortal decides to spend their life with either another immortal or human, they create a Bond by feeding from each other at the same time during sex. The Bond is forever, and it creates a link whereby the couple can sense each other's emotions and feelings, and they can communicate telepathically. If one of them is human, the blood they ingest from the immortal one will stop them from ageing and keep them healthy—just like my blood does for my staff. Apparently, sex is off the charts good if both parties take blood from each other when they are intimate."

"Keeley tried to explain this to me, but she didn't tell me everything. Is that what she and Josh will do? And have Alex and Julia, Nik and Gina done the same?"

"Yes. Through the Bond, they've committed to being with each other forever. There is no divorce or anything like that for a Bonded couple. It's a lifelong commitment. And because they never age or die, as long as the human continues to take the immortal's blood, it really does mean forever."

I was quiet for a while, thinking about the enormity of such a thing. My mum and dad were so happy together and were great parents. When Mum died, my dad was never the same. He would have loved to have forever with her. It always got to me when I found out people were getting divorced, although they often had good reason to go down that road. But it seemed like a lot of people didn't appreciate what they had at home.

"If I commit to someone—you know, marriage and all that—I want it to be forever. So being Bonded appeals to me. My mum would still be here if she and Dad had Bonded—if he'd been a vampire, I mean. Then she wouldn't have got cancer, and my dad wouldn't be a drunk."

"I know it's early days for us, Dan, but I know you'll

make a great Bonded mate, and I'd be proud to call you mine."

I tugged Freya towards me, slow dancing with her around the kitchen without the need for music.

"I've always been yours, Freya, but now I get to show everyone you are mine," I told her.

After kissing her softly, I whispered, "I love you." Then I smiled contentedly, knowing I'd be saying it to her every day for the rest of my life.

Chapter Thirty-Four

Keeley

I'd been working with Gregor for the last three hours. We sat at the kitchen table, our laptops and diaries open as we caught up on the previous few days. I knew Gregor's Russian PA had been checking his overseas business dealings, and I felt guilty about enjoying his hospitality while not giving anything in return.

Ever the gentleman, Gregor said I'd been through a terrible experience and should take all the time I needed before returning to work. Yet I wanted to work. This little bit of normality made me feel like myself again.

Just as we were finishing up the morning's business, I heard the noise of a vehicle pulling up the gravel driveway. While my new vampire hearing helped me detect that noise before it even approached the front of the manor, Gregor went one better when he announced, "That's Nik's car. He and Gina have been strawberry picking, and she promised to bring me a few punnets."

Gregor's ice-blue eyes were almost glittering with expectation, and his enthusiasm was contagious. I heard Josh open the front door, so I waited before I walked down the hallway to greet them. Gregor got there first and embraced Gina quickly before taking the strawberries from her.

"Gina, my darling, you brought cream as well. Thank you. You are so good to me," he declared, kissing her cheek. Then he darted off to the kitchen before anyone could steal one of the mouth-watering berries.

Gina smiled and shouted, "You're welcome, Gregor. But save some for Keeley and Josh."

Gina hadn't taken her eyes off me. She stepped forward and threw her arms around me, hugging me tightly. Tears fill my eyes, clouding my vision, but not before I'd seen the way Nik looked at me when I hugged Gina back. He feared I'd hurt her. And with the way Nik tensed and gritted his teeth, I knew he held himself ready to separate us in case I went into blood lust.

Gina's much shorter than me, and I didn't know she was crying until I felt her tears soak through the front of my T-shirt.

"Hey, come on, girls." Nik came towards us, enveloping Gina and me in one of his big, brawny hugs. "You'll get there, Keeley; it's just going to take some time. But you have lots of that now, and more love and support than you could ever know."

Gina and I still couldn't let each other go. It was the first time we'd seen each other since she'd staked Maxim and tried to save my life. A few days ago, I wished she'd let me die, but now I was grateful for her intervention.

"Thank you, Gina, for saving me. I hope you're feeling okay now. Sergei's been keeping us informed about your recovery, and I know I did nothing but blubber when we tried to speak on the phone the other day," I said as I took the tissue from Josh and wiped my eyes.

"That was nothing," replied Nik. "Gina cried for forty minutes after that call. It was awful. I've never seen so much snot in my life…oww!" Nik yelped as Gina nipped him.

"I don't know why I love you, Nik. You're such a pig sometimes," Gina declared. But she was smiling when she said it, and we finally let go of each other.

"Do you all want a drink?" I asked when Josh took my hand and led me back to the kitchen.

"Something cold," replied Nik. "It's not as sunny outside today, but it's still hot and quite humid."

I agreed with him. Even though my body temperature was lower now than when I was human, I still felt warm.

"There's a thunderstorm forecast for later this afternoon," Josh informed us. He handed everyone a glass of cloudy lemonade.

A good thunderstorm should settle the humid weather, but I worried about Daisy being scared because she didn't like thunder and lightning. I hoped the storms didn't reach her at Aldbrough.

I desperately needed to talk to my friend alone. Gina had been a bit of everything to me over the years. First and foremost, my best friend, even with the nineteen-year age difference. She was also like a mother figure, especially with all the help and advice she'd given me since I got pregnant with Daisy. Gina has a good way of delivering help and advice—not excessive or overbearing. It's always given from experience and straight from the heart, just like I thought my mum would have done.

I could also talk to Gina about men and sex, something I don't think I'd have felt comfortable talking to my mum or

Aunt Mags about. And even more so Freya, now that I'm engaged to her brother.

Sensing my need to talk, Gina asked, "Shall you and I have a cosy, girly chat in the dining room, Keeley?"

"I'd love that," I replied. She turned to Nik to stop him following us.

"I'm not leaving you, Gina. You know what we talked about earlier," Nik reminded her.

"As you can see, Keeley is fine. Now please, let us have half an hour of girl time. I've missed her," Gina said, pouting and pleading with her eyes.

"Okay, but I'll be right outside the door if you need me. Sorry, Keeley. Although I'd like to trust that you'll not go into blood lust, you did ingest quite a bit of Gina's blood and could suddenly start to crave it. I can't let Gina be hurt. I'm sure you understand," Nik said, half apologetic, half determined.

I didn't blame him for trying to protect Gina. It was admirable, really. But honestly, I just didn't crave blood like they all thought I would. Sometimes I wish I did, then I could recognise the start of blood lust and learn to stop it before it became too bad. But so far, I'd had nothing like it since I woke up that first morning, and even then, it wasn't that bad.

I told Nik I understood his concerns, but they weren't warranted. When he finally acquiesced, I led Gina into the long dining room and took a seat by the window.

"I'm sorry about Nik, Keeley. I know you wouldn't purposely hurt me."

"I understand his concerns, Gina. I wanted to talk to you about them if that's okay."

"About the risk to Daisy?" Gina questioned. Though I

could tell she knew my answer would be yes, I nodded anyway and hung my head low while I spoke.

"They said I could hurt her because a child's blood is more tempting to a newly transitioned Made vampire than an adult's. I don't want to put her at risk from me, Gina. If something happened when she was in my care, I would never forgive myself. I love her so much and I miss her terribly, even after these last few days. But I would forgo any further contact with her if it meant she was safe. When I first found out I was a threat to her, I wished you'd let me die. I brought her into this world, after all, so to think I could be the one to remove her from it cuts me to pieces."

Gina didn't say anything; she just placed her arm around my shoulders and let me speak.

"I made a decision a couple of days ago. People aren't going to like it, Gina, but I'm going to ask if Freya will keep Daisy for me. At least for a year, maybe more. I don't know yet. Before I have any physical contact with her, I need to know I'm safe for her to be around. I hope she won't hate me for it, but in the end, I would rather have her safe and hate me than be scared or dead after I attacked her. I can't even go out during daylight with her. What kind of life is that for an almost five-year-old?"

"I know what you mean, Keeley. I've thought about it non-stop since this happened. If this is what you want, then I'll fully support you. But you'll have to think of something to tell Daisy, so she doesn't think you've just abandoned her. You're such a good mum, Keeley, and she'll really miss you. Maybe you'll be able to have her back in your life sooner than you think?"

We heard a loud clatter and raised voices outside the door. Seconds later, an angry-looking Josh stormed into the room.

"So you want to give our daughter away, Keeley? Just give her away like an unwanted pet you've grown tired of taking care of. Well, what about me? I'm her father now. You shouldn't be able to make these decisions without consulting me."

"You were listening outside the door," I said flatly. "Why am I not surprised at that, Josh? Oh, I know. It's because everyone keeps telling me what a risk I am to others in case I go into blood lust. You stood outside the door in case I hurt the best friend I've ever had. How the bloody hell do you expect me to let my daughter be put at risk when I can't even be trusted around an adult? Your actions don't inspire confidence in my abilities as a vampire mum," I yelled, no, screamed at him.

"Josh, listen to Keeley. You know what she's saying makes sense. She's only doing this because she loves her daughter and wants to keep her safe," Nik insisted, trying to calm Josh down. His eyes had taken on a red rim around the iris, and his voice was almost a growl. But Nik's words didn't help.

"She's my daughter too, Keeley, and I'm not giving her up. I made a promise to you and Daisy, and I will not be the one to break that promise. You can give her up, but I won't. She can live with me in my cottage. We'll be okay."

He almost spat the words at me, but I wouldn't back down. I knew if Daisy were nearby, it would be too much for me to keep away from her.

"It breaks my heart to do this, but she's my everything, Josh. I love you so much, but I won't be moved on this decision. I'm her legal guardian and what I say is final. We aren't married, and you have no legal rights because you're not her biological father. I want Daisy kept away from me until I know I can control myself. My job is here, and I don't have any other finances to live off, so I need to stay near the village to keep working.

"I appreciate that you're thinking about Daisy's feelings," I told him. "She loves you so much, and I wasn't going to suggest that she didn't call you Daddy or not see you. But I want her to have as normal a life as possible. You can only have two and a half hours in the sun before its effects become dangerous for you. How would you cope when she needs you to accompany her on a school trip or sports day? You would send for Freya, Gina, or Julia. What about all the girly stuff she'll need to do, or when you work your night shift? Who will you call then? She needs a woman around her too, Josh. Freya will make a good mum for her while I can't be one."

"Keeley, if you ever loved me, you wouldn't break my heart like this," Josh groaned desperately.

"And if you loved me, you'd respect this decision and the reason I made it. I won't stop you from being her father if that's what you want. But give her a normal life, Josh. Let her live in the light as much as possible while she's still a child. I was going to be the one who could give her that, but neither of us can do that now."

His features showed anger, hurt, and something else I found intimidating. I fiddled with my engagement ring nervously, wondering what he would do or say next.

"Are you trying to take that off so you can give it back to me?" he snapped, pointing at the ring.

"I wasn't going to. Why? Do you want it back?" I asked, praying the answer would be no. But all Josh did was raise his eyebrow and glare at me, which gave me my answer. I took off the ring and placed it on the dining table at the side of him. I already had tears in my eyes, but I was determined not to let him see them fall. So I headed straight for the door, with Gina following close behind.

Gregor was at the door to the dining room and took my hand in his when I reached him. He led me to the stairs, and when I stumbled, he lifted me in his arms effortlessly and carried me to the guest room at the side of his bedroom.

"I'm sure he doesn't mean it, Keeley, but I want you to know you are welcome to stay in my home for as long as you need. I was going to give you one of the coach house cottages to live in. After your attack, that would be inappropriate. I have other properties on the estate yet to be renovated. You can have your pick of them, but do not make a hasty decision that you will regret. Give yourself at least a few months to adjust. You are welcome to come to Moscow with me when I leave."

He was so sincere about everything he said. I nodded and kissed the back of his knuckles. The light that was there earlier in his pale blue eyes had been extinguished with all the arguing he'd overheard.

"Gregor, I'm so sorry you've had all these problems brought to your home. I know I've told you this before, but I appreciate everything you've done for me. I think it's best if I return to my dad's house. It isn't fair that you keep getting caught up in all my drama."

"Nonsense, Keeley. I would be lonely if you were not here. And besides, I do not want you to stay on your own while Maxim is unaccounted for. No. You will stay here with me. I will protect you."

And with that, Gregor got up and left Gina in the room with me. Standing at the foot of the bed, she said, "I'm so sorry, Keeley. I can't believe what just happened. I'm sure Josh didn't mean it."

I shook my head and wiped away my tears. "Don't worry about it, Gina. I'm just not meant to be in a happy, committed relationship. I thought it was all too good to be true anyway, and we did rush into it. It just wasn't meant to be, that's all. I'll bounce back; I always do. And I have Gregor and my job, so at least that's something."

"Don't say that, Keeley. You *are* meant to have a happy and committed relationship, and as much as I love Josh, he was so fucking wrong down there," Gina stated angrily.

"He loves Daisy, though, Gina, so I knew this would hurt him. I thought it would be a temporary thing, and once we were sure I wasn't going to harm her, we could get Daisy back. I just didn't want to commit to a timescale in case that couldn't happen. I honestly believed he loved me, but now I'm wondering if that was because of Daisy. Like his need to be a father to Daisy made him fall in love with me."

"That wasn't the case at all, Keeley. Anyone with eyes in their head could see how he's looked at you for so many years. Josh loves you! Trust me on that. He could never physically hurt you; it's not in his nature. But because he was hurting emotionally, he lashed out at your feelings, too, so that you could hurt as bad as he did. If he didn't have a man's brain, he could see that you're hurting much more than him. Men will never know the full extent of what being a mother means. If someone were out to harm Daisy, he would expect you to fight to the death to save her. So why can't he see that this is you fighting just as hard to save her life now?"

"I *can* see that, Gina," Josh proclaimed, walking into the room.

Gina looked at us both, then asked if I wanted her to stay.

"It's okay, Gina, you can go. I'm sorry you had to see all this," I told her, and then I hugged her before she left.

On her way out of the door, she turned to Josh. "You're on my shit list, Josh, and if I find out you've hurt my friend any more than you have already, you and I are done. Start to think before you speak and say hurtful things to someone you're supposed to love, or it will be too late. Some words and actions you can't ever take back."

After glaring at him for a moment, Gina left the room.

Josh sat on the bed beside me. He leaned over to the bedside table and placed my engagement ring on it. It caught the dull light from the window and sparkled. It was such a beautiful piece of jewellery, and something I was so proud to wear. I wanted to look at Josh and ask him why he'd brought it back to me, but I couldn't do it. I suddenly felt exhausted and wanted to be left alone.

Josh broke the silence first.

"I bought it for you. The ring is yours if you want it, Keeley." His voice was quiet, and it didn't give me any indication as to how he felt.

"It's just a ring, Josh. It's beautiful, but you gave it to me because you wanted me to become your wife. If that's not what you want anymore you can take it back. Because without that, it holds no meaning or worth to me."

He picked up the ring and clenched his fingers around it. Despair gripped my chest and wouldn't let me breathe.

Had I done something terrible in a previous life that warranted so much pain to be sent my way in this one?

I contemplated throwing open the window and leaping down towards the solid drying room roof, and then sunbathing until I burned from the inside out. Being a Made vampire, I'd be unable to tolerate more than a few seconds of sunlight. I knew it would hurt, but it couldn't be any worse than what I was feeling already. Then at least it would be over for me. Daisy would be safe, and Josh could be her father, just like he wanted.

There was something I needed to know.

"Josh, if I ask you a question, will you answer me truthfully?"

"You know I will, Keeley."

"Did you ever love me for me? Or was it because I had Daisy and you wanted to be her father?"

"I can't believe you're even asking me that," he answered angrily. "I tell you how much I love you every day, and I mean every word. I love you for you, Keeley. For everything you are as a person. Your strength, your personality, your beauty inside and out. All that time I was dreaming up ways to be near you, to kiss you, and make love to you, I never once thought of being Daisy's dad. You were enough to occupy all my thoughts."

I smiled at that. At least I knew I had genuine love from him, even if it was only for a short while.

"Thank you, Josh. Even though I'm heartbroken, knowing you loved me helps. I'm sorry that it wasn't meant to be, and I hope you'll find happiness with someone in the future. You deserve it."

I meant it, too. As much as I was hurting, I didn't want him to be suffering. I loved him too much for that.

"Hang on a minute, Keeley. What's with all this '*loved*'? The correct term for my feelings is love, not loved. Loved is past tense. Don't you ever listen to what I say? I just told you I love you for you, and it's not just friendship love either. It's a deep and lasting love that's captured my heart and soul, keeping them bound with yours forever. That's why all this hurts so fucking bad. I can't walk away from you, Keeley; I love you so much, though I know I upset you terribly downstairs. Do you know how I know that? Because every time you hurt, I hurt. It's like one of those voodoo dolls. You get upset; I get upset. Your heart hurts; my heart hurts. I understand the *what's yours is mine* concept of marriage, but I didn't think it would include this much pain."

What could I say to that? I still didn't know what he wanted from me. I was happy to hear he loved me, but I also felt confused.

"What do you want from me, Josh?" I almost whispered it because it scared me to know the answer.

"Everything, Keeley. But I know that's not possible right now. I want to be a family with you and Daisy, but that's not happening either. I don't want to hurt Daisy's feelings. God, that's the last thing on this earth I would ever want to do. But I understand we can't all live together as we planned. I want to be with you, though, Keeley, because if I don't get to hold you in my arms at least once a day, my life won't be worth living. Will you forgive me for hurting your feelings again? I seem to keep fucking up around you. Even when I know it's happening, I can't seem to stop myself. I think it's because I didn't prevent your attack that I'm getting like this.

"My life was stolen from me, Keeley. They took me away from my family, home, and country. I had no control over what was happening in my life. I was chained like a criminal and whipped and beaten for trying to protect the innocent. I love Alex and Freya more than words can express, but I spent years grieving the absence of my biological family. I could never replace them, just like Daisy can't replace you.

"I like to have things planned and to know that I can make life good for you. Maxim took that away when he took your human life, and I have no control over anything once again. I wanted to give you and Daisy a life full of love, happiness, and everything you could ever need. I was going to share all those proud moments of Daisy's new achievements with you and the other kids we would have. I had it in my head what our life would be like, and I vowed to put a smile on your face every day. I haven't been doing such a good job of that so far, have I?"

"I think we've both contributed to that, Josh. You can't take all the blame," I told him.

"Well then, we are a pair together, aren't we?" He took my left hand in his and slipped the engagement ring on my finger. I looked up at him, questioning with my eyes.

"The meaning behind this ring will never change for me, Keeley. I shouldn't have goaded you downstairs, but when I saw you messing with it, I thought you wanted to take it off. It was like a stake through my heart."

"That wasn't the case at all, Josh."

"I know that Keeley, and I'm so sorry. Will you wear the ring as my fiancée? Will you let me be the one who puts a smile on your face every single day?"

"What about my wishes for Daisy's well-being? Will you respect those? Because if you won't, being with you is pointless, and we'd better make a clean break of it now." I told him.

"I will respect you on this, Keeley. Your reasons are valid. I don't have to like it, but I respect why you came to that decision. I want her safe, too. But I do think you'll be okay. Nothing about your transition to a vampire has been typical, but I know you want to be sure. Will you at least let Freya bring Daisy to see us so we can explain that she has to stay with Freya for longer? I think she'll accept it more if it comes from both of us. We can say it's because you're still unwell and tell her she can come to see us regularly. I'll make sure there are enough of us here to keep her safe."

I visibly shivered at that statement. Josh put his arm around me and pulled me close.

"You'll be fine, Keeley, I promise. You were great with Gina today. Did you ever think of feeding from her at all?"

"God, no! It never even crossed my mind," I said with a grimace. I wouldn't like to feed from anyone other than Josh —apart from Gregor, maybe. But I wouldn't tell Josh that. It's a thought he wouldn't appreciate at all.

"Gina was close to you on so many occasions today. You've also been extremely distressed, which could have made you crave more blood. Yet here you are, absolutely fine and able to cope without going into blood lust."

He sounded so proud of me, and it gave me a bit of a boost. Although I still felt tired, I didn't want to curl up in bed and sleep anymore.

"Will you come back to the cottage with me?" he asked, stroking his hand down my arm, smiling at me as if I wasn't going to refuse him.

"I thought we were staying here."

"I'm no longer welcome," Josh said with a sigh. "Gregor's kicked me out. I was only allowed up here to apologise to you."

"Really?"

"Yeah, he pinned me up against the wall in the hallway and threatened he'd come after me if I hurt you again. Gregor has such a soft spot for you, Keeley. I think he's taken to you like he took to Freya."

"I like him too. He said I'm welcome to stay here for as long as I need, and I can go back to Russia with him if I want."

Josh pulled his arm away from me and turned my face to look at him.

"Tell me you aren't going with him, Keeley?" he pleaded.

"I'd like to see what it's like over there and to meet his other staff."

"No," Josh cried. "Please, Keeley. We don't know where Maxim is, and if I'm not there to keep you safe, I'll not rest."

"I won't put myself at risk, Josh. I'm not stupid," I said with a huff.

"I know you're not, babe. I just… I didn't protect you last time, and look what happened. I can't go through that again. Your safety has to be a priority from now on. Yours and Daisy's."

"I know, and I appreciate that," I told him. "But I'm much stronger now, and I can take care of myself."

"I know you are, love, and you're getting stronger every day." After a few seconds of silence, he asked, "So, will you come back to our cottage tonight?"

"No, Josh. I'm going to stay here for a while. I think it's for the best."

I expected him to be shocked, but he wasn't. He kissed me softly on the lips, then got up to leave.

"I'll call Freya when I get home and tell her you want her to be Daisy's guardian for a while. And I'll ask her to bring Daisy over so we can talk to her about it."

"Thanks, Josh. I'm not looking forward to that conversation. I could cry just thinking about it."

Josh smiled sadly. "I know, love. But even though I hate it, I know you've made the right decision."

"Thank you. It means a lot to know I have your support in this."

"Walk me out, Keeley. I know it's still light, so you can't go near the door, but at least I'll have your company for a little longer."

I did as he asked, and we parted company in the hallway. He waited until I'd gone into the kitchen before he opened the door and left.

Gregor was in the kitchen eating strawberries and cream.

"Would you like some, Keeley?" he asked. "These strawberries are delicious."

He offered me a strawberry dipped in whipped cream and held it in front of my lips. I took a bite out of it and savoured the taste. It was sweet and juicy. I went to take the rest from his fingers but he popped it into his mouth.

"You can get your own," he said, smiling. "That one looked way too tasty to let you have it all." I laughed while grabbing a bowl out of the cupboard and filling it with strawberries before Gregor ate them all.

I hadn't mentioned to Gregor about him making Josh leave. I missed him, but I thought the break would do us good. After all, it's what I'd been trying to achieve a couple of days ago.

I'd been so used to making my own decisions and found it hard to let other people do that for me. As Josh said, I need to feel like *I'm* in control, too. I think it comes from being a single parent, or maybe all mums feel this way.

I've never been one of those *"it's my way or the highway"* types. But when you balance being the parent of a small child, little or no spare money, a drunken father, plus a job, then a bit of control makes you feel as though you're keeping on top of things—even if you aren't.

Gregor and I were watching a Mafia film on one of the movie channels. I loved this movie, and so did Gregor. We sat together on the sofa with the last few strawberries and some ridiculously expensive champagne from his cellar. I asked him about the bit that had been sectioned off for a *different use,* but he declined to tell me anything about it.

We talked about the movie, and he told me about how the Russian mafia or the "Bratva," had been active in Russia since the time of the tsars. Gregor said that organised crime had gained in number and power every year since the Second World War and had infiltrated many other countries in the West, including Britain, Germany, and America.

I knew very little about it and was appalled by the stories he told. His country had experienced several major political events over the last two centuries, and the issues that these political factions brought about had caused their own set of problems for the people of Russia. Gregor said without the political issues, the Bratva might not have gained such great power and numbers within Russia.

The problems his country had faced, as well as all the various uprisings that came about because of them, saddened him. I hated to see him looking so dejected and wanted to offer him comfort, so I linked my fingers with his and rested my head on his shoulder. Thinking about everything that Gregor had seen in his life, I wondered how he remained such a nice guy.

He'd been around for over five hundred years, and a lot of the history he'd personally born witness to should have left him quite jaded. But Gregor had an almost regal quality about him. Something about being in his presence commanded your full attention. I asked if he had any royal blood in him; Gregor winked at me and said, "Not recently. Why? Are you offering, princess?"

I laughed, but winked back at him and answered, "Anytime, Tsar Gregor."

The atmosphere in the room changed, and Gregor held my hand a little tighter.

"Would you like more champagne?" he asked.

"It's lovely, Gregor, but I've had two glasses already. I don't want to stand and have it hit me all at once like alcohol normally does."

"Keeley, as a vampire, you can tolerate much more alcohol than you did before. But do not trust Sergei's alcohol. His friend, who is a Born Immortal, makes it, and it is very strong," he warned.

"Too late for that, I'm afraid. Ryan and I had some the last time he brought it over. I was in a terrible state. Josh took us back to his cottage to look after us because we were so drunk. I lost one of my high heels and my bra, although I still wore the rest of my clothes, so I don't know how the bra went missing," I admitted.

"Keeley, that kind of behaviour is so unbecoming of a female, and it also puts your safety at risk. I shall have strong words with Sergei about this," Gregor said crossly.

"Why? He didn't force me to drink it. I knew I shouldn't have had the second glass, so it was totally my fault."

I could see Gregor still shaking his head at me, not accepting that I would willingly get totally wrecked like that. He obviously held a very high opinion of me, and although I liked that he thought of me that way, it wasn't right to blame someone else for my actions.

"After we'd taken my dad into rehab, I decided I'd be more careful when I went out drinking. But it feels good to go out and forget about my responsibilities for a few hours. My ex's parents take Daisy overnight now that she's older, and I can let go for a change."

"I can understand that, Keeley. I know you haven't always had it easy, and I am sorry for that. A woman like you should only ever have the finest things in life and should be cared for by a man who worships you. Your ex was a poor excuse for a man; I am glad you've made a better choice with Josh. He would give you the moon and stars if he could. Your Bond will be a strong one when you finally take that step."

I could tell he meant it, although I still questioned him.

"But that's the same man you made leave your home this afternoon."

"And the very same man who's been parked outside my home for the last fifteen minutes," he replied.

"What? Where?" I asked, getting up from the sofa and walking over to the window. Sure enough, I saw Josh's Honda parked on the other side of the driveway.

"He pulled up when the man in the movie shot his boss. I thought you may have heard, but you were too busy being horrified by the film. This is why you need to be with one of us instead of alone at your father's home. Your senses are much more heightened now, but you still need to be more aware of your surroundings until we catch Maxim." Gregor continued, "You were occupied by the film, and that's how it should be when you have others to take care of you. But if you are ever on your own, you need to be constantly alert until the vampire who hurt you is truly dead. Joshua is here because he fears for your safety. He knows I'll watch over you, but because you are his, he feels that no one can protect you as much as he can. He is both possessive and overprotective of you and your daughter. That is why your decision today was hard for him. He wants to love and protect both of you because you belong to him now. Once everything settles and you become accustomed to your immortality, you will feel the same."

Gregor was at my shoulder, peering out of the window at Josh's vehicle.

"I love Josh, Gregor, and I feel possessive of him too. But I also need a little independence, and it irritates me when he assumes I'll let him make all the decisions for us."

Gregor rested his chin on the top of my head and wrapped his arms around my waist.

"Keeley, I want you to think about a few people and how they cope with certain aspects of this life. Firstly, think of my lovely Freya and how strong and independent she is. A good role model for any woman, immortal or not. Then think about your friends, Gina and Julia. Both women are human, with immortal men who show the same sort of possessive, overprotective nature that Josh displays. But tell me, who do you think is in charge in their relationships?"

"Nik and Alex like to think they're in charge, but I know they'd do anything in their power to keep their women happy. So I suppose it's a little of both."

It was an honest answer based on my observations and my talks with both Gina and Julia.

"Exactly. It requires give and take from each person in a relationship to make it work, but an immortal male is a dominant force. Through the Bond, they become more aware of their woman's feelings. The immortal male will act accordingly when he senses his woman is upset or in distress, which can often lead to him toning down his possessive, obsessive, overprotective behaviour."

"Why can't they just listen to what we tell them in the

first place, human or immortal?" I rolled my eyes in exasperation.

"My darling Keeley. That would make things a little too easy now, wouldn't it?" Gregor sighed, then said, "Let me ask you this. How many times have you been angry or upset, and when a man asks you how you are, you say '*fine*,' when clearly, you are not? Then the man has to work out why you are upset instead of just being told."

He was right, of course. I'd done that many times with Dan over the years when he'd pissed me off, and more recently, with Josh.

"Gregor, how do you know so much about relationships when you have no significant other in your life? You seem to be good at reading women."

"It is good to study people and their behaviour. After all, it's part of what makes a good businessman or woman. You need to study their tells, like when you are playing poker. You need to read their actions to see if they are bluffing or have a hand that could steal the game. You will get the very best out of a business meeting by doing so. It is also how I like to study women. That way, when I am with a woman sexually, I know how to get the most out of them."

Gregor turned away; as if realising he'd said too much. I let the curtain fall back into place and turned around to face him. He stood in front of the unlit fireplace with his back to me.

"Gregor, show me the secret room you had built downstairs." It was a command, not a question.

"It is not for a woman like you to see."

"What's that supposed to mean?" I asked, surprised by his words.

"The type of sex that the room dictates is not for someone as nice as you," he declared adamantly.

"When it comes to sex, it's up to me to decide what I see or do, Gregor. Do you think it's only sluts who like a bit of kink?" I challenged.

He stared straight at me for almost thirty seconds without blinking. I thought he'd deny me access again, but he took my hand in his, leading me down to the secret room he had in the cellar.

The wine cellar had been cool as we passed through it, but the room he led me into after that was pleasantly warm. He flipped a couple of switches that lit the room in an ambient light, which came from amber spotlights overhead. Of course, I knew what this room was supposed to be from what Josh had said, but I expected something similar to a very famous book I'd read. This room was nothing like that.

There was no bed covered in red satin or silk sheets. In fact, the only piece of normal furniture was something that looked part sofa, part chaise, which was against the wall on the left-hand side of the room.

To my right was what I knew to be a St. Andrew's Cross. However, it appeared as though it was attached to steel girders. The cross itself comprised of thick, highly polished oak and had leather padding around the middle and halfway along each end. I ran my hand over the wood and leather, both of which felt beautifully smooth.

Even though it was varnished, the wood had a just chopped smell to it, and the scent of the leather reminded me of an expensive handbag I'd wanted but could never afford. There were various holes and fixings running along it, and I wondered what they were for.

"I know what this is, Gregor. But how does it work?" I asked.

"Would you like a demonstration, Keeley?" he questioned, smirking at me, expecting me to say no.

"Yes, I would," I replied, trying to replicate the same smirk back at him.

He hesitated, and I could see he didn't want to do it, so I walked over to another piece of equipment.

"This looks like something we used to have in the gym at school," I told him as I tried to figure out what it was.

Gregor came up behind me and pushed on my shoulders. I dropped to the floor, my knees resting comfortably on padded black leather. The piece was similar to a vaulting horse or pommel horse, although it was only around three feet in height.

Once again, the wooden structure was made from highly polished oak, and instead of the soft suede we had at school, the top of this one was finished in padded black leather. There was a dip in the middle of the padding; Gregor pushed my shoulders forward so that my body leant on the wood and my head rested in the dip. He ran his palms over my arms and placed them on the other side of the horse, or bench, or whatever it was. Gregor walked around the other side and slipped both my wrists inside two black leather cuffs, which were firmly attached to the wood.

"Gregor, what is this thing used for?" I asked, trying not to sound nervous but failing miserably.

"Anything I want, my darling," he whispered in my ear before running his nose down the side of my neck and inhaling deeply. There was a comfortable piece of black vertical leather about a foot long and two inches wide through the middle of it. I felt a pull low in my belly, but when the structure suddenly started to move, my tummy flipped completely.

"Gregor, what's happening?" I yelled. I felt my body being lifted when the wood began to rise. Looking over my shoulder, I found Gregor with a remote control.

"I prefer to move and alter the equipment to suit my needs and the height of the submissive. With this, I can deliver any punishment the submissive requires, sensual or not. There are ankle cuffs and wrist restraints to keep them in place."

Gregor dropped down behind me and pressed his groin into my bottom. Whispering in my other ear, he said, "When I think my submissive is right where I want her, I can allow myself to fuck her and take her blood."

Just then, the vertical leather piece that was resting against my core began vibrating with hard, pulsing movements. I couldn't help the moan that slipped out of my mouth as Gregor thrust against my backside, and when his teeth scraped against the side of my neck, I felt myself become wet.

But this was wrong. As much as I was enjoying the experience, it was happening with the wrong man. When I felt Gregor shift slightly behind me, pressing his erection between the cheeks of my bottom, I panicked.

"Gregor, this is wrong," I said breathlessly.

"And that is exactly my point, my darling. It is not right for a woman like you to be in a place like this."

"That's not what I mean, you bloody fool," I yelled. "I should be down here doing this with my fiancé, not my boss."

Gregor quickly jumped to his feet and released me from the cuffs. He rubbed my wrists, then kissed each one.

"I am so sorry, Keeley. Please forgive my actions. I

should not have done what I did, and it will never happen again." He was so worried about what my reaction would be that he couldn't look me in the eye.

"Gregor, look at me, please," I demanded, stepping closer to him.

When he finally raised his eyes to mine, I smiled at him, then winked.

"You'll be pleased to know that a *'woman like me'* found that pretty hot, and if I were here with Josh, I'd have begged for him to do what you said. All this," I gestured around the room at the equipment, "is something I find thrilling, and it's a turn-on just knowing what this room is for. Does that make me a slut in your eyes? If it does, so what? I'm still a good person who would never willingly hurt anyone. I'll openly admit I like sex, kinky or not."

"Joshua isn't into bondage," Gregor stated.

"I know that. We've already had that discussion. Although he said he'd be happy to try a few things. But if Josh wanted to do this with me, I'd be more than willing. It wouldn't affect any other aspect of our relationship if we did. He'd still have the same respect for me, just like I would for him, too."

Gregor began pacing the room.

"I saw you flirting with Chloe from the flower shop the other day," I commented. "She seems such a lovely person, from what I know of her. Kind, hard-working, friendly, and very pretty. Are you going to ask her out?"

He stopped pacing and looked back at me before saying, "Maybe. Why?"

"Let's say you take her out somewhere nice, for a meal maybe. You get along well, have easy yet interesting conversations, and find that you're really attracted to her. If she agreed to come down here with you afterwards, would that mean Chloe wasn't a nice person?" I questioned.

"Keeley, I understand what you are saying, but I find it hard not to separate the two. I like the company of women. I love everything about them and always treat them well. But I find that once I have a sexual encounter with a woman and she submits to me completely, then my interest wanes."

"So you're a love 'em and leave 'em type, just like my ex was with me," I said sadly.

"No, Keeley. I am nothing like your ex. He left you pregnant and alone and refuses to acknowledge his child. I would never do that. I would have made sure you were cared for—both of you. You wouldn't have wanted for anything."

"Except for you in my bed. I'm right, aren't I?"

He stared at me as though trying to figure me out.

"I enjoy getting total sexual submission from a woman. Their blood always tastes so delicious when that happens. It becomes addictive, but then anything other than that starts to bore me. I lose interest quickly, and they only ever see me as their Dom after we have sex," he stated.

"Gregor, women of today are much savvier and more aware of all things sexual. Women work hard at their jobs, at being a housewife, and bringing up kids. Don't you think it's possible that this kind of sex would be an outlet for some of those women? We're expected to be able to do it all, so can't we have it all and be it all, too? We can be the nice girl, sweet girl, and supportive girl. Mothering, generous, sexy, kinky, submissive, or dominant. We should be allowed to be whatever or whoever we want to be, instead of having just one or two labels or roles in life. How many labels and roles do you have, Gregor?"

He was quiet for a moment, so I answered for him.

"Businessman, friend, boss, generous, kind, trustworthy, thoughtful, dominant. That's a good start, but there are lots more. So why do you expect women not to have more and embrace them all?"

"I see what you have been trying to do here, Keeley. But I have been this way for so long, and I enjoy what I do. Why should I change?" He almost huffed out his defensive words.

"Because I think you want more than that. I'll be living with Josh soon, and Freya has Daniel now. Freya and I will always be here for you. But no matter how much our other halves know what you mean to us, I don't think they'll appreciate us sitting and holding hands with you while we watch a movie, for instance. But that's something you could do with Chloe, either before or after you've been down here with her."

"I will miss spending so much time with Freya," he said. "I wish there had been more to our relationship, but we were better off as friends. I wanted to want more, and so did she. But it didn't need to be anything more, and Freya would not have let me have free rein with my dominant nature. But I have always been close to her, and I am beginning to feel the same type of attachment to you, too.

"Sometimes, immortal males can have that with a female and love them dearly," he added. "It doesn't need to be anything physical. I have a feeling that Sergei has the same sort of thing for Gina. Why this happens to us, I do not know, but human males do not seem to have that kind of relationship with women."

I nodded in agreement. "I feel that same pull towards you, Gregor. And you're right in saying it wouldn't happen to human male and female friends. But it feels deeper than friendship, somehow."

I didn't understand this thing we had going on, but I found it comforting to know I had Gregor in my life.

"I will try to have more of a relationship with someone, Keeley. I admit I am set in my ways, but for you, I will try," he said in a determined voice, although the look on his face told me he didn't think he could do it.

But there was nothing more that I could do. Any changes that Gregor made to the way he viewed women had to come from him and no one else. However, it didn't mean that Freya and I couldn't secretly help along the way.

"Let us go back upstairs, Keeley. We must take pity on Joshua and invite him in for a drink. It is best you take a shower and dress in different clothes, though. You are covered in my scent, and my demonstration aroused you. Joshua will know this." Gregor raised a brow and gave me a sexy smile when he said that, leaving me highly embarrassed.

After showering, I joined Gregor and Josh in front of the TV. Gregor had brought up more champagne, and we all settled down together as a family would. I sat between two of the greatest guys ever on that sofa. I know they both cared about me in their own different ways, and it comforted me to know I wasn't alone.

Josh didn't go back to his cottage, and I didn't stay on my own in the room next to Gregor. Instead, Josh and I went back to our original room and made love until the sun began to rise. It was a beautiful experience full of love and acceptance, and I never wanted the night to end.

Chapter Thirty-Five

Keeley

While going through business with Gregor the next morning, I received a phone call saying that the Volvos we ordered were ready to be delivered. I arranged for the vehicles to be brought to the manor, enabling them to collect the ones on loan to us. Gregor told Yuri to return the one he'd been driving before midday.

Yuri had been down to Southampton tracking Maxim from his last known whereabouts, but he'd returned to the Red Lion in the early hours. Josh said the sale of the pub was going through swiftly, and Yuri would become the new owner in around four weeks.

Just after I'd hung up, my phone rang again. It was the rehab clinic where my dad was staying. They informed me that Dad's treatment was going well and said they'd relaxed the contact stipulations they first set out, so Dad had written us a letter.

They said if we'd like to write one back, they'd pass it on to him. I thanked them for their call, and as soon as I hung up, I rang Dan to let him know. He didn't answer, and neither did Freya. I began to worry, but Gregor assured me I was probably worrying for nothing. They were most likely out of cell service on one of their many outings with Daisy.

Gregor was probably right, but the mother in me still wanted them to have answered straight away and let me know my baby was okay.

I had an email listing the meetings that were taking place in Rothley Community Centre next week. They were brought about at the request of local businesses to see what impact the new supermarket would have on their economy. I expected it to impact Barrowfield and Rothley's food shops more than other companies. But all the local ones had been informed and were asked if they'd like to attend.

Gregor and Alex were going, and as Gregor's PA, it would have been beneficial for me to attend. But it was summertime, and it would still be daylight at 7.30 p.m. when the meetings were due to take place, so that ruled me out.

I tried to call Dan again at noon when Gregor and I stopped for lunch, but there was still no answer. The same thing happened when I called Freya. I was anxious and frustrated by the time Yuri arrived with fish and chips from Barrowfield chippy, but I agreed with Gregor that I'd wait until after lunch to call them again.

Josh had left to collect more clothes from his cottage, so Gregor and Yuri kept me entertained by trying to teach me Russian. Sergei had tried it on a night out around Barrowfield, but I didn't trust the phrases he taught me weren't rude.

To say hello would be, "Zd`rastvuyte," and how are you is, "Kak de`la."

This went on for over an hour, and my attempts at proper pronunciation provided quite a lot of laughter for Gregor and Yuri.

When we heard two vehicles pull up the driveway, I assumed it was the Volvos. So while Gregor and Yuri went to sort that out, I cleared away our plates and began loading the dishwasher. A few minutes later, Josh called my name as he entered the kitchen, and at the same time, I heard the one little voice guaranteed to make me smile.

"Daisy's here," I announced, surprised yet nervous, knowing I hadn't prepared enough to see my little girl.

"Did you know they were coming today?" I asked suspiciously.

Josh shook his head. He seemed as surprised as I was. "No, I didn't," he said. "When I told Freya what you'd decided yesterday, she said she'd bring her over in a couple of days. But apparently, Dan was upset with your decision and wanted to talk to you about it."

I couldn't believe this was happening. We hadn't even decided what to tell Daisy.

"Don't let them in yet. Please, Josh. Give me a chance to think of something to say to her."

Josh pulled out his phone and sent a text to Freya. Seconds later, he received one back. Gregor was taking them on a walk around the secret garden to give us some time, and to get to know Dan a little better.

I walked into the sunroom and watched Daisy through the French doors, grateful for the special tint that Gregor had put on the windows—making them safe for Made vampires. I watched Yuri swing my daughter high enough to carry her on his shoulders.

"Don't cry, Keeley. I promise everything will work out okay for us soon," Josh assured me.

I wasn't even aware I was crying until Josh mentioned it, probably because I felt completely numb. Like my body was made of stone, and the only way to get any feeling back was to be cuddled by the little girl on Yuri's shoulders.

"Are you expecting visitors?" asked Josh. The sound of vehicles pulling up the driveway brought me out of my melancholy.

"That will be the SUVs," I said flatly. "I'm sure Gregor will have heard them, but could you just go out front and greet them until he gets there, please?"

"Of course," Josh replied. "Do I need any paperwork?"

"On the desk in my office. It's in a blue folder with the Volvo emblem on it."

I didn't even turn to watch Josh leave. Instead, I looked towards the secret garden where they had taken Daisy. A few seconds later, I saw Gregor and Yuri reappear and make their way to the front of the manor.

I was trying to think of what I would say to Daisy about why she had to stay with Freya, when I suddenly heard her scream, "*No! Get him off me,*" and my first thought was that Maxim had attacked her.

Without even thinking of the consequences, I threw open the French doors and ran with vampire speed towards where my daughter was still screaming. Josh and Gregor called out my name, but I didn't stop. It only took a few seconds to reach her, but it felt like an eternity.

Dan and Freya held on to Daisy's arm as they looked up at me in horror. When I grabbed Daisy and tried to pull her close, both Freya and Dan threw themselves over me, covering as much of me as they could. But I couldn't see what was wrong with Daisy that way, and I quickly threw them off me.

"What happened, Daisy?" I cried, looking into her beautiful, tear-filled eyes.

"Mummy, a buzzy mister wasp stinged me. Look," she said in a babyish voice as she pointed to her arm.

"Kiss it and make it better for me, Mummy," she sobbed.

Something covered my head, and for a moment, I couldn't see Daisy. I reached up to throw the item away, only for it to be replaced by something else until Freya yelled, "Stop it. She's fine. The sun isn't affecting her, Josh."

As I looked around, I saw Josh picking up his and Gregor's shirts that I'd thrown on the ground, trying to cover me again with them. Gregor, Yuri, Freya, and Dan just stared at me, their mouths hanging open in shock. Freya stepped forward and took the shirts away from Josh, and he finally stopped to look at me.

"How do you feel, Keeley?" Freya asked curiously.

"I'm all right," I answered truthfully. "I heard Daisy scream, and I thought that Maxim had come back, so I ran out to get her away from him."

"I don't understand it, Keeley. I mean, I'm so glad you're okay, but you shouldn't be able to tolerate any sun at all," Freya remarked while touching my face and arms.

I bit into my finger until it bled and told Daisy to kiss it better because *I* had a poorly, too. When she complained that my finger tasted funny, I took it away, satisfied she'd had a couple of drops of blood to take away the nasty-looking stings the wasp had given her.

Sure enough, a few seconds later, her pain was forgotten. Daisy began telling me about her adventures with Auntie Freya and Uncle Dan. As per what usually happens when Daisy's overexcited, she didn't seem to take a breath between sentences. Everything came out jumbled up and too fast for most people to understand.

Not that anyone other than me was listening to her. No. They were all still staring at me.

Josh dropped to his knees beside Daisy and me.

"It was your mother, Keeley," he exclaimed as he looked from me to Freya. "The woman that the vampire Brandr forced to Bond with him must have been your mother. He said he knew she was pregnant, but then she disappeared, and he couldn't find her. So he didn't know whether he had a son or daughter. But she was pregnant with you and Dan. I can't believe we didn't think of it earlier."

"Josh, I don't know what you're talking about. What has my mother got to do with this?" I asked in confusion.

"Yeah, Josh, and who is this Brandr bloke?" Dan demanded.

"Yuri, take Daisy into the house and get her a drink of juice," said Gregor.

Yuri took Daisy's hand, and reluctantly, I let her go with him. Freya linked her fingers through Dan's before she spoke.

"Brandr was the man that Alex and I thought was our father. He was a Viking warrior—tall and handsome with blond hair and blue eyes, a bit like you, Dan. He was married to my mother, although, as I remember, he had many affairs. But my true father was a Born Immortal vampire who used mind control to stop Brandr from being with my mother. Brandr sailed to England with my father and other men from my village, so they could build a settlement for us to live in when they brought us over."

"So what has this Brandr got to do with our mum? I still don't understand," Dan questioned.

Josh spoke this time. "Before they could return for their families, Freya and Alex's father attacked Brandr and turned him into a vampire. He bound him, leaving him weak and out in the open so he'd burn from the inside out when the sun rose. But before that could happen, a warrior loyal to Brandr saved him and took him to safety. He returned to take revenge on Sebbi years later but found that he was already dead."

Freya tried to walk away, but Dan pulled her close, offering her comfort.

Josh carried on. "Brandr then decided to take revenge on Sebbi's children, Alex and Freya. But Freya had lost her family, so he couldn't make her suffer any more than she already had. Brandr decided to wait until Alex found someone to Bond with, then he would take them away, just like Sebbi had taken Alex and Freya's mother."

I recalled the rest of the story from what Josh had told me before and was starting to piece together the association with my mother. But I let Josh explain it to Dan.

"As you know, Alex didn't Bond with Julia until last year, but Brandr had been coming back for centuries, watching and waiting, which brought him to Barrowfield around twenty-five years ago. He was fed up with waiting for Alex to find someone, and he forced a woman from the village to Bond with him.

"This woman was already married, and her new husband had been working away when Brandr took advantage of her. He said the woman reminded him of Freya's mother; she had the same blonde hair, but her eyes were blue, not grey. Through mind control, he forced her to Bond and have sex with him repeatedly, and eventually, the woman became pregnant.

"Brandr had to leave the village for a while, and when

he returned, the woman had left. He said that because he was still Bonded with her, he felt it when the woman died years later. If I'm right, and I truly believe that I am, then that woman was your mother, which makes Brandr your biological father. It also means you're both Born Immortals, like Freya, Alex, Sergei, Nik, and Gregor. And that's also why the sun isn't affecting you, Keeley."

Everyone was quiet for a moment, not knowing what to say. But Gregor spoke up next.

"After Maxim had attacked you and Gina had staked him, she gave you her blood. She was still doing so when I arrived. She had cut her wrist too deep and almost died from the amount of blood she had lost. If Gina hadn't made you swallow her blood, you would not have been able to make the transition, and you were very nearly dead. Our vampire blood may not have been enough to save you without Gina's, because a Born Immortal cannot make the change without human blood."

"Where is this vampire that raped my mother?" asked Dan angrily.

"He's dead. That's the guy who tried to kidnap Julia. He wanted to do with her what he did with our mum, but he was killed last year. Am I right, Josh?" I asked.

"Yes, love, he's dead now. He can't hurt anyone else."

"I wonder if Dad knows any of this," Dan pondered with tears in his eyes.

"I don't know. But I don't want anyone to tell him that we know," I croaked, wiping away my tears. "I heard from the rehab place today. He's doing well at the moment, and they asked us to write him a letter. He's sending us one too. I don't want to set him back in his recovery, and as far as I'm concerned, my dad is the only dad I've ever wanted or needed."

"I agree," said Dan, also wiping tears away. "He's my dad, and despite his problems, there was no better dad in the world before Mum died. He can be like that again now he's getting the right help."

"Did you hear what I said, Dan? You're a Born Immortal, too. If you drank human blood, you'd undergo the transition from human to Born Immortal vampire—if that's what you wanted," Josh stated.

"You don't have to think about that now," Freya told him. "Let's all get used to this and let the dust settle before any hasty decisions are made."

Dan let go of Freya and pulled me close, enveloping me in the best brother-and-sister hug ever.

"Keeley, as a Born Immortal, you won't be subject to the same blood lust as a Made vampire. That means Daisy can come home and stay with us," said Josh, smiling from ear to ear.

That's all it took to set me off bawling like a baby. Freya joined me in my crying, and it looked like Josh and Dan had shed a few silent tears. Gregor was clearly overwhelmed and tried to hug us all over the next few minutes. But I could tell seeing Freya and I cry like that broke his heart, even though they were tears of joy.

When I could finally stop crying, we went back into the manor to find Daisy and Yuri playing 'go fish.' From the number of cards Daisy had at her side, it looked like Yuri was letting her win. When she turned to look at us, she threw her cards down on the table and jumped up to hug me.

"Mummy, why have you been crying? Are you sad?" she asked.

"Not anymore, sweetheart," I answered, hugging her tightly. "Would you like to go home with Daddy and me?"

"Yes!" Daisy smiled and hugged me tighter, playing with my hair like she used to when she was a baby.

We said our goodbyes, and I hugged and thanked Gregor before leaving. I told him I'd pick up my things when I returned to work in a few days. For now, I wanted to go home with my fiancé so I could mother my daughter forever.

Chapter Thirty-Six

Josh

Looking around at everyone enjoying our engagement party gave me an immense feeling of hope for the future. All our friends and family were here in the secret garden at Rothley Manor, which I suppose is a silly name for somewhere everyone knows the whereabouts of.

Gregor had hired a marquee, but since the weather was good, Keeley decided it would be nice to have everyone in the garden itself. And Keeley always gets her way around Gregor, just like Freya has over the years.

Chloe, the florist, had brought new plants from the local garden centre and attached solar and battery-powered fairy lights all over the trees and hedges. Daisy loved it and said it was like a magical Queen Ellie fairy grotto.

I could tell that Gregor was enjoying all the ladies' reactions to the lights, flowers, and glittery stuff. With every gasp and awed expression, Gregor's smug grin grew wider.

It had been four weeks since we discovered that Keeley

was a Born Immortal vampire instead of a Made one. Although I knew what happened to her mother at the hands of Brandr was terrible, it meant that Keeley could walk in the sun and take care of Daisy as any human mother would.

Since finding that out, Keeley hadn't wanted to be away from Daisy. There had to be another vampire involved in her care, or Keeley just wouldn't leave her. Not until Maxim had been located.

It caused a few issues with Daisy's grandparents on her biological father's side. They'd been used to having Daisy on overnight visits to their home, but with Keeley's paranoia over Maxim's return, we could no longer let that be an option. So instead, we invited them to our cottage to see Daisy and meet me.

The look of surprise on their faces when they first met me was laughable. Keeley had failed to mention the colour of my skin. If only they knew our other secrets.

I don't think they liked hearing Daisy call me Daddy, but what did they expect? Their son wouldn't claim her, so a better man stepped up…and he was loving every minute of it. What did impress them was my wealth. That stuck in my throat because it shouldn't have mattered if I was a multi-millionaire; it should have been about my love for Daisy and her mother. But as long as they accepted me and didn't make trouble for us, it was enough for me to let that go.

I took them on a tour around the Night Movers compound at Daisy's grandfather's request. As he'd worked in the transportation and warehousing sector before, it gave us some common ground, and we began to relax in each other's company.

Keeley and I agreed that we'd allow them to take Daisy to France on a long weekend later in the year. We were desperate to Bond but knew how insatiable we'd be for each other in the first few days, so it was best that Daisy wasn't around then. But we couldn't confirm an exact date until we knew Maxim had been eliminated.

Another obstacle that could have been in our way was Keeley's father. He'd been out of rehab for nearly ten days and was doing really well. Derek's a handsome bloke without his bloodshot eyes and ruddy complexion.

As part of his programme, the rehab centre offered him access to their facilities once a week for ongoing counselling. It didn't come cheap, but it was worth every penny to see Keeley and Dan so happy and proud of their father's progress.

He'd even met a woman while he was in there, and she seemed to give him the extra push to overcome his problems. Marion's a lovely lady who lost her way after her son died in a motorbike accident. I think she and Derek can offer each other support and understanding because they both know how hard it can be to fight ongoing battles with grief and addiction.

They were both here tonight, and because of them, Keeley and I were going to make this a no-alcohol party. But her father had insisted we didn't do that. He said he had to learn to say no to temptation, and he couldn't do that if he avoided it altogether.

Derek had been dancing with Keeley and Daisy and was now walking towards me.

"Derek," I said, acknowledging his presence.

"Josh, I want to apologise for my behaviour the day you came to my house before I went into rehab. I'm not racist and obviously haven't brought my children up to be that way, so I'm sorry I said those vile things to you."

I looked him over before nodding my head. "Apology accepted."

He carried on looking at me. It was unnerving, and it took a lot to hold his gaze.

"I also need to thank you for getting me into rehab. I was causing myself so much harm and upsetting Keeley and Dan. You didn't do it for me, but I'll thank you anyway because you did it for my daughter—to make her happy. And she is happy, Josh. Just look at her," he said, gesturing towards the dancefloor where Keeley and Daisy were dancing with Freya and Gina. "I want to pay you back when I get the money together. I could sell the house, and when I'm recovered enough, I could get a job and—"

I held my hand up in front of him, stopping him in his tracks.

"There's no need to pay me back. Just make it work for you. As you said, I did it to make Keeley happy, and to give Daisy the grandfather she deserves. Don't let me down with this, Derek. Be the man they need you to be," I told him.

The next thing he said shocked me to the core.

"I know the man that fathered my children was like you…a vampire."

I turned to look at him and saw the pain in his heart reflected in his eyes.

"Josie and I got married three months before I had to start my new job in Gainsborough. The company I worked for sent us to their other depot for training. As it was in Kent, it was too far for me to travel, so I stayed in digs with the men who were training with me. I didn't come back to Barrowfield every weekend because we needed every penny we could get to put away for our new home. It was a new build property on the outskirts of Gainsborough. Josie worked at the bakery in Rothley until the house was ready, and we saw each other every weekend.

"It was while I was away doing my first week's training that he met her. She told me she didn't want to sleep with him or drink his blood, but something he did to her made her do anything he requested. He threatened to kill me if she told anyone about him and what he was, so she daren't report it to anyone or even tell me. Josie wasn't sure if anyone would believe her if she did tell them. So she suffered what he was doing to her until he suddenly left the village.

"She wasted no time packing our things and headed to a bed-and-breakfast near our new home. Josie sold the furniture we had here in Barrowfield and used the money to help pay for her accommodation. When she told me what had happened with the vampire, I didn't believe her at first. I mean, never mind that she was saying vampires existed; she was also telling me she'd been having sex with another man, willingly or not.

"I'm ashamed to say that I thought about divorcing her. Josie was distraught and frightened that he'd find her. In the end, I believed her about him forcing the sex on her. It was after she told me why he'd come to Barrowfield. He told her he was watching someone at the Night Movers' company. He was waiting until he could hurt them the way he'd been hurt. My sister-in-law had been working for you for a good few years by then, and I knew there was something different about her employers. I'd asked my brother about it once or twice, but he was being cagey and told me I was better off not knowing."

Derek sighed and looked at Keeley and Daisy before carrying on.

"Josie said the vampire had told her he'd scented a pregnancy on her before he left, but she said it should have been too early to tell. Three weeks later, the pregnancy was confirmed, and it felt like someone was trying to tear me in two. My wife cried and cried and promised me she'd have an abortion if I stayed married to her, and I agreed. I loved her too much to leave her. But bringing up another man's child after he'd been forcing my wife to have sex with him was something I just couldn't deal with. So she got a date for an abortion on the NHS.

"Three days before that was due to happen, Josie started bleeding heavily. We'd just got the keys to our new home and had bought some cheap second-hand furniture to tide us over until we could afford what we wanted, and we were carrying it into the house. I took her to the local hospital, and they confirmed she was having a miscarriage. While we were there, she became dizzy and passed out. They said she was anaemic, which was probably because the vampire had been feeding from her for weeks. The bleeding stopped, but they still gave her a blood transfusion. She needed two pints before she was anywhere near stable.

"After the transfusion, they did a scan to make sure the miscarriage was complete, but they found two live embryos still in the womb. I looked at the images the radiographer was pointing out on the screen, and I knew those babies were trying so desperately hard to live. I looked down at my wife and said, 'I'd better get some overtime in if I've got to buy two of everything.' I think I was won over by those little wonders before she was, but in the end, we both knew those babies were meant to be born and loved by us.

"The day they came into the world was one of the best days of my life. I had a son and daughter. Two beautiful blond-haired, blue-eyed babies, and I was thoroughly smitten. I was their dad, despite not being biologically related to them, and nothing would change that.

"Life was good for us until we learned that Josie had breast cancer. She had surgery, chemo, and radiotherapy, and all was going well—then we found it had come back in her other breast. When they did more tests and scans, they found it had spread to her lungs and liver, too, and there wasn't much they could do for her. They tried chemo again, but it wasn't doing anything other than making her sick. We had to move back to Barrowfield so Maggie and Dave could help us with the kids. I nursed the only woman I had ever loved until she took her last breath."

I put my hand on Derek's shoulder when I saw him trying to hold back tears.

"Derek, you don't have to tell me any of this," I told him while trying to find a tissue in one of my pockets. But Derek found his voice again and carried on speaking.

"When Josie died, I had a full-on breakdown. Not only was my wife dead, but we were now living in the same place where the vampire who attacked her last saw her. He'd told her she was pregnant, and I thought if he came back, he might have been able to recognise somehow that Keeley and Dan were his biological children. I started drinking to block out those thoughts, but it never worked. Now and again, I'd think it was okay, and I would stop all the alcohol. But the thoughts always came back, and I'd drown them out with whisky when they did."

"You don't ever have to worry about him finding them, Derek. The vampire who hurt your wife was called Brandr, and I had a hand in ending his life last year," I assured him.

The look of peace that came over Derek visibly transformed his features. He no longer had that pinched look on his face, and I saw the tension leaving his body right before my eyes.

"Thank you for telling me that, Josh," he said as he looked me square in the eyes. "Can I ask that you don't tell Keeley and Dan about this? I don't want them to know I'm not their biological father?"

I tried to protest, mainly because they already knew, but he cut me off before I could get any words out.

"Please, Josh. I'm doing well in my recovery so far. I'd hate for all this to come out and jeopardise that."

What could I say to that? I didn't like keeping secrets from Keeley, but I also didn't want to harm Derek's progress and recovery.

"Okay, Derek, I'll do as you ask. But I don't like keeping secrets from your daughter. All I ask is that one day you'll consider talking to them about it."

He nodded his head and said, "Maybe."

Keeley came over to where we stood and hugged her father tightly.

"Come on, Dad," she said, smiling while she pulled him back onto the makeshift wooden dance floor. "Just have one more dance with me."

"You'd better get used to this, Josh," shouted Derek as Daisy grabbed my hand. "If my granddaughter is anything like her mother, it will be *Just one more dance, Dad,*' until the DJ packs up for the night."

Epilogue

Sergei

Most of the guests were up dancing, singing, and having a great time, although Alex and Julia sat at a table to my left.

Julia was due to give birth soon, and she tired easily. Her ankles had swollen, so Alex had them resting on his knees while he rubbed the ache in her feet. She put her hand on her rounded belly, then laughed when it visibly lifted with her baby's kick. Alex leant forward to place one of his hands where hers had been, and he smiled when he felt his child move around. It was a touching moment, and one I felt compelled to observe. But Gina interrupted me by grabbing my hand and tugging me onto the dance floor.

She seemed a little drunk, and as she'd been drinking with Ryan—the interior designer Gregor hired to work at the manor—it was safe to say she'd probably had more than enough alcohol tonight.

I noticed Yuri giving me the signal I'd been waiting for all night, so I spun us around, giving me a direct view of all the guests. I noted where Keeley and Daisy were before focusing on the intoxicated Ryan, who stumbled out of the garden away from the party. The song ended, so I kissed Gina on the cheek before walking over to Nik.

Taking my friend's arm and pulling him away from the crowd, I said, "Keep your woman close tonight, Nik, until you get a call from me."

"What's going on, Sergei? Is there something I should know?" he asked, frowning.

"Don't let her out of your sight until I tell you it's safe. I must leave for an hour or two, so I need you to keep Gina, Keeley, and Daisy close." Placing my hand on his shoulder, I added, "Be my eyes for me this night, Nikolas. We must put our fears to rest, once and for all."

A moment of silent understanding passed between us before he nodded in agreement. Taking a deep breath in, I let a feeling of calm wash over me before heading in Yuri's direction.

I waited in the shadows of the small copse by the coach house cottages. They were fully completed now, with no trace of what had happened on that terrible day. No evidence of Keeley and Gina's blood littering the walls and floor.

Lights were on inside the property that Gregor's drunken guest was staying in, and after a few minutes, I watched the curtains close. I hoped we didn't have too long to wait tonight, and I was glad that the warm night air carried no breeze. Our scents would be almost undetectable from this distance. I couldn't see Yuri, but I knew exactly where he would be from the plans we'd made, just in case.

Ryan opened the front door and leant against the door frame. He was drunkenly trying to light a cigarette, and it took four attempts of his swaying hand to do so. After he had taken a few drags, a dark figure appeared in front of the building, making its way towards the door.

"Ryan," said a voice I recognised. So did Ryan, apparently. Jumping with fear, he dropped his cigarette, trying unsuccessfully to close the door.

"What the fuck are you doing here?" Ryan hissed, still struggling with the door.

"I came back two weeks ago to see you, but you'd left. Then I overheard someone in the next town talking about this party, and I knew you'd come back for it. So I came to find you again."

"Why?" Ryan asked.

"I wanted to thank you—for what you did for me that day. And I wanted to ask *why* you helped me?"

"I don't want your thanks, Maxim, because I shouldn't have done it. You nearly killed Keeley, and for what? Because you were jealous of what you thought she had going on with Gregor?"

"Why did you remove the stake from my heart if you felt so angry about what I had done?" Maxim asked.

"Because I know what it's like to have such a deep, unrequited love for a straight man, and I felt sorry for you. But I want you to go now, Maxim. Go far away and never come back. And whatever you do, please don't contact me again."

Maxim walked away with his head hung low, near where Yuri waited.

Within the blink of an eye, Yuri grabbed him from behind.

Using my vampire speed, I was with them a second later, while Maxim tried freeing himself from Yuri's hold.

I didn't waste any time giving a long speech about why I was doing this—like killers do in the movies. Instead, I said nothing as I rammed the stake deep into his heart.

We carried Maxim's body behind the old gardener's potting shed, both of us satisfied that we'd prevented any further hurt and disruption in the lives of someone we loved. I texted Nik to let him know, and to tell Gregor and Josh that Yuri and I were having a bonfire tonight, and both Gina and Keeley would no longer have to live in fear.

Next in The Night Movers Vampire Series

vinci-books.com/gregorsreason

Can she trust the vampire who stole her heart?

From the quiet town of Rothley to the busy streets of Moscow and St. Petersburg, Chloe's hard-earned inner strength is put to the ultimate test with Gregor, the billionaire vampire Dom, who challenges everything she believes. As their intense connection grows, betrayal strikes, forcing Chloe to decide if she can trust the man who has captured her heart.

Turn the page for a free preview…

Gregor's Reason: Chapter One

Chloe

The orders had been coming in since the shop opened at 8.30 a.m. I'd had others coming through by text on my mobile before that, since getting the news that Julia Staithes had her little boy, Rory, at 10.36 p.m. last night.

My assistant, Pam, worked all day instead of her usual six hours, and Emma, my Saturday girl, covered the till and gift areas.

Pam and Michelle—my young apprentice—were helping with the orders for the new mum and baby in the back room of my shop.

I'd taken over the little flower shop in Barrowfield when my aunt Joyce left it to me just over a year ago. I wasn't sure what to do with the place at first. When I'd gone through the books, it didn't seem like my aunt had made much of a profit in the last few years. Still, I didn't have the heart to change the little shop into something else.

I'd spent lots of happy school holidays here making up

bouquets with my aunt, and she'd always told me the shop would be mine one day. Sadly, Aunt Joyce suffered a massive stroke last July and passed away a week later without regaining consciousness. When her will was read, it revealed that my aunt had left me the flower shop, the flat above it, and her little minivan. She'd also left me her extensive earring collection, a pair of which I was wearing today.

I retained Pam and kept the shop as a florist for a while. After I'd sorted out all the legal paperwork, Pam and I sat down and discussed the ideas we had that could bring in more customers.

We diversified a little, adding various gifts, candles and small decorative items to our stock list—as well as party products. We also redecorated and gave the shop a new name, Chloe's Flowers and Gifts, and have been doing well financially for the last ten months.

I've taken a few floristry courses, and I really enjoy my work. I just wish my aunt Joyce could see how well her little shop was doing now.

I relish the challenges my new business has given me. I love what I do, and although the shop came to me in sad circumstances, it also came at a time in my life when I needed a change: a new direction and purpose.

I married my now ex-husband, Craig, when I was a loved-up twenty-six-year-old. We'd been engaged for over two years beforehand, and I thought I was so lucky to meet such a sweet guy after a previous abusive relationship. The boyfriend before Craig had become violent towards the end of our time together.

The emotional scars from that relationship lasted longer

than the injuries he gave me, and I swore off men for a while. So when Craig came around with his thoughtfulness and gentle ways, I thought my dreams had all come true. Granted, there wasn't as much passion as I would have liked in our sexy time, but I thought we could work on that, and passion wasn't everything, right?

Craig's family was quite wealthy and gave us enough money to buy our first home as a wedding gift. His mother and father were wonderful people and had Craig—who was an only child—later in life.

They were very much in love, and after being married for fifty-two years, they passed away within four months of one another. His father had a massive heart attack after losing Craig's mum to bone cancer.

That was three-and-a-half years ago. A month after his father's funeral, Craig sat me down to discuss something. I thought it would be about his parents' home and belongings; what I didn't expect him to tell me was that he was gay.

To say I was shocked was an understatement. I was so stunned and unbelieving at what he'd said that I burst out laughing. Afterwards, when I realised he wasn't joking, I went through a whole range of emotions and actions.

I cried, screamed, and shouted; I also threw a cream cake at the wall before ordering Craig to leave our home, but he wouldn't. He kept saying he was sorry; he didn't want to hurt me, and he would always love me—just not how a husband should love his wife.

It took over a week for me to calm down and at least two months to accept the unwelcome development. As I've said, Craig and I had very little passion in our relationship. I used to think he wasn't as attracted to me as I was to him.

Craig is tall, fit, and good-looking, with blond hair and

baby-blue eyes, and he often turned other women's heads whenever we went out.

Being short, plump and pear-shaped, I never felt confident about my looks. Although I'm not unattractive, my light brown hair and pale freckly skin make me a little ordinary, yet my blue-green eyes are quite pretty. But as it turned out, I could have been a Playboy model, and I still wouldn't have made Craig get all fired up and passionate. I didn't have the right genitalia to get his motor running.

After six months of coming to terms with Craig's sexuality—and with divorce proceedings underway—I moved out of our home. We sold Craig's parents' house, and I used some of the money from the sale for the rent on a modern apartment close to where I worked, and Craig was happy for me to do so.

My parents own a B&B on the Costa Blanca in Spain. They offered me a room in their home, but I wanted to stay in the UK to keep my job as a medical secretary, which I'd had for years.

Craig eventually met Jake, a great guy who made him truly happy. When we finally divorced, Craig ensured I had a reasonable settlement, so I was okay financially. Some people think I'm crazy to remain such great friends with Craig, but I still love him dearly—although only as a friend—and I adore Jake.

They helped me decorate the shop, and we still see one another regularly. Their friendship helped a lot when I gave up my job and made the sixty-mile move from the outskirts of Nottingham—where I lived previously—to the little flower shop in Barrowfield, South Yorkshire.

I've made quite a few friends in this village, the new mum Julia Staithes being one of them.

Gregor's Reason: Chapter Two

Chloe

After Julia's husband, Alex, sent me the text last night to let me know about baby Rory's safe arrival, he was the first to place an order for Julia's flowers. Of course, this order also had to include a helium balloon, as was customary for the couple. Julia had bought Alex one on the day she proposed to him.

Alex wanted to say thank you to his wife for making him the happiest man on earth, for loving him and making him a father. I suggested red carnations instead of roses for the flowers because they were Julia's favourite. I also included baby's breath and various bits of greenery to bring out the red in the bouquet. Inside the arrangement was a small, heart-shaped red and white balloon on a stick that said, *"Thank You."* The customary helium balloon was white with red lettering that said, *"I love you."* Alex wanted this to be all about Julia, as he knew baby Rory would end up spoiled by everyone else. He was right about that.

The next order came from Joshua York and his fiancée, Keeley, not ten minutes after Alex sent his text. They requested a blue floral arrangement with an *"It's a boy"* helium balloon. Keeley also wanted to send a blue teddy from her daughter, Daisy.

Keeley and I are also friends. I'd provided the floral arrangements and fairy lights that decorated the secret garden at Gregor Antonov's manor house, where her engagement party was held.

Gregor was next to request an arrangement. Unlike everyone else last night, Gregor's request came via a phone call. What made this even more special was that Gregor was in Russia at the time, so it was good to hear his voice.

He's flying back to Yorkshire today, and he'll stay at his home in Rothley for at least two months. I was glad. I missed the flirty friendship we had going on when he wasn't around, and I hoped we would get the chance to spend more time together while he was over here.

I first met Gregor when I called at Rothley Manor to deliver flowers for Keeley—Gregor's PA—who was staying at the manor. Gregor took me on a tour around his home and flirted shamelessly while we discussed what type of floral arrangements would suit each room.

I couldn't believe it when, after my tour, Gregor asked if I would go out to dinner with him. I wondered why he was asking someone like me. I mean, Gregor is a tall, good-looking, sexy Russian billionaire, and I'm just a plain nobody who happens to own a flower shop.

Since moving to Barrowfield, I've taken more care of my appearance. I keep my hair short and styled in a pixie cut, and it's a shiny chestnut colour right now instead of the dull brown it once was. I have a healthy tan from all the time I spend outdoors at the flower markets and garden centres. Yet, for all that and the twice-weekly swimming sessions and Zumba class I attend, I'm still a little too chunky in the hips and thighs, and at nearly thirty-five years old, my boobs have started to gravitate in a southerly direction. So why would Gregor be interested in flirting and spending time with me?

Whatever the reason, I've been extremely happy about it. Gregor's not only nice to look at, with his short brown hair that has just a few flecks of grey at the sides, piercing blue eyes and GQ model looks, but he's also intelligent, charming, generous to a fault, and always treats me with the utmost respect.

Of course, I'd love him to rip my knickers off and take me up against the nearest hard surface whenever we're alone, but that's never going to happen. Unless I suddenly grew a few more inches in height, lost thirty pounds in weight, and got a head transplant. But a girl can dream if nothing else.

Gregor's bouquet for Alex and Julia has white carnations and deep blue gerberas interspersed with blue irises. He said he'd bought Julia sapphire and diamond earrings to celebrate the birth and show her how special she was—another reason women seem to swoon when in Gregor's presence.

Yet, for some reason, even though Gregor has all these outstanding qualities and was more swoon-worthy than a handsome A-list movie star, I found myself wondering just what his dark secret was. I suppose from my track record with men, anyone would understand my wariness. But there was just something different about Gregor; something that I couldn't quite put my finger on…

Gregor's Reason: Chapter Three

Gregor

We landed at Doncaster Airport at 6.30 p.m. after a flight with the worst turbulence I've ever experienced. Even the ordinarily laid-back Sergei had looked anxious and worried until the aircraft came to a stop. Only Yuri hadn't seemed affected by our troubled flight.

Yuri loved the Gulfstream jet we'd flown in on. It was the four-fifty model, so it wasn't our largest. But it was still very comfortable—luxurious even, and I was reminded again how fortunate it was to acquire this fleet of planes at much less expense than buying them outright.

Yuri was a trained pilot, but he'd flown nothing near the size of this aircraft and hadn't yet expressed any interest in doing so. Perhaps I should ask why and encourage him to try it?

We collected our luggage from where we'd stowed it. There wasn't much, as we'd left a lot of our belongings behind on our last visit.

The pilot and cabin crew were staying here for two weeks—transporting another Born Immortal from the UK to Barcelona during this time. The immortal in question had used our services several times, and the pilot and crew we employed told me that he was a favourite passenger of theirs. This was good to hear, as we had only one other immortal on this crew, and I liked to know that the humans I employed were safe.

Exiting the aircraft, I immediately spotted Keeley waiting in the VIP area. Her smile was infectious, and my spirits lifted as I walked into her embrace.

"It's great to see you, Gregor," Keeley said while kissing my cheek.

Before I could reply, Yuri picked her up and twirled her around.

"Keeley, you are more beautiful than ever. How is my little Daisy, and the new baby, too? I cannot wait to see them," he voiced loudly.

"It's good to see you too, Yuri. Daisy and Rory are both good. We can call over to see them before I take you to the manor, and I have photos of the new baby on here," Keeley said, sliding her thumb over her phone screen.

Sergei snatched the phone up first and flicked through the photos with one hand, grabbing Keeley by the waist with the other.

"He is very cute. How much did he weigh?"

"Nine pounds, six ounces," said Keeley with a beaming smile.

"So, has he done it?" questioned Sergei with humour in his voice.

"The earring? Yes, he's wearing it, Sergei. But I have to say, it's so not Alex. I can't believe that's what you bet him," Keeley replied.

"What did you do now, Sergei?" I asked, but he couldn't answer me for laughing. Yuri spoke instead.

"Sergei bet Alex that his baby would be a boy over nine pounds. I bet a girl about eight pounds, and Nik and Josh bet girls, too. Alex said he thought a boy about eight pounds." Yuri laughed, then added, "Alex was so sure he was right from what they said at the last ultrasound that he told Sergei he could name his forfeit. Sergei said if he won the bet, Alex would have to wear an earring again, as he did in the 1980s. I didn't think he would do it."

"Alex wanted me to shave off my hair if I was wrong, and I accepted his bet, so he had to accept mine," Sergei insisted when he finally stopped laughing. Keeley shook her head at him and proceeded to show me photographs of Alex and Julia's son as we walked through the airport.

Keeley insisted the baby had Julia's mouth but had a look of Alex and Freya around the eyes. Yuri and Sergei nodded, agreeing with Keeley. But to me, he just looked like a baby, albeit a chubby-faced one. Perhaps I would see a difference when we saw him face to face. I've never been the biggest fan of babies. I haven't had a great deal to do with them. I visited and brought gifts to celebrate their birth, but nothing more than that.

Not many in my circle of friends have become parents over the years. Still, my human employees have families, and I ensure I welcome their safe arrival into this world with a monetary gift for their future.

I wouldn't need to do that with Alex's son, so I'll have to be more inventive with little Rory's gift. On the other hand, Julia will be given sapphire and diamond earrings to show how special she is to me—for loving one of my best friends and making him a father. Two very precious things.

I brought Chloe a gift, too, and it's one of many that I

have stored away at my favourite jewellers in Russia. It is a gold bracelet with floral charms made from various coloured precious gems. Flowers for my little flower girl. It's a nickname I gave her during the time we spent together on my last visit to the UK.

I was ever the gentleman with her those few short weeks ago. With how I was feeling now, I wouldn't stay that way much longer.

During my last stay, I took her out to dinner several times. We also went to the cinema, which I detested due to the number of noisy people who kept insisting on getting up and squeezing past us. I should have hired the whole cinema that night, and if Chloe wanted to go again, that's just what I would do.

I was hoping, however, that she would be agreeable to becoming so much more than just my friend. I could not wait to explore more of the witty and intelligent Chloe, who'd become such an obsession to me. I wanted to touch her constantly, even if it was just holding her hand, and while I wasn't sure at first that I would be attracted to someone as full-figured as Chloe, I found myself lusting after her ample curves.

Usually, the subs I take in my club are a little lither, which helps them hold a position easier and for much longer. But I long to see Chloe and her generous curves strapped to the St Andrew's Cross in my cellar at the manor. Her breasts have also appeared in many of my fantasies, bound in leather and sporting clamps on what I guess will be rosy-brown nipples.

I turned to look at Keeley and realised she had been speaking to me. We had walked to the SUV I'd bought her a few months ago, and I felt a little ignorant in not paying her my full attention.

"I am sorry, Keeley. It has been a long day with a particularly gruelling flight, and I wasn't giving you my full attention. So what were you saying, my dear?" I asked, stroking her hair back from her face affectionately. We got into the vehicle and started the drive to Barrowfield.

"I was saying that Aunt Maggie's niece, Chelsee, is moving into the bungalow that Josh is renting her tomorrow. I know she's looking forward to having lunch with you next week. Sergei and Yuri have offered to help her move in, along with Josh and Nik."

"I offered her a cottage on my land, but she wouldn't take it," I told her, still a little put out that Chelsee hadn't wanted me to help her. She's Maggie's—Alex's PA—sister's girl. Although, she's not a little girl anymore.

Chelsee is twenty-eight now, but when she was nine, she came down with an autoimmune illness called pars planitis, which was caused by sarcoidosis. This attacks the eye, and sadly, in Chelsee's case, she lost her sight. She's been so brave in her short lifetime, and it doesn't look as if that's about to change anytime soon, even after her sixty-five operations since being diagnosed. I offered her a home on the Rothley Manor Estate that I own, but the stubborn girl turned me down.

"Gregor, Chelsee said that she appreciated you offering her a home, but she wanted to be in the village so she could use public transport and have easy access to the shops," Keeley said.

"I would have provided transport to anywhere she wanted to go. She knew that."

"That's not being independent, though, Gregor, and it's what Chelsee has strived to be above anything else. It would have helped if she'd stuck it out on the two-week *Guide Dog*

Matching Course, but she came home after just one day," Keeley muttered.

"Why didn't she stay the full two weeks?" asked Sergei.

"Chelsee said she didn't stay because they treated her like a blind person, which she objected to," I answered, shaking my head in bewilderment. I knew it would have been a real boost to her independence. I told her this, but she told me to *"butt out"* because I didn't know what she went through on a daily basis, which was right, I know, but I only ever wanted the best for her.

When she was first diagnosed, we tried our best to heal her, but unfortunately, our blood didn't have any effect on the autoimmune disease that ravaged her sight.

We had seen her grow from a determined young girl into an exceptionally tenacious and strong-willed young woman. She had her mother and aunt's beauty, but with stunningly silky, long dark hair: the kind you want to run your fingers through. I was surprised she hadn't got herself a husband already, but Chelsee has concentrated on building her career and recently qualified as a counsellor. She's secured two positions of part-time work: one at Rothley Medical Centre and one in a private practice in Barnsley. I am immensely proud of her achievements, even if she doesn't let me help and spoil her anymore.

Traffic had been minimal due to the time of day, which I appreciated. I felt quite weary, and I was anxious to get back to my new home—amongst other things.

My mind wandered yet again back to the delectable Chloe. I hoped she wasn't busy tonight. She was always a little vague on our phone calls and messages; perhaps that's why I found her so appealing. Maybe it's the chase? It's the first time I've ever had to do it. I have to keep guessing as to her moods and feelings and find her so hard to read.

I long to take her under my command and have her obey me, naked and wanting. I would be a gentleman no more where Chloe was concerned. But how do I approach the fact that I am immortal? And that I would like to take her blood as I take control of every inch of her body?

I took out my phone to send her a text message, but as we pulled up to Alex's home, I saw her little white van with Chloe's Flowers and Gifts written on the side. Josh was helping her carry large floral arrangements into the cottage.

Chloe glanced at our vehicle and smiled when she noticed me in the front passenger seat. That one thing lifted my spirits higher than they had been since I last held her hand in mine.

We all got out of the vehicle and said hello to Josh and Chloe. I took the floral arrangement from her as I leant to kiss her cheek. Before I pulled away, I whispered in her ear, "Come and see me at the manor later, Chloe. I have missed you."

"I've missed you too, Gregor, but you'll have to wait until after nine o'clock for me to join you. There've been so many orders for Julia today that we're running behind with the rest of our work. I have Pam doing some overtime, but I'll have to finish up, get a shower, and have something to eat before I come over," she said as she followed me into the cottage.

"I will order something from the Italian restaurant in Rothley," I told her, my eyes scanning over her full hips and bottom as she walked in front of me. Chloe and I had been to that restaurant a few times on my last visit. I knew her favourite dish because she would never order anything else.

"Gregor, that restaurant doesn't do food to take away," she stated.

"My darling Chloe, for the right price, I am sure they

will," I said as I winked at her. Chloe huffed and shook her head.

Alex stood beside the fireplace, smiling broadly, his son in his arms. Something hit me deep in my gut when he looked at me and found my gaze. Like he was communicating without words that this is what life was all about. And if I wanted to see true happiness, I should look no further than the baby in his arms and the woman sitting on the sofa looking radiant, wearing the same expression as her husband.

Sergei and Yuri went straight to Alex to take the baby, so I crossed to Julia and sat beside her.

"Congratulations to you both," I said as I kissed Julia's cheek and shook Alex's hand.

"My darling Julia, you look more beautiful today than ever, although a little tired, so we won't stay long. I couldn't resist buying you a gift to celebrate the birth of your son. I hope you like them."

I handed her the sapphire earrings and said, "Blue, for a boy," as she opened the box.

"Thank you, Gregor," Julia said as she wiped a tear from her eye. "They're beautiful. While you're here, there's something we wanted to ask you. Alex and I have discussed it, and we would love it if you'd be Rory's godfather."

I was taken aback for a moment. I looked from Alex to Julia and then to the baby, who was currently in Yuri's arms.

"If you don't want to, that's okay," said Julia quickly, taking my lack of speech to mean that I wasn't interested. But that couldn't be further from the truth.

"I would be honoured to be his godfather," I declared,

swallowing hard to dislodge the lump that had suddenly appeared in my throat.

Yuri came over and handed me the baby. It took a few moments to get him cradled correctly in the crook of my arm because holding babies didn't come naturally to me. But when I looked down at him—my precious little godson—I was overwhelmed with emotion.

He stared at me, unblinking. His eyes were a mixture of his mother's blue and his father's grey, and his little rosebud mouth pursed as he studied my face.

I smiled down at him and said, "Hello, little Rory. You have my love, my protection, and anything else you will ever need."

He wore a blue sleepsuit and was loosely swathed in a blue and white blanket. He raised his arm, opening and closing his tiny fist. I dipped my head and kissed it before lifting him a little and kissing his forehead. I saw a couple of flashes and looked up to see Keeley and Chloe taking photos of us on their phones. I smiled and turned Rory slightly so they could get a better picture.

"I want a photo of him on my desk, and we will get a professional in to take some for the walls and cabinets in the sitting room," I told Julia. Chloe took a few more photographs and told me she had the perfect frame in her shop.

"Would you like to hold him, Chloe?" Julia asked.

"Oh, I would love to," she said, taking him from my arms gently.

I inhaled both Chloe's and the baby's scent, and it stirred something inside me. I looked at her, gazing down at him so sweetly as she cradled him. She was doing a half-bounce, half-rock sort of thing while singing the Judy Garland song "Over the Rainbow."

Chloe has a beautiful singing voice, more so than any professional female singer I'd ever heard. Everyone in the room stopped what they were doing and stared at her in awe.

"Wow, Chloe!" exclaimed Josh as he looked at her admiringly. "I didn't know you could sing like that. How come you aren't singing professionally or even doing the odd gig around the local clubs?"

Chloe looked embarrassed at Josh's question and avoided everyone's smiling faces when she spoke.

"I used to sing when I was younger. I've done a few open mic sessions in a bar where my mum and dad live, but I'm not good enough to sing professionally, and I wouldn't be confident enough to do it either."

"I beg to differ," said Josh. "I think you're a brilliant singer, and I'll be doing a duet with you on the next karaoke night at the Red Lion now I've heard you sing."

Everyone joined in with the compliments, but Chloe was clearly uncomfortable under all their scrutiny. I stood and took my beautiful godson back from her arms and kissed her cheek, whispering in her ear that she should accept their compliments because they were well deserved.

She blushed before making her excuses to leave. She told Alex and Julia that their little boy was beautiful, and if they needed a babysitter, they should give her a call. Julia smiled and said she would. Then Chloe left, waving goodbye to everyone as she did so. I missed her presence immediately, and so did little Rory. He began to cry and turn his head towards me.

Grab your copy...
vinci-books.com/gregorsreason

About the Author

Helen Bright was born and raised in Yorkshire, UK, and often bases her novels in and around the county.

Whether she's writing paranormal or contemporary romance, her novels often have darker elements hidden inside a deep and meaningful love story.

www.ingramcontent.com/pod-product-compliance
Ingram Content Group UK Ltd.
Pitfield, Milton Keynes, MK11 3LW, UK
UKHW041512100326
468839UK00004B/1251